THE HAND OF AN ANGEL

MARK BROWNLESS

www.markbrownless.com

ISBN-10: 1976248744
ISBN-13: 978-1976248740

SIGN UP TO THE NEWSLETTER AT
www.markbrownless.com
AND GET

MARK'S NEW SERIAL FICTION

FREE!

Be careful what you wish for

Prologue.

2013 – Eighth International Congress of Clinical Psychology, Granada, Spain
The printed A3 sheet clipped to a folding stand outside the lecture theatre
announced the afternoon sessions.

Shortlist lecture series:
Elspeth Dickson Award for New Research Areas

A list of research papers and their presenting authors followed; two
investigating clinical depression in relation to other medical conditions, one
looking at the mental health issues of repeat offenders, and the final paper
was listed as:

Professor Magnus Stephens, Mr Tom Boyand (Consultant Cardiologist, UK – Presenter)
and Dr Mike Chu – 'Near-death experience: the collected testimony of 240 subjects.'

Inside the air-conditioned auditorium, steeply sloping rows of
folding seats were packed with delegates. Notepads, laptops and phones
rested on the slim wooden plinth that curved along the length of each row,
ready to record, in their own ways, the salient points of the work being
presented. Tom Boyand stood at the lectern, his dark brown eyes looking out
across the room. He was tall and slim with a naturally athletic build, more
from good genetics than honing in the gym. His hand periodically clicking a

dongle to change the PowerPoint presentation up on the big screen.

'...and that, ladies and gentlemen, is our study, which I can summarise as the collection of testimonies from two hundred and forty subjects worldwide, across a number of partner centres, from those whom have had a so-called near-death experience. We defined this as the absence of vital signs capable of sustaining life, and the absence of medical intervention in order to sustain life, for in excess of ten minutes. The data shows that the vast majority of subjects describe a sensation of falling, of being drawn towards somewhere and ultimately a white light and feeling of well-being. We have concluded that the biochemistry and physiology of cell death – hypoxia, cellular breakdown and associated release of what are effectively toxins to the surrounding tissue – would be the same in every individual, and that these chemical reactions are therefore directly responsible for causing the similar experiences we have found. Our proposals for further work would be to look at blood and tissue analyses immediately on admission to emergency rooms, to study the exact chemical soup that is causing this.' He paused, studying the faces staring back at him. 'You know, ladies and gentlemen, as we can see from our study, most of our subjects have had the same experience. By defining the chemical and physiological reactions at the time of death, we are closer to answering the question of where do we go when we die... and what happens to *us*? Thank you.' Tom stood back from the platform. Realising how hard he had been gripping the lectern for the last twenty minutes, he flexed his painful fingers and felt every one of his forty years. Without prompting, a number of hands went up, and he started to field questions.

'How did your research group come together?' asked one delegate.

'Whilst researching biochemical and physiological aspects of cell death and still having a clinical practice, I guess I was always balancing life and death. Where the two meet became of compelling interest to me and I was drawn to various cases of near-death reported in my hospital. I expanded this to look into groups across the United Kingdom, then Europe, then worldwide, and got in touch with similar, like-minded colleagues who were investigating the subject. We shared cases and eventually, over time, came up with the standardised interview questions I have described.'

'And specifically, what were your inclusion criteria?' Another delegate wanted to know. *Did you listen to what I've just said?* thought Tom.

'We clearly needed to standardise a number of factors to differentiate our subjects from those who were temporarily unwell. We therefore decided on a cut-off of at least ten minutes without cardiac output, preferably confirmed, without any kind of supplementary life support such as receiving piped oxygen, during that time. This also included those who were being treated mechanically with heart massage and defibrillators, because those individuals were no less dead.' Tom paused to take a breath himself and a sip of water. 'The absence of any identifiable mental impairment after the event was vital, because we needed subjects whose brains made a complete recovery, to optimise their memory of their experience. For obvious reasons, this also *excluded* those who were completely anaesthetised. Determining levels of anaesthesia was very important.'

'The data seems to be exceptionally consistent, Mr Boyand, particularly for a questionnaire study and taken from such an unusual model, namely test subjects being on the edge of death.' Another delegate commented, with a suspicious tone in his voice. 'In the circumstances, wouldn't you have expected a much wider range of data – a scattering of results one might say?' The older man was reclined in his seat with his legs crossed, commanding some authority in the room. Tom was concerned about the question and how it had been received by the audience, but he'd known that something like this would come up and had planned a response.

'Yes I agree, and that is the real crux of the study – that the results are so narrow. In my opinion it reinforces just how strong, consistent and predictable this reaction is within everyone, when placed in such a situation...'

Suddenly a man stood up in the centre of the auditorium. In his early fifties, his wavy dark hair loosely eased back from his face with wax, giving it a sheen that framed his olive-skinned complexion. He wore a black shirt, opened to three buttons down – one too many – exposing his thick gold rope necklace. His suit matched the shirt. He looked every inch the rock star psychologist at this meeting. 'Hi Mr Boyand, my name's Bob Wauberg and I'm a Professor of Psychology at Penn State University. I'd just like to congratulate you on your paper, and on putting together such a series of testimonies from across the world.' His comment stimulated a couple of audience members to politely start to applaud. Wauberg liked this, joined in and led the cheerleading. 'Yeah. YEAH!' He turned to the other delegates, nodding for them to join in with him – most did. This was the first time Tom had ever received applause at a scientific meeting, and it was certainly an eyebrow-raiser for him.

'I think it's amazing that you've been able to put together data from across six or seven centres worldwide,' Wauberg continued as the applause died down. 'Although I do think this raises questions as to how easy it was to control things like inclusion criteria, for example. It would obviously have been much more satisfactory to have just one centre where one research team would analyse the data, and the reliability of these data wouldn't be open to question. I understand that you've even visited individuals across the world – speaking to them in person – which again does raise a concern.' His soft, southern drawl lengthened the vowels as he spoke.

'What do you expect us to do, Professor? Unless you've got two hundred and forty people in *your* centre queuing up after having a near-death experience?' Tom responded, sounding a little more aggressive than he intended. 'We have to study these people from all four corners – sometimes quite remotely – because it's still a relatively rare presentation. That said, it has given us an insight into what people experience at the time of death.'

'You said – during your very well delivered presentation – that the consistency of the observations you have made reflect your earlier work on cell death; how the biochemical changes of the dying cell will, if extrapolated up to the level of a higher organism, result in the same experience by everyone.'

'Well, I didn't think I presented it as hard and fast as that, Professor, but, yes I believe that could be the case.'

'I would suggest, Tom, that you have not considered the individual's perception.'

Tom smiled. 'I suppose I should've expected a question on perception from the expert.' Bob smiled back before Tom continued. 'But in that case, why should so many people perceive the same thing, it doesn't make sense to me.'

'It makes every sense Doctor! This study could simply be showing us that the brain reverts to a familiar and comforting series of images when faced with the overwhelming fear of our own death. The accepted norm is falling, tunnels of light, being reached-out to, it's a familiar perception of people in dreams of death and in these so-called near-death experiences. It's almost cliché! All you are identifying is that people's minds seek comfort when they die, and leaving alone any religious debate, the familiar images you mention are what they create. You have proved little else. Perception is a three-dimensional construct that denotes the personality and the 'soul' if you like, and this aspect of perception is designed to ease their passing from life to death, to make it more acceptable, and it's a fairly commonly reported event.'

'I disagree. Perception reflects all aspects of a person's consciousness – mood, past experience, people's background, their social circle, their standing – thousands of variables. The consistency of our results across the world doesn't support your argument. We have found similar experiences across cultures, genders, socio-economic backgrounds and levels of intellect, when it's known that different cultures view death in different ways. Some will revere it and therefore not wish to create a 'comforting construct' as you put it, but actually wish to embrace the next stage in their soul's existence. Are you suggesting that their perception of death would create the same old construct as those who are terrified of the end being a blank – a nothing? I can't see how they would be the same. Our work shows that there is one constant that is the same for all, and I am suggesting that that constant is the biochemical processes involved, having the same local cellular effects in everyone, which ultimately drives their experience. We have anecdotal evidence from cultures that don't typically see white light, tunnels, God, that kind of thing, and have no accepted norm of that in their belief systems, who describe near-death experience of white light and tunnels and so on.'

'Well exactly, Tom, *anecdotal* evidence. Analysis of trends from a survey is all very well, but it's so much less compelling or powerful than hard numbers. Where's your *actual* data?' Bob raised his arms out to the side, palms raised and shrugged, playing to his audience.

The whole room had become quiet and tense, the atmosphere thick and heavy as the audience watched the tennis match before them, wondering who would emerge as the victor, each delegate taking sides and rooting for their man.

'But no matter what you say,' Bob continued. 'Whatever your study claims to show, you can never prove or disprove it. You could say that the gate-keeper to the afterlife was a giant pink walrus riding a pony and nobody can prove otherwise.'

Tom concluded. 'I guess we need to do more research at the edge of life then.'

Later, in his hotel room, he Skyped home. Seeing and speaking to Sarah and the boys back in England gave him some perspective, but he was still bothered by the exchange between him and Wauberg. He had known about him beforehand, had heard that he liked to strut around at these meetings as the great 'I am', and tear down any ideas different to his own. Tom's argument was actually the better one during their exchange, until he'd stupidly mentioned the anecdotal data. He sank a large Scotch that he'd poured from the mini-bar and, hey, the world seemed a little better. Conclusive proof, folks, that we don't need psychologists, just strong drink. Tom showered and let the scalding water jets blast away at his forehead and neck, and at his concerns about the meeting. He carefully massaged moisturiser into the early signs of crow's feet around his eyes, then dressed in jeans and a casual shirt, smoothing his hair back from his face and tucking it behind his ears. Short hair had never suited him, but he never grew it long enough to tie back, so it always stayed at a floppy somewhat unmanageable length.

There was a drinks reception that night in the main bar. Tom didn't really want to attend and would have preferred to be on the first plane out of there – schmoozing wasn't his thing at all – but it did mean he'd be able to eat some canapés, which would at least solve the dinner dilemma. He lifted his jacket from the back of the dressing table chair, swirling it around his shoulders as he slid his arms in. He tucked his reading glasses into his inner jacket pocket – the only glasses he had ever found that didn't make him look like Garth from *Wayne's World* – grabbed his wallet and room card and left. *Perhaps a liquid dinner might work better.*

The main bar of the hotel was accessed through a number of terracotta tiled arches, where the floor stepped down from the foyer into the cooler, open space. The middle of the room was packed with small tables, each surrounded by high stools. Small, more secluded booths were secreted in the shadows off to the sides, lit by the orange glow of table lamps. The place was packed, bustling and noisy, with what seemed like all the delegates from the symposium in attendance. It wasn't exactly what Tom had wanted, but he grabbed some tapas from a passing waiter and made his way to the bar. He found the last bar stool available and ordered a glass of Rioja.

When in Rome.

The food was exceptional and he asked the bartender if he would get him some more. Tom didn't notice the older Spaniard's disappointment in him for not getting off his backside to find the finger-food. The man acted like the perfect host and managed to direct a waitress over. Tom accepted some more food and a refill for his glass, raising it in thanks to his new Spanish friend.

'Muchas gracias!'

'¡De nada, cabron!' The barman smiled, covering the insult.

Tom finished his nibbles, and all that left him to do was to work through his host country's wine cellar, which he managed with some aplomb. For the first time in a while he emptied his head and thought about nothing, becoming oblivious to the comings and goings of people at the bar around him, enjoying being anonymous and the solace of the grape. After a while he became aware of someone standing next to him. For most of the evening, people had ordered drinks over his shoulder, so he thought nothing of this new presence until it spoke, breaking his relative isolation.

'Good evening.' Tom recognised the voice as unmistakeably Bob Wauberg's. He turned to look half over his shoulder, nodded very slightly, and replied. 'Professor.'

Bob smiled, nodding his head in return and said. 'I don't think there's any need for us to be so formal anymore, do you Tom?'

'Was there any need for earlier?' Tom said bitterly, looking back at his glass as he responded.

'Just a little Q & A,' Bob shrugged by way of response.

'Oh really? Felt to me like you were really going to town on my work just because I was taking a different standpoint to yours. They were *your* crowd and you played to them by starting on me. Didn't seem to me like a little Q & A. Or is that just my *perception*?' The wine had taken him to the point of slurring his words, petulantly so, but he focused enough to get his point across.

'Well, if you *are* gonna put your work out there, there's going to be debate. If you are gonna put your work out there and make *conclusions*, there're going to be people who shoot you down.'

'And that was your job,' was Tom's immediate retort, even though part of him realised there was no need for this, and that his colleague was trying to offer him something.

Bob raised both hands defensively. 'Tom, I meant what I said. It's a great effort that you put together this piece of work. I just think you're making too many leaps and connections between changes happening in people's cells and how they perceive things – that's all. There are too many pathways and processes from a cellular point of view, and in terms of their higher functioning there's their consciousness and perception that you don't consider. That's all I'm saying.' Tom sat motionless, listening to Wauberg speak. Some of what he was saying was exactly the same as earlier, but it also sounded like Bob was trying to give him some advice.

'Would it be possible to see some of the raw data – the questionnaires themselves? I'd be really interested in the minutiae of the testimony and see how one reads compared with the next, being that they are so similar.'

Tom's eyes widened slightly. 'Sorry, I didn't keep them – didn't see the need when we'd transferred the data to computer and got the paper out. With major refurbishment happening at work and moving offices, and our renovation work at home, space was at a premium, so they were an easy thing to trash to free up some room.'

'Pity, would have been interesting to see. The data is compelling though, Tom, such consistency of results across everyone...' Bob turned his hands palm upwards.

'So you're coming around to my way of thinking?'

'That there is one reason why they all have a very similar experience? Sure. It's just that our reasons differ.' A smile lit up the older man's face.

'I don't want to go through this again, I couldn't really have more convincing results if I'd made them up. And the patients involved are such a broad spectrum of people that I don't see how it can be anything else other than biological.'

'Well, maybe. It's like I said, we'll never know until we can actually send someone into that situation with recording equipment.'

'At least we're agreed on that – it's the next natural progression.'

'You know what, Tom?' Bob continued. 'We should work together on this.'

Tom shook his head and turned properly round to address the more experienced academic. 'The thing is, Bob, I already know enough overbearing pricks with an excess of personality – I don't really need another one.'

'Just trying to help by pointing out the counter-argument!' Bob smiled at the somewhat inebriated younger man.

'Devil's fucking advocate, eh?'

***

Within two months, Bob Wauberg was offered the post of Chair of Clinical Psychology at St Catherine's University Hospital NHS Trust. Tom Boyand's hospital.

1.

September 2016

Monday morning yawned and rubbed the sleep from its eyes after a heavy weekend to find Tom Boyand sitting in his Cardiology clinic bright and early – before the rest of the hospital had put the kettle on. He'd already been reviewing and examining patients so they could be waiting first in line for tests across various departments by the time they opened at nine. His was a hugely busy clinic and needed the highest calibre of staff to make it run efficiently. Tom had spent the three years he'd been in post hand-picking his staff, choosing the best people, those who could cope with the workload and fit in with the rest of the team.

The clinic was a happy place – everyone knew everyone else so well that news, gossip and humour flew around. News items came, were dissected, debated and embellished, then jettisoned by the time anyone got their first cup of coffee. The staff were as intense socially as they were with their work. New members sometimes found it tough – you had to sink or swim in the group dynamic. Some sank.

Tom didn't shout or scream like some of his prima donna bow-tie wearing colleagues, and like his old boss, Professor Dakin. He didn't stay aloof from his team either, he had barbecues for them at his house and they went on nights out and got drunk together. The clinic was a well-run place, well respected in the hospital. But the real reason people wanted to work for Boyand was because they liked him.

By mid-afternoon, as he sat in his room reviewing patients and dictating letters, he was acutely aware that he had to leave shortly to do the school run. Mrs Iris Chase sat in front of him, dressed in her Sunday best as older people often do for hospital appointments, anxiously awaiting his verdict on her problem. He smiled his best reassuring smile, explained that all her tests were normal and that her palpitations were nothing to worry about – more likely an indigestion problem – and she should return to her family doctor should they continue. She thanked him nervously and left.

Tom dictated a letter to Iris' GP, explaining her ECG and blood tests were normal and that she would be returning to his care for further management. He pressed stop on the digital dictaphone.

Why can't bloody GPs do a bit of diagnosing for themselves once in a while rather than panicking that everything is a cardiac event? 'Dear doctor, please prescribe an indigestion pill – a burp and a fart and she'll be right as rain'.

Tom liked to take all of his patients on face value; if they were sitting in front of him in clinic, they'd decided to make a change and that was good enough for him. There were no-hopers of course – you could spot them a mile off – those that turned up because they were told to by their doctor, and by doing so, through some sort of clinical osmosis, expected to get better. His friend Scott called them the 'couldn't wait to die' bunch. Obese, not taking exercise, not changing diet, not listening to advice, smoking heavily – ticking every box going. Tom would look at them and think they'd either end-up on *his* table or an undertakers', depending on whether Lady Luck smiled on them on that day or not. He took his laptop and slotted it into the pocket of his satchel, along with his notebook and dictaphone. He would email his clinic notes to Mags later. She'd then upload into the transcribing software, so all she had to do was edit, punctuate and mail merge.

'Going somewhere are we, Doc?' Nurse Shirley Wilmslow popped her head round the door of the clinic room, with a beaming smile.

'Ye-es, why? That smile isn't fooling me, sister, what's up?' He smiled back, with a comically suspicious expression.

'You've got another one.'

'I don't.'

'You do.'

'*I don't.* Hang on, this is becoming a pantomime.' *He's behind you!* 'It doesn't say so here?' He looked down at his clinic list for the day.

Shrugging slightly-built shoulders in blue theatre scrubs, Shirley said, 'A Mr Dodds?'

'Dodds. Dodds... Nope, don't remember. Notes?' He shrugged back.

'Heart attack. Builder. Northerner. DNA'd last week.' Shirley handed him a green folder full of medical notes, letters and reports.

'Was he re-booked?' He skipped through the notes to the Cardiology section, recognising his own letters, test results and started to remember the mysterious Mr Dodds.

'No, he got his dates wrong – thought it was this week. Re-book him, it's his mistake?'

Tom sighed. 'No send him in – we'll never get him back again if we don't. Will have to be quick though.'

'Okay – I'm sure you will be...' Shirley smirked as she left and Tom studied the last few entries in the notes, familiarising himself with the case. She reappeared a few seconds later with the patient in tow, ushering him into the seat next to the desk.

'Mr Dodds – good to see you again!' Tom beamed at the wiry, round shouldered man sitting in front of him. *Hang on does he really? Yes, he actually does have a cloth cap actually held in his hands in front of him, and all of a sudden I'm in an episode of* Heartbeat.

'Was you leaving, Mr Boyand?' Mr Dodds clearly didn't want to be a burden.

'Eh? Oh. No, well, yes. I do need to be somewhere else.' *To pick the kids up from school.*

'I could come back, Doctor, I know yer a busy man.'

'Not at all, Frank, the most important thing right now is how you're getting on.' Tom smiled.

'I been fine, Mr Boyand, really I have. Takin' it easy, exercising every day – nothing too much, like – but slowly building myself up, and I feel great.' Frank's enthusiasm was encouraging. 'Thanks to you o'course,' he added deferentially.

'Are you going to cardiac rehab?' Tom made some unintelligible notes on his jotter.

'Yeah, but that's just finished, so I've joined t'gym – me and t'wife, you know, are gonna go together.'

'Well that will be a nice thing to do – something together – share an interest.' *Am I really giving out marriage guidance to a middle-aged builder from Yorkshire?*

'Yeah well she's a big ol' girl, Mrs Dodds like, and needs to ship some timber, so it won't do either of us any 'arm.'

Tom sighed. 'How about diet?'

Frank paused and looked straight at his doctor. 'I won't lie to yer, Mr Boyand, but I've never been one to take any notice of what I eat, like, and t'balance of things and that.'

Here we go.

'But I'm a changed man. I've done some reading, me and t'missus are looking at a better lifestyle with our diets – less fatty foods and fried stuff – she *is* a big girl, yer know. I reckon I eat healthily now, more fruit and veg – even trying to have some of my diet with uncooked veg – been reading how that's better for yer.' It was obvious that Frank was very proud of his efforts and wanted his doctor to know it.

Pleasantly surprised, Tom reflected that sometimes it was the most unlikely patients that came up with the best results. 'Well that's marvellous news, Frank, delighted to hear it!'

Shirley busied herself with taking Frank's blood pressure and pulse. As she did so, Frank leaned conspiratorially toward Tom. They made eye contact, then Frank very deliberately looked at Shirley, then back to his consultant, and leaned in closer. Tom did likewise.

'Wor about...' he whispered, looking back at Shirley again. 'Yer know... Shagging, Doc?'

'Oh, right,' Tom whispered back, suddenly having an image in his head of skinny old-man Dodds and his apparently overweight wife going at it. Now there was a thought he didn't want to have.

'Mrs Dodds said it weren't a good idea, risky for me heart, but... well...'

'Frank. Sex is fine – it's good exercise. Just take it easy to start with.' Tom smiled at Frank, and out of the corner of his eye he noticed Shirley's shoulders shaking as she bent over to write the observations in Frank's medical record.

After a cursory examination of Frank's heartbeat using his stethoscope – window-dressing, really, given all the previous tests they had run on him – and final reassurance that he was doing okay, Frank left with a handshake and a smile on his face. And why the hell not now he could plan his evening's entertainment?

'The old dog,' said Shirley, still smiling as Tom once-again packed his bag.

'If she is a big girl that doesn't exercise, I'd be more concerned that the next time I see a Dodds on my list, it will be his missus and not him! Good luck to 'em anyway.'

Ten minutes later Tom was running down the main corridor of the hospital from the clinics to the foyer and off to the underground car park for the life sciences research staff, where he always parked out of habit. Frank Dodds had made him late and he was trying to make up some time.

**

Tom was thankful for the parking assist as he reversed the Grand Cherokee into an impossibly small space, surrounded as he was by all manner of similarly expensive vehicles. He didn't want to nudge into one of them in full view of what Sarah called the 'yummy mummies' standing across the road at the school. He got out of the car and wrapped his suit jacket around him against the drizzle that was falling and, head down, ran across the road, dodging slow-moving traffic as he did so. The late summer sun had, for today at least, given way to more typical British September weather. Head still down he turned and mounted the pavement to be greeted by a pneumatic pair of breasts threatening to break free from the restraint of a flimsy top. He looked up, his heart already sinking. 'Hello Kelly.'

'Hi Tom!' The breasts were attached to Kelly Tomlinson, and by default were associated with her annoying voice. Kelly was a single mum of one of the kids in Ben's class, well known for chasing anything in trousers, and even better if it was a man. The presence of a wedding ring on one's finger was simply more of a challenge in Kelly's eyes and she'd rather obviously wanted to get to know Tom 'better' for some time.

'Why don't you bring the kids round for coffee one day after school? It would be nice to catch up, if you're at a loose end or something.' She smiled her most appealing smile. 'Thanks Kelly, do have a huge amount on at the moment though, so maybe some other time.' He rushed past her to join the mob of parents who were waiting by the gates to pick up their offspring, irritated that he was blushing, knowing Sarah would find his embarrassment funny when he told her later. Tom felt the daily bunfight of parental rugby to get one's kids out of school before anyone else was some kind of metaphor for the state of society. Fortunately today, both Ben and Liam were waiting for him, avoiding the need for strained politeness. Liam was clutching a piece of A3, covered in a kaleidoscope of still glistening paint, seeking out any unsuspecting fabric upon which to become permanently ingrained.

'Here, Daddy,' Liam declared, solemnly presenting the picture to his father as if making a religious offering.

'That's amazing, mate!' he said, wondering if he should really tell his son not to give up the day-job, but deciding to let it go for now with the five-year-old. Besides, it might be destined for the Tate Modern.

'Right lads, hold my hands! Let's cross the road and jump in the truck.' They walked away from the school at a brisk pace, leaving behind the heaving parents and their heaving bosoms, back to the relative sanity of his world. He enjoyed the days when he picked them up, and returned home to do some work while they played around him. It often wasn't the most productive of times, work-wise, but as the head of his project and main driving force behind it, nobody could object to him taking a little downtime.

They lived just over a mile from the school in an imposing Edwardian townhouse, a double-fronted brick building with white-painted wooden fascias and sills, separated from the road by the narrow drive which ran across the front and around the left of the house to a garage at the back. Mature trees and large bushes screened the house from the street. Tom reversed the car round the side of the house, stopping short of the garage. The jeep came to a halt right outside the side door leading into the kitchen – the postman used their front door more than they did. He jumped out of the car and quickly walked around the back to let the boys out. He looked across to his left and got a glimpse of the garden with more mature shrubs and small trees surrounding the lush green lawn he had replanted and nurtured from the weed-infested pile that it had been when they bought the place. Tom bounded up the three stone steps to open the kitchen door, dumping his keys and laptop bag on the worktop as he went in. Experience told him to move out of the way to avoid being trampled to death by rampaging children as they quickly followed him inside, racing through the open-plan kitchen to the den. Within seconds, the sounds of the finer works of *Spongebob Squarepants* could be heard. The boys had kicked their school shoes off on the black slate floor, the white grouting something Tom and Sarah continually regretted now that the boys seemed to get it filthy on a daily basis. It was a total bastard to clean. Their schoolbags were tossed in well-practised fashion onto the work surface between the kitchen and the den as they ran past. Liam's painting had landed butter side up next to the bags, Tom was pleased to see. He busied himself with tidying their shoes – *they could really do with a clean, but, hey, they'll go another day* – and unpacking their schoolbags and lunch boxes – *no canteen food for my lads*. The boys had no idea how it happened, but as if by magic two small bowls of sliced apple and cups of orange juice materialised on the wide coffee table on which they were playing. They were great kids – a two-year gap between a five and a seven-year-old sometimes seemed a big one, but they were the best of friends and Ben liked being able to regress and play 'little' kids games with his brother.

Tom put the impossibly heavy kettle on the hob and then put away the lifting gear he had needed to get it on there. He always thought it ironic that Sarah, who rarely cooked, had chosen the pans. She liked how they looked, which was fine if you didn't have to lift them.

It wasn't long before he was sitting on the sofa in the den, the laptop on the oversized coffee table that served as both play surface and desk on days like today. He was ready to start some work. He opened the document containing the scientific protocols that would end his life, and the roles of his colleagues in managing his stasis so he could be brought round again. It was strange to be reading that while the boys played with their Power Rangers figures around him. He sipped steaming, hard-wrangled coffee from his 'Top Dad' mug and watched the Power Rangers football team take on the might of the Jurassic Stars, a common fixture in their household. Ben, who loved his football, manoeuvred the ball skilfully around Liam's dinosaurs, whilst Liam, who couldn't care less about sport as long as there was violence, tried to eat as many of the Rangers as possible. He stared across the table at their game for a little longer until his gaze was drawn back to the laptop screen.

'Woah, careful boys!' Tom raised his voice as the Red Ranger flew across the table, almost knocking the coffee mug over. Startled to hear Daddy shout, Ben was immediately contrite and Liam, even more so, came over and put his arms around Tom's neck.

'Sorry, Daddy,' he gave Tom a soggy kiss on the cheek, leaving a little string of snot behind where his nose had been running.

'No problem, guys – be a bit more careful of Daddy's laptop, okay? And can you play a little quieter?'

'Okay!' They both 'shouted' in a stage whisper and ran around the table to fetch the Thomas trains from the toy cupboards.

Tom settled back into his protocols – dispassionately writing how to react if he wasn't responding to the efforts to revive him, with separate notes and checklists about equipment and people to check and check-in with tomorrow.

Tom had just finished preparing dinner for the boys and was getting on with making food for the grown-ups when his wife Sarah walked in – Monday being a day she could work later at the art gallery while Tom had the kids. She came in to a fairly familiar bustling scene; the noise of the TV as the kids watched while they ate, and steam rising from pans on the cooker. She saw the chaos of toys, games, schoolbooks and various items of clothing scattered around the sofas and coffee table in the den with an open laptop at the epicentre of the scene of carnage.

'Had a good evening, boys? Tight ship as usual...' She smirked as she took off her jacket and hung it on the pegs by the kitchen door. When she turned back round to engage with her men-folk, a glass of fruity red Cabernet was placed in her hand and a kiss administered to her cheek. This one without snot.

'Nice day at the salt-mines, babe?' Tom asked as he returned to monitor the stove.

'Same old, same old,' she replied. 'How did your day go?'

'It went.' The same mantra they always shared after work rather than boring each other with this happened and that happened.

'And how are my big boys,' she gave her most winning smile to the kids while they sat at the table eating their pasta. Well, 'eating' was more of an abstract term in Liam's case, rather more like 'wearing'.

'Mmmffmfmm,' said Ben, his mouth full, and not wanting to break the new rule of not talking with your mouth full.

'I did a picture!' said Liam, flouting all authority and spraying tagliatelli over the table to Ben's disgust, pointing at his masterpiece on the kitchen worktop.

'Yes you did, my darling, and it's wonderful!' She was as enthusiastic as any mother would be when she looked at the further addition to her son's portfolio.

'F,' said Tom, incurring a gentle elbow in the ribs from his wife.

'What're you working on?' She nodded to the still open laptop. They never talked about their respective jobs, unless there was something specific they needed to get off their chests – work stayed in work. But this had a lot more riding on it than usual. She took a sip of her wine.

'Protocols. Want to make sure that everything's right, so everyone knows what they need to do.'

'And tomorrow?'

'Meetings, meetings, meetings! I'm gonna sit down with the whole team and run through it – like a walkthrough – test some of the kit.'

'Kit? Oh you mean like the cooling suit?' Sarah was repacking the boys schoolbags as they talked, putting Liam's PE gear in his bag – Ben wouldn't need his until the day after.

'Yeah all that. The defib as well – that's gotta be working!'

'Do you have a spare one, just in case?'

'No. They're like rocking-horse shit as it is, so no, make sure it's charged and off we go!'

Tom split his time between working on the laptop and fussing over the evening meal – he was making boned-out roast rabbit legs wrapped in pancetta on a simple mushroom risotto. Meanwhile, Sarah supervised the boys in the bath upstairs, which usually had Tom concerned that the tidal wave of spilled water would come right through the ceiling. Today was no different. The three of them re-appeared half an hour later, Ben and Liam wrapped up in superhero robes, Iron Man and Hulk, respectively. Liam decided that now was the time to open his robe and strut his stuff, flashing his manliness at everyone. Ben found it hysterically funny, as did his parents, doing their best to ignore their son and hide their smiles.

'Wow, as impressive as his father,' said Sarah, holding finger and thumb about an inch apart.

'Am I not IMPRESSIVE!' roared a comedically shocked Tom, in his best 'This is Sparta' voice. 'Never had any complaints, love...' He turned and looked at his son, parading semi-naked around the den. 'Although, you might be right...'

Sarah quickly restored order, and before long the two boys were dressed in pyjamas, had read their schoolbooks and were giving Daddy a kiss before teeth-cleaning and bed. She was back downstairs twenty minutes later.

'So how're the protocols going?' she relocated her wine glass – which she hadn't seen for some time – and took a long draught.

'Okay, it's just there's a lot to write before we go through them tomorrow,' he pulled a face, nodding towards the laptop, which now sat on the kitchen worktop.

'Do you need to have them completely done by then?' she asked, switching into her ultra-organised, let's-make-an-action-plan voice, while leaning against one of the stools at the breakfast bar.

'No, not really, I s'pose,' he took a gulp of wine. 'But I want as much as I can written down so they can pick holes in them, *and* give me enough time for revisions.'

She looked down at the laptop and absently started to read what was on screen as Tom returned to the cooker...

***

Tom and Sarah met at a music bar when they were at university, and had been almost inseparable since. Tom was on a Hawaiian-themed MedClub night out alongside a mob of drunken medics, in the inevitable fancy dress. The future of medical science walked into the place, and were assaulted by the sound of the guest band running through a deafening set of 70s and 80s pop hits. The place was packed, and to get to the bar Tom waded through a sea of half-drunk students swaying from side to side, either to the music or because of cheap cider. He eased his way through the throng, when the group of girls in front of him parted and he saw her. Her piercing blue eyes opened wider than anyone's he'd ever known as he was pushed forward by the sway behind him. Her tightly curled blonde hair hung down in ringlets, framing her face and accentuating her brilliant smile and full lips. The rest of her hair was loosely tied back and cascaded over her shoulders.

'Easy, tiger,' she smiled and put a hand on his chest to stop him stumbling any further forward.

'Wow, sorry,' he yelled over the sound of the band. 'And I'm not even that drunk!'

Her playful smile widened. 'You're not trying hard enough then!'

Tom was dressed in the loudest yellow, green and orange shirt he had been able to find in a charity shop, straw hat, grass skirt and a garland of fake flowers round his neck. Sarah's friend, who Tom later found out was called Gemma, leant across and shouted in his ear. 'Are you gonna wait any longer to give my friend those flowers on her birthday?' She slurred ever so slightly – *thoshe flowash*. Tom looked from one girl to the other, mock surprise on his face.

'It's your birthday?!' He tried to look genuinely taken back. 'Nobody told me! If only I'd known...' he shook his head as if disappointed to be kept out of the loop. Sarah was clearly enjoying this playful banter. Tom reached up, lifted the flowers over his head and carefully lowered them, with some ceremony, over her shoulders. He then leant forward and gave her a chaste kiss on the cheek, whispering, 'Happy Birthday,' as he did so. Sarah blushed slightly but her friend was having none of it.

'Is that it?' Gemma responded, now the official spokesperson for her friend. 'Is that as good a kiss as you can manage for my friend, on her birthday?' She looked somewhere between angry and disgusted.

'Was it not very good?' More feigned surprise from Tom. 'Wasn't it?' He turned to Sarah. 'Wasn't it?' Her smile slowly pulled into a sceptical expression.

'Maybe, maybe not,' she said with a slight shake of the head.

'You've got to be able to do better than that!' goaded Gemma.

'Yes. You're right of course. Must try harder, must try harder,' he said to no one in particular, lifting and lowering his shoulders, breathing in and out noisily, puffing his cheeks out, looking like a long-jumper preparing himself to race down the runway.

'Kiss her, kiss her, kiss her,' chanted all of Sarah's friends in unison. Tom pretended to spray an imaginary breath freshener in his mouth, then his eyes met hers and his playful expression became deadly serious. *If you want a proper kiss, you'll get a proper kiss.* Placing his hands on her shoulders, he bent forward, his mouth closing in on hers. He stopped about an inch away, as her head tilted backwards, accentuating the curve of her neck. He paused long enough to see her eyes had closed, and her lips were pursed to meet his. She started to smile as he made her wait, and with that he crushed his lips to hers. She pushed up to meet his kiss and they held the pose, far longer than a simple birthday kiss might have permitted. Encouraged, he opened his mouth to allow the tip of his tongue to touch her lips, waiting for her reaction – *how far did she want to go with this*? She responded immediately, opening her mouth and pushing her tongue forward to meet his. The girls around them gave a loud cheer and were whooping as their tongues danced together for the first time. Her arms slid around his waist and his did likewise, pulling her hips firmly against him. They were oblivious to the raucous noise and cat-calls all around them and the deafening strains of the band covering Gloria Gaynor's 'I Will Survive'. He pressed against her belly, no longer hiding his interest, but rather wanting to see what she did in return. She responded by pulling him tighter to her and pushing back even harder. He finally broke the kiss and pulled away, looking at the lust in her eyes – never breaking eye contact.

'So,' he said, his voice tight and thick. He cleared his throat and tried again. 'So, is that all you were wanting for your birthday? Or was there... something else?' Their hands clasped.

'I'm sure I can think of something,' her eyes glinted at the prospect of what that might be.

'Me too.' He leaned in and whispered in her ear. Her expressive eyes widened as she listened.

***

Sarah's eyes widened now as she read the protocol. Tom had listed every task to be performed, with the initials of those responsible in brackets afterwards, referring to everyone as 'all hands'.

...Confirm & record 'no output' – note time
- *Start 20' countdown (SK)*
- *Continue ice water pump (CB)*
- *All spare hands pack ice packs around body (AH)*
- *Check all monitors – observations, EEG, ECG, videos, pumps (AH, SK)*
- *Manually record core temperature each minute (CP)*
- *Begin blood and tissue sample collection as per separate protocol (CP)*
- *Prepare warm water tank and manifold for switchover. Check tank temperature = 37.5° (CB)*
- *Anaesthetics – prepare drugs as per Drugs Protocol (SE)*
- *Defib team on standby – check battery levels – ready to charge (SE, AD)*
- *Coffee and doughnuts if you get a minute (AH)*

T- plus 20 minutes
- *Remove ice packs ASAP – care with disposal (AH)*
- *Switch-over cold pump to warm – manually check pipes are pumping warm water (CB)*
- *Remove chest section of cold suit, dry skin if necessary (CP)*
- *Commence Defib and Drugs Protocols (AD, Al)*

Sarah read this dispassionately-written laboratory methodology with her heart being squeezed tighter and tighter in her chest. She hated how he'd referred to himself as a 'body' and his flippancy about getting a coffee, which she knew he'd included to lighten the mood on the day. Tears rolled down her cheeks as she read about drying his skin ready for the defibrillator. She bit her lip, exhaling through her teeth and looked to the ceiling to try and fight them back. Tom had finished cooking and was ready to serve when he heard her sob, saw what she had been reading and wrapped her in his arms in a second.

'Hey! It's okay,' he whispered in her ear, holding her close as she clung to him.

'I'm sorry. It's just I know what's going to happen, and I'm glad you and everyone else are so organised, and that there'll be a lot of people in that room to help you, but...' she sobbed into his chest again. 'Seeing it written like that...' she breathed out hard and wafted her hands in front of her face to cool herself down.

'Well I didn't particularly want you to see that–' he said sheepishly.

'So close the bloody laptop!' she said, angry for both her and for the kids, who had been playing obliviously around Tom as he worked.

'Okay, yes, you're right, I'm sorry. And you're right again, it's because of all these protocols that the day will go smoothly and everything'll be fine.' He gathered her in his arms again.

***

Dinner was a more muted affair than usual; Sarah seemed very distant and didn't really engage in any conversation that Tom tried to start. He had wanted to broach the subject of his Will, but decided to put that on hold and not push her any further. They tidied the kitchen together in silence then sat down to watch some TV – selecting the next in the series of *24* they had been watching, but not even Jack Bauer could lift the atmosphere by single-handedly taking on the might of the North Korean Special Forces. In bed, they lay reading, side by side, but Sarah couldn't concentrate on her book for long and switched her light off. She turned to kiss him goodnight, rolled over but immediately turned back.

'Hold me, Tom,' she said. He switched his light off and they spooned, his arms wrapped around her vest top and pyjama shorts, his hand cupping her breast and his other arm resting on her lower abdomen. He pressed himself against her, his arousal obvious, her body warm and pliable. On any other night it would have been a recipe for not going to sleep just yet. Tonight he resisted and just held her, feeling her breathing and her warmth, smelling the conditioner in her hair. They both lay awake with their thoughts; Sarah thinking that he would get a hard-on anytime, anywhere, before thinking that she couldn't manage without him, she couldn't *live* without him. Tom enjoyed her *feel* first and foremost, then thought about *her* and them as a family, and how he couldn't imagine not being with them. And it was with these most uncomfortable feelings that he drifted off to asleep.

2.

Tom pulled the Cherokee out onto the road from the driveway, with Sarah about to leave right behind him to take the boys to school. Just before he left, in a scene from some old utopian movie, Tom kissed both of the kids as they sat at the breakfast table and was handed his coffee flask by his wife, who in turn kissed him on the cheek.

'Safe trip,' she said as always, smiling.

'You too,' replied Tom who didn't think for a minute that Sarah had been replaced by a Stepford wife.

He drove along the quiet leafy street, overhung by large oak and beech trees. Tall hedges framed the gardens with overgrowing buddleja and cotoneaster spilling around brick walls creating growing obstacles for unwary dog-walkers and pavement cyclists. The cooler drizzle of the day before was long gone, with another balmy day forecast, more like early August than the second week in September. Watery morning sunshine created sunbeams on the road as it diffused through the leaves. He turned right onto Southern Way, the main road heading into the city. The Jeep steadily picked up speed through the suburban green-belt and climbed the hill. The road twisted through heavy woodland, with the old hall emerging from the trees on the right. A once stately building with pillars guarding the entrance, the place was now in need of at least a little love and a coat of paint, but Tom suspected it needed a lot more than that from the glimpses he could get through the trees. The road curved as it crested the hill, a stone wall alarmingly close, following the road like the crash barrier on a race track. Descending, the road meandered slowly downwards through the woods, before dropping more steeply and emerging from the greenery to give a view of the wide basin that was the city in front – civilisation rising from the ground.

Tom approached the hospital grounds of the newly re-built and modernised St Catherine's University Hospital NHS Trust. The old Victorian hospital had been a sprawling thing of tarnished tiled corridors and endless anti rooms, of cubbyholes on ever-changing levels linked by non-disabled-friendly steps and stairs, with the odd sweeping staircase and massive church-like open hallway. Oh yes, and then there was the asylum in the back half of the site, where unspeakable things had been done to inmates with electrodes and leeches, often at the same time. The whole place had become unfit for purpose, but, it seemed to Tom, when they closed the madhouse, they transferred the crazy people to the board of trustees of the university, who thought it best to try and preserve at least some of the old building for historical and 'lest we forget' purposes. The kind of purposes that cost twice as much as simply levelling the place and starting again. For ten years, building and renovation had been inconveniencing both staff and patients alike but was at last nearing completion. Peripheral buildings had been flattened some time before and modern, state-of-the-art pathology labs, maternity suites, education and rehabilitation centres built in stand-alone blocks, all with crisply modern architecture of glass and zinc, mosaic tiles and white render. It looked like the kids had been given a massive pile of new Lego and invited to go for it after being fully revved-up on high octane sweets. All of the unmatching blocks were cleverly linked by walkways and corridors which made it much more convenient for patient and visitor movement, even if it was often quicker to cut across the car park to get to wherever you wanted to be. He looked now at the centrepiece of the whole site, the imposing Victorian stone front of the old hospital, with its main elevation up to six floors. A large stone arch curved over the front entrance which was now an illuminated 'Welcome' sign, matching the hospital logo. The painstakingly restored masonry was fitted with huge new sash windows and overhanging oriel bay windows on the upper levels, supported by specially commissioned stone gargoyle corbels – just the right tone and atmosphere for a healthcare facility. The new copper roof, with its complex lead work for the now-defunct chimneys, had begun to fade from the original shiny orange. In places it was already green, as it would all be, eventually.

The old building was undoubtedly impressive, and a lot of work had gone into restoring its imposing exterior. The integrity of the brief was maintained inside as well, radiators refitted with heavy, old-school designs, and oak doors throughout. Hospital networks and cloud systems or not, Tom mused that the admin staff should be obliged to use typewriters and pen and ink to maintain the authenticity.

The giant main building of the new hospital stretched across the site, rising to five storeys of ultramodern glass and steel, topped by a football-pitch sized flat roof. To the left it joined awkwardly with the six floors of the old building, the research facility drawing the short straw in transitioning new to old with corridors sloping at angles to integrate the differing floor levels, and the roof above trying to fit with the copper of its neighbour. Between the research block and the main hospital sat the vaulted atrium of the main entrance and further to the right were the wards and theatres.

The last of the building work had just been completed on the main hospital. The tower crane was still in place, bolted to the roof, where it had lifted in the triangular sheets of glass for the frameless, self-supporting domed roof above the main entrance. The whole atrium space and glass roof did look incredibly impressive, but every single pigeon and seagull in the city was storing up a shit to completely whitewash that glass inside the next three months. Pete's Windows round the corner had been looking forward to a bumper contract to keep that thing clean from the moment the glazing lorry arrived on site.

Joined to the left of the old hospital sat the round, four-storey medical school, bulging out in front and behind the old building like a buttress and looking like the old was hiding behind the bushel of its shiny new friend, the slate roof leaning against its neighbour. The medical school wrapped around the back of the original building, linking walkways and corridors that ran the length of the whole hospital. These were matched at the front to form main arteries and thoroughfares. The whole slightly concave structure appeared to have a large Victorian stone wart about a third of the way along that really didn't belong there at all.

Like any civilised piece of architecture, nobody had considered the smokers who congregated outside the main entrance to properly aerate their lungs before an anaesthetist did it for them – or to fill them with 'proper' gases again, washing away all the pure oxygen crap they had been fed. People in pyjamas, dressing gowns, on crutches and in wheelchairs were congregated just to one side of the revolving doors, the hospital having reluctantly added a few cigarette bins retrospectively. Perhaps the idea was that everyone would be so in awe of the new building they would instantly lose any cravings they might otherwise have had. They should have talked to the pigeons first.

Tom swung into the main hospital grounds and drove by all the shiny glass, taking in the smell of cigarette smoke, the wart on the landscape, and the bulging curve of the medical school, giving way at the mini-roundabout at the end to a hospital services truck, its back open and full of yellow and red plastic waste bags. He turned right and drove around the gently curving back of the building, all white painted and crisp, turning down the ramp and through the security barrier to the underground car park reserved for staff of the Life Sciences Research Institute. He parked and punched in the code for the lift that took him to the top floor – so much for the 'take the stairs not the lift' signs everywhere. The lift opened out into the reception area for the Human Physiology Research Centre, from which numerous corridors led, like the arms of an octopus. He nodded to the receptionists, Helen and Denise, who, as usual, barely acknowledged him. They'd worked for Tom's predecessor, Professor Dakin, and had fawned over him. He'd ruled his department like a tyrant and was older than Yoda when Tom worked under him as a registrar. When he finally retired, neither woman had any time for Tom, giving the impression that they thought he was too young and inexperienced, and too 'nice' to people.

Tom strode across the small foyer, its brown leather sofas and mahogany coffee tables looking like refugees from a high-street coffee shop chain. He pushed through the double fire doors which swung shut behind him, satisfyingly sucking together as they did so. The corridor beyond the modern sleek café charm of the foyer was now building-site chic, with barely finished walls simply boarded out, and electrics contained in trunking yet to be sunk behind wall panelling. The university's redevelopment budget was not a bottomless pit and more and more additions were being made as people thought of them. Departments like Tom's, at the bottom of the food chain, were glad to have a roof over their heads. It might get finished – one day – but don't hold your breath. He walked down the slope as the levels changed half a floor – one of the internal compromises needed to accommodate the old building next door. The floor, of temporary boarding prior to tiles being laid, was stained and marked with black rubber lines – the tyre tracks of trolleys. The surfaces of the boards had been worn away in places or partially torn off, exposing screw heads or the loose fibreboard below. As the floor levelled out he could march along at his normal fast pace and he pushed through the final set of fire doors to his domain.

The lab was actually a series of laboratories and storage areas arranged around two corridors that crossed one another. The main administrative section was in the centre of the cross which everyone now called the 'hub' and had arisen out of both chance and necessity. When the research group first moved into the facility, electric cables still hung down from the roof and there was no running water. Boyand had equipped his office, and the others just set up their own workstations in a haphazard manner outside the office in the intersection of the two corridors. The workstations remained, everyone became used to the ad hoc arrangement so that when other office rooms were finished and made available, nobody wanted to move. At least this area was finished, but more from grant funding than the university putting its hand in its pocket.

Tom was at his desk by just after eight, putting the final touches to his protocols. Unusually he'd been the first in and grabbed the opportunity to re-dot some 'i's and cross some 't's for the third or fourth time. Scott Knowles arrived shortly afterwards, and Tom could hear the banging of doors getting closer, his telltale tuneless whistle in evidence whenever a door was opened. He popped his head round the perpetually open office door.

'Morning, boss. Coffee?' he enquired, raising an eyebrow above the rims of his small round glasses. He ran a hand through his floppy blond hair, cut short at the sides and with a lazy centre parting.

'Erm erm erm, make a decision Tom for Christ's sake. Erm... no, thanks Scotty – I'll leave it until the meeting. But while you're there, would y'mind filling the kettle after you so we can have a big pot going for nine o'clock, please?'

'Sure. Everything okay?' Scott was looking over his glasses slightly at Tom, like a concerned school teacher.

'Yeah, no, everything's fine mate – just a thousand things going on in my head this morning is all. Complex stuff like whether I want a drink will have to book some thinking time!'

'Chloe says I get that kind of delay *normally*, let alone if I have a lot going on!'

'Smart girl that Chloe!' Chloe Palmer was Tom's research assistant, whom he'd brought in at the start of this study. She, like the rest of them, was a qualified doctor who'd drifted more into research than clinical practice *per se* from a Cardiology rotation. She was looking to extend some of the current work into different avenues of post-doctoral research. 'Not that smart, though!' Chloe and Scott had just started seeing each other. Scott turned away in search of caffeine.

'Hi Tom!' Chloe replaced him in the doorway. She was bright and full of energy, easy with her smile and easy with other people, she could brighten up a room by walking into it. Chloe was all flouncy skirts and dark tights with boots or clumpy heels like today, long curly dark hair cascading over her shoulders. She was wearing a black skirt with a red and yellow pencil design, accompanied by a snug-fitting grey cardigan on top that flattered her figure and left her neckline exposed. He caught himself looking, and so did she.

'Er, yeah, sorry, morning Chloe – just a bit pre-occupied this morning – all okay with you?' Tom blushed.

'Fine by me, Chief,' she beamed, leaning forward with her hands flat on his desk, the two open buttons at the top of her cardigan inviting his gaze. 'Anything I can get you?' Chloe loved to flirt, and when they first started working together, Tom wondered if she might have wanted to do more than flirt with him, but, it seemed, that was just Chloe, and he was wise to it by now.

'Yes! Could you get the spec sheets on the cooling and heating pumps, please, I want to check the turnarounds on them before Charlie comes over to the meeting.' Flirting over, Chloe stood up – all business-like and professional – and left to pull the data he needed.

Mags came in just after eight as usual and was surprised to find other people in before her. That *never* happened, in *her* department, where she ruled the admin and so ran the place, no matter what the medics might think. It was still early and the rest of the team gradually trickled in. They were joined by staff from other departments who would provide cover in their own specialist areas on the day of the experiment. Charlie Broadshaw was from the Engineering department of the main university. Tom had met with Engineering's research team some months ago to discuss how they might cool him very quickly and then reverse the process at the appropriate time. Using a hoist-like lifting rig to take him into and out of baths of ice cold, and later warm water was the preferred option for some time. It became clear, however, that the logistics of working on a 'body' immersed in water would be difficult. Problems were raised, such as infection risk from the water, the presence of electrical apparatus when someone was immersed, and time lost using a hoist when they were going through the resuscitation process. The idea was finally consigned to the recycle bin. It was Charlie, a research student and keen rugby player, who came up with the idea of the 'cold suit'. Two years ago he had undergone surgery to repair the front part of his shoulder after dislocating it while playing for the university. During his immediate post-op care he wore a neoprene compression cuff wrapped around the shoulder attached to a tube and a small tank containing iced water. He could circulate cold water around the harness by raising the tank above the height of the shoulder, and drain warmer water from it by lowering it. Charlie expanded on this and had worked on designs of a whole-body suit of a similar design. Ultimately, he and Tom decided that it was too unwieldy and instead opted to attach a mesh net lined with close-packed rubber piping to Tom as he lay on the hospital bed – like covering him in under-floor heating pipes. Charlie designed a system to continually pump cold water around Tom's body by dividing it into sections, supplied by separate pipe work, all attached to a central manifold and pump that would ensure all parts were continually flushed with cold water. Just like after Charlie's own surgery, the pump would re-circulate the water – refreshing in a large tank full of ice. His idea won the day and Charlie himself got the gig of technician on the job.

Charlie had only been to the unit once before, and was wandering around like a little boy lost when Chloe guided him to the hub. He looked like he'd slept in his clothes in the tumble dryer, so crumpled were his brown cargo pants and black polo shirt. His dark curly hair was similarly styled and even his expression had all-night-bender written all over it. Puffing out his cheeks, he set down the large cardboard box he'd been labouring to carry.

'You okay, Charlie?' Scotty asked, shaking his hand.

'Yeah fine, just up late working on pump pressures and turnarounds,' he looked around, familiarising himself with the place.

'Snap!' said an enthusiastic Tom, holding up the pump schematics from Chloe. 'Great minds and ours think alike!' In an instant they commandeered the nearest desk and started pointing at various aspects of the pump drawings and cross-referencing these to pump spec data.

'This place is gonna be like nerd nirvana!' Scotty smiled happily to himself.

More and more people gathered in the hub for the meeting. Professor Andrea Dent arrived with nurses Shirley Wilmslow and Cath Griffiths, who together would form the resuscitation team, along with Sigurd 'Aliens' Edmunsson, the anaesthetist on Tom's research team. Two porters arrived as well.

'Thanks for coming everyone,' Tom stood slightly off-centre in the middle of the hub, his office door to his back and his audience informally scattered around chairs and desks around him. 'I think you've all got some coffee, but do feel free to get a refill if you want.'

'Are you gonna be *that* boring, Tom?' Bob Wauberg had been the last to arrive, and he was typically lounging at Chloe's desk at the back of the group. Everyone turned to look at him.

'I never could be as eloquent as you, Bob!' Smiles rippled through the assembly. 'I'd just like to say that we appreciate and value everyone's input into today and also for the coming days of the experiment. So much so that one day, soon, I'll choose a bar and there'll be drinks all night with your names on!' Some weak cheers rang around to signal the end of the preliminaries.

'As I know Mike and Dave need to be in clinics this morning, I'll get the ball rolling with them. Will you guys be able to collect some of our equipment, please? That includes our bed. It's currently being stored in Storage Hall 3, which is the new and far more romantic name for what used to be called the Wessex Building back in the day, at the far corner of the campus beyond the Med Club. It'll be separate from whatever else is stored in there, wrapped in plastic and has my name and the name of the unit on it. If you wouldn't mind getting that as soon as you can, today or tomorrow, please, that'd be great. Apparently the two old chest freezers we managed to 'liberate' from the kitchens before their refurb should be there too, so can you bring them as well please?' The two porters waved in agreement and then left, nodding at people as they passed, making their way back up the corridor.

'Charlie, what about the tanks?' Tom continued, looking across at Charlie, who perked up.

'Yeah the tanks are finished, we've done the water-tests on them and they worked fine. I can have our own estates people on the main site load them and the pump onto a van and bring them over, maybe tomorrow? That's if you'd like?' In his excitement, Charlie wasn't sure when he last took a breath.

'Yeah that should be fine, if you get them to bring 'em to the loading bay in the underground car park.' Tom moved on.

'I'd like to thank Cath and Shirley, my nurses from clinic, and Prof Andrea Dent, our Head of Emergency Medicine, for agreeing to come over to be our resus team for the day. I know Andrea had some issues with the project at its inception, but I'm delighted to have somebody with her expertise and experience, hopefully looking after me!' Tom and Andrea exchanged a nod and a smile. Indeed, during the Ethics Committee phase, where Tom presented the project to the select board of the medical school – who would judge the study on its merit, request changes or simply throw out the proposal – Professor Dent had been vehemently opposed to the study taking place at all.

***

When Tom first came to work at the university, it was as a registrar on the cardiology team. Within a year he'd been given a consultant's post, and his stock was rising within the department. He then branched into research, working on the area of cell death; looking for markers and the potential for reversibility of some processes. His work had far-reaching implications for both medicine and biotechnology, and was starting to draw worldwide interest. As a clinician and a researcher, he was regarded as one of the 'bright young things' in the corridors of power and the university was happy to fund his work. All of that changed, however, when he became more and more interested in near-death experience and his study of those claiming to have had one. When he proposed his new study to the Ethics Committee, Andrea Dent had petitioned to have the idea thrown out, feeling that the ethos and experimental design were pure folly, and potentially very damaging for the credibility of the medical school, whatever the outcome. Andrea had been bitterly disappointed and somewhat cynical when the Committee actually approved the project. She was right to feel that way – the study hadn't been passed because the Committee liked the idea, but rather so the university could be seen to be supporting one of its young researchers. They knew full well, however, that the project would stall because there was no way Tom would get any kind of research grant to pay for it. What they hadn't counted on was Kyle Solomon.

The previous year, Kyle Solomon, a young Hollywood actor, starred in a remake of an airport hijacking movie from the 70s. More disaster movie than *Die Hard 2*, it had been a box office smash and propelled Solomon onto the Hollywood A-list. Visiting his parents in Colorado at the start of the winter season, Kyle, driving in bad weather on an icy road, lost control of his Ford Explorer, which slid off the road and onto a frozen lake, breaking though the ice crust and sliding into the freezing water beneath, submerging the vehicle completely. Local people saw the accident happen and so help arrived on the scene almost immediately, but it was twenty minutes before they could hook-up a truck with a winch and fix it to some stout trees to stop it too sliding in. By the time they got Kyle's body clear of the water, into an ambulance and in transit to the local trauma centre, being warmed, pumped with oxygen and shocked by a defibrillator, forty minutes had elapsed. It was due to the efforts of the paramedics on the scene, the staff at the hospital and his immersion in ice-cold water – preserving him so efficiently – that Kyle Solomon not only survived, but stayed in hospital for just one night, and was none the worse for his icy adventure. As his story had been very big news across all media at the time, Tom made contact and invited him to take part in the 'near-death' survey. In turn, when Solomon found out that Tom was planning his own study that needed funding, the now wealthy A-lister was only too happy to write a cheque.

In typically 'Tom' fashion, after the project was given the go-ahead, he sought out Andrea Dent, not only to bury the hatchet with her, but also to bring her on board as the clinical lead in resuscitating him in the experiment.

With the surprise funding of the project, the hospital went into full-on defensive mode. Use of equipment and other members of staff was denied, previously open doors closed and the 'welcome' mats taken away. It became very obvious to all involved that management didn't want the study to go ahead. Tom could get around equipment issues because the funding would allow it, within reason It was also relatively easy, with the building work going on, to 'acquire' things. The old Wessex building became like the warehouse at the end of *Raiders of the Lost Ark* – an Aladdin's cave of old equipment that the hospital didn't want to dispose of but also didn't know what to do with. The store was poorly catalogued and so people in the know from across departments in the cash-strapped hospital stripped the place like locusts. Tom quickly got to be in the know. He even managed to obtain a defibrillator, condemned by the Estates department because of a persistent series of reported faults, and because the new Emergency Unit wanted more modern kit. Strangely, when the defib arrived at the hub, it worked perfectly, with none of the previously reported problems.

The real headache for the group was staffing. Ordinarily they would approach a member of staff and the manager of their unit to ask if they could be released – 'borrowed' – for a short period. It would never usually be a problem provided enough notice was given to allow for cover, or shifts to be swapped. Now, with the hospital management telling all to close ranks, every request was refused. This sent Tom into guerrilla mode, calling in favours, asking staff whom he knew, asking those who would be off duty, or were prepared to swap shifts ahead of time without explaining why. They were still getting a lot of interdepartmental help, but this was without the knowledge of those departments.

***

'I've handed each of you a protocol for what will happen next Wednesday. Some of this I've obviously discussed with you, and it might seem strange to be handed back your own work, but it's simply because these protocols will form the basis of both the medical notes for the procedure and the methodology for writing up the study. We've protocols for anaesthetics – before and after – resus, thermal, blood and tissue samples, general staff, telemetry recording and aftercare. None of these are set in stone, guys, all I've done is taken the discussions I've had with all of you these last few months, cross-referenced them with the literature and written them like this. Please feel free to make any changes you wish and flag them up to me by close of play tomorrow so I can look at them over the weekend. On the day, I'll ask each of you to sign the protocol for your section, which'll bind you to undertaking it. You'll obviously have read them so it shouldn't be a problem.'

Tom spent the next two hours moving between groups in the hub discussing various aspects of the protocols. Most of the issues were simple mistakes, typos or creating slightly more logical timelines – do *this* now and *then* that. He had with him his master copies and was gradually covering them in red ink as he walked through the experiment with everyone. Occasionally something more significant arose – an oversight or other scenario that hadn't occurred to him.

'Hang on, how do we monitor the temperature of the warm water?' Scott looked up from his handout.

'There's a thermostat built into the immersion system,' said Charlie.

'Does it have a fail-safe and an alarm or something?' asked Chloe.

'No,' Charlie was disappointed at this oversight.

'Can it have?' Tom paused with his pen over the relevant section on his notes.

'Yes! No problem, will sort it by Monday!' Charlie replied, triumphantly, his mind already designing the modifications needed.

'Thank you,' Tom ticked a box on the additional check-list he was writing as he went along.

'What do we do with all that ice?' asked Andrea.

'Put it back in the freezers at the time, easiest place to dispose of it,' Tom made a note to add this.

'Aren't those bags going to leak melting water and condensation all over the floor, though?' This was the crux of Andrea's concern.

'Yes, that's true – we'll need a supply of paper and ordinary towels just to keep the floor dry... Chloe, can you raid one of the wards for some towels, please? And can we get some towel rolls ordered sharpish?'

'Okay boss, check.'

'What if the resus protocol doesn't work?' Aliens stopped the room dead.

There was no answer, no protocol, nothing written. Tom had thought long and hard about the consequences of what he was doing but, apart from arranging his personal affairs, he hadn't committed anything to paper. Up until now this had felt like just his experiment, his design, the culmination of three years of planning based on previous data that he knew better than anyone else. As such it couldn't fail. And now the realisation struck that, during the experimental phase, he would be the one person who couldn't influence the outcome, and he was relying on everyone else.

What if the resus protocol doesn't work?

What if the resus protocol doesn't work?

'Improvise,' said Tom, not bothering to write it down.

***

By the end of the meeting, it seemed every possible question had been asked and every base covered – Tom had now signed a consent form to just about every possible medical procedure including surgery if needed, which gave the team (and anyone else they might need to draft in) carte blanche to do what they wanted. The rest of the delegates drifted away by lunchtime, leaving Charlie as the only non-member of research staff.

'Okay Charlie, what's in the box?' All morning, Tom had barely been able to resist asking what it was that Charlie had staggered in carrying.

'Your cold suit!' Charlie said, eyes glinting as he smiled.

'Really?! Let's take a look.'

Charlie opened the box and lifted out a disorganised mess of plastic and mesh, setting it on the floor. He placed each section in heaps according to their labelling, opening them out to lay flat, looking like someone had tried to install under floor heating pipes on a fishing net in someone's garage. That wasn't too far off because the pipes were simple rubber hosing – more flexible than under floor heating pipes – and he had used the Engineering department's garage in which to build the device. The mesh onto which the pipe work was clipped with cable ties was from a garden centre – the kind used to keep birds off crops and fruit trees. It had been painstaking work, making two sections for each arm and leg – upper and lower – along with two for his torso and a bespoke 'helmet' that would ensure Tom was completely surrounded by the suit. Charlie laid the sections out on the floor to give Tom an idea of how the suit would look and work.

'So the pressure in the pumps will have no problem surmounting the twists, turns and angles of all the pipes, Charlie?' Tom asked, his hand cupping his chin as he studied the system.

'No, no problem. They aren't rigid pipes, so the back pressure in the system isn't too high. The mesh will distort, though, as the pipes try and straighten themselves out, so I've reinforced some sections with wire running along the pipe to improve the rigidity. No issues other than that.'

'So, get the tanks in and the manifold and we're –'

'– Good to go!' Charlie finished for him.

3.

The glass door creaked open as Boyand entered the storeroom – technology in sealed, dust-proof lab environments not extending to quiet door hinges. Tom breezed in, wanting to check for himself – again – that the medical paraphernalia was as it should be; saline, adrenaline, atrapine, and Zol. Zol, the drug developed by Aliens as his primary research interest – his life's work – developed back home in Iceland and now primed for its first human trial.

Sigurd Edmunsson was a brilliant anaesthetist. Tom read his work on resuscitation several years before in the medical journal *Acta Anaesthesiologica Scandinavica*, whilst researching something else. He'd made contact, and it hadn't taken much correspondence before they both decided they shared a common research interest and wanted to work together. Along with Scott at the beginning, Sig became a permanent member of the team. When he first arrived in the department, one of their undergraduate students at the time mis-heard his name and said, 'Sigourney? As in *Aliens*?' The name stuck. For Sigurd himself, a serious clinician and academic, the flippant side of the banter in the unit didn't sit well, but he accepted his nickname because it meant he belonged, like a tribal badge.

Sig's research developed new stimulants to use primarily within resuscitation, but now for use in re-starting the hearts of those recently dead. Hydroxyphenylamine xydol was the class of drug and bastardised name that Sig came up with for his stimulant. A mouthful for anyone, Sig christened his drug 'Zol' from day one. Part of the same catecholamine family as adrenaline and noradrenaline, Sig had modified its chemical structure, 'bolting' an extra oxygen molecule on the side to act as a magic bullet in stimulating the heart. It was the culmination of three years development work for him and colleagues in other labs worldwide. The group designed numerous new compounds but none of them delivered satisfactory results. Sig's trials, however, at a time when serious questions were being raised over the efficacy of adrenaline in resuscitation, were successful. The final trials, whilst representing a bad time for a variety of mammals in the university labs, allowed him to perfect dosage algorithms for body weight. These final experiments had startling results. Sig, of course, hadn't informed his international cohort of his success, 'not just yet' anyway. Human trials were a long time away... or next week as Tom preferred to call it.

The door closed silently as Tom headed through the equipment racks – metal cages arranged in parallel rows containing everything from barely portable centrifuges to test tubes, packs of sterile disposables and glass containers of chemicals. The main lights in the store were switched off, so the blue-white neon glow from the bank of fridges at the far end of the room provided ambient lighting. For their laboratory studies on cellular breakdown, the group had a range of glassware from petri dishes to large volumetric flasks on shelves that would keep any drug-dealing chemistry teacher happy. The fridges along the back row contained perishable items such as blood and platelet packs, including ones earmarked for Tom, ready for re-introduction into his body if required. He had been regularly donating samples for months now to build-up a significant stockpile – just in case. He checked the labels on each pack, cross-referencing them with the check-list on his clipboard.

A sliding noise caught his attention. Turning to his left, the glare of the fluorescent light from the fridges blinded him to anyone's presence in the gloom of the rest of the store. He trailed his hand along the glass doors of the fridges as he tiptoed along. There couldn't be anyone else in the store other than one of his team, yet paranoia tickled the edge of his consciousness. He turned the corner at the end of the cold 'deli' section. Silhouetted by the fridge light, a large figure loomed above him, and Tom's breath caught in his throat. He took one more step and realised that the mysterious figure was Aliens. He was looking through his own inventory of vials and fluid pouches, the harsh neon glow enough to illuminate his work area.

'Hey Sig,' Tom said, matter-of-factly.

'Hello Tom.' Sig replied, eyes remaining fixed on his clipboard. He was wearing the 'This time it's war!' T-shirt they'd bought him for his birthday.

'Is everything okay? You were quiet in the meeting yesterday, and again today?' The concern was evident in Tom's voice.

'You know why Tom, and what I think.' Sig looked up from his chart for the first time, half his face in shadow. 'I don't see why you brought in Andrea, that's all. I understood that I would be taking care of you and bringing you back, not someone else.'

Sig's Icelandic accent had a typical Nordic tonal stress, although softer than the similar sounding Swedish and Norwegian. Most of the time his accent was difficult to pick up apart from an almost lispy Icelandic 'th' sound. Today he was rolling his Rs more because he was angry.

'Yes, but I need someone there who can open my chest to massage my heart if need be. And there is a certain inevitability of someone of her standing naturally sliding into the clinical lead position when you bring her in.'

'Okay, but I feel a bit marginalised is all – I'll get over it but I'm pissed off.'

'You're not a surgeon are you, mate?' Tom asked patiently.

'No and never have been, so why hire me in the first place?' He met Tom's gaze – questioning him.

'Because we've been friends for a long time, you're the best anaesthetist around... And you have Zol!' Tom smiled.

'Oh, so you only want me for my drug?' Aliens looked fiercely at Tom, then gradually his face lightened into a smile and he laughed.

'Well, now you mention it...'

'Okay,' he smiled again.

'Yeah? You sure?' Tom needed to be certain he was on side.

'You are a bastard con artist, but sure it's okay.'

'Takk,' said Tom, in his limited Icelandic. 'Does Andrea know about the Zol?'

'No. At least, I haven't told her.'

'Shouldn't you?'

'An unlicensed drug..? She'd have a field day.' Sig didn't hide the surprise in his voice.

'That's true, but when you bring out a vial of something she's never heard of on the day, she might be even more freaked out.'

'So what do we do?'

'I'll speak to her, skirt around it a little so she doesn't ask too much, say you're looking at different combinations of stimulants or something. By the time she really starts to get suspicious, you'll have used it on me and I'll be sitting up with a coffee.' Tom smiled.

'Okay, that sounds good, if you speak to her.' Sig effectively dismissed Tom as he completed his list, then moved on to check the dosage calculations for his wonder-drug based on Tom's body size.

'Oh, and one other thing, mate.'

'Yes?'

'Next time you come in here, put the fucking light on – you scared the shit out of me!'

***

Tom arrived home to find domestic bliss in full swing. The boys had just eaten and were playing on the PlayStation in the den while Sarah looked on over the top of her laptop. This, it seemed, was how they spent their time watching the kids these days. The organised chaos of Tom being in charge had been replaced by the calm serenity of Sarah's captaincy of the good ship Boyand. He never could work out what the x-factor was. She looked up and returned his kiss, looking studious in the new reading glasses she'd taken to wearing for computer work.

'All okay?' she asked.

'Fine – ticking boxes all day. You?'

'Some fun and games today, but fine in the end,' she smiled. 'Went down the docks, with all those hunky sweaty men in overalls. Whew.'

'Oh yeah, how much did you make?'

'Thirty quid as you're asking.'

'Wow, a record.'

'Cheeky bastard.' They both smiled. 'But not as cheeky as the bloody loading guys have been.'

After studying a combined degree of Ancient and Art History at the university, Sarah's PhD had involved dating and cataloguing a collection of Ancient Greek artefacts from a recently discovered site between Corinth and Nemea on the Greek mainland. The site included a temple, small arena and palatial building forming the estate of a local landowner from the Mycenaean Period. The research would bolster the already extensive collection from that region of the country. She developed new theories to enhance the understanding and importance of the local artistic styles, giving further insight into the structure of the society of the time. The catalogue and its descriptions formed the basis of her PhD thesis. Ever pragmatic, Sarah realised that research into ancient antiquities was a financially unsustainable career and she started to trade in some of the artefacts she studied. From her knowledge and contacts within the ancient history community, and the respect she had earned for her academic work, Sarah was soon able to pick and choose pieces from collections to which other traders could only dream of getting close to. She named her studio gallery, Aglaea, after one of the three Graces and goddess of beauty, adornment and splendour. It had held numerous exhibitions of works never before shown publicly, and her star was rising.

Sarah's business changed over the years. Ten years ago her business began simply – in person in her studio – people viewing and even handling pieces of interest. It seemed, however, even this specialised area of retail could move online and now her collections were just a click away on a smart phone. She found it a strange development, having envisaged herself as the curator of a beautiful museum-shop when she started the business, drifting between groups of customers, explaining and pointing out aspects of history and authenticity for the items of interest. Now most items remained boxed and crated in the warehouse behind, or, increasingly, in the studio itself. This lent a certain *Indiana Jones* to the space – not at all what she had imagined. Stock would arrive in a shipping container, and Sarah and her staff spent their time taking detailed photographs of the items from all angles to either email to specific collectors, or to put on the Aglaea website and Amazon page.

Sarah gained a reputation as a highly specialised agent and buyer for wealthy collectors. Some people might see her as the 'trophy wife' of a successful surgeon. In reality, Tom was a researcher with no private practice, meaning he earned nowhere near as much as his potential. Sarah did, however, which was fortunate given that their mortgage was the size of the national debt of a small nation. Now she no longer had to travel to look at stock, she worked far fewer hours than she had in the early days, which allowed her to be just like the other mums and pick the kids up from school.

All her business was now just a click away.

'Who was giving you the trouble, the Poles?'

'No, the Polish guys are as good as gold. It's a stereotype, but they really are hardworking, and why wouldn't you want them on your workforce? No, this was the bloody locals.' He sat down beside her on the sofa, glancing across to the boys on the game console, immersed in the *Ratchet and Clank* universe. 'Remember the Monolith exhibits I've been putting together?'

'Yes,' he nodded unconvincingly, searching his memory.

'The twelfth century Monolith relics from Shaanxi province?' she reminded him

'Yep, I remember now.'

'They were due in last week – I was going to be late home Tuesday when they came in?'

'Yep, your mum was going to pick the kids up, and didn't need to after all.'

'Yes, because the container never bloody arrived. Or so I thought. I phoned the Chinese supplier and the shipping company last week. It took a while because of the language, but thankfully they have computerised rosters, so when I finally spoke to someone in English, they told me it had been delivered on time.'

'You better start learning Mandarin.'

'It's on the list...'

'So your cargo had been there at the docks for a week?'

'With my collectors wanting to know if the exhibits had come in, with the museum wanting to see them, and I'd been fending them off! So I went down there and got nowhere with the foreman who said he couldn't see my container on the roster – *again*. In the end I went out onto the quayside to find it myself.'

'Needle. Haystack. Discuss.' Tom pulled a face.

'Right. There were thousands of containers. I found my container ready to go, right at the front beside a container that was about to be lifted onto a trailer. The dockers were stood around doing jack-all. I showed them the paperwork and asked to check the container. They weren't happy but I told them if they wouldn't let me approve the goods, they'd stay there, which changed their minds. The crates were fine but they didn't want to load the container onto a truck for me, they were putting chains on the container next door, ready for the crane. You can imagine what sort of attitude they were giving me as the only woman down there, and I lost it.'

'Oh God, what did you do?' Sarah's temper was legendary.

'I climbed up a ladder onto the top of the other container and unhooked all the chains. By which point they were yelling at me, telling me they had to get the load out.'

'What did you say?'

'I told them there was a load they had to get out last week, and it was going first.'

'And nobody tried to stop you?'

'No, they were really taken back and they don't *really* give a shit either. I threw the chains over onto my container, climbed across and hooked them on. Then I went back and dragged the crane hook across. It was so heavy that I wasn't sure I could lift it, let alone jump across with it in my arms. In the end the crane driver took pity on me struggling and lifted the pulley across for me. He was laughing his bloody head off.'

'I bet. Hope you weren't wearing heels.'

'No flats, thank you very much.'

'And you got your container?'

'In the end. Then I had to persuade a driver who thought he had another job, to do mine first. And *then* I had my container.'

'And was it worth it?'

'Oh yes! Some of the exhibits are incredible, giving insights into a civilisation we thought was lost – this is all pre-Ming. This will be huge. You wouldn't believe the amount of swearing though.'

'From you or the dock guys?'

'Funny man.'

'Weren't you getting a lot of pieces for this exhibition?'

'Yeah, supposed to be in that container, but only about a third of it turned up. Apparently the other items are on two separate cargo ships due over in the two weeks.'

'Sounds like you'll be hanging round the docks a bit more then.'

'Well, times are hard...'

***

The living room was bathed in a warm yellow glow from numerous strategically-placed table lamps. Sarah flopped down on the sofa next to him, as he furtively clacked away on his laptop keyboard.

'You okay?' she said, rubbing a hand across the top of his shoulders, his face half in shadow from the low light of the lamp on the table beside him.

'Yeah,' he paused, nodding. 'Yeah, I'm good.'

'You *sure*?' she said in a tone that said *I know you're not*. 'What's up?'

'No, nothing, but –,' his eyes searched back and forth across the room, trying to find the right words. At that moment he wanted to tell her – wanted to be straight with her – they never kept secrets. But he wasn't ready, it wasn't something he could just come out and easily say. So he chose something else that was on his mind. 'You know what it's like when you're desperately trying to get everything right?' He made eye contact with his wife. 'That's where I'm at. Apart from some protocol work that will write itself, I'm really done, but I can't help feeling there's stuff I've missed.'

'Have you been through it all, start to finish, to check?'

'Oh, only about six thousand times, and every time I close my eyes, and every time I go to sleep, and every time I wake up in the morning. I don't think there's anything I've missed, but I can't help being a bit paranoid.'

'Missed? I know you'll have checked and double-checked everything – you always do. You won't have missed anything.'

'Hmmm, you're probably right.' He left the keyboard and embraced her, holding her close, enjoying her familiar smell.

***

On the Saturday morning, Ben's football team, The Hornets under 7s, were playing their usual matches. Supposed to be a series of 'friendlies', to watch the commitment of the players, it seemed anything but. Tom was delighted to see that the coach employed the 'flies around a light bulb' formation that had served them well so far this season, as opposed to the 'flies around shit' that didn't work so well. Ben went into a big booming tackle – his foot blocking that of the opposition player as he swung to shoot. The crunching noise could be heard echoing across the field, raising gasps from all the parents, but the boys just got up and carried on. Ben maintained a permanent, determined expression on the pitch that disguised how much he loved to play. After six keenly fought ten minute games, the Hornets were unbeaten with four wins and two draws. Ben's friend Kelo was the Hornet's best player – really classy on the ball, good in defence and with a fierce shot. Ben was a reasonably close second and quite happy to play second fiddle to allow his friend to do his thing. Tom always thought he had a very mature attitude for one so young, while Sarah just told him them they were kids having fun.

'Do you fancy going to Sheilagh's tonight?' Tom asked as they stood on the touchline, his fingers intertwined with Sarah's. Sheilagh's was an Irish bar-restaurant in town where they sometimes went. The boys liked it because it seemed like a grown-up actual pub, Sarah liked the grown-up actual food for the boys without a chicken nugget in sight, and Tom liked it because they served a nice pint of grown-up actual Guinness, the head of which Liam liked to draw smiley faces in.

***

Even though it was far from a dressy place, that evening Sarah decided to make an effort, putting on a short dress that she knew Tom liked. Completely independently, Tom decided to make an effort as well, putting on a proper shirt rather than a 'Keep Calm or you'll Have a Coronary' t-shirt like he normally would, and his smartest black jeans.

'We scrub-up pretty good, babe,' Tom said looking in their bedroom mirror as Sarah put the finishing touches to her hair for the evening – she had put it up, with thin wisps pulled down to frame her face, almost like when they first met.

'Yep, we don't look bad at all,' she took a cursory glance up and down at the full magnificence of her husband. 'Well – I look nice at least.' she smiled.

'Damn cheek – I'm lovely,' Tom grabbed her, arms round her waist, and pulled her back to him. She wiggled slightly, knowing how he would react.

'Uh oh,' she wiggled again, a quizzical expression on her face for the benefit of his reflection in the mirror. 'Uh oh, Houston, we do have lift off.' Another wiggle and this time she felt him press against her. 'You know what this will mean...'

'Staying in, kids in bed early..?' He gave a thumbs up to the mirror, and his most winning smile, wrapping his other arm more tightly around her.

'No python-boy, we are going out.'

'Python-boy, eh? Heh heh,' he said, pleased with himself.

'*Referring*, of course, to you snaking your arms around and trapping me.'

'I think, for the record, there were other snake references in there. Even if just implied,' he wore his most earnest, 'if it might please the court' expression.

'Snake? Really? You?' She held up her pinky finger to the mirror and wiggled it up and down.

'Cheeky bitch,' he said, nuzzling her neck and pressing against her, trying to prove his was more python than wormy-finger.

'Get off, teenage boy!' she managed to wriggle free and turned and kissed him long and slowly , her tongue slipping in to meet his, her arms wrapping around his neck. 'Sheilagh's first, shenanigans later.'

'Nice, liked what you did there. Okay let's go... maybe skip dessert...'

***

The next morning, Tom got up with the boys while Sarah had a lie in. They routinely watched yesterday's *Match of the Day* together, Ben and Tom absorbed by the games, while Liam played Lego. He still claimed to love his football and to know exactly what was going on, but just wasn't quite as attentive as the others. Afterwards, when the boys went upstairs to snuggle in with their mum, Tom searched the cinema listings for something to please everyone. Their local Film Planet multiplex had a Film Club showing of *Finding Nemo*. He took the laptop upstairs with a cup of coffee for Sarah and saw the three of them cuddled in under the blankets despite the warmth of the morning. The boys pretended to be asleep, laying on either side of Sarah, both doing comical pretend snoring of 'Snort – pheewww', 'Snort – pheewww.'

'Okay,' said Tom, setting the coffee down and sitting on the edge of the bed and opening the laptop. 'Don't tell the boys, babe, but they're showing *Finding Nemo* at the cinema and I thought we could all go – what do you think..?' The blankets were immediately thrown off and the boys both ran off shouting excitedly about their trip to the cinema. The film was a family favourite, but they'd never seen it on the big screen.

He sat, half watching Nemo getting annoyed by Dory, and half watching the delighted looks on the boy's faces as favourite lines like 'Fish are friends, not food,' were played out across the auditorium. He took in every expression – savouring them like the sip of a fine wine or a delicate canapé, wanting to remember everything as clearly and in as much detail as he could. Ben was taking in some of the finer points of the story he'd never noticed before and Liam was scaling the north face of a massive box of popcorn – so big he could barely see over the obstruction. Sarah caught Tom watching them, smiled to herself and said nothing, knowing that Tom was reflecting on them, on what was about to happen. *Good, I'm glad*, she thought. Tom was too pre-occupied to get anything out of the film, but today wasn't about that. He caught Sarah's gaze at one point and they exchanged smiles, albeit somewhat forced on her part. As it faded she reverted back to her current default state of worry and fear, for Tom, for them, for the future, for the kids, all in the melting pot this coming week.

With Nemo well and truly found and the boys happy, walking slowly back to the car hand in hand with their parents, all was definitely well with the world. About half a ton of popcorn had negated the need for any form of lunch, but when they got home, Tom began to prepare food for later. He took onions, garlic and ginger from the larder and began finely chopping them.

'What's for tea, Dad?' Liam came over to see what he was doing.

'Curry, mate. That okay?'

'Oh yeah!' came his reply, and he marched off, repeatedly chanting. 'We havin' cur-ry, we havin' cur-ry,' and his brother duly joined in. Tom toasted and ground some whole spices before quickly frying them off, releasing their oils and flavours into the room, before adding the chopped vegetables. The smells permeated the kitchen and reminded Sarah of Khans across the park.

'We should be going to Khan's tonight, rather than have you cooking,' Sarah said.

'No this is good – I want to cook for you.'

'No I'm sure it will be fabulous, but, you know, no washing up and no lingering smells in my kitchen.'

Tom looked down at her, over the top of some imaginary glasses. '*Your* kitchen?'

Later that evening, after clearing up the pans from their curry, rice, vegetable bhaji and Bombay potatoes, jet-washing the kids and getting them into bed, Tom and Sarah snuggled together on the sofa.

'Okay, what's up?' Sarah tapped him on the nose with her finger.

'Nothin', why?'

'Yes there is, you've been quiet all evening. So, what's up?'

'Just a bit pre-occupied, that's all.' Tom set his wine glass down on the adjacent table and rubbed his eyes.

'Gemma says that whenever Paulo gets bothered by something, he doesn't talk to her for days and days. Like, total silence.'

'How can she tell?'

'Tell what?'

'Well, I imagine the poor bastard can't get a word in edgeways at the best of times, living with her. Just wondered how she could tell?'

'Very funny, mister.' She punched him playfully on the arm. 'Why are *you* pre-occupied?'

THE HAND OF AN ANGEL | 53

'Oh you know, there's this experiment going on next week, and –'

'Okay, arsehole, you can do all your bravado, and maybe anyone would be pre-occupied at this point, but, are you getting cold feet about next week?' She put her legs up on his.

'Oh I don't know, babe, maybe. It was just something that Sig said on Friday, and it's just been there on my mind.'

'What did he say?'

'Oh nothing,' Tom lied, not wanting to mention to Sarah about how Aliens had thrown him completely when he'd asked about the potential for resus failing. 'It's just brought it home to me really, I guess.'

'But you're so certain about your numbers from the near-death project that you know what you are going to see and it's worth taking all this risk that you insist isn't a risk?'

'Yes I'm happy with the set-up,' Tom replied evasively, not looking at her but instead reaching for his glass to swallow down half its contents.

Sarah frowned. 'That doesn't quite answer the question though. The near-death results were pretty fucking comprehensive. I mean, you saw the raw data, you must've have had an idea fairly early-on what the overall results would be, when all the data was so similar? But you don't seem quite so sure right now. What's going on?' She looked at him with a suspicious expression.

Tom smiled and finally met her gaze. 'No I'm happy, course I'm happy, they're fine. The results are fine. They are what they are. It's just a bit of cold feet I guess.'

'What do the other guys think – the ones who you did the first NDE study with?'

'I don't really speak to them much these days.'

'But you did get on well with them, right? You could talk to them, maybe, if everyone else is a bit too close to the experiment?'

'Well our association was purely to extend the size of the data set – the patient population. Essentially I wrote the paper and it was just approved by the others – I don't really know them at all.'

Sarah's eyes widened. 'But you weren't down as the lead author on the paper.'

'No, Magnus Stephens was. It's a bit naughty, but I thought if we had a professor as lead author, the work would carry more weight.'

'Won't anyone find out about it? What if they ask Magnus?'

'They won't. It's my contact details on the paper, not his, so he won't get asked anything about it.'

'There's me thinking you were friends with these guys and in touch all the time – you think you know someone! Any other little surprises that you've got lined up for me?' she said with a half-smile.

'If there are, they're so secret that even I don't know about them. Sure I could think of some though...' *Yep, I probably could.*

4.

Tom rose just after the alarm at 6.45am and pissed like a horse in the en-suite toilet, waking Sarah from her slumber.

'Nice,' she muttered.

'What?' he asked, sitting on the side of the bed to put on some thick socks which he wore instead of slippers.

'You could wake the dead when you pee.'

'Oh. Yeah. Sorry, half asleep,' he said sheepishly.

'Yeah well, I was all asleep... Just like in the films though.'

'Yeah? What?'

'You know, Brad romantically pissing Angelina awake in the morning – the hell with coffee, crumpets and flowers – who needs that?' she yawned and stretched languorously.

'Do you think it's what finished them off?'

'Very likely.'

'I was about to do the coffee bit anyway.'

'Yep, you crack on big fella.' The stretch seemed like it had been too much for her as she flopped back onto the bed to await her caffeine shot.

Tom walked along the hallway, certain he could hear bursts of electronic gaming noises coming from Ben's room. The front spare bedroom door was shut, and he turned at the top of the landing, heading down the long curving wooden stairs into the den. He hit the floor almost at a run, striding straight across into the kitchen to the non-fast-boil kettle, to ask it nicely to put on a brew. Looking out over the patio, overnight rain was already drying under the warmth of the sun, with no apparent sign of the chill mornings of September yet. He moved back into the den and through the partition into the lounge, opening blinds. With a flourish, he flung open the curtains in the front bay window and was startled by the sight of the assembled photographers camped at the edge of his driveway, so much so he jumped backwards, still holding a curtain in each hand. There was a sudden scramble of activity as cameras were brought up, lens caps removed, power switches flicked and TV cameras primed. Tom quickly closed the curtains again before the photographers got a shot of him shirtless in his lounge trousers. He could still see through a narrow gap between the drapes, and counted about ten press photographers, a few folks without cameras who must be journalists, and two TV camera crews. They must've been there early to all be set up like that.

Shaken, Tom carried a steaming mug of coffee up to his lounging lioness who almost purred as he sat the cup down.

'Thanks babe,' she muttered in a thick 'yep I really did go back to sleep' voice.

'No problem. Sorry it took a while –'

'Not the kettle again,' she interrupted.

'No, not at all. I had to make a load of drinks for all the fucking press parked outside on our driveway.'

'What?' she muttered again, barely registering this any more than if he'd said it was raining outside.

'The media, my love, camped outside our house.'

'Are you having me on?' she propped herself up on one elbow to take a slug of her essential morning stimulant.

'Only about making them drinks – go take a look. They're out the front so take a look out of the spare room window. But –' he indicated her naked breasts, exposed by the bedclothes as she sat up, 'You might want to decide which of the papers you want to appear in.'

'You're winding me up,' she said, wide awake now. She slipped on a baggy t-shirt and, accompanied by Tom, carried her mug to the spare room at the front of the house. He caught her arm so she'd go more slowly toward the window, to spy on the spies without being spied. 'Jesus. When did they get here? What do they want?' She was at a loss.

'It must be the experiment. Unless your crane antics caused an international incident.'

'Shit, how're we gonna get to work?' she asked, suddenly thinking of practicalities.

'Run'em over I guess.'

'Very helpful. I thought the experiment was low key – that the university didn't want a big hoo-ha?'

'You and me both, babe. You and me both.'

The telephone rang downstairs and Tom turned and headed down to the kitchen to answer it. 'Tom, where the hell've you been, I've been trying to get you all morning?' The voice on the other end of the line was shrill and urgent.

'All morning, Mags? It's barely seven o'clock.'

'I've been trying your mobile for half a bloody hour, Tom.' He looked across the worktop at his phone, plugged into the wall to charge.

'Oh. Sorry. Not had it on me –'

'Forget about all that Tom – have you seen the papers?'

'No,' he said slowly, but he suspected he knew what was coming.

'You need to – I'll bring one in – there's a story about you coming back from the dead in an experiment.'

'Shit.'

'Yep.'

'They're all outside my house.'

'Who?'

'The media – TV cameras, the lot.'

'Oh God. What're you going to do?'

'Run the bastards over,' he said acerbically.

'Really?'

'I'll get through them and then we'll see how the land lies.'

***

Tom was at work within the hour, having run the gauntlet of cameras and shouted questions as he left the driveway and turned onto their quiet side-road, feeling like Harry Redknapp on transfer deadline day. A few photographers had run after him as he drove off – why did they do that, as if they could catch up with a car? Tom pulled over just before the main road and phoned Sarah.

'You get through okay?' she asked, sounding relieved.

'Yeah, it's like driving through some shouty bushes, or maybe belligerent sheep. Point the car at the middle of the drive and go steadily. They move! Although how I didn't run over anyone's foot I'll never know.'

'Okay, I'll do that. I've told the boys it's an adventure – hope they don't get freaked out.'

Mags greeted him in the hub with the paper in question, Boyand making the front page; 'Dr Death plans to come back from the grave.' shouted the headline. Tom sighed, it was hardly an accurate or reasonable way to introduce the story, but typical of the red-top papers.

'Henry's been on already – he wants to see you right away.'

'I bet he's shit a brick. I've got a patient list though.'

'You did have – will either have to get Scott to run it or cancel.'

'No, can't cancel folks,' Tom said. 'Shit. Okay. Will talk to Scott.'

'There's another thing about Henry, though. He asked Gilly, his secretary, to try and get hold of Magnus Stephens.'

'Why?' Tom could feel his heart rate rising.

'I don't know for sure, Gilly told me on the weekend when we met up, and she doesn't know either. Maybe he wants to gauge someone else's opinion about your study.'

'Or stoke the fires a bit. He wants to see if Magnus thinks it's a good idea, and whether he'd support it.'

'And would he?'

Tom looked at Mags. 'I don't know. Him sending me a pile of data from the States for me to number crunch isn't exactly a close working relationship.'

'Would you be able to contact him?'

'Why? It's not me that's got his knickers in a twist and wants to speak to him. Besides, it's from years ago – I bet he hardly remembers me.'

'Really?'

'Yeah, like I said, we had a bit of contact, I got some data and sent him a copy of the paper, end of.'

Scott was serenity itself – he must've taken some kind of pill, Tom thought – and was happy to step in and run the clinic. It had been a while since his last cardiology gig, he said, and so he was going to have a coffee and Google things like 'heart' and 'valve'. It was far from an ideal scenario, and Tom was concerned about a lack of continuity with his patients. Scott was perfectly qualified to run things, of course, and Chloe could look after routine cases if it got busy or behind time. Brooding, Tom left the office. Scott was right – between his own research and helping with this project, he hardly did any clinical work anymore. But it couldn't be helped.

Tom left the hub, walking briskly into the main foyer of the research unit, turning right through the security doors and onto the 'umbilical' – the link corridor between the new hospital and research block, and the old building and medical school. It was always a busy thoroughfare, and today was no different; medical staff in various uniforms hurrying one way and the other, several looking at tablets with clinical information or x-rays accessed via the hospital's cloud system, others carrying older records in paper form. The hospital was in the process of becoming completely paperless, gradually transferring more and more clinical departments over to the electronic system. It wasn't very efficient – in fact, more were lost or just not delivered from Records than ever before, resulting in clinics descending into chaos. Administrators in suits wandered past at a more sedate pace – no lives in their hands to rush for, Tom thought. He turned off the umbilicus through the double doors, crossing the threshold into the old building, and walked back in time. The brilliantly lit white-painted corridor with its cleverly hidden strip lighting and wide glass window on one side gave way to dim hallway lights, like gas lamps, casting long shadows. Old highly polished parquet floors echoed as he walked along. The walls were of ceramic cream Victorian tiles that looked like they might once have been white and perhaps had discoloured with age like stains on teeth. The tiles rounded off as they approached doorways, leaving no clean lines like in the umbilicus, no sharp angles but soft curves. At the end of the hall he left the original parquet floor tiles and sank into blue carpet, with a pile deep enough that small children could disappear, never to be seen again.

With the building of the new hospital, all senior administrative and clinical staff were given the option of relocating to brightly lit offices with large glass walls, new furniture and all the latest communication systems readily in place. Most chose this option but Henry and a couple of others elected to stay in the old building, their offices as much a relic of a bygone era of medicine as they were. When everyone else moved out the remaining relics went into full-on dinosaur mode, having carpet installed.

Carpet? In a hospital?

Floors were restored and absolutely no modernisation was done. In fact, some more modern strip lights that had been added over the years were removed and more authentic lighting used instead. In contrast to the latest technology on show in the rest of the hospital, this area did well to get a reliable email connection, and nobody could get a mobile phone signal.

This was no simple corridor now, this was a hallway, and a grand one at that; Regency chairs were placed outside office rooms and paintings of alumni of the medical school were lined up like soldiers, inspecting whoever was walking past. At the end, the hallway opened into a wider space containing two secretarial desks, with oak doors leading from it.

The secretary directed Tom to Henry's office, telling him to go straight in. He walked in through the heavy oak door and took in the room in front of him. Across the wide, dark-wood furnished room was a large desk at which Henry sat, leafing through some documents. Sunlight filtered through vertical blinds on two wide windows to Tom's left, illuminating the darkened room a little, the windows framed by heavy burgundy drapes. Behind Henry were large bookshelves, heaving with medical tomes and volumes from the annals of specialised literature. Professor Henry Dawson was a haematologist by trade, who had pioneered work on the prevention of blood clotting when the first heart-lung by-pass machines were used. His drug protocols quickly became the standard to avoid complications when using these first devices, and were still not hopelessly outdated decades later. His research awards and certificates adorned the room. No mere administrator, Henry was a heavyweight academic in his own right, pushed 'upstairs' when the need for academics on the Board was increasing, and now he was the Chairman.

Henry was reading by the light of an antique banker's lamp, its curved green glass shade and brass stand dominating the left side of the large desk.

'Research isn't of interest to the new breed it seems, Tom,' Henry said matter-of-factly, without looking up. He waved in the vague direction of one of the heavy chairs opposite him, the ancient brown leather carefully riveted to the stained oak arms by countless metal studs.

'Oh?' Tom sat as instructed, aware that Henry was deliberately making him wait.

'Apparently they want a fast-track to consultant, make their name by trying a brand new procedure nobody has used before, shag some pretty nurses and drive an Aston to their private practice.' Henry looked up for the first time, snatching his half-round glasses off the end of his nose. Henry liked everything to be just so. He liked his academics to be academic, liked his clinicians to be clinicians, he liked his office to be old-fashioned, imposing, suggesting of by-gone days at the dawn of medicine. Henry wrote letters. He didn't email. He didn't text.

'It doesn't really say that in there does it, Henry?' Tom said, indicating the *British Medical Journal* on the desk.

'I may have been paraphrasing somewhat,' Henry said grumpily. 'But where is the future? Who is going to do the next wave of groundbreaking work?' Henry stared straight at Tom, eyes boring into his.

'And this leads us on to my work I suppose,' Tom gestured lightly with a winning smile.

'Oh really? I'm talking about quantifiable, provable, reproducible work, not some flight of fancy, Tom.'

'Given the telemetry we've set up for this, Henry, it will be quantifiable, provable and reproducible – we've talked about this. In fact, after the first successful test, we'll run the same battery with a number of subjects to get a cohort from which to draw stronger conclusions.'

'Do you really think the university will let you do this more than once? We didn't want you to do this one, let alone anymore.'

'Well, that goes without saying doesn't it?' Henry's obstruction over recent months meant Tom's patience was running out. 'What if we find definitive results in our bloods, of threshold data for cellular survival after death, for example? What if we can ultimately pioneer new and better ways of bringing people back after prolonged periods of stasis without permanent damage? What if we can determine new resuscitation drug protocols? There are innumerable possibilities in the science of this, Henry, once you see past the headlines and start to see it for the research it represents,' Tom emphasised, indicating with his outstretched hand the academic paper Henry had been reading.

'And your rather unhealthy obsession with near-death experience of course.' Henry smiled smugly.

'Yes, I'll freely admit that I'm interested in the events that occur after system death, and the relative involvement of biochemical reactions versus perception that Bob Wauberg and I've been working on – that's part of this design too.'

'Oh fuck off, Tom!' Henry dismissed this with a wave of his hand. 'We all know you're obsessed with finding out what these people from your survey have seen, and whether you can predict what comes next. You want to open the gates of heaven, and don't have the decency to admit it. Don't you find it ironic that the same chap with whom you crossed swords only a short while ago is now a collaborator on your project?'

'Not at all. Bob and I have very similar beliefs and goals, we approach them differently is all. Anyway, is it irony, or coincidence, that Bob gets offered the Psychology Chair here shortly after our first altercation? Particularly when my study was being looked at by the university with some distaste and the favourite for the post was Marilyn Marsden from Edinburgh? Bob's obviously more than qualified to do the job, and now I'm glad he got it, but the conspiracy theorist in me thinks that his appointment was another way of making my life difficult. I bet it pisses some people off that we're friends now.' Tom shrugged, staring at just one of those people.

'I'm not sure whether it's your over-inflated ego or paranoia saying all that, and that's before you get irreversibly brain damaged. I can only imagine what you'll be like afterwards.' Henry sat back and interlocked his fingers over his rounded abdomen. 'Anyway, that brings us round to this whole bloody mess of this morning. You are obviously aware of what's hit the press?'

'I was made acutely aware of it by the dozen or so reporters camped outside my house when I got up this morning.' Tom replied, irritated again.

'Quite. The first thing to do is to determine how this got out to the newspapers. Somebody from your team, presumably?'

'Somebody in my team? My team has been hand-picked, they're people I trust, with whom I've worked for years, who're interested in this particular area, are excited about this project and who fully understand the need to keep the study in-house beforehand. There's nobody who would breathe a word of this outside our circle, let alone say anything which might lead to the press. There's no way it's an inside job. It's not. And remember the only people who really know any details about this project are my team and your office. So, therefore, if it's not my team, then it must be someone from your office that's leaked it.' Tom sat back having lit the blue touch paper.

'My office? You are accusing me? You're accusing *my* office of leaking this to the press?' Henry was so angry now he was spitting when he talked. 'How fucking dare you!' he raged, bouncing around so much that he could barely keep himself in his chair. 'You should think very fucking carefully about making wild accusations. It would be a shame to spoil your future career just because you shot your mouth off one too many fucking times.' He leaned forward to emphasise the point, and it was received loud and clear.

'I'm just answering your question. You said we needed to find out where the leak came from and accused my office. I'm telling you it's not, so you can remove that from your line of enquiry. All I did was return that to you about your office.' Always be measured and reasonable in a disagreement, Sarah always said, it will infuriate the other party while you stay icy calm. 'Besides, it's no secret that you've never liked this project from day one. So, if someone with similar feelings, leaked something to the press, it would certainly make my life more difficult.'

'I don't see the point of your project, Tom – whether I like it or not is irrelevant. It's a high risk experiment with little chance of great success and a good chance of catastrophic failure.'

'But look at how much information we will be gathering – this is an amazing opportunity. And where would your work've been if you'd listened to the nay-sayers who talked about the heart being the soul and that bypassing it was a Godless act?'

'Oh, don't give me any of the self-righteous Jonas Salk shit again, Tom, I had to put up with enough of that during the bloody Ethics Committee. This is hardly his bloody polio cure, now is it? Everyone knows if he'd anything about him he would have experimented on the disadvantaged like everyone else. Save that sort of thing for the press conference.'

'What press conference?'

'The one you're giving this afternoon. The press officer is at your disposal – no doubt delighted not to be covering up removing the wrong kidney or who the Chief Executive is shagging at the moment. We've got such a compensation culture that people sue about everything these days, and we take a hammering for it in the media. Now, all kinds of other nonsense has been written in the press today about you, as you've no doubt seen. The university needs you to stop all the conjecture and gossip at source before it gets even further out of hand, and starts to paint us in an even bleaker light.' Henry sat back, enjoying Tom's discomfort at the thought of it.

'I'm not doing a press conference.' Tom held his hands up defensively – aghast at the prospect.

'Oh yes you fucking are, Tom.' Henry leant forward in his creaking Regency leather chair, a much grander version of those outside in the corridor. 'You are if you want to keep this little charade of yours going. I've set it up with Kate Delaney, the press liaison, she'll meet with you at two and brief you thoroughly. The press conference is at three. Make sure you deflect as much attention away from the university as possible and towards you and your 'work'. If anyone's going to have paparazzi sneaking around their gardens I want it to be you and not me, understand?'

'Henry, I can't give a press conference, I've got my final follow-up clinic before I go on sabbatical for this study. I can't cancel those patients.'

'Then your registrar is going to be a busy chap, isn't he?'

5.

Tom entered the briefing room – part of the main press suite off the main foyer of the hospital – just before 2pm. After storming out of Henry's office, Mags had calmed him down and Chloe and Scott had come back over from clinic for lunch.

'How was it?' Tom asked, apprehensively.

'Piece of piss, boss,' Scott replied in the most relaxed way.

'Really? Who did you see?' Tom was ready to have a blow-by-blow account of the whole clinic, to reassure himself that all was well.

'Relax, I prescribed everybody statins – how hard can it be?' Scott shrugged, pointing his palms to the ceiling, with Chloe nodding sagely by his side.

'Diuretics too – I did them...' she nodded, almost to herself.

'All right, all right, I know you can run these things. Sorry for checking on you.' Tom forced a smile. 'The bad news is that I need you to do the same with the afternoon clinic.'

'Yeah, Mags texted me. Gonna be on the telly. Woo-hoo!' enthused Chloe with a big sarcastic grin.

Tom was distracted at lunch – still annoyed but also apprehensive about speaking to the press – so much so he hardly touched his burrito. Today was Chloe's turn to go out to Pablo's for their order. Of course, Chloe would argue it was always her turn, and it would probably be her turn again next week. And should cardiologists have an account at a Mexican place?

Being in the bosom of his colleagues went some way to calming Tom down. Henry was all teeth and trousers, but he had to be the one behind the leak to the press. He'd also been the main dissenting voice on the Ethics Committee from the start. *Fuck him. Let's see him stop us now*, Tom thought, becoming even more determined to continue with the study rather than cave in to the pressure, as Henry and his cronies were obviously hoping.

He walked into a sterile meeting room with white painted concrete walls, suspended white roof tiles, blue carpet and a small oval boardroom table of light oak veneer. It could have been any meeting room on the planet. White plastic ducting masqueraded as dado rails, covering electrical and network feeds for the myriad of power points along the middle of each wall. In the corner was a water cooler and little containers for tea and coffee, along with bottled water and small clear plastic cups. The room was occupied by one other person, sitting at a Macbook at the head of the table, facing Tom as he came in through the door.

'Hi, you must be Tom,' she stood, maintaining eye contact as she reached toward him with a firm handshake. 'Kate Delaney. Good to meet you.' She was firm, clipped and to the point, immediately exuding an air of confidence and authority that told him she was in charge. Tom returned her gaze as they shook, remembering a former colleague whom, whenever he met Sarah, addressed himself to her chest and not to her. Tom had always made a point of not doing that. He could still take her in, however. She was younger than he had expected – maybe mid to late twenties – immaculately dressed in figure-hugging navy pinstripe skirt, her matching jacket currently draped over the back of the chair. Her flattering cream blouse, tailored without being tight, had just two buttons undone to avoid showing any cleavage. She wore her hair up, neatly clipped back, and her earrings and necklace were simple and unobtrusive. She was the ultimate elegant professional, clearly the right person for this type of job, Tom concluded, given his vast experience of press officers. He found himself with an immediate schoolboy crush.

'Is anything... wrong?' she woke him from his daydream, her lips curling into the faintest of smiles – he had evidently been staring.

'No, sorry, a bit distracted with this whole press conference thing

Henry's dumped on me.'

'Well you *are* the best person to brief the press, in fairness,' she smiled diplomatically. 'My job today is to make sure you don't sully the good name of the hospital and to put a stop to all of these screaming headlines.' She held up a couple of tabloid newspapers from that morning.

'Your job is to make sure I divert the 'gentlemen' of the press away from the current glut of clinical negligence cases and to give them something different to write about. You're to take the flack away from senior management for a change. That *is* why Henry leaked the story isn't it?' Tom said bitterly.

'I don't know what you mean – nobody leaked the story – it just broke today.'

'Somebody must have leaked it otherwise it wouldn't have broken, and he did leak it, largely to build the pressure on me. He wants to discredit me – hoping that I might pull the plug on the experiment.'

'Look, I'm not sure I want to get into this, but if Henry was so set against this from the start, why did he let it get through Ethics?' She had a disapproving look on her face that made him feel like he was twelve. She had clearly been well briefed. Had she been tracking him and the potential news story for long? Was she in cahoots with Henry?

'That's because some other people on the Board felt that it might be worthwhile to support more innovative research, so they voted him down. Henry didn't like it, and he's never liked it since.'

'Okay, we need to move on without the conspiracy theories,' she said with finality, trying to draw a line under the matter.

'I'll give you a conspiracy theory. Why, on Friday, did Henry book time in his diary to talk to me this morning? *On Friday*. My secretary Mags is friends with his PA and she told me after I spoke to him. He knew what would happen this morning, wanted to throw me to the wolves, and planned just how to do it.' In the battle over who will have the last word, Tom had won.

'Your meeting, whatever, was probably coincidence – you're being paranoid, and that isn't going to help you come across at your best in a few minutes. Besides, I hardly think it was Henry who was the leak, Tom.'

'That's what *he* said – are you sure you weren't involved too?' He half joked, but she didn't notice and he let it slide – *wouldn't do to get off on the wrong foot now would it?* 'Look, I don't normally do this kind of thing,' Tom said nervously.

'What?' she was slightly confused over his change of tack.

'This.' he indicated the press room.

'You aren't used to speaking in public?' The surprised tone in her voice was not disguised.

'Well, yes at academic meetings, presenting papers to experts in my field, hugely knowledgeable people. And to funding bodies, research institutions...' he gestured with his hands.

'You just aren't used to speaking to 'normal' people?'

'I'm not used to speaking to people who's target audience can't wait to see the tits on page three, that's all,' he said, matter-of-factly.

'Well, you'll have to bury that, and come across as passive and charming and as earnest as possible,' she shrugged slightly with a thin-lipped take it or leave it expression. When he heard her say 'charming' he immediately pictured Anthony Hopkins training the young Zorro.

'Christ, we're in even deeper shit than I thought! At least you didn't say I had to be nice to the bastards,' he smiled grimly as they got down to the business in hand. They went over Tom's work, the main plan for the experiment and what he wanted to get across to the press now he was forced to speak to them.

'You'll get the broadsheets asking you some technical medical questions. Go into as much detail as you want with those. You'll also get the red-tops asking complete rubbish.'

'Like what?' asked Tom with genuine curiosity.

'Personal stuff. Things they don't need to know and are none of their business, but they can shout about in a headline – like about your sex life. That kind of thing.' She gave an apologetic shrug.

'Well, I'm happy to answer a question that's sensible and normal, but anything that starts getting ridiculous or personal like that and I'm going to walk. Henry can throw his weight around as much as he wants, and bang on about how he's got me by the balls. All I need the university for is the room. I sourced the funding for the study privately and paid for all the equipment. I've recruited staff to come in when they're off duty. So I'm doing this to smooth the water. But anyone takes the piss and I will leave.' Tom's intense gaze was intended to leave Kate in no doubt as to his sincerity.

As they talked, the noise levels from the neighbouring press room gradually increased. The muffled noise of a few individual voices grew to become a cacophony. There were the sounds of chairs being scraped as they were removed from stacks, the crashing of lights and cameras being set up on tripods. It sounded like there were a lot of people next door.

At two minutes past three, Kate led Tom through the fire doors and across the corridor into the main press room, her final instructions ringing in his ears. A wall of noise hit them. The hubbub from too many people talking at once, shouted questions from a few seasoned hacks who should know better, the metallic whine and snapping of camera motors. Television cameras tracked Kate and Tom as they took to the makeshift stage platform and sat down. Tom looked at her like a rabbit in the headlights and she gave him a calming smile. They had agreed that, as the senior clinician, Tom would lead the press conference from the start, with Kate only stepping in if she felt she needed to.

'Let them settle down first,' she said out of the corner of her mouth. The fifty or so journalists and technicians were focused entirely on him. It looked as though, at least for these fifteen minutes, he was the star of the show.

'Good afternoon – thank you for coming today. My name is Tom Boyand and I am a Cardiologist and research fellow at the university… er, St Catherine's University Hospital I should say,' he cleared his throat, nerves making him stumble through his opening. Two microphones taped to the desk in front of him were feeding back, causing a loud squeal over the speakers in the room. A technician and a journalist, to whom one of the mikes belonged, rushed forward to adjust their position. 'I've called this press conference to announce a research project on which we have been working… that we're about to progress to the next stage. And to correct some inaccuracies that appeared in the press this morning.' He paused to take a breath, to clear the tightness in his throat, and to take in some of the people in the room. 'As a cardiologist, one specialises in the heart, the organ that gives life and which is the engine room for the very existence of the organism. In a perfect balance of yin and yang, however, one must also consider and confront death. For the past five years, I've had an interest in the end of life; what happens to the physiology – the cells of the body – when the supporting organism, dies? What are the processes? What shuts down permanently, and what can be recovered? We now know how the cell decays – the toxins that are released, the order in which things stop working. We know less about how this affects the organ or the system involved, however. How does an organ itself die – what are the catastrophic events that happen and how is this perceived by the rest of the organism as a whole? This led me to become interested in the existential perception of death – what happens when we die, how does the body react?' The room was silent, hanging on his every word, the occasional electronic shutter clicking the only sound other than his voice.

'More recently I have been interested in what happens to the mind, the consciousness if you will, at the point of death. Where does our consciousness *go*? Both at this centre and with colleagues around the world, we have collected testimonies from two hundred and forty people who have had what might be described as a 'near-death' experience. My research findings show that in almost every case, subjects report the same thing, the same experience. This generated the idea for the current project.

'First of all the idea was to examine the physiology of cell and system death and analyse, in a host of different ways, the nuts and bolts of dying. But it's become much more than that. It has become more about the perception of death, not on a cellular or organ system level even, but on an organism level. How does someone perceive their death? By definition, the vast majority of people are in a medically poor condition when they reach this point, and so even recorded testimony may be flawed. The most logical step is to take a perfectly healthy subject and bring them close to death in a controlled clinical manner. This pilot study is using me as the subject and we will record both my physical responses and, later, testimony of my experience. We hope that we'll start to understand whether what people have reported in the past is real or whether it's simply a construct, generated by the dying brain to create acceptance. And beyond this, in some ways the most interesting aspect of the project, is that it might allow us to gain some insight into the definition of existence itself. What defines us? Philosophers and existentialists will tell us one thing, pragmatists another, religious groups will tell us many different things depending on their own ideology. But no matter what your faith, belief system or scientific training, nobody knows. I find that fascinating.' He looked up for the first time. He had been hunched over his microphone, staring at a spot on the floor between him and the reporters, and had focused entirely on this while he spoke.

'So you're going to willingly have your heart stopped for the sake of this experiment?' someone called out.

'Yes, yes I am – that is the whole purpose of the experiment.'

'But you're just one guy aren't you – that's not very scientific?' another journalist asked.

'Yes, it will be hard to make major conclusions from my results alone. We hope to extend the study over time to include a number of subjects, so we can compare results.'

'You seem very calm, about this whole thing.'

'I am calm,' he smiled in response. 'We have a whole series of protocols and fail-safes developed and researched in the recent months by my team, whom I trust with my life.' He gave a snorted laugh which was not lost on some of his audience, who smiled back. 'And yeah, I am calm about the whole procedure and what the outcome will be, yes I am,' he beamed at the female journalist who posed the question.

'Isn't it incredibly dangerous to stop your heart? I've looked at survival rates for patients who have had cardiac arrests, and they seem, well, low,' she asked.

'Ah yes, you are looking at people who have had a cardiac arrest. People whose bodies have become so severely compromised that their hearts go into arrest, and the subsequent damage that their heart muscle sustains as a result of that. Trying to bring those people back is problematic because of the compromise their bodies have undergone. Even so, with modern medicine, if we get to people quickly enough after they arrest and can get their heart pumping in an organised rhythm, the mortality rates are relatively low.' He looked around the room, holding everyone's attention in the palm of his hand, his previous nerves having evaporated. 'We're talking about taking someone who is not medically compromised, taking an otherwise healthy person and flicking a switch – not causing significant heart trauma. So all the data you mention doesn't apply. Our prospective data and case study evaluations of people who are otherwise healthy and suddenly put into extraordinary circumstances, such as drowning or being immersed in ice cold water, for example, show high survival rates if the right things are done at the right time. We've used this model and extrapolated that to the laboratory environment. As such we should minimise risks even further and we're confident that the experiment will be a success. It's really very simple and controlled. Bear in mind that the whole point of the experiment is that I get successfully resuscitated – it will be a failure if I don't, because we won't be able to fully understand both the mental and physical effects of the study without that.'

'Can I ask you about your protocol?' she probed further.

'Yes, but people will say that I've planted you in the audience to ask me these things. I won't elaborate too much until we publish the scientific work from the results. What would you like to know?'

'How will they stop your heart?'

'With an electric shock from a defibrillator, to knock my heart out of normal rhythm – not to stop it. It's worth remembering that the heart *wants* to beat, it wants to keep beating and will do so after the rest of the body is 'dead'. The heart spontaneously contracts even when there is no other stimulus to make it do so – that is the nature of heart muscle. So, my heart will want to start back up again and the whole point of this protocol is to ensure that it does so.'

'And then, after you knock it out of rhythm?'

'And then, after a specific period of time where I will be thoroughly monitored, my colleagues will 're-start' it again, if you will, in the same manner.'

'Simple.' She smiled.

'Simple.' He smiled back – he decided he loved press conference flirting.

'How long is a specific period of time... to keep your heart stopped,' the man next to her was less of a flirting target, Tom thought, and seemed irritated that they'd been having their own private Q & A.

'I can't reveal that I'm afraid.'

'Well, thirty seconds, ten minutes, two hours, a day?' There was a slight hint of sarcasm about these timescales.

'It will be a period of some minutes.'

'Won't your brain get damaged without oxygen for any length of time – that is a concern in this sort of thing isn't it?'

'Yes, absolutely, but not just the brain, all the major organs will start to degrade and die if left without oxygen. Taking them to the edge of this is one of the key investigative roles of this study – to analyse the composition of blood and tissue samples to see how they change. But to preserve my body as intact as possible, we will be cooling it using ice.' Tom could see how this might start to go and decided to head a line of questioning off at the pass. 'It probably is worth saying at this point that you may be interested in the minutiae of how we are going to do this. Please be aware that I have a team of people around me, all experts in their own right, who have spent the best part of a year researching best practice and have gradually honed what we are going to do. Our literature count currently sits at around six hundred research articles from which we have taken information. In fact, one of the positives from this work is that several of my colleagues will be publishing literature reviews in areas such as resuscitation and drug protocols that haven't really been collated before. We've even designed new engineering systems in relation to cooling and heating the body. My colleagues are also looking at numerous practical applications for these following on from our study. So the conclusions from our research so far will certainly benefit our patients, and that is before we have our main study results.' He looked across the room. Most of the hacks had stopped writing and were just watching him – looking bored. Exactly how he wanted it; make the act seem dull, boring and matter-of-fact, and *stop asking mindless questions about the protocol.* 'In terms of the exact nuts and bolts of what we're going to do, we'll hopefully be publishing our physiological findings shortly after the completion of the study. That work will contain the methodology, so I would steer you to that at the appropriate time.'

'Does your wife understand the risks?' A short blonde woman in the front row asked, looking back down to her note pad as Tom started to answer.

'I would estimate that the risks are no more than somebody doing a parachute jump. I can understand how people can get... excited by the concept of this –' he instantly regretted using the word, knowing someone would turn it against him. '– and hence the headlines, but, taking a healthy body and stopping and re-starting the heart is reasonably low risk.'

'So what if the experiment 'doesn't work' as you put it, what if they don't manage to bring you round?' The reporter looked up at him, seeming genuinely concerned for his welfare.

'Well,' Tom replied with a snort. 'My wife did threaten to kill me the other day, so, it would save her the job.' A snigger rippled through the assembled press corps.

'What about your heart, isn't that the basis of what makes you?' someone else asked.

'No, that's a romantic misconception. As I said the heart is an organ that wants to beat. It's a simple pump that's very hard to kill. Take it out and put it in a supportive medium, an oxygen soup if you will, and it continues to beat. All the body does is regulate and control its beating. There's no soul there, if you are looking for one.'

'So where *is* the soul?'

'The concept of the soul is just a construct to explain our existence. But as animals with self-awareness, it would make more sense for the brain to be the home of whatever it is that we call 'the soul.' When we look at a pixel, or a dot on the wall, we see one dot. When we look at two pixels, we see two dots, and so on. Yet when we see a million pixels on the wall, we see a complex picture or painting or landscape made up of those dots. Our brain constructs that picture by merging the dots into something it can recognise. Television works the same way, we see dots on a screen, each one of which changes colour repeatedly, but that isn't what we see. We see a series of moving images of people kissing, birds flying over mountains or a game of football. It's the dots we see, but our brain assimilates them into the images we understand based on our experience and understanding. Our soul? It's a construct of our brain and the biological activities occurring there. It's millions of nerve cells firing in certain patterns, switching themselves on or off depending on that which is required. There are so many, such a huge number of them, that our brain assimilates their interactions, cross-referencing them with our experiences and memories, our beliefs and morals, our hopes, aspirations and understanding, into what seems like a physical thing that we call a soul.'

'So if your brain is affected by this experiment, you might come back a different person?'

'My wife is hoping so.' Some laughter rippled through the room. 'But yes, you're correct. If some of those nerve cells stop working because of this, and there are enough of these cells affected that the construct becomes different, then yes, essentially I'll be a different person.'

'Does that worry you?'

'No.'

'Why not?'

'Because I won't know anything about it – as far as I'll be concerned, I'll still be me.'

'Matthew Dennison, *The Times*.' A tall thin man, all crumpled corduroy suit, short greasy hair with a side parting, but with an air of gravitas. 'The reason that we are, er, *excited* by your work, as you put it, is more because of its questionable morality of switching life off and on again at the whim of one man.' Tom stared at him, saying nothing because the reporter hadn't asked him anything and was merely stating his opinion.

'Are you a religious man, Mr Boyand?' He did finally ask a question.

'I'm sorry, I don't understand the relevance of the question?' He smiled through gritted teeth, this was interminable.

'If you *are* going to be the first person in history to meet God, and plan to return to tell the tale, I wonder if the representative of the human race should be a Christian?'

'Very Carl Sagan, Mr Dennison. I think if 'the human race' sent a devout Christian into this experiment, one would immediately lose objectivity as to the outcomes, and to the definitive existence of God – that person would almost certainly perceive God to be the Christian projection of Him. Secondly, if a devout Christian went, what if the god they meet was Allah or Buddha? The proof of one definitive God would obliterate quite a lot of other religions, don't you think? In this case I prefer to remain an objective agnostic.' He said with a smile, having expected this type of question.

'Aren't you playing God though?' A middle-aged man wearing thick rimmed glasses asked from the back of the room, an iPad resting on his extensive paunch.

'What do you mean?'

'Aren't you playing God by deciding whether you live or you die?

Isn't that going too far?'

'But isn't that the very nature of medicine? Aren't a great number of patients in this hospital examples of how we've 'played God' with them?' He emphasised the point by making quotation marks with each hand. 'We play God every day, some die, some don't, some recover where they otherwise would not, and yet we're not accused of heresy in that.' He looked accusingly at the writer, who wouldn't meet his gaze. *These fuckers are just trying to get a rise out of me to make a headline, they don't really care what they ask or write.*

'What will you say to God?'

'What? WHAT?' Tom stared down the tabloid journalist who had asked the question. 'What will I *say* to God? Wow.' He threw his hands up in the air, looking around the room for some semblance of sanity. 'Next question, please.'

'Sorry? You aren't going to answer my question?'

'Oh you actually *want* an answer do you?' Kate put her hand on his to try to calm his reaction as they had talked about before the conference. He felt the warmth of her and the softness of her skin. He was distracted enough to wonder if she was the first woman to hold his hand since he had met Sarah. It certainly distracted him, but it didn't work as a calming influence. 'Let me tell you something...' Tom squinted at the name badge. 'Jim – from *Breaking News*. I will be dead, hopefully to be revived by my colleagues a short while later. We are conducting a proper, grown-up study of the early stages of cell death and breakdown. My consciousness will be dying and we're not even sure that I'll have the power of memory or cognitive thought, let alone speech, during that time. You are once again assuming that there will be a God, and not nothing, or Buddha or Shiva or someone else. You confidently predict that there will be a meeting between said God and me, and during that meeting I will be allowed to speak. You somehow know a lot more about this than I do because I can't even begin to see how any of those events will happen... What would you say?' He looked up at the whole press pack in front of him, his arms opened wide to invite a response. The room was silent. 'No?' he scanned the faces in front of him, daring anyone to speak. Jim was the only real candidate.

'C'mon Jim, God hasn't got all day!' Kate stared straight ahead with a fixed smile on her face, completely horrified.

'I just meant that… everyone would want to meet their maker and…' Jim knew when he was beaten and he backtracked, but no referee was going to step in to stop this fight.

'Oh I can assure you everyone *will* have the opportunity to meet their maker, should their maker exist, that is the one absolute in this world!' A few people laughed quietly at this.

Kate leaned in to whisper to him, covering the microphones as she did. She moved her lips to touch his ear, so no one would be able to lip read what she said. The touch of her lips on his ear was delicate and soft, and he could feel her warm breath on his skin. 'Just answer the fucking question will you?' She returned to her upright sitting position, beaming her best press officer smile at Tom.

'Yes of course,' Tom smiled back at her. He turned to the journalist. 'What would I say to God? What would I *say*?' he paused for the final time, enjoying the hold he had on his audience, but also knowing what the reaction was likely to be when he responded. 'I'd say you don't exist.' And with that Tom stood up, noisily kicking his chair backwards to collide with the university backdrop behind them. It wobbled satisfyingly, and he valiantly resisted the urge to put his foot through it. Cameras began clicking wildly as he stood, and a host of questions were thrown at him, so intensely that it was just white noise. He smiled and quickly waved to the assembled press as he walked back out of the room, Kate following closely behind.

Elsewhere in the hospital, a TV feed into Henry's office had played the whole conference live. The single occupant of the office had watched the discourse play out with a degree of frustration and annoyance. His mood had improved as the questioning progressed and he'd smiled a broad grin as Boyand kicked back his chair.

'Just what the fuck was that?' Kate Delaney caught up with Tom in the corridor, grabbing his shoulder as he tried to stride away.

'*'Answering the fucking question!*' As instructed.' Tom was more than irritated. 'This whole thing is a ridiculous exercise anyway, but that last question put the tin-fucking-hat on all of it.' He turned and marched off before she could infuriate him any further.

***

Tom's mood hadn't improved much by the time he got home. The attendant press corps were thinner on the ground than that morning – some being satisfied with the copy they'd posted from the press conference, but others wanted to milk all they could from this particular cow. Tom ignored the reporters as he turned in, scattering them like skittles as he swung the car around and angrily reversed back along the side of the house. Fleet Street's finest unhappily picked themselves up from the pavement and nearby bushes, muttering that there was no need for that sort of behaviour, as they went back to training their zoom lenses on the windows of the house. Not one shutter opened, however, as he got out of the car and climbed the steps up to the side kitchen door.

'Daddy!' The boys shouted in unison as Tom dropped his satchel onto the kitchen worktop. 'We saw you on TV!' They were very excited.

'You are... famish now,' Liam said the line he had been carefully rehearsing. Tom snorted and smiled down as he ruffled both the boy's hair.

'Famous, mate. But might also be a bit famished.' He directed the second comment to Sarah who smiled a welcome and kissed him.

'Hi superstar, are you okay?'

'I've been better. The *Jonathan Ross Show* haven't phoned have they?' He smiled and shrugged, shaking his head.

'Not as yet, but it is quite early. Wine?' She held up a bottle of Shiraz.

'In a pint glass.'

'What was it like being on telly, Daddy, was it coo-oo-el?' Ben said, having fun with his words whilst wearing Heinz's new range of spaghetti hoops clothing.

'It was okay, mate, just a load of people asking me stuff, really,' he smiled down at the serious expression on his son's face.

'Oh,' Ben looked disappointed. 'Being on telly must be rubbish. A bit like school then?' A thought occurred to him and his darker mood vanished. 'I can't wait to go in tomorrow and tell them, 'my Dad was on telly.'' He stood upright and spoke slowly and clearly, as if addressing an audience.

'Here you go – a nice big glass of wine,' Sarah handed him a large glass, but not a pint.

'You let them *watch* it?' Tom whispered to her as he took his drink.

'No! Course not. They watched the first bit, got bored with all the medical stuff and went off to play. I was ready to turn the sound off if the questions were getting too close to what was going to happen to you, but there was no need in the end and they didn't hear anything we wouldn't want them to. Now, how do *you* think it went? Really?' They turned away from the boys at the table, Sarah watching him intently as he took a large gulp.

'Shite. It was like a brainless mob. I reckon they had a sweepstake beforehand to see who could ask the most stupid question. Should've just read a statement,' he shrugged.

'I thought you looked great on TV – really. That twat who asked you about God at the end was stupid –'

'Yeah but I shouldn't have reacted, it wasn't very smart. He reeled me in for a headline and I bit. I was just getting tired of the bullshit.'

'But I thought what you said was okay, broadly. Might have annoyed a few of the more pious folks out there but nobody else. 'Course you can't defame God or religion on the TV, and the networks are going on a bit.'

'Are they? What are they saying?'

'That you shouldn't be allowed to do the study, that the university should withdraw your funding and cut you loose.'

'Well, that's alright then – they obviously don't know it's not their money, it's mine.'

'That's not strictly true, now is it? Have you heard from Kyle Solomon?'

'No, but he's not a God-botherer as far as I know, so it shouldn't be a problem. Besides, he's too excited about the study and what we might find to let anything spoil it,' he smiled.

'And Henry?' She took a sip of her wine.

'Nothing. I expect he's lying down in a darkened room to let his blood pressure come down – but he's got what he wanted anyway – the press slating me personally and not the university.'

'Well yeah, but if they're clamouring for you to be taken off the study, he's gonna be under some pressure.'

'So hold all my calls?'

'I would... but what if it's Jonathan Ross?'

'Ask him what he'd say to God first.' He looked down at his wine glass which had apparently emptied itself and reached for a refill.

6.

'Hello?' The man walked cautiously down the slight slope of the corridor leading to the hub. None of the people sitting at workstations in front of him seemed to take any notice, however. 'Hello?' he asked again. Chloe looked up and saw the man in his early sixties with neat, side-parted grey hair and trimmed goatee beard approaching. He wore a grey tweed jacket and charcoal trousers. His black shirt and white clerical collar gave away who he was.

'I'm Simon Ardent, the Hospital Chaplain,' he said stopping by her desk.

'Oh hi,' she looked puzzled as if he expected her to know why he was here. 'What can I do for you... Reverend?' She wasn't sure how to address the chaplain, but that couldn't be far off.

'Is Mr Boyand available? I wondered if I might have a moment of his time?' he said patiently.

'I'll see if he's free – he is pushed for time today though, we have a procedure planned for tomorrow.' Chloe pushed her chair back and started off to the lab, with vicar in tow.

'Yes I know. That's why I'd like to see him,' he replied.

She went through the observation room and into the main lab. Tom was with Charlie, unpacking the tanks for the thermal system. They had teased Charlie that he spent so much time over here at the moment, he must want a job in Life Sciences. Charlie had lifted the second of the plastic tanks down from a trolley and Tom was picking up the twin pump apparatus.

'Jesus Christ.' He struggled to lift it. 'How bloody heavy is this, Charlie?' he huffed and puffed as he put the pump between the tanks as Charlie indicated.

'Well *you* wanted a heavy-duty system with flow and return pumps – just doin' as I'm told, boss.' he smiled. They both looked up as Chloe and the chaplain came through the main doors.

'Tom, this is Reverend Ardent,' she indicated her companion. 'He wondered if you had a minute?'

'Simon Ardent, Hospital Chaplain,' the priest stepped forward and had a firm handshake for Tom. 'Call me Simon.'

'Hi, er, sorry about that,' *you picked a great time for a bit of blasphemy, son.*

'It's fine – I'll say a prayer for you later to clear things up,' smiled the clergyman and Tom, who was already planning a way of getting out of seeing him, relented.

'Simon, I am pretty pushed for time today, but seeing as how you've made the effort to come over, I can spare you a few minutes if that will do?' Tom said, leading the way to his office.

Tom's plan for the day was to catch up with everyone either in person or on the phone to make sure they were happy with tomorrow's schedule; when they needed to be there, going over what was expected of them and of course to discuss any last-minute reservations they might have for their department or the experiment as a whole. The lab now looked like an operating theatre, although more cluttered, with partially unpacked equipment that still needed to be unwrapped for final testing tomorrow morning. He had planned to supervise hardware in the morning, followed by final protocol checking and emails this afternoon. The arrival of the chaplain added the smallest spanner into the works. Tom hoped that there wouldn't be a toolbox more of them.

'What can I do for you?' Tom asked as they both sat in his office, the door unusually closed.

'I heard about your... experiment tomorrow.' Simon sat with his hands folded.

'From the press conference?' Tom said, his expression saying *why am*

I not surprised?

'Mainly, yes.'

'Well as you can see, we're making the final preparations now, and there's still a lot to do.' Tom smiled his best 'cut to the chase' smile.

'Mr Boyand –'

'Tom.'

The chaplain nodded. 'Tom, I wanted to come and speak to you today to ask you to reconsider your position on this. Please don't carry out the experiment tomorrow.'

'Okay. Why?'

'Yesterday, there were amateur theologians in that conference and frankly some ham-fisted questioning, but their sentiment was right. You are playing with the sanctity of life in the first instance, deciding when you die, and in this case, that you also return. That is essentially playing God.'

'I did go over this yesterday, but that *is* the essence of medicine – many more people would have met their end much sooner without people like me. Nobody from the church objects to that.'

'That's quite different.'

'Is it? Someone who's about to be *called* by God, whose time has otherwise come to be taken into eternal rest or whatever it is you believe, suddenly has that spoiled by a guy like me with a defibrillator. Am I not playing God then?'

'You are using the skills that God has given you to help people and by doing so you are celebrating God.'

'And will I not be using those skills tomorrow?'

'One must always use one's skill and judgement, Tom, to determine the boundaries, and I feel very strongly that this is going too far, blurring the boundary between man and God. I question the morality of the enterprise. You will be entering God's realm, if you like, and I fear for your immortal soul if you do.'

'I am intending to stop my heart. To allow slight changes to happen to my body as a result, to record those physiological changes and to record my personal experience as a result of those cellular changes. It's essentially a physiological experiment, a lab study with me as the guinea pig.'

'And what is the value of it?'

'To understand the reversible effects of cell death on the local system and the organism as a whole. To understand how changes to the body at the edge of death shape experience and to hopefully better document that experience.'

'And why does that experience need to be documented – why must we reveal the pathway to God? And you just referred to yourself as an organism?'

'Is that not what I am? A bag of cells that's seventy percent water.'

'You are a father, a husband, a doctor, a *person,* and a child of God.'

'We're conducting a simple physiological experiment. There is risk, I'll give you that, but it's a controlled risk and we've made every possible contingency for that. I'm not the most devout of individuals –'

'I did sense that from the press conference.'

Tom winced. 'But with respect, a lot of people are jumping on the theological or moral bandwagon for this. In terms of me as a person? I answer to my wife and she's fully supportive of what we are doing.'

'Is she? Have you truly spoken to her?'

'Yes, I have, of course. She isn't one hundred percent happy about it, but she is behind me.'

'Well that is somewhat reassuring, I hope that God feels the same.'

***

It suddenly felt like there was a lot to do – like the realisation you're going on holiday tomorrow and you've barely started to pack, or download the pictures from your camera so you can wipe the memory card, or the thousand other things you wanted to do before you left. The number of things on the 'To do' list for the afternoon now looked like a couple of days' work and Tom started to panic a little. He and Charlie were filling tanks with water ready for the next day. There was no running water in the room, so they were using large plastic crates, half-filling them in the shower room before staggering back under their weight to deposit the contents into the tanks. Tom looked up and saw Bob at the lab door. He was immediately soothed by the American's presence.

'It's pre-game nerves, Tom and it's just how it's manifesting itself.

It'll get done – everyone else is pulling hard and will stay until it has been. Can I help? These are yours,' he held up his hands, palms facing toward Tom as an offering.

'Thanks Bob, yeah it'll get done and maybe some things don't really need to be until morning, but...'

'You want to feel you've got to a certain place, and you wanna have got there tonight.'

'Yeah, exactly that. Now you've offered, could you give me a hand moving those chairs and this monitor screen into the observation room, please, mate?' Bob looked at his friend, the offer of assistance being largely rhetorical because Bob didn't do physical work. He always had staff to do it for him. In this case, however, he was prepared to make an exception.

In spite of Tom's fears, by five o'clock the lab was ready to go. The heavy equipment – the bed, tanks, thermal pumping system, biopsy fridge, defib and so on – was all present, although pushed against the walls to keep the middle of the room free. There would be time tomorrow morning to position everything. Drugs trolleys, monitors and camera gear were waiting in the hub, gathered together like some kind of medical yard sale. Satisfied with his final adjustments, Tom printed the latest protocol sheets for every station and shut down his computer. Everyone else was slumped at desks in the hub, tired and emotionally drained as they thought about tomorrow. Yet another big pot of coffee was being shared around.

'So anyone having trouble with the whole God thing?' asked Scott, kicking back with his feet on the desk.

'What?' asked Sig.

'You know, Tom tomorrow, meeting his maker.'

'God?' Chloe raised an eyebrow. 'When did you start getting religion?'

'Oh I don't know, just with the realisation of someone about to shake hands with the guy upstairs, and it makes you think, that's all.'

'Does it?'

'I think reflecting on one's own mortality is a perfectly reasonable thing to do when faced with this type of scenario,' Bob replied, opening a packet of dry-roasted peanuts from the stack of stockpiled snacks, brought in to get them through the next day. He shovelled the contents into his mouth. 'Has anyone thought,' he continued, covering his mouth to prevent the others being sprayed with peanut shrapnel. 'That we are all potentially complicit in an assisted suicide? Any thoughts on that?'

'Jesus Christ on a fucking bike, Bob! Now there's a thing to lay on us.' Scott stared at the older man.

'I just think you need to be prepared for what might happen tomorrow, is all.'

'Tom's protocols, and the disclaimers all exonerate us from any wrongdoing provided we follow them.'

'I'm not saying you need to cover your ass, Scott, I'm saying *you* might need to prepare *yourself*.' Bob emphasised his words.

'It's a bit late in the day for me to get into that now, mate. Que sera sera and all that.' Scott sighed.

'God probably wouldn't say; 'oh Jesus Christ on a bike' either. Not unless he was really up himself,' said Chloe.

'No, not unless said offspring was attempting to learn how to ride a two-wheeled form of self-propelled transport at the time.' Bob smiled.

'Sorry, who was up themselves?' asked Chloe.

'Anyway, any thoughts on God?' Scott was determined to get an answer.

'I think if you're a believer, Tom could definitely do with a few prayers in the locker for tomorrow,' said Chloe.

'What was the question again?' Tom asked, as he came out of his office, finally ready to leave.

***

At home that evening Tom and Sarah busied themselves in the kitchen. The main lights on low and the surfaces ambiently lit from spotlights under the cupboards, creating two pools of white light on the worktop. Tom prepared dinner while Sarah tidied the detritus of the day and organised the laundry. A simple ragù sauce had been cooking down on the hob for an hour or so while half a pork shoulder slowly roasted in the oven. He poured a red Bordeaux from a small chateau they had visited last year on holiday. They settled into an easy rhythm and with the familiarity came conversation.

'So, how was your day?' he asked, stirring the sauce.

'Fine, always fine,' she replied in their familiar mantra. 'I got a new phone though, it's work only, so there're no excuses if people can't get hold of me. Can do my emails too – properly synched up.'

'Hey, and it's tax deductible too.' A man can never be regarded with any seriousness when he gestures with a wooden spoon in hand. They both took up their glasses.

'Well,' she said raising hers in a toast. 'Here's to tomorrow.' Their glasses chinked. 'Are you ready?' She looked at him the way she always did, as though she couldn't quite believe he could do the work he did when he was the guy she married. She knew he was extremely bright, and was involved in groundbreaking work, but it was difficult to believe when he forgot to put the dishwasher on before coming to bed, or hadn't remembered to phone the plumber.

'Christ, I hope so. Spent the day going through the systems and equipping the lab and I spoke to just about everyone. Went through the protocols at the end of the day, too, so there's not a lot more I can do.'

'You don't have to do this you know,' she said, waving her glass expansively. 'You could put it off, get someone else...'

'We've been through this, babe. You know it's the only viable option. You agreed with me three months ago,' he reminded her, shrugging.

'That was three months ago, before it was the day before. Most guys *would* be happy that their wife *wasn't*, about them dying.'

'There's quite a lot of women who *would* be happy if their husband was gonna die.' He smiled at her.

'But you aren't gonna die.' she stood close to him, her hands against his chest, her voice breaking, the banter and bravado falling away.

'Well, technically I am, but they'll bring me back.' He was wondering how wise it was to be having this light-hearted discussion about his potential fate.

'Promise me you'll be back?' Her eyes were pleading, filling with tears.

'Of course I'll be back, I wouldn't be going anywhere near this if I wasn't one hundred percent sure. It's just an experiment – a simple experiment. It's like getting a runner to stop and then start running again. If he's been running non-stop for a while it'll be harder to get going again, but there's no reason that he won't.' He had, as usual, been using his hands to talk, taking the time to taste linguini from a large steaming pan as he did so, noting that it needed another minute. 'None.'

'That sounds like a press conference speech.' She leant her hip against the worktop, sipping her wine quietly.

'Yeah, shoulda used that.'

'Shoulda –'

He kissed her, suddenly, passionately, catching her so unawares she almost dropped her glass. She quickly put it on the worktop without spilling any of the contents and responded as his tongue found hers, her arms snaking round his neck. He clasped her hips, pulling her firmly against him.

'Mmmm, you're not just thinking about cooking are you?' She smiled against his lips, a tear streaking each cheek. 'Or if you are, you've got some real issues.'

'Yep 'cos that's me,' he said, grabbing a quick kiss of her bottom lip. 'Not enough issues...'

'No.' She kissed him back, her breathing coming faster and harder. 'Not enough.'

'The pasta's ready.'

'Christ, it *is* the cooking isn't it? Weirdo.'

'I'm the weirdo that keeps you from living on toast.' He pulled her close to him again.

'But toast doesn't take all this time and cleaning up, when we could be doing... other things.' Her eyes were glinting now and a playful smile on her lips.

'This won't take *any* tidying up; look there are some pans I *haven't* used! And I need an early night before tomorrow.'

'Yep, definitely an early night for us.' He lifted her onto the worktop, standing between her parted nylon-covered knees, pushing her short wool skirt up her thighs as he did so. They kissed again, tongues dancing together. He reached beneath her jumper. She moaned as he cupped her breasts.

'Tights or stockings?' he breathed in her ear, pulling her hips against his.

'Tights.'

'That's... disappointing,' he said, with his best hurt look, before he nuzzled her neck.

'In a skirt this short? It's not like I can try for promotion you know... I could always change though...'

'Well, hold that thought or dinner is ruined.'

'Mummy kissing Daddy! Mummy kissing Daddy! Mummy kissing Daddy!' Liam stood in the doorway, sleepily rubbing his eyes with one hand, dragging the floppy dog he had had since he was a baby with the other, its bedraggled and now largely de-furred body trailing along the floor behind him.

'Oh God.' Tom disentangled himself from his wife and pulled her skirt down.

'Mummy kissing Daddy. Mummy kissing Daddy. Mummy kissing Daddy. Shit. Shit. Shit!' He said.

'Sorry?' Sarah said, looking from Liam to Tom and back again.

'Ah.' Tom had a sheepish look on his face. 'Someone cut me up on the way home the other day, sorry.'

'C'mon big fella, let's get you back into bed,' she said, sweeping her son into her arms, shaking her head at Tom as she looked over her shoulder at him. 'While Daddy concocts an explanation as to the other bad words he uses around my children'.

'Mmmmm?' a sleepy Liam said, his eyes already closed as his head rested against his mother's shoulder.

'Won't be long – get me my dinner!' she winked at her husband as she carried Liam back upstairs to bed. Tom sliced bread and then shredded the pork, tossing it with the ragù and the linguini.

'All is good,' Sarah said as she came back into the room, the steaming bowls of pasta already on the table. 'And you better be good too, now I'm wearing these,' she said, quickly lifting the side of her skirt to expose a creamy white thigh above the top of her stockings.

'We'd better eat quickly.'

After eating, they made a cursory effort at tidying up, but it became increasingly difficult to keep their minds on the task at hand. In the end they couldn't stop touching each other and almost made a run for the stairs. In their bedroom they took their time, undressing each other slowly, knowing each other's bodies so well. He told her he'd kiss every inch of her, and, as a man of his word, he did. Some inches did receive more attention than others, however. Her moans increased in frequency as she thrashed her head from side to side, lying on the bed in just her stockings. He paused, changing position and moving back up the bed, kissing her hard, his hand entwined in her hair. She returned his kiss just as urgently. They made love slowly and tenderly, fighting the urgency they both felt, knowing this might be the last time. Anything could happen tomorrow; who knew how their lives might be affected? With Sarah's final passionate cries, tears rolled down her face and they held each other. They stayed entwined for a while, shutting out everything else and imagined themselves as the only two people in the world.

7.

The alarm went off at ridiculous-o'clock, or 5.30am as Tom read it. He needed to strike it twice to hit the snooze button, somehow resisting the urge to smash it into oblivion, before rolling onto his back. He saw Sarah stirring.

'Coffee?' he asked. 'Oh, fuck!' he answered himself as he remembered his protocol was for him to be nil by mouth. Well, a little black coffee wouldn't hurt, would it? Be gone from his stomach long before he was anaesthetised. He sighed. No, he would stick to the plan, otherwise, what was the point? 'Do *you* want coffee, babe?'

Sarah's face was buried in her pillow. She moaned her response, reminding him of the night before. He padded downstairs to make his wife her drink, the rest of the house in silence. When he returned, she was sitting up in bed, the sheet around her waist and her hair falling over her shoulders.

'Morning, sexy,' he smiled, leaning to kiss her good morning as he set her coffee down on the bedside table.

Sarah self-consciously ran a hand through her hair, unconvinced. 'I'll bet,' she said. Tom busied himself putting together some clothes and toiletries into a holdall and then went for a shower. Their en-suite bathroom had a walk-in shower for two, all black mosaic tiles, curving glass walls and twin chrome shower heads. An ostentatious design that Tom had insisted on when they renovated the place. Examining himself in the long mirror stretching across the large rectangular 'his' and 'hers' sinks, he poked at his skin, examining blemishes and stretching his eyelids. He looked in good shape if you ignored the bags under his eyes. He reminded himself to moisturise after the shower – he'd need to look his best to meet his maker. The shower sprang to life as he turned the chrome dial, the large head deluging him with scalding hot water, just as he liked it. Shortly after he had stepped into the water spray, Sarah joined him. They stood under the powerful jets and helped soap each other's bodies. It became increasingly clear that at least one part of Tom was interested in a re-run of last night's entertainment. Sarah looked down, then back up at him, a soapy hand playfully rubbing back and forth, one eyebrow quizzically raised.

'Really?' she said with a smile

'No,' smiled Tom, gently pulling away from her grip as he resumed washing her back, wishing his body didn't have a mind of its own.

Tom finished packing his holdall and was about to go downstairs when Sarah came up behind him and wrapped her arms around his waist, resting her head on his back. He overlapped her hands with his, and turned to gather her in closer to him, wet ringlets of her hair dripping onto his t-shirt. He squeezed her tightly – maybe as tight as he had ever done, wanting the moment to last forever, to be something perpetual, that no one could break other than them.

What God has joined together, let no man put asunder. The lines from his wedding vows popped into his head. *Where the hell had that come from?* He must have spent too much time considering religion these last few days.

Eventually they pulled away from each other, both with tears glistening in their eyes and both unable to articulate anything of any great worth. They embraced again, whispered that they loved each other, then went to rouse the kids. From very early on they'd decided not to tell the boys about the experiment – they were too young to understand. Sarah continued to struggle to understand it herself, so what chance did the boys have – and there was no easy way to explain it to them so they wouldn't be afraid. The boys, therefore, knew nothing about the day's planned events, and Sarah and Tom intended to keep it that way. As far as Ben and Liam were concerned, it was just a day like any other.

Mags Chesterfield pulled into the driveway, scattering reporters and TV crews as she did so. Like anyone familiar with chez Boyand, she pulled in turning to the right, stopping before the bushes to reverse back round to the left of the house. She stopped opposite the kitchen door – getting out would be so much easier now she was facing the right way. The door was already open, and Mags waved at Sarah as she walked round the car and up the steep steps. She walked straight into a noisy bustling kitchen – all the time knowing that cameras were trained on her movements. Ben and Liam sat at the table in their pyjamas, both nonplussed at breakfasting at this hour – 6.30 was an hour early for breakfast, and nobody had come up with any kind of explanation. Today certainly didn't seem like a normal day to them. They put their heads together and began to giggle as the grown-ups looked on.

'We are definitely going on holidays,' Ben whispered with the solemn certainty of the older sibling.

'Oh... How d'you know?' Liam said, his mouth half-full of cereal.

' 'Member last year? They woke us up in the middle of the night to go on holiday, and we went on a plane and a bus and everything!' Ben's eyes were wide with excitement.

'Oh,' Liam's blank look encouraged his sibling.

'We went to a holiday house. We had our own pool and you pooed in it on the third day. Or maybe the fourth?'

'I remember. Where are we going this year?' Liam brightened as he considered the opportunities for al fresco bowel movements.

'I don't know. They never tell me anything. But look; the taxi driver's here and Daddy's got some stuff packed in that bag,' Ben indicated one of the two holdalls sat next to two large crates by the kitchen door. 'And he's been on his laptop a lot, so he must've been using it to buy our holiday. And they've been acting weird the last couple of days, like they're not telling us something.'

'Def-nit-telly going on holidays then,' Liam declared to his brother, the great detective, thus writing these facts in stone.

***

Mags noticed that Tom and Sarah were much more subdued than usual, lacking their usual warm, effusive greetings. Sarah was quiet and withdrawn, and whilst it was early in the morning, looked particularly tired. Tom busied himself around the kids, helping wherever he could, attending to their needs, his hand lingering on their shoulders or ruffling their hair, savouring every touch. Mags tried not to interrupt the family scene and remain in the background. Tom had asked her to come over, but even so she felt like she was intruding. He sat with the boys, not eating, but focusing all his attention on them. After all, this might be their last breakfast together.

'Ready?' Tom asked suddenly, looking up at Mags from plying the boys with more fruit juice.

'As I'll ever be,' she said with a forced smile. She really didn't like this.

'Can you open all the doors and the boot, please?' Tom asked, indicating the luggage at the back door. He got up from the table and followed her down the steps, lifting one crate into the front passenger seat and the other into the back. They both returned to grab a holdall, and these too went in the back. Tom returned to the house, bending to kiss each of the boys, ruffling their hair once again. He embraced Sarah, the two of them clinging to one another all too briefly. Mags had to turn away and walk down the steps, unable to watch. As planned, and on a signal from inside, she made her way around the car, taking her time and closing the doors in sequence, starting with the rear passenger side, walking round to do the front doors and finally the driver's side rear door. She made her way round to the boot, reached up to grab the tailgate, and with one look down inside, slammed it shut. With a last wave to the family inside the kitchen, she climbed back into the car and fastened her seatbelt. She followed the drive sharply to the left around the house, then immediately right through the gateway, not even pausing for the press pack, who'd been most interested in her visit. Cameras of all kinds were pushed against the windows of the car as she drove by, shutters clicked and motors whined. The footage later revealing a couple of bags and crates no doubt destined for the lab and the experiment. Seeing nothing else of interest, the crowd of journalists and photographers parted for her, allowing the car through, and she turned onto the road and began her journey towards the hospital. She checked the rearview mirror. No one was following her, and a mile down the road she pulled over and texted Tom to say so. She drove past the park and the neat rows of large detached houses with immaculate gardens and expensive cars, up and over the hill to descend into the deep basin of the city. Victorian houses gave way to old stone buildings from almost every era in the last three hundred years. Civic buildings sat side-by-side with a modern cricket stadium, the new leisure centre next to a Victorian private school. Ugly concrete flyovers and underpasses were overshadowed by giant billboards with ever-changing adverts for celebrity endorsed fragrances, Hugo Boss clothing and the new Range Rover. Whole streets were composed of bauble-shaped office complexes reflecting the early morning sun in various hues and at infinite angles by the millions of panes of glass cladding their walls. She turned right across the park at a giant estate of tower blocks, noticing a man walking his dog, and a couple dressed in lycra out for an early-morning run. At the end of the road, the hospital campus came into view, the road passing a series of entrances. The first and main entrance had a smattering of press people and a TV camera, waiting to capture Tom's arrival. No doubt there was more media interest now after Tom's performance at the press conference two days before. Mags continued along the campus' feeder road to the main staff entrance, which had a large concentration of journalists, photographers and two TV camera crews, the TV anchors periodically delivering pieces to camera for breakfast TV or twenty-four hour news shows. Yellow-vested security were on hand to do very little – porter staff drafted in to look official and to prevent the press from taking over the hospital. To her right, she could see the main hospital and university buildings – the ultramodern and the significantly older, jostling for prominence in the public view. She continued along to the university entrance, seeing the proof of Tom's theory – there were no reporters here, just two bored-looking porters who waved her through after spotting her car parking pass. This entrance meant she had to drive all the way back behind the main medical school and administration buildings to get to the research block. There was plenty of other traffic using the roads on site that morning so her car didn't stand out, and the reporters at the house had obviously not tipped off their colleagues about her.

Mags pulled into the underground car park of the Life Sciences Research Institute. She parked the car, carefully driving into a space rather than reversing in as she normally would, so as not to block the boot. She got out and popped the boot release. Tom lay on a duvet with a pillow under his head and squinted at the light streaming in from the strip lights overhead.

'Do you think we could go round again Mags, I think there were some potholes you missed on the road back there... not many though...' he reached his hand out and she helped him unfold himself from the boot and stand up, stretching his legs. 'It worked,' he said, pleased with the subterfuge.

'Yes it did, it was worth all that planning yesterday,' she said as they walked across the parking level to the concrete foyer with a lift at the end.

'I was almost crawling when I came around from the patio doors just to make sure they didn't see me above the car. I was worried that they might notice the car bounce when I got in.'

'Shoulda been on a diet for the last few weeks since you came up with the idea then, eh?' Mags replied pithily as she punched in the key code next to the polished aluminium doors – after half a minute or so the lift arrived and the doors hummed open. On the top floor the lift opened out into the foyer of the Human Physiology Research Centre. Two security guards, normally stationed at the central foyer of the building were, today, patrolling here to prevent any journalists from gaining access to the research area. Management had drafted in some further private security staff for the main foyer to be on the safe side. The receptionists, Helen and Denise, were in overdrive today, scanning everything like velociraptors on the hunt, ensuring that the hospital gossip trail would be continually fed – this was their moment. They even found time to politely acknowledge him, which was unusual. Tom usually made a point of being overtly nice to them – he wasn't going to let it bother him that they found him second best to his predecessor. And it had the added advantage that it might win them around, eventually.

Tom and Mags walked through the main doors into a wide hallway, lined with plywood, which sloped down to the main corridor. At the far end were two sets of double doors, those in front leading to the hub, those on the left into the main 'theatre' room. Tom pushed the theatre doors open, leaving Mags to stride purposefully on towards her desk. Despite it being just after seven, the whole team had arrived and were bustling around their own stations in the brightly lit room. Tom had left named protocols for the experiment at every station before leaving work the previous evening. He was pleased that everyone had taken them and were working through checklists, readying and calibrating equipment one more time, and stockpiling drugs and fluids. The hospital bed in the centre of the room was covered in the cold suit, the central torso section having been attached to the bed frame by straps. He looked at the network of white plastic pipes attached to the mesh. The separate arm sections hung off the sides of the bed and the rugby skullcap helmet curved off the mattress at the head of the suit. Each section had flow and return pipes that were now being bunched together and plugged into the manifold system on the far side of the room by Charlie's control desk. Charlie's assistant Ray was doing the plumbing, checking each pipe connection so that 'flow' and 'return' matched that on the manifold. Charlie was sitting at his desk, running tests on the pump system. Ray offered occasional words of encouragement and advice. Both looked uncomfortable dressed in blue theatre scrubs like everyone else.

There was little small-talk – everyone was quietly focused on their job. The significance of getting everything right was not lost on anyone, and for once, nobody minded repeatedly checking and re-checking that everything was just so. Tom nodded to those who looked up when he entered and walked over to the bed. He exchanged thin smiles with Chloe and Scott and lay down so they could practice covering him in the cooling system, pulling the helmet system into place as he did so. Scott pulled the network of pipes over him and tightened the straps around his arms and legs so Tom was strapped to the bed. He felt confined, uncomfortable, trapped in place and helpless. Suddenly he started to panic, claustrophobic surrounded by the pipes with everyone milling around him.

'Get me out, Scott.'

'Give me a second longer Tom, wanna check all the strap tensions for later–'

'No. I need to get out now, Scotty, just do it will you!' Agitated now Tom struggled to free himself, arms and legs shaking to get free. Quickly releasing all the straps, Scott and Chloe helped him up into a sitting position, still wearing the head section, looking like the Professor from *Back to the Future*.

'You okay, boss?' Scott bent forward with his hands on his thighs, keeping eye contact with Tom.

'Yeah, fine.' Tom gave a humourless laugh. 'Been strapped there before, but just got the yips or something today. Fuck. Can't be letting this get to me already.' he smiled at them both, and Chloe put her hand on Tom's shoulder.

'There's a lot going on in your head, Tom. When you see that everything's done and ready in a couple of hours' time, you'll be just fine.'

'I'm sure you're right. Struggling with a lack of coffee as well. Where's Aliens?' he slipped the skullcap off.

'In the storeroom, stocking up on drugs.'

'Think I might join him.'

They spent the next hour populating the room with equipment, drip stands, computers, camera gear and tripods, and the anaesthetic trolley and defibrillator. Equipment built up around the bed, like a concert stage being filled with monitors, guitars and Charlie's water-baths being the bass drums. All that it lacked was the lead singer. The pump for the cooling system was tested and re-tested, and the warm and cold reservoirs brought to temperature. This took time as Charlie had specified a large volume of water to buffer each tank to ensure that the overall temperature of the reservoirs didn't fluctuate. Charlie sat at his desk behind the tanks, side-on to the room, Tom wishing he had a pair of drumsticks to give to him. The bespoke telemetry software ran continually on screen with data for pump velocity and pressures, tank temperature and volumes. They ran test pumping of the pipes for both hot and cold once again, trying to avoid spraying water all over the floor as Andrea ran checks on the defibrillator. Hatim sat at a computer terminal on the opposite side of the room to Charlie. His on-screen software showed an array of camera feeds, the viewing angles from which he painstakingly adjusted by getting up and slightly turning a tripod or tilting a camera until he was happy. He chided technicians and other members of the team if they moved one of the two free-standing towers arching over the bed, and used a joystick to position the three CCTV cameras mounted on the walls. Hatim had plugged all the cameras into his central desk, recording each feed separately in real time. Another screen would take a feed from the medical monitors displaying Tom's vital signs during the procedure. All the camera and telemetry data would be recorded and stored for later analysis, so nothing would be missed. Hatim and Charlie sat at their respective drum kits on either side of the room, surrounded by their monitors, ready to launch into the mother of all drum solos. Tom looked on, directing the positioning of every new piece of equipment and checking it off on his list.

Predictably, they were not left alone to prepare, with a steady stream of visitors passing through to take in the freak show. Some, like Bob Wauberg, came to wish Tom well, and to settle himself in the observation room next door. Others were purely voyeuristic and were summarily dismissed. On cue, Henry arrived with Bill Samuels, the Dean of the university. Tom intercepted them at the door so that the royal visit didn't distract anyone while Henry clearly wanted to poke his nose into everything.

'No cold feet? Not tempted to call it off?' Henry sneered at him, as if he expected nothing to go well today.

'Not at all,' Tom lied. 'We couldn't be better prepared and all our systems are coming together and online. You'll watch remotely as planned?' Henry was chairing a screening of the CCTV feed in his office. Tom didn't know whether they had ordered popcorn.

'I wouldn't miss this, Tom.'

'I'm glad.' *You bastard.*

'I can't pretend that I was wholly for this project, Mr Boyand, but you do have my warmest wishes for a good outcome and a speedy recovery,' said the Dean, pumping his hand, and showing which of the two of them was the most statesman-like.

'Thank you, Dean Samuels,' said Tom with a formal nod, but curtly added. 'Would you gents please excuse me, though, must crack on.' And with that Tom ushered the two men out of the room and shut the door, leaving Henry with a furious expression on his face.

Fully equipped, the room now properly resembled an operating theatre, with the addition of miles of cables linking to the two consoles. Between them were the two chest freezers full of ice, surrounded in an arc by rows of stainless steel medical trolleys.

'Just how the hell do we get to those trolleys if we need the kit from them?' whispered Scott conspiratorially to Sigurd as they stood alongside the drugs trolley at the head of the room.

'I don't know, but I also don't know where the hell else they would go. Too much kit, too much cameras...' Sig said with a small shake of the head. 'Circus.'

'Yep.'

Tom toured round his team, checking and re-checking that

everything was in place, before retiring to his office for a few minutes to clear his head. He opened the door and Sarah suddenly stood up from his chair, a guilty expression on her face, knowing she shouldn't be there.

'Sarah! Hi. Erm, I wasn't expecting you. Have you been here long..? Coffee..? Who let you in? Did Scotty organise this –' He was so surprised to see her that he was gabbling like she had caught him doing something he shouldn't be doing.

'Sorry, Tom, I had to come. I can't sit at home while this is going on – you can say goodbye to the kids, but not to me.' They embraced, and she squeezed him hard, her body pressed close to him. They kissed and Tom went to pull away, but Sarah's arms stayed locked around her husband, refusing to let him go.

'Is everything ready?' her concerned face angled up towards his.

'I think so – I've been fussing around all morning and honestly haven't done much at all – everyone is set up and knows what they're doing. I think I'm just getting in the way. We *have* done some dry run stuff though, so that's positive.'

'You don't have to do this, you know?'

'Oh babe, we've been through this, I know how you feel, but –'

'Do you? Do you really? You're an arrogant bloody scientist. It's not an average day for most people when your husband goes to work, and not only do you not know when he's coming home, but if! That the *idea*, the whole *plan* of the day is for him to die!' Sarah was crying, angrily cuffing at the tears running down her face. She'd planned what she was going to say and this wasn't it.

***

Andrea called a team meeting in the central hub to which Tom wasn't invited – she told him it was for medical staff only, and he was the patient. Sarah was fielding email queries on her new phone in his office so Tom went into the experiment room to get changed. He'd brought an old t-shirt and some shorts to wear on the bed. Dropping his boxer shorts to stand unencumbered it amused him that the room had been full of people earlier. He was bending forward, putting one foot into the leg of the shorts when Kate Delaney marched into the room, announcing her entrance with her heels click-clacking on the floor. None of the women who worked in the unit wore heels like that. She got a good view of the Boyand buns as he hopped around to turn his back on her, swearing at her intrusion as he wrestled the shorts into place to cover his modesty.

'Jesus, Kate, I'm stark bollock naked here!' he complained.

'Then put a 'Do not disturb' sign up next time,' she smiled. 'Besides, I don't see what all the fuss is about.'

'Can I help you?' Tom replied in an exasperated, cut-to-the-chase manner as he pulled on his t-shirt.

'Yes, well I wanted to say, first of all, that I'm sorry about the press conference. I've reflected on my actions and I think I dropped you too far in at the deep end, and I'm sorry to have done that.'

I've reflected on my actions? Who says that?

'Okay,' he said, as if to say, *and?*

'Well, I also wanted to make sure we're on the same page for press involvement for the next few days?' She almost breathed a sigh of relief now she had said it, even though Tom didn't have any idea what she was talking about. He just sat and smiled at her. 'My office..?' she added, as if being completely clear. Tom remained impassively vacant. *God, for a press officer, you really are fucking terrible at communicating*, he thought.

'As in..?'

'As in, making sure that any press statements go through my office and there are no random releases put out there. We don't want contradictory statements, mixed messages, anything inappropriate that hasn't been thoroughly considered getting released.'

'So you'll decide what's put out and how?'

'That isn't how it is, Tom —'

'Oh? Sounds a little like we're being censored.' He stared at her, throwing down a challenge.

'No, Tom, we just want consistency. If you write a statement, we might adjust the wording if need be, but I don't see why it wouldn't go out. Unless you call Henry a twat that is.'

'So why go through your office at all? Some of us can even spell you know.'

She ignored the sarcasm. 'It's just so we know what you've said, and we can make sure any official hospital statements back that up, that's all. It really isn't unusual for press releases to go through my office. We need to calm the hysteria of the last few days.' She had gradually drifted closer to him and he detected the same perfume as she was wearing the other day.

'I'm with you on that. Does the same go both ways?'

'I don't follow.'

'Will you run your press statements through us?'

'Why?' she said, curling her mouth downwards and shaking her head.

'So you don't get anything wrong. Think how bad the place looks if you announce something that's wrong on a technical level – would be all over the news in an hour.'

'We do have medical people to advise us on that sort of thing.'

'Yes. Us. Who better?'

'Okay,' she laughed. 'All right – why not? I'll send any relevant releases to your office for your approval.'

'Andrea, Scott, Chloe and Sigurd can all approve things in my... absence. No problem.'

'Okay, well I'll make sure that happens.' Kate turned to go, paused, then turned back, her hand reaching out to touch his arm. 'And you were right.'

'Oh?'

'It was Henry who leaked the story. Sorry.' She looked suitably contrite.

'The wrinkled fucking ballsack,' Tom spat with some venom.

'Good luck, Tom,' she found it hard to maintain eye contact. 'I hope you find whatever it is you're looking for.'

'Thanks,' he replied, getting used to how heavy people's gaze became when saying goodbye. He watched her walk to the door.

'Oh, and Tom?' She turned again as she pulled the door toward her.

'Yes Kate?'

'Nice bum.'

***

Tom lay on the bed and started to pull the mesh of the cold suit over him. Funny how it was the 'cold' suit, when it would actually be the cold then the warm suit, he thought. Charlie and Scott fussed around him, helping lift the pipe and mesh equipment where Tom didn't have the leverage to fold the stiff pipes across his body. Tom's nurse colleagues – Shirley and Cath – busily checked output readings on the monitors surrounding the bed, to make sure nothing was dislodged as the suit was attached. Finally, when all were happy with the set-up, his entire body covered head-to-toe in netting and plumbing supplies, they were ready to go. Tom suddenly realised that they still needed someone to direct traffic – something he hadn't protocoled for. Ready, steady, go. Perhaps..?

'Is everything set, guys? Thermal system online?' He spoke loudly, too loudly probably because his ears were covered by the helmet.

'Yes boss,' Charlie said.

'Reservoirs ready?'

'Check,' Charlie didn't even look up from his computer. The large white plastic tank to his right contained equal amounts of ice cubes and cold water. The pipe manifold was attached to this and the pump and linked to the flow and return pipes of the various sections of the 'cold suit'. When his body was being cooled, the freezers would be emptied of dozens of bags of ice cubes which would be packed around him, effectively immersing Tom in ice. When this process was complete, the pumping system would run continuously to pump the cold water around his body to keep him cold. The returning water would be deposited back into the cold tank, made a little warmer from Tom's body and from the friction of its journey through the pipes. The skill for Charlie was to maintain the tank at a steady temperature.

The warming tank sat next to its cold counterpart, containing water maintained to a steady thirty seven degrees. The clumsy part of the whole operation was that when it was time to bring Tom around, the ice packs would need to be removed from his body and cooling switched over to warming. This required the pump manifold to be manually unplugged and moved across from the cold tank, with all its suit pipes still attached, plugged into the warm tank and the 'warming pump' started.

'Cameras and telemetry?'

'Check.' Hatim was flicking between cameras and monitors on his desktop, with more windows open than most normal folks could monitor.

'Anaesthetics and life support?'

'Yes.' Aliens busied himself with a collection of drugs sat in small trays and pouches on the anaesthetics trolley.

'Defib kit ready?'

'All set, Chief.' Scott smiled down at him, Andrea nodding from across the room.

'Okay then, Charlie, can you start the cooling system, please?' Tom was focused on the matter at hand, not thinking of what was really about to happen or Sarah watching from the observation room, as she had insisted. They had shared a quiet and quick goodbye in the room shortly after Kate left. There was little else left to say.

'Okay,' Charlie said nervously as he activated the pump to send cooled water through the pipe network. There was complete silence aside from the mechanical hum of the pumps as they started their circular motion, and the bing of the monitors reading Tom's heart rate and blood pressure.

'I can feel the cooling... bloody cold!' A few nervous sniggers came from the group. 'Mr Scott? You have the Conn,' said Tom as he tried to turn to catch his friend's eye.

Scotty smiled at the Star Trek reference. 'Aye aye Cap'n. Aliens, can we have the sedative, please?' Sig was already at the drip stand and administering the dose. There had been great debate in the previous weeks about how much anaesthetic to give. Too little and the anxiety state might cause genuine pathology, too much and it might fog any results or memories and render his experience as unrecordable.

'Still want to do this?' Andrea smiled down at him, her hand on his shoulder.

'Was there a consent form?' Tom smiled to hide his nerves.

'Last chance, Doctor.' Andrea needed an answer.

'Gotta do it now, I'm on the front page of *The Sun*.' She nodded, broadening her somewhat tight-lipped smile, patted his pipe-covered shoulder and stepped backwards. She nodded to Scott, happy that she had given Tom every opportunity to back out should he want to, even at this late stage.

'Count backwards from ten for me.'

'See you in the next life! Ten, nine, eight…' He closed his eyes, aware of the effects of the sedative as he did so, and concentrated on his breathing which grew louder in his ears as his nostrils flared. The darkness had blurred, fuzzy edges. Slowly, he drifted backwards, being accepted deeper and deeper into the pillow and mattress which seemed to soften and dissolve away under him. He slipped through their foam and feather fingers, falling through into the void. The lights from the recovery room had cast an imprint on his retina and he saw ghostly trails rearrange themselves into a criss-cross yellow mesh, fading in and out of focus at the periphery of his vision. He fell faster, the mesh becoming a blur, encroaching more and more into his field of 'vision'. The abyss into which he dropped becoming colder and colder, the air temperature surrounding him dropping gradually. He started to shiver. Tom heard a buzzing in his ears – maybe machinery in the room or wind rushing by as he fell. More importantly, he could also hear the strong reassuring beat of his heart, loud in his ears and chest.

He began to spin about his axis, arms drifting outwards with the motion, almost acting as stabilisers. The light surrounding his vision became a spinning kaleidoscope, shapes overlapping and changing, morphing and twisting from the almost recognisable to the amorphous and back again. He was spinning faster and faster, tightening the shapes around into a funnel, a spinning vortex which wrapped around him. The lights ever-changing forming new and different shapes. The funnel closed around him, the vortex snapped shut like a spinning trap, completely enclosing him. He was in complete silence and was colder than he had ever experienced.

'*Shock him.*' Already connected to pads on Tom's chest, the defibrillator was building charge. A steady series of beeps increased in their frequency and pitch until they made a continuous shrill noise.

'*Stand clear.*' A hand pressed a button and Tom's body arched off the bed. The trace on the monitor screen showed a disorganised inconsistent line indicating that his heart was completely out of sync and therefore not working. The heart muscle tissue continuously tried to contract but needed a coordinated signal to keep it working in an organised manner to be an effective pump of blood around the body. Without such coordination, no real circulation could be maintained – the defibrillator taking away life as easily as it could give it. Tom Boyand was dead.

The funnel released its hold on him, folding back on itself, peeling away like a banana skin, then gave him a huge kick in the chest. He was knocked backwards, disorientated, wheeling around and around, and was eventually left floating... somewhere. It took a second for Tom to orientate himself before he realised he was looking down at his body in the medical room. He had been right to refer to himself as a 'body' in the protocols. He was unrecognisable as a person, covered by dozens of bags of ice as he lay on the bed. Aliens was busy intubating him to prevent him swallowing his tongue and to maintain a patent airway for when they revived him. Meanwhile, Scott and Chloe carried more bags of ice to pack around him. Chloe placed one on the right side of his chest to pack between the rest – one of the last pieces of the jigsaw. She tried to push it into the gap, quickly turning away to get the next one, but the bag hadn't become wedged in, and as she turned it fell to the floor. Tom watched all this unfold from above, floating, looking down on the scene, but he was being pulled away. He was dragged upwards through the ceilings and walls of the Research Block until he flew clear of the roof, looking down at the solitary crane that remained from the construction work – only now being dismantled. He flew over the curved top of the glass atrium, and saw pipes and crane parts scattered on the flat roof, the scaffolding in the distance marking the new Health Education Block due to open next year. He turned away from all of this and flew upwards. The weather had stayed clear, and he ascended into blue sky, dotted with fast-moving cotton wool cumulus clouds driven by the stiff breeze.

The city receded beneath him as he climbed. He gazed across the high-rise buildings of the city centre, shining and reflecting the midday sun, to orderly rows of Monopoly houses. His ascent seemed to accelerate. He could see the hill climbing up and out of the basin of the city, the woods at the top jutting out of the last of the morning mist, individual trees reaching up to escape the grey blanket. Tom spread his arms wide and spun, pirouetting through a cloud, the freshest dew spraying on his face, causing him to break into a beaming smile. Spinning to the left, through 360 degrees, then back again he tested his powers of flight before buzzing past a flock of birds who seemed not to notice him. He continued to climb and accelerate, at speeds impossible to estimate, the wind resistance on his body, shaking and vibrating, his t-shirt flapping like a skydiver's in free fall. His cheeks being pulled backwards into a sneer. The atmosphere became thinner and colder, water vapour froze into ice crystals on his face. He blinked rapidly to prevent an ice wall accumulating in front of his eyes and leaving him blind. Frozen vapour sloughed off the rest of his body leaving a trail behind him as he was propelled forward, like Iron Man without his jet boots.

Above him was the giant curving snow globe dome of the sky, the brilliance of the light incredible to his eyes, as if he had never looked up before. The sky was light blue as it met the horizon, deepening to azure in the middle. High cirrus clouds formed a thin folded sheet across half the roof of the world, looking like ripples in the sand on a beach at low tide. Tom imagined leaving a hole in the cloud sheet as he flew through and pictured some kid on the ground – miles below – seeing the cloud formation collapse and the sky fall in. Beyond this the sky grew darker, the temperature dropping. His widespread arms had frozen in place, they refused to move even when he told them to, rigid like the wings on a plane. The blue gradually gave way to black, the world that surrounded him growing dark and filled with stars. Tom looked down and there he saw the Earth, its vast curving beauty glowing brilliantly green and blue in the blackness of space. He saw a giant tropical storm, brooding grey clouds covering almost half a hemisphere gradually rotating, increasing its force and destructive power as it did so. He saw darkness in the east being pushed back as the sun rose on a new day. The colour contrast was incredible – the purest blue of the oceans, the greens of the land in temperate zones and the brown of the desert at the equator. And then, the massive brilliant-white polar ice cap of Antarctica. He gazed on the majesty of Mother Nature and reflected that it might be his last ever view of home. The pull of the universe was inexorable, however, and he turned reluctantly away from the Earth, toward the vastness of space laid out in front of him. The utter darkness punctuated by what must be millions upon millions of pin-pricks of light. In front of him was the International Space Station, and he glided past a large window showing what looked like the living quarters. There was no sign of anyone at home as he zipped by a solar panel, almost clipping it.

With no close points of reference, his forward flight was almost imperceptible – but he knew he was moving. Air seemed to rush past him, like when riding his bike as a small boy. It was just as real now as then – impossible, of course, in the vacuum of space – yet there it was. He realised he was steadily accelerating, first slowly approaching, then flashing past the eerie white glow of the Moon, flying by the Sea of Tranquillity, spotting large deep craters as he flew overhead. Soon the Moon was a speck in the distance and Mars approached, glowing red like a sunset before it disappeared in a flash. Even at speed it seemed to take an age to reach the next celestial body.

Christ space travel must be tedious.

He closed the distance to Saturn, then Jupiter, seeing them appear in the distance and counting what seemed like days as each one grew larger in his field of view, before giving him the briefest of close-ups and then they too were a memory. He saw a comet in the distance, its vapour trail of ice crystals arcing across the whole horizon. Tom twisted and weaved joyfully in and out of its tail, gaining every second on the ball of ice and rock at its head. He was disappointed that he couldn't fly alongside or surf on it, but it too flashed by in a blink and with that he left the solar system altogether. He'd travelled further than any human ever had, and it had happened in a matter of, what? Days? Weeks? It should have taken him years to get this far, but surely that long couldn't have passed, could it? As long as it had taken he also knew he was flying impossibly quickly.

What if this was his ending, what if this was what he was destined to do for eternity, slowly dissolving into the insanity of isolation? He'd certainly had time, time and space one might say, to think about his life, about Sarah, Ben and Liam, about his friends, his work, his choices. He remembered them, all the people that mattered, but it was an effort. The memories were two-dimensional, like there was no depth or flesh to them, like a picture on the wall – images without story, faces without recognition. His memories of his old life were fading with the distance from home.

8.

'Fifteen minutes in, prepare for switchover and standby on resus – no time for donuts, guys,' Scott smiled, allowing himself to relax as the process went to plan, but still nervous about bringing Tom back.

'Check your protocol – it's changed!' Aliens exclaimed, staring at his hand out. There was rustling of paper as everyone checked their own documents.

'It's gone to forty minutes?' Chloe replied, confusion in her voice.

'It should be twenty! We all agreed twenty,' said Andrea.

'What has he done?' Chloe looked around at every face that would meet her gaze.

'He's pushing the envelope as far as he can – if he's going, he might as well go as far as he can,' analysed Scott.

'You knew?' Andrea accused him.

'No, not at all, just surmising – I know how he's wired up.' He shrugged.

'Well, I didn't sign up to this,' said Andrea, holding her hands up as if to say she was about to leave.

'I think you probably did,' Aliens responded.

'What do you mean?' Andrea looked at him.

'He made changes.'

'Yes, the changes we agreed on at the meeting.'

'And did you re-read your protocol when we got it this morning?'

Did you check it?' Sig had a thin-lipped smile.

'No, I... I suppose I didn't.'

'Then he's got us,' Sig said.

'He doesn't, we just have to stick to what we originally agreed and what we signed up to,' Chloe's matter-of-fact tone made it clear she didn't understand why they were having this conversation.

'Have you signed your protocol?' asked Scott.

'What?'

'Did. You. Sign. The. Protocol sheet. This morning?'

'Well, there's no need to be so fucking patronising. Yes I did, but –'

'Then you did sign up to this, and he has got us,' Scott shrugged again and looked through the observation room glass at Sarah, whose hands were at her mouth. The minute hand of the clock flicked around to twenty minutes. Scott stared through the glass at Sarah, their eyes locked together, hers pleading, his unreadable, and he said:

'That is twenty minutes in everyone... halfway.' There was a combined gasp in the room. Sarah's head dropped into her hands, her body shaking.

'I don't see why we should just accept changes that Tom has hoodwinked us into – he knew damn well we wouldn't read them again this morning.' Andrea was angry.

'I understand what you're saying, but these protocols form the exact experimental design we're bound to and that we've agreed with the university and the funding body. If we vary from them and something goes wrong, we could have a problem with our employer or Mr Solomon.'

'Oh Jesus, I'm not hanging around for this,' Andrea decided, stepping back from the bed.

'So you're going to leave him dead on the table?' Aliens queried.

'This isn't professional or ethical,' she said firmly.

'No, it isn't, but *it* doesn't matter anymore, you might be the only person who can bring him round.' Scott looked across at Sig. 'No offence, mate.'

'None taken, I'd prefer Andrea to be here if he's out this long.'

***

Tom's acceleration was increasing exponentially, and soon he was racing past neighbouring stars and flying through tomorrow's horoscopes, climbing higher and higher through the celestial roof. He flew through a nebula, clouds of dust particles, gas and debris from dead stars coalescing together to form new stars and systems – a brightly coloured nursery for the newborn stars blinking forth for the first time from within. The gasses and massive dust clouds – as big as the solar system itself – refracting light in different ways to create a huge canvas of blue, green and pink. The rushing sound had returned. Perhaps it was the sound of his super-fast flight being bounced back off the heavenly bodies he flew by. Or maybe it was just his imagination. A star in the distance went supernova, creating a giant flash far away somewhere, sending a shockwave across the cosmos. From his elevated viewpoint the wave moved slowly, spreading out at a crawl, but he was so far away and travelling at such speed now, even the speed of light seemed slow to him.

Stars seemed smaller and closer together, forming interlinking chains of constellations, like fairy lights at Christmas. He ascended until he flew clear of them and looked down in wonder at the spiral arm of the Milky Way he called home. He saw the impossibly massive collection of billions of stars curving away into the distance, converging with the other arms of the spiral galaxy far in front of him. At the periphery of his vision were other galaxies that he vaguely remembered Professor Brian Cox mentioning late at night on the BBC. Names like Andromeda and the Magellanic Cloud floated like a distant galaxy at the edge of his memory and then disappeared. He was drawn, inexorably, toward the huge black hole at the centre of the galaxy. The super-massive gravity well was the size of our solar system, it sucked all life and light into itself, taking matter beyond the event horizon of time and gravity. And yet there, in amongst the maelstrom, was a star – a giant ball of white energy – seemingly unaffected by the gravitational pull of the black hole, sitting impossibly in orbit around it. The strange star emitted more light and power than a thousand of the suns he had already encountered. He was drawn toward it, his flight bringing him in closer. The heat struck him like a hot wind on a summer evening and grew warmer still, becoming uncomfortable. As he was drawn closer, and stared deep into the shimmering white fire, he noticed movement, swirling and twisting. The incredibly hot gases roiled, twisting and combining, creating new elements as they did, writhing like vipers in a nest, sliding and moving over each other. It was almost like they were taking on form, or perhaps it was a trick of the intensity of the light on his eyes. Tom saw other things flying into the giant sun, glowing shapes that might represent bodies – souls on their final journey. Were they all human? Were they souls of any living being from Earth or were they beings from other planets, souls of all living creatures in the cosmos?

The twisting mass below had coalesced into solid forms. They looked like arms, thousands and thousands of white, ethereal arms, like rhythmically beating cilia. They waved with indistinct hands reaching up and out like the tentacles of an anemone, waiting to draw in and cushion the landing of any soul on its final journey. He smiled, his heart ached with joy. All thoughts of death, the experiment and his revival were long gone, replaced by the majesty of the cosmos, by a feeling of oneness and belonging to every atom of the universe itself. Enraptured, he longed to be caught and welcomed into the glory that this surely represented. He reached out with both hands like a child reaching out to it's parents. He had flown through the galaxy at faster than light speed and yet now he crawled. The final part of his final journey taking forever, and perhaps it was, perhaps this would be his forever – always out of reach. The distance closed and as the light of the star filled his vision, an arm reached out from the others and a hand clasped his. It looked just like a human hand and closed gently but firmly around his right wrist, drawing him slowly in. He somehow knew he was meant to be here, that he had come home after flying thousands of light years from Earth. The welcoming hand promised everything; comfort, protection, warmth and a thousand other things just beyond his reach, and he longed to be enveloped.

Suddenly, the blackness of space beyond the curve of the star was replaced by a flash, sending a ripple through space-time, radiating out like a pebble dropped in a lake. The ripples bent and folded his view, distorting the spiral arms of the galaxy, the shape of the giant star, and the hand holding his wrist, before converging on him and punching him hard in the chest. He was flung backwards, but the hand gripped onto him with increasing force, squeezing hard. Tom drifted back towards it, unsure of what the shock wave had been, but just as quickly dismissing it as an irrelevance. He readily gave himself to the moment again, forgetting the annoyance of the interruption. Another shock wave vibrated the whole universe again – stronger this time – hitting his chest, throwing him backwards hard, almost dislodging the grip of the hand on his. The hand squeezed harder, crushing his wrist, bone breaking and splintering as the joint collapsed, sending searing white hot pain up his arm. The hand held on. He looked down at the restraint and it had become a hideous claw, thick and strong with coarse black hair on the back, sharp red talons digging into his flesh and crushing the bones. He was jolted from his reverie, from his hallucination of drifting into some form of nirvana or heaven and he realised what it truly was. The end of days – his descent into hell.

We're losing him

I thought he responded to the Zol, his brainwave activity peaked

But it's still working overtime

Hope he remembers what he's seeing

Hope he wants to come back

We've got to shock him on max and hit him with more Zol

He's already had the max Zol dose – we've not tested any higher than that on anything! It could kill him

He's dead if we don't – he might be already

We waited too long, we shouldn't have changed the protocol

Can't we keep shocking?

We're protocoled for another regular shock

Fuck the protocol that's long gone

He's not responding at all physiologically now – no one's been this far before and come back – draw me up 30mg of Zol please. And charge 360 joules

That's three times the dose

Any better ideas would be welcome right now. Your objection is noted

Fuck

Sig was handed a kidney bowl with a syringe containing the drug. He grabbed the barrel, flicked it up in the air, spinning 180° to point with the needle downwards. Sig plunged it hard and fast down between his index and middle fingers each covering a rib, through the inter-space into the chest cavity and into the heart itself.

Delivered like Fed Ex – shock him!

***

The claw had almost pulled him all the way in, and no amount of struggling could resist. Tom felt or almost heard a muffled explosion across the horizon and this time saw a massive shock wave travel across the galaxy, folding and enveloping all in its wake, bending space-time into a giant tidal wave, destroying all before it. The wave-front completely enveloped him, tearing him free of the claw and the star, leaving them far behind. It was like being tied to the front of a thundering juggernaut that was sweeping across space. The cosmic energy battered Tom as it surged across half the galaxy, tossing him around with universal debris, spinning him over and over. So pummelled did he become over time that Tom's mind became dulled to the beating. His senses switched off from the spinning chaos outside of him and he retreated inwards, desensitised to all that was happening to his body. He was being tumbled through space at the front of a giant cosmic tidal wave at a million miles an hour, just after being snatched from his final descent by something unknown. That was a fair summary of recent events, he thought grimly. He kept his eyes closed, the blur of spinning stars and clouds and debris making him nauseous whenever he opened them. He tried to think, tried to work out what was happening, whether this would be his last ride? And when the wave deposited him, would that be it? He tried to reflect, tried to think back to what his life had been before he became a celestial body, but it was too hard. His memory wouldn't stretch back that far – he could barely remember the concept of being on a planet and having a life, let alone what that life had been. Who had he known? What had he seen? Was there anything left behind to care about?

He's responding

His battered brain had struggled against the dizzying action of the wave for too long, and his mind slowly began to shut down. He still tried to think, tried to focus, remember things he had seen, comets and planets, even back as far as flying through the Earth's atmosphere.

Earth! That was it, that had been home, but...

He faded again, blackness invading his thoughts, and he could fight it no longer as he continued to turn inwards. His consciousness started to fade, and he guessed this must be the end, his thoughts becoming unclear, foggy and abstract, seeing fleeting images of people he didn't recognise, places he didn't know and memories that weren't his. As the final blackness enveloped him, his mind was no longer his either, his thoughts no longer coherent, and his awareness of who he was and who he had ever been was gone.

We're losing him again

Do something

Tom was no longer being battered by the wave, but was totally submerged by it, like a surfer trapped under the force of the water. He fought to free himself, fighting for air, tumbling over and over in the chaos, struggling against the impossible current and force of it. He swam upwards, to see if he could find the surface, lungs bursting, suddenly aware of how long it had been since he had breathed, his chest feeling like it would explode.

He's responding, we've got him!

Suddenly Tom was being pulled forwards and upwards, yanked bodily up. He was at the bottom of the cosmic ocean, submerged in eternity, the water dulling his senses and now he was ascending, heading for the surface, the light above him, the noise. The assault on his senses came at a rush as the water roared over him, deafening him as he broke the surface. He took a breath, a single sharp deep breath, filling his lungs with sweet air from which they had been deprived for so long. Even knowing how harsh it would be, he had to see, he had to gaze upon his surroundings, to process where he had landed.

Sinus rhythm

His eyes flickered open for a second, not even long enough to focus, before he collapsed backwards again. The cosmic wave had subsided into a giant black lake on which he floated, enveloped completely in totally sensory blackness in a starless sky. He was alone with only the sound of his breathing and his heartbeat and the pain from his ruined hand.

9.

It took time for Tom to come to his senses, his consciousness pushing through the blackness and the cobwebs. He had no idea how long he'd been lying there, time was an abstract concept to him. It could have been forever. His awareness returned, and he began to process all he knew of his surroundings, realising he was lying in a lake, the gentle waters supporting and holding him, lapping around his spread-eagled body. He had no real recollection of how he had come to be there or where indeed *there* was. The place was in complete darkness, no light, no stars in the sky, no shades of grey or depths to the blackness to suggest shape or texture. He faded in and out of awareness, remembering the claw and the wave, piecing together his consciousness and rebuilding his most recent memories, more distant ones being just out of reach. The lake was silent. He tried to lift his arms to make a splash but his limbs wouldn't move. He wasn't tied or trapped, he just couldn't physically send the messages through to his body.

Beep beep

More of an awareness, not a sound, a man-made noise, totally out of place in this most isolated of surroundings.

Beep beep

Beep beep

The sound again and, now he focused on it, he realised that it was there all the time, a regular noise, but in the background like it didn't matter, like it belonged with all the other sound. And when he concentrated, there *were* other background noises – humming and whirring noises that must have been machines but which meant nothing to him. And then he heard more organic sounds, not as synthetic or artificial as the first things he had heard; sweet, delicate sounds that floated to his ears, that almost sounded like words. Words! Of course they were words. He heard someone speaking – distant, too far away and through too many layers of fog to understand – but still unmistakable – the wonderful magic of a woman's voice.

He tried to absorb what he heard, it seemed there was a lot going on around him and it felt closer to him now. He realised he could move his limbs a little, and whenever he did, it changed the *beep*, and caused the voices to respond. This was amazing, he was communicating with something, someone, although where to go from here? He tried to speak, tried to articulate words of his own, forcing himself to remember how to make the sounds. His mouth was dry, his throat acutely painful and he gagged on his attempt, causing further excitement in the voices, the people evidently watching him. Something was restricting him, making it harder to move his mouth, like a gag tied across his face. He tried again, licking his lips to moisten them, swallowing to lubricate his throat and once again tried to force out a sound.

Hello

Tom opened his eyes. Or at least he tried to, but the brightness of the light in the room made him wince and close them again. The sweet, deep breath he had taken hit the back of his throat and his lungs, and, like a heavy smoker first waking, he collapsed into a coughing fit that gripped and twisted his body.

'Tom!' a woman standing over him cried, waving to the observation window to get the attention of some other people, but Tom didn't recognise anyone. She went closer to Tom's bedside, placing a reassuring hand on his shoulder as he coughed.

'It's okay, Tom, take your time,' she said to keep him calm.

He opened his eyes again, his vision swam, unable to see clearly. The light was still painful, and he flopped back onto the bed again, losing the consciousness he'd only just regained – the oxygen mask still in place over his mouth and nose.

When his eyes next opened, he turned his head away from the glare of the overhead lights, blinking repeatedly as they watered, giving the impression he was crying. Someone quickly pushed the lights away, and he saw a little more, his face relaxed as he tried to take in his surroundings. Slowly the people in the room came into focus – there were more this time, three or four. The same nurse smiled down at him and a man turned and spoke.

'Hey Tom,' he said and Tom realised that he must be back on Earth – back home. He remembered an experiment, but frustratingly nothing else, the memories seemed just beyond the reach of the outstretched fingers of his mind. He *did* remember flying through space, remembered seeing the wonders of the universe laid out before him, and he remembered the claw. He looked around at the people in the room trying to place them, to see if he recognised them. They certainly seemed to know him, or maybe not, maybe his brain was reading too much into their expressions. The effort of concentrating became too much, and his eyelids fluttered, once again falling back into a deep sleep.

'Did he recognise *any* of us?' asked Scott. 'What're his EEG readings?'

'Off the scale,' said Chloe.

'So at least his brain's working,' Scott looked in turn at all the monitors in the room.

'Yeah it's working, but that doesn't mean that there isn't any damage there,' Chloe replied as she recorded some data onto an iPad.

'What do you mean?' Scott looked up.

'Well, the actual brain function's there, as far as electrical activity goes, but what about all the complexity, the connections, the links and pathways, the memories and structure that he's created all through his life – is that intact? He was gone for a long time, Scott, *twice* as long as we planned for. Can the things that make Tom survive that? And is an EEG gonna tell us that?' Chloe's large eyes were solemn and concerned.

'Still early days yet, babe...'

Tom drifted and time passed. The beauty of sleep was that one never perceived time, so that eight hours in bed passed in an instant. He woke again, not knowing whether he'd been asleep for seconds or hours, the head of the bed had been raised so he was no longer laying flat but reclining, the electronic bed control placed on the blanket next to him. The same people were still in the room. He looked at the man, and he recognised him somehow, some strand of memory he found himself reaching for, like a rope disappearing off into the void. He clung to it, pulling hard on it, reeling it in. It came closer and closer and suddenly he remembered.

'Scotty?' he questioned, not sounding too convinced.

'Yay, boss,' Scott said with a grin and sat down on the side of the bed. 'How you doing?' The flood gates opened and Tom's brain suddenly remembered Scott, all the memories of their association together over the years rushing back at once. Snapshots of Scott, variously in the lab and at home, like a collage on a wall, from different angles with different expressions; with beard and without, with different girls, images of working with him in the lab, of him huddled over a microscope, and an image of him and Scott out in town, very drunk, with Scotty pissing against a wall. *Why would he remember that?*

'Scotty, I –' he struggled to speak, his mouth being so dry. He could barely free his tongue from the roof of his mouth but found no moisture with which to lick his lips. He looked at the nurse in the room. 'Water,' he croaked. 'Please, Chloe.'

She smiled down at him. 'It's Shirley, Tom,' but she reached across and handed him a clear plastic cup half-full of water with a large black straw sticking precariously out of the top. 'Chloe's in there,' Shirley pointed to Chloe who was sitting in the observation room with another woman. Chloe smiled and waved, the woman next to her looked upset. Lifting the cup in his left hand, Tom took the first drink he had taken in this lifetime. He gulped the water down like it was the finest thing he had ever swallowed, draining the cup in a few mouthfuls. He wiped his face with the back of his hand and sank back against the pillows.

'Thank you. I remember, Scotty.' He smiled at his friend. His head was thumping and his right wrist sore. Then again his chest ached like someone had dropped a weight on it and he had pins and needles in all his limbs, like bolts of lightning shooting around his body. 'I couldn't remember at first – I've been gone for so long –'

'Yeah well, both Andrea and Sig are gonna wanna talk to you about that.'

'Really?' Tom was wistful, seeming far away again. 'I can't... remember... things before I left...'

'Before you left? Okay. Is that how it seemed?' He stared at his friend, watched his facial muscles twitch into life, his expressions changing like switching channels on a TV; from serene to troubled, to a smile.

'Seemed, Scott?' He had a dreamy expression as he remembered. 'I've been to the stars!'

As the two men talked, Shirley reached down to take Tom's pulse. Her fingers closed around his wrist on the radial side, feeling for the telltale beat under one of them. Tom screamed as she gripped his wrist, the pain shooting up to his elbow. He yanked his arm free as a startled Shirley released him, using his other hand to protectively cradle his injured one to his chest. The venflon remained fixed to the back of his hand with a tube connected to a bag of saline on a drip stand. Shirley looked at Scott, both with equally surprised expressions on their faces.

'What was *that*?' asked Scott.

'I don't know, I tried to take his pulse, and he screamed,' Shirley's eyes were full of apology.

'Okay, let's take a look,' Scott leaned over the bed and looked at Tom's wrist, immediately noticing diffuse bruising throughout the hand and arm, but faded, yellow and green. 'I didn't see any of this when we prepped him – did we photograph his wrist?'

'I think so – Chloe took pictures and video of him all over before you wrapped him in the cold suit,' Shirley leaned in to join Scott's examination.

'It's swollen too – look how puffy it is around the wrist and it's spread to the back of his hand.'

'What the hell did he do?'

'I don't know, he was thrown around a little when we were using the defib, but I don't remember him hitting his arm.'

'Me neither – we would have noticed that, would have been concerned about the venflon.' They both looked through the glass partition to the others in the adjacent control room. Sarah was wide-eyed, wanting to be with Tom, but she'd agreed to let everyone work on him to get him stable before she went in. After watching Tom jerk his arm away, however, and seeing his pain and confusion, she decided to act.

'I'm going in.'

'Sarah, I don't know if that's such a good idea –' Chloe was interrupted as Sarah opened the observation room door and immediately pushed through the double doors into the med lab. She rushed in, stopping a few steps from the bed. Scott turned to see her come in, only surprised that she'd waited this long. Tom saw her too. A very attractive woman in her early forties, slim, curly blonde hair, forced smile and looking drained. He knew he must know her, knew she was probably close to him – maybe she was his wife – but he had no memory of her.

'Hi,' he said brightly, wanting to please her, searching his memory, stalling for time.

'Tom?' She approached the bed, perching on the edge of the bed next to Scott. 'Tom, do you remember me?'

'Sarah, I'm not sure that this is such a good –'

'You've had him for long enough, Scotty, now it's my turn.' She looked at Tom again, past the attempted goofy grin put on for her benefit, but not seeing any recognition. Tears flowed down her face.

'Tom, I love you.'

Tom stared at Sarah's face – it was a stranger's but he focused on her and searched his memories. He wished he had created a memory palace to structure his brain. Somewhere he could walk into a virtual room and pick something out of it. He had always dismissed that type of thing as psychology mumbo jumbo, the kind of shit that Bob would champion. *Bob? Now who the fuck was Bob?*

'Brain activity off the scale, Scott.' Shirley noted.

'Take it easy Tom, just allow the memories to come back,' his friend said reassuringly. Tom frowned, screwing his face up as if fighting with himself mentally.

'Oak tree,' he said after what seemed like an age.

'What?'

'An oak tree, when we got married,' Tom said triumphantly.

They had got married at a stately home near Sarah's parents' house with a huge spreading oak tree in the grounds that was a favourite location for wedding photographs. He held that picture in his head now. Sarah was definitely his wife.

'Yes! Our wedding day. Yes.' She reached down and hugged his chest, being careful of his cradled arm.

'Ben.'

'Yes! Yes?'

'Ben... my son,' he said solemnly.

'Your only son?' She was pushing him now that he was on a roll.

Another? He searched the furthest corners of his memory. Images were flowing through his consciousness now, like a river that had broken its dam, the plains being suddenly and quickly flooded with water. His brain seemed to fill with noises and conversations and days out and laughter and Power Rangers and kids' football matches and yummy mummies at the school and Christmas day and blue birthday cakes and what seemed like every memory from the last few years. It was as exhausting as being battered by a cosmic wave, and now he felt that he knew what a hard-drive went through when it was rebuilt with data.

Can't remember

Come on.

Can't remember

Think, damnit.

Can't remember

Yes, I've got something.

'Liam!' He suddenly realised that his memories of what he thought was one child at two different stages in his life, were actually of his two boys. Now they separated and became distinct, and he saw their faces in his mind's eye. Sarah put her head flat on his chest, being careful to avoid the burn marks from the defibrillator.

'Sarah. The places I've been... the things I've seen... I have to tell – it's incredible – I can't begin to tell you, I –'

'Shhhh.' She put her fingers on his lips. *Fingers on lips,* he remembered they used to say to the kids when they were being too noisy, although it never seemed to make them any quieter. 'You can tell me again – we have all the time in the world.'

'Hi Chloe,' Tom said brightly as Chloe came into the room carrying another two bags of saline. Looking away from Chloe his eyes met Sarah's and she looked a little hurt, as if she was reading too much into how pleased he'd been to see his colleague.

'What happened?' maintaining eye contact with his wife.

'What do you mean, pal?' Scott said over his shoulder as he was disassembling the water pumping kit which had succeeded in creating a small lake on the floor.

'What happened to me?' Scott stood up, looking odd in theatre scrubs with grease down the front and a wrench in his hand. He and Sarah exchanged glances – there wasn't a protocol for this.

'Do you know what your job is, mate?' said Scott, putting the wrench on a worktop.

'I'm a doctor... right?' Tom replied, looking around the room for confirmation.

'This,' Scott indicated the room and all the equipment surrounding them, 'is your baby. Your idea. You wanted to see what happened to people at the edge of death, what they experience and what happens to them physiologically.' He indicated the equipment again. 'Remember?'

'Maybe a little. My memory faded so much while I was away – it was so long.' Tom's frown told Scott that he was wrestling with his memory, trying to dig things out.

'So you killed me?' Tom's eyes bored into Scott's.

'Yep, we did,' Scott replied, as if it happened all the time.

'And then resuscitated me?'

'Yes, but you changed the protocol this morning, on when we could start resus,' Scott was chiding him now, which was probably a little unfair as Tom had just been dead.

'What? Did I?'

'You changed the protocol – the one you wrote – so instead of being out for twenty minutes, you were gone for forty before we could start to bring you back.'

'And how long was I out in total?'

'Just under an hour.'

'Wow. What's the longest anyone has been gone for?' Even in his newly re-booted state this mattered to Tom.

'Not exactly sure – forty minutes we think. Wait a minute. You didn't change the protocol just so you could break the record, did you?' Scott's raised his eyebrows in surprise.

'I would,' Tom replied.

'You bloody did, you muppet.' Tom was pleased with himself, some of his frown had disappeared and recognition was lighting up his face. 'You remember don't you?'

'Yes. Yes I do. It makes sense,' his eyes were wide and scanning backwards and forwards, thinking, recalling, his memory returning as he did so. He was aware that his returning memories might superimpose themselves over those of his journey, and so needed to record these while they were fresh. 'Can I get some paper, please? I need to write some things down,' he asked Scott.

'Can do better than that, boss,' he said, and raised the head of the bed a little more to make Tom more upright, before picking up the laptop and headphone-mike set from the worktop next to the bed. 'As per your own protocol, voice recognition software all ready for you, just talk away.' Scott opened the laptop and put it on Tom's abdomen, plugging in the headset. Although Tom had no recollection of having voice recognition software, without pausing, he opened the application and created a new document ready for him to dictate.

'We'll leave you alone so you can get some thoughts down – but not too long, though, you still need to rest.' He turned to leave, ushering Chloe and Shirley with him. Sarah was last, kissing him on the forehead.

'Not too long, okay?' she reinforced to him and he nodded. Tom put the headphones on, clicked the record button on the screen and began to talk.

Sarah sat down in the control booth and watched Tom through the glass.

'So, what do you think?' Scott asked, handing her a mug of coffee.

'I was freaked out when he didn't remember me or the kids. I wasn't expecting that, and I was worrying that he might have brain damage or something,' she added a spoon of sugar and took a sip of the strong, pungent liquid. 'You?' she looked at him over the rim of the mug.

'Well, he's weirder than ever, that's true, but it's still Tom, so I'm glad about that.' Scott sat next to her as he set his mug down on the desk. 'Aim for home tomorrow? He should be okay by then.'

'Okay. Is he going to eat tonight?' She asked absently as she watched Tom dictating on his headphones. His eyes were drooping as the events of the day caught up with him again.

'Yeah, we'll grab an early takeaway or something – his stomach should be fine,' Scott said brightly – takeaways when working late tended to be a standard thing for them. They both watched as Tom's head nodded towards his chest a couple of times, before he caught himself and continued his dictation. On the third occasion, his head stayed drooped. The laptop, having slid sideways off his belly, was hanging at a precarious angle at the edge of the bed, ready to fall and smash on the floor.

'My cue to rescue a laptop,' said Scott, leaping to his feet and bounding out of the room.

10.

Everyone left Tom in peace and Sarah too stayed out of the way, catching up with her messages as she waited for him to wake up. The main lights in the room were turned off to help him rest, a couple of reading lamps left on to give some low light in the gloom. After an hour or so he stirred, his awareness of his surroundings came first, conscious that he wasn't in his own bed, before realisation of where he was. He immediately looked for the laptop and spotted it on the worktop next to him. He heard a faint hissing noise – the sound of the nasal oxygen cannulae that looped over his head, under his ears and across his top lip, a squat pipe poking into each nostril.

They must have changed my oxygen when I was sleeping, he thought. He didn't need it though, and he pulled the tubes out of his nose so they hung down round his neck like a piece of jewellery. He noticed something else, something almost intangible, like a change in the atmosphere. Immediately he became more alert, his heart beating faster, the monitor giving a soft 'bing' as a gentle warning – there was definitely a presence in the room. There was no way to be certain, but he wasn't alone.

'Hello?' he called out in a croaking voice. 'Hello!' More forceful this time. Suddenly the room grew colder, as if all the windows and doors had been opened, the sheet covering him now inadequate in the cold air. He tried to turn around to see if anyone else had come in.

'Hello?' he said again. No answer.

He sensed someone else was there (or was it some*thing*?), watching him, sensing their breathing, aware of their movement displacing the air, their density almost palpable.

'Who's there?' His mind was still somewhat groggy, still not quite itself, some of it scattered across the galaxy. He had an inkling that this might all be in his head and he was still comatose. He pinched himself with his right hand, regretting it straight away as his painful wrist protested, causing him to cry out. At least that proved he was awake. The awareness of a presence became greater, they were behind the bed, and he wanted to reach around and touch them. He was afraid, afraid of what might be in the room with him, afraid of what he might see. His heart raced as he panicked that they would jump out and grab him. The warning 'bing' increased in frequency, like a teacher starting to lose patience with mis-behaving children. The coldness seemed to drift over his shoulders as if whoever was behind him had just walked in from a sub-zero outside, trailing the frost in with them.

Fuck this. Taking his time, Tom sat up, pulling himself upright with his left hand, head thumping and a wave of light-headedness washing over him. The room spun, his vision blurring as it took trips on the fairground Waltzer, faster and faster. At the periphery of his vision, however, there *was* something, just beyond the corner of his eye. A figure. Nothing more, nothing distinct, just the dark outline of a figure standing in the corner of the room. The room was spinning so fast now that his eyes almost met themselves on the way around again giving him a panorama, unable to get anything into focus – the lamps left a trail, the neon of the Exit signs and the illumination of the monitors blurred across his view. And way out beyond that, just beyond reach, something was watching him. The room spun more quickly and became indistinct, he saw black spots in front of his eyes and heard the monitor alarm going off. The world became a fog, and he sagged from his semi-upright position, slowly starting to pitch forward, the hard tiled floor filling his vision. Scott caught him as he fell, rushing into the room in response to the alarms. Shirley and Chloe followed at a run, resetting the monitors and checking the reason for their alarm – as Tom swung his legs over the side of the bed to get up, he'd pulled off his oxygen, and his blood pressure had dropped. Tom had fainted – too much too soon. They laid him back on the bed, Tom struggling with them, still trying to get up.

'Tom, relax, you've just come round, you need to rest.'

'But I saw –'

'There'll be plenty of time to tell us what you saw, but now you need to rest, okay?' Shirley stroked his forehead which seemed to comfort him a little as she replaced his oxygen pipe. It did seem that it had all been too much, because within seconds, Tom was asleep.

***

'All I want to do is patch the CCTV feeds through my laptop, that's all, Scott.' Tom shrugged his shoulders. He'd woken after an hour of heavy and dreamless sleep.

'And *I* don't think *you* should be working today, boss.'

'Your opinion is noted, now would you patch the recordings through for me, please?' Scott knew when he was beaten and he made ready to download the files onto Tom's computer. Paranoia of prying eyes and stolen data had led them not to use the hospital servers to store their information. Hatim's job has been to create a local server network using a separate PC with a large storage capacity. Tom's laptop wasn't yet configured to this server so he needed to download individual files. He searched through video files as they came in – backed up onto a file every fifteen minutes – looking for the most recent ones.

The team were milling around the room, tidying up around Tom as he sat up in bed looking at a large window filling most of the computer screen before him. A trolley ferried away the pile of wet towels used to mop up where the manifolds had leaked. A number of different coloured bags were filled with the detritus from around Tom's bed – plastic containers from which instruments had been pulled, empty saline pouches, drug vials and used plastic utensils. Clinical waste went into a red bag – blood and body fluids from setting up central lines, taking routine bloods and some of Tom's personal care – and these were bagged and tagged ready for pick up. Aliens was replenishing the drugs in his trolley. Tom enjoyed the bustle around him, finding the presence of others comforting. Scott had not only patched through the previous recordings, but had by now given him access to the server so he could watch the 'live' feed from the cameras. In reality the footage was thirty seconds old because of a slight delay in processing and caching the video before releasing it to any device on the network running the software. Watching the feed amused him. People left the room who had subsequently returned and people repeated jobs they had already done. He rewound the feed, quickly at first, going back until the point when he'd tried to get out of bed and Scott had caught him. After that he slowed it down, watching events in reverse at only double speed. He didn't really know what he was looking for, but when he found it a chill ran down his spine. The screen showed him asleep after dictating some notes. All was still in the room, only a tiny movement of Tom's chest in grainy blurry-vision showed that it wasn't a still photograph. At the top left of the picture Tom could see the lower part of the double doors that led into the room, and, through the narrow glass panels, the floor of the corridor beyond. He watched in reverse, and then repeatedly in normal motion, the right of the two double doors being opened, enough for someone to go through, held open for six seconds, then released to allow the door to close. The door would have needed to be physically held open during that time otherwise it would have swung shut. But that was it – no sign of anyone in the corridor, no sign of them coming into the room, just the door opening. Tom was sure that he must be watching something coming in through the door, holding it open as it did so, then releasing it again. Something *had* been in the room with him.

'That could be anything,' Scott said, when Tom insisted the group gather round his bed to watch the feed.

'Like?' Tom turned his hands palms up and raised his eyebrows, offering the floor to anyone with a suggestion.

'Like someone going through the double doors at the other end of the corridor – you know what it's like in there – like an air-lock, the other set of doors is always moving.' Scott gestured for effect.

'And the door holding halfway open for six seconds? Really?' Tom shook his head. *You'll need to do better than that.*

'Has someone pushed the door open, ready to come in, then gone back to get something and so the door closes again, maybe?' Chloe was watching the feed loop around the incident.

'First of all, there's the glass in the door – we'd see someone through it if they were pushing the door open from the corridor. Second, did any of you start to come through the door then decide to do something else?' Tom said scanned everyone, knowing the answer. Nobody said anything.

'Okay, Hercule Poirot, what do *you* reckon it is?' Scott invited Tom's explanation.

'I started to get up out of bed because I felt something in here, you know when you can just feel that someone's there? It's like one of you guys were hiding in the room or something. It was a... presence, but it was cold, *really* cold. There *was* something out of the corner of my eye, but it was too far out of my line of sight and I couldn't turn around enough from the bed, so I tried to get up. That's when I got dizzy, my BP dropped and you all piled in. And thanks to Scotty, I didn't do a face plant on the deck.'

***

Sarah stayed at his bedside as everyone continued to clear up around him. They chatted and he rested, not sleeping now, but lying with his head on his pillows and watching the floorshow. He was quiet but he was also thinking.

'I wanna go home. I don't want to sleep here tonight,' he looked at Sarah, then across to Scott who had overheard and came across.

'Because of what happened in the room and the CCTV?' Scott leant an elbow on the counter above the bed.

'Maybe, but that just put the tin hat on it. I don't want to sleep here, it's not my own bed, it's not cosy. I want to see the kids and be with Sarah.' She squeezed his hand. 'I've been gone so long...' Scott and Sarah exchanged a glance at his last comment. What did *that* mean?

The Boyand's were well-known stay-at-home-bods; never wanting to go out if they could help it and just wanting to lock the world out when they got in at night. Occasional romantic weekends away were great but they always thought it 'nice to get back to your own bed'. Sarah always said that soon they would do nothing and go nowhere. In a way Tom reverting to type was good news.

'Your protocol says you stay here – you're not supposed to be going home,' said Scott.

'I don't care. I wrote the protocol, I'm changing it... Not for the first time apparently. I'm going home.'

'It's not as simple as that – there are further bloods and tissue biopsies to be done, and there's monitoring you..?' Scott shrugged his shoulders in a 'what can you do?' kind of way.

'I'll take a couple of needle biopsy kits home with me and refrigerate the samples, same for bloods. Sarah has brought up two kids and she's smart – she knows enough to call for help if I go off.'

'It might be too late if you *do* go off.'

'But you and I both know I'm not going to, don't we?' Tom smiled at his friend. 'There's nothing wrong with me.'

Scott sighed in resignation. 'Are you happy that you'll be able to take the samples and it won't mess the data up?' In reality he was questioning Tom's continued interest in the study, checking his hypoxia hadn't made him apathetic to the whole thing.

'Yes, quite happy, I don't see why I can't do that – I determined the intervals and I'll set reminders.' Andrea had walked in as the two of them were talking and she looked between them.

'What do you think, Doc?' Scott asked her.

'That you should stay in, where we can keep an eye on you as Scott said. On the other hand, if you sleep better and are more comfortable at home, there's a lot to be said for that. I don't think you'll go off again, but I am concerned about you becoming unwell overnight.' She looked at Sarah. 'Why don't you take the monitor home with you – it belongs to the project anyway, doesn't it?' Scott nodded. 'And if the alarms go off, Sarah, you call Scotty, Sig and me, okay?' Sarah nodded her agreement.

'There's no need,' said Aliens who interrupted his drug audit and came across. He stood up from the defibrillator trolley and moved to the monitor as everyone turned to look at him. 'This a new monitor – from the States. It's got wifi – it's why we ordered it – to download all of the observation data straight to our systems without having to put it onto a zip drive and copy it across.' Everyone was still staring at him, as if waiting for him to clarify his point. '*It's got wifi.* All we do is put in our phone numbers – mine, Andrea's, Chloe's, Scott's – link it to the alarm system, and the monitor itself will message us if the alarms go off.'

'You sure it can do that?' Scott asked in surprise.

'Yes, of course, it's part of the software. I never thought we'd have a use for it, but I remember reading it in the manual. I guess they use it in hospital hotels in the US when patients aren't on the main ward, so their medical teams can get to them if there is a problem.' Aliens turned to Sarah. 'All you need to do is go into this menu here.' He touched the screen with Sarah watching him so she knew what to do. 'Open up wifi selection, and it will automatically detect your home network.' He pointed to an address on screen. 'See, here's ours in the research unit. At home, yours will come up and you'll select it. You happy with that?' Sarah nodded. Scott looked down at his clipboard.

'The only thing now is to brief the press.' He said, looking round at everyone else. 'Kate Delaney said that bulletins should go through her office. But we've already protocoled the statements and have them ready to go.'

'So let's go,' said Tom with finality.

'You'll be popular.'

'Story of my life.'

'So I guess I better do it.' Scott said with some reluctance, holding the piece of paper containing the statement and pulling a face.

'I'll do it,' Andrea reached over and grabbed the piece of paper from Scott's hand.

'Really?' said Scott.

'Yeah, I don't mind. You'll get far more questions about the minutiae of the research than I will, and if you've brought me in as emergency medicine consultant it makes sense that I do this statement. I do these things all the time when people get brought in who become a news story. So, yeah, I'll do it.' She smiled at Scott.

'Thanks Andrea, thanks, I didn't fancy it, I'll be honest.' She smiled at him again and walked towards the door, stopping as she reached it.

'I'll see you tomorrow – take it easy, Tom.'

***

Tom needed to get up, get dressed and check he was mobile enough to get to the car. They also had to work out a 'protocol' for getting him out of the hospital and down to the car without the media finding out what was going on – the statement Andrea would give was a perfect cover. Tom slowly got himself up and started to move around the research room that was once again more representative of a lab than a hospital room. He took a few tentative steps and waved away assistance from Sarah who was fussing around him. He slowly walked across to Chloe, who was finishing the other half of Aliens' drug inventory.

'I saw you when I was out.' He said, wobbling as he approached.

'Did you?' She said, distracted by the list in front of her, as if a five-year-old had just told her that he had gone to the bathroom by himself.

'I left my body when I died, and I remember floating above it, looking down on it as you guys were packing me in ice.'

'The out of body experience is a classic thing people describe – you know that,' Chloe smiled at him.

'Yes, I looked down as I left my body and flew away. I saw you drop an ice pack as you put it on the –' he paused, looking down at himself to make sure he wasn't getting his left and right mixed up, '– right side of my chest. All I could see of me was the breathing tube going into the ice where my head was. Then I was gone.' *Breathing tube? What the hell is it called?*

'I did drop some ice when –' she blanched a little. 'How could you have known that?'

'I told you, I watched you – from up there.' he pointed to a place on the ceiling that approximated to where he had earlier looked down upon his colleagues.

'Look Tom, today has all been a bit weird from where I'm from, and I'm struggling to get a handle on it if I'm honest,' Chloe was clearly uncomfortable and busied herself finishing her task so that she could leave as soon as possible.

'You wait 'til tomorrow, when I tell you where *I'm* from.' Tom walked off toward the bathroom carrying his clothes under his arm. He returned ten minutes later, dressed in baggy blue tracksuit bottoms and a faded brown hooded top – looking every inch the same old Tom.

'We ready to do this?' he asked and everyone nodded.

***

Andrea was the perfect person to speak to the press. She had reached middle-age with two grown-up kids and still forged a successful medical career. Her husband Tony had easily dropped into the role of house husband when she went back to work after both kids. A writer, although by his own admission, not a terribly good one, he could work from home and run the house – he wasn't terribly good at that either – but somehow it worked. Andrea knew she liked rather too much wine, and should probably take a little more exercise. Or maybe just *some* exercise would be a start. Currently middle-age spread was of the low fat variety smeared thinly on your toast, but it had the capacity to be full fat butter, spread everywhere if she wasn't careful. The message had gone out to the press corps around the hospital that they were going to get a statement, and they had gathered on the green in front of the main entrance. Andrea approached feeling self-conscious, having not taken any care with her appearance today or checked how she looked on the way down, she realised she should maybe have changed, or done something with her hair. She quickly discounted the idea, however, as dishevelled implied she had spent all day working hard, looking after patients and not in front of a mirror like that press officer woman – she had dealt with her before and had about as much time for her as the morons she was about to speak to. The media throng had set up cameras and sound booms to the side of the large sign carrying the name of the hospital. Andrea stepped up onto the grass carrying the prepared statement, her face illuminated by the glare of some portable lights used by a TV company.

'Good afternoon, my name is Professor Andrea Dent, I'm the Head of Emergency Medicine at St Catherine's University Hospital NHS Trust.

'As you are no doubt aware, earlier today we conducted a controlled experiment to stop a volunteer's heart, to monitor their body's response for a fixed period, and to re-start it again. I am pleased to report that the experiment ran exactly as per protocol and the volunteer patient is resting as planned. We collected a large amount of data during the experiment and will spend the coming weeks analysing this, along with testimony from the subject. We would hope to publish the findings of the study in medical journals at a later date.' She looked up at the TV cameras pointed at her, taking off her glasses as camera shutters clicked and whirred. She was deluged with questions.

'How is Tom?'
'How long was he 'dead' for?'

'Is he brain-damaged?'

'Is he awake?'

'Has he spoken yet?'

'Will he make a complete recovery?'

'When can we speak to him?'

***

Mike the porter had been called, to take away a trolley ostensibly carrying dirty laundry, but which would be carrying a very different cargo. Sarah had gone ahead to check that the coast was clear and to get the getaway car started. With some help from Scott and Mike, Tom climbed over the side of the trolley into the heavy canvas bag suspended from the frame. He lay down on a bed of soft clean towels that had been prepared for him, while the others scattered a few remaining towels and a sheet over the top. *Mission Impossible this isn't*, thought Tom, but with him hidden, and the hope that his weight didn't rip through the bag and leave him lying comically in a corridor somewhere, they were on the move. Mike pushed the trolley with Scott and Chloe following behind, carrying Tom's belongings in a satchel and holdall. They made their way through the department and up the slope of the service corridor, with Scott giving Mike some help to push.

The central foyer receptionists were well known for their noisiness. In order to spread news throughout the building, all one had to do was casually mention something in their vicinity and the next day, everyone knew. Mike pushed the lift call button and Sarah and Chloe stood side by side in silence. They needed to be particularly careful here. The additional security guards sat around on the sofas looking bored as the receptionists looked on – they had noted and catalogued who had emerged, but seeing nothing desperately exciting other than people leaving for the day, they resumed telegraphing and embellishing the gossip doing the rounds from earlier. Tom lay in his cocoon, aware of his vulnerability even though he was surrounded by padding. He was concerned that another porter might collide into his trolley with a theatre bed, or a cleaner might push a heavy polisher into him by accident. As well as mangling his body some more, it would also mean their game was up, and it would be particularly bad if it happened here.

Denise, the statuesque, older receptionist, hadn't been due to work today, but had insisted on coming in to 'help manage the security situation'. She beckoned Scott over to the desk.

'How is he, Dr Boyand?'

Mr Boyand, it's Mr fucking Boyand, Tom thought. *I don't mind if patients get it wrong, Mister becoming Doctor then becoming Mister again might be a bit tough for the great unwashed, but you've worked here, with me, forever! You ought to know how medicine works.* Tom made an even worse passenger when pushed around in the belly of a laundry cart than he did in a car.

'He's fine, thanks, Denise,' Scott smiled falsely at her, not giving her a morsel.

'And you're leaving him here?' She was already planning what she would tell Sue in Radiology.

'A nurse will be with him at all times and the medical staff are just a call away, so he'll be fine. But no visitors at all please.' He tapped his nose in a 'confidential' type gesture.

'Absolutely not, doctor, you can rely on us.' To leak something to the press if they get the chance, Scott thought, and left the two women to their gossip network. He crossed the foyer to the lift as the others helped Mike push the mobile Monty Python sketch into the elevator car. They managed to sneak across the car park with relative ease and unloaded Tom from the trolley and into the boot of the Jeep without being spotted. Man-handling him out of the trolley was a struggle, but Sarah helped keep him steady and between them they eased Tom into a wobbling upright position as he stood on the canvas bottom of the trolley before shakily climbing out. Sarah had moved the car over to the far side of the garage, at the far range of the CCTV cameras, so it would be impossible for Security to pick up what they were doing. They used the clean laundry to make him a bed on the floor of the Jeep, to make him as comfortable and padded as possible. Reluctantly, with a sorry wave of her hand, she shut the boot lid on her husband.

***

'Mr Boyand is in remarkably good health considering what he's been through. He is tired, however, and is resting in a specially constructed patient room in our secure research facility. I would anticipate that it would take him one to two weeks to recover sufficiently to be able to speak to you. As an aside, however, much of what you may wish to know, as Tom has previously said, would be experimental findings and so will not be released until we publish. What I'm saying is, please don't expect too much when he does finally speak to you.'

'Have you spoken to him?'

'Yes, yes of course, I've been with him all afternoon.'

'Has he discussed what he experienced?'

'As I said, he's tired and that kind of discussion can come later, when he's well enough.'

'Was he foolhardy to conduct this type of experiment on himself?'

Andrea bristled. 'Tom Boyand is an incredibly brave and resilient man. Regardless of the purpose of the experiment, not many people would put their lives directly on the line in such a way in the name of science.'

'But didn't you oppose this work in the early stages?' The same man called out from the throng.

'Yes, I opposed it at the Ethics Committee phase. On its approval, however, Tom was gracious enough to ask that I look after him during the experiment and I was delighted to be able to do so.'

'So even though you didn't agree with the experiment, you helped him do it?' He continued to push.

'My participation wasn't a matter of whether I agreed with the study or not, it was whether I could help make sure he got through it safely.' Andrea hoped that she had finally closed that chapter.

'Is his health still at risk – is there a possibility he could deteriorate or his heart stop again?' *Somebody new, thank Christ for that.*

'The simple answer is that we can't be certain, because this type of work hasn't been done before. We can only look at those patients who have had cardiac arrests, for example, and how they may react in the first forty-eight to seventy-two hours post-event. Given that Tom is medically stable, I'm fairly confident that he'll be fine and make a full recovery. The lack of data on this, however, leads us to be particularly cautious in his initial recovery.'

***

Sarah picked the kids up from after-school club and they sat in their car seats, just inches from Tom as he reached out to them, listening to their excited stories of their day at school as Sarah moved off again heading for home. She reversed around the side of the house, under the watchful gaze of the few hardy reporters remaining outside chez Boyand. The Jeep stopped and the kids piled up the steps and in through the kitchen door, following behind Sarah. She came back out to the Jeep and opened the boot, Tom shakily climbing out and disappearing round the back of the house, the car completely screening him from the view of the press at the front of the drive. He walked in through the patio doors to surprise the kids – for Tom it'd been so long since he'd seen them, almost feeling like years. He had wondered if he'd ever see them again when struggling to hold on to his memories of them, and of Sarah, as his consciousness flew far from his body. They stood awkwardly by the coffee table in the den – about to get the Lego out. Tom dropped to his knees and embraced them, arms wrapping them up, pulling them in close to him, burying his face in their hair, inhaling their smell, squeezing them to check if they were real.

***

The boys were in bed and sleeping soundly. Tom spent a long time standing at their bedroom doors, watching them sleep. His head was resting against the doorframe of Liam's room as he watched his little chest rise and fall under his duvet, his *Star Wars* pyjama top in evidence with his arms thrown above his head. Tom smiled as his son let out a loud, relaxed fart in his sleep, his grin broadening as he thought of how funny Liam would have found it if he'd heard it for himself. Sarah came up behind him and put her arms around his waist, pressing herself against him, wanting to make sure that Tom was still Tom.

'You okay?' she whispered, meeting his gaze as he turned to look at her in the soft glow of Liam's night light. He turned back to look at his son and ignored the question as an irrelevance, enjoying the pressure of her arms, but enjoying even more the presence of his family, without having to rack his brains and think back over time and space to what they looked like, sounded like and smelled like. Even their farts.

'Don't fucking ignore me, mister,' Sarah whispered, persisting, biting his earlobe. 'Are you okay?'

Tom again turned his gaze away from his son and looked at his wife. 'No,' he said and started to sag into Sarah's arms. She helped him away from the boy's rooms and into their own, sitting him on the bed.

'What's wrong?' she asked, her hands in his. He looked down at their intertwined fingers, and paused, thinking about all she meant to him and to the times they had spent together.

'My hand's throbbing, it's weak and aches when I move it.' Inwardly he was worried about it, but until now he'd been putting on a brave face, or so he thought. As usual, however, Sarah had seen right through him.

'Have you taken anything for it?' She asked.

'Some codeine,' he replied.

'Do you want to go to A&E?'

'No. God no, it just got bashed or something. I'll go and see Mike Hughes tomorrow – he'll look at it.'

'Everything okay apart from that?' she asked again, searching his face, knowing the telltale signals.

'I'm really tired – more than I can ever remember. It feels literally like years since I've slept.'

'So let's get you to bed then – you do need some rest,' she took his hand and he dumbly followed.

'I've seen some amazing things, Sarah,' he muttered as he looked around their bedroom, which he barely recognised.

'Tell me in the morning, baby.' She put her index finger on his lips.

'No, I need to,' he insisted, 'I flew, Sarah, I flew across space, and I saw the origins of the universe. I've seen the most incredible things…' he sagged onto the bed and slowly peeled his t-shirt over his head, reaching across to re-start the heart rate monitor that Sarah had registered with their home wifi. 'But I was a fool for doing it.' He looked up at her with tired eyes.

'Yes, you were.'

11.

Tom arrived at work the next day in what was becoming routine fashion. This time Sarah dropped him off, or rather, prised him out of the boot of her car in the underground car park. Andrea's press statement of the night before had done nothing to calm the media frenzy and the press were becoming frustrated by the complete lack of Tom-action. Sarah had been scanning news reports and web stories as this escalated and in a shocking turn of events for the British press, they had advanced from rank speculation to making things up.

Was Tom dead?

Had the experiment gone catastrophically wrong?

Was he in intensive care?

There had been several reported attempts by reporters to gain access to ITU, where they mistakenly thought Tom might be, so security had been increased across all hospital departments. Still, it seemed, their subterfuge worked, and the reporters showed little interest in the car beyond a few pictures as they left the driveway.

Tom rode the elevator to the top floor by himself, nodding to the women on reception. They looked as if they'd seen a ghost. He walked onto the hub which was in starkly quiet contrast to the previous day.

'How you feeling?' Mags asked from her desk, with too-big a smile on her face.

'I'm okay thanks, Mags. At least I think I am. Listen, before the meeting and everyone is here, I want to speak to Mike Hughes about my arm. Shouldn't be too long – okay?' Tom smiled apologetically at Mags, as if to say, you'll have to stall them for me.

'Okay.' He turned and hurried through the rear fire doors. He went down the fire escape stairs to avoid the eyes of the receptionists who had no doubt told the world of his appearance by now.

***

The bustle and chaos of an orthopaedic ward in the early morning was something Tom hadn't witnessed in many years. A convoy of heavy catering trolleys were parked along one wall, obstructing that side of the corridor. Nursing assistants in drab brown uniforms unloaded them, delivering plates of lukewarm scrambled eggs and bacon to patients. A nurse stood by a drugs cart she'd had parked opposite the food trolleys, narrowing the channel even further. Yet more nursing assistants pushed used commodes out of six-bedded side wards, right next to where the food was being removed from warm storage, their fragrant contents mingling with the delights of the kitchen and making Tom wish he'd missed breakfast altogether. Further down the corridor, a cleaner was pushing a heavy polisher, the cleaning company having decided it wise to deploy their domestic staff at the busiest time of day on the ward. Amongst all of this, Enid Jones, an eighty-two-year-old music teacher, three days post-op following her knee replacement, was attempting to take a short walk up the ward, pushing her wheeled Zimmer frame in front of her as the physiotherapist had instructed. It looked, however, as though Mrs Jones might be about to have a nasty altercation with a patient hoist that was being wheeled up the ward from the opposite direction.

Tom marvelled at all of this as an outsider looking in, so many staff and yet nobody to ask as to the whereabouts of his colleague and friend. More people joined the throng as a haematology technician emerged from a side room, pushing his collection of vacutainer tubes and glass vials on a rickety cart. Tom looked beyond all of these people for a member of the orthopaedic team he had come to see. The technician pushed the cart across the corridor to the opposite side room, and as he did so revealed a figure behind him, standing in the middle of the corridor with its back to Tom. It was wearing navy tracksuit bottoms, baggy at the knees and hips, and a faded brown hoody with the hood raised over its head. The figure stood motionless for a second then slowly turned to face him – its face partly hidden, but with a certain familiarity he couldn't place. The figure's arms were bent at its sides like a gunslinger waiting to draw, waiting for Tom to make the first move. The drugs trolley nurse had packaged up another plastic cup of pink and green painkillers for the next patient on the list and turned to walk into the opposite six-bedded unit. She walked in front of Tom's eye-line, obscuring his view for a second, and when she passed, the hoody had gone. Tom looked from left to right for a second, as if expecting the figure to re-appear, and when it didn't–

Why am I thinking of it as an it, not a he or she?

– he ran forward to where it had been standing. Tom didn't know who the hoody was or why they were there, but somehow he thought it important and he wanted to speak to them. To his right, the link corridor leading to the parallel orthopaedic ward was deserted. He ran down it to the other ward, looking up and down, seeing nothing that shouldn't be there, the ward just as busy with trolleys, food, washing, dressing and drugs as its neighbour. Retracing his steps, he looked in the laundry store, the cleaning cupboard, staff room and the now somewhat fragrant sluice where he disturbed a nursing assistant cleaning a commode. Again he walked back to the second orthopaedic ward, and seeing a nurse at the station, he asked. 'Have you seen a visitor come onto the ward, perhaps from the connecting corridor, wearing a brown hoody?'

'No I haven't, sorry,' the nurse looked at him quizzically, spotting his staff badge but otherwise not recognising Tom in any way.

Tom turned away from the nurse's station and almost ran into Mike Hughes, the orthopaedic surgeon with whom he'd been to medical school.

'Mike!' Tom exclaimed, slightly out of breath from running up and down the wards. Mike 'Shagger' Hughes was with some students on a ward round.

'Ah, our superstar zombie. How is life after death?' He held out his hand to his long-time friend, who instead raised his right hand in front of his face.

'Complicated to say the least,' Tom replied.

'Well, you only live twice, Meester Boyand!' He smiled his most winning or cheesy grin depending if you were Mike Hughes or not.

'It's what I've come to talk to you about.' Tom looked at his friend, whose smile was fading. 'I need your help.' Mike looked at Tom's raised hand for the first time and saw how swollen and discoloured it was, patches of bruising scattered between red blotches. He stepped closer and saw that the lower arm looked almost deformed – not the elegance of two long bones held together by ligaments and joints, but a more twisted looking appendage with tight patchy swelling.

'Come with me.' Mike said, immediately switching into his doctor voice.

Ten minutes later – with the students hastily dispatched to study x-rays with his registrar – Tom sat in a clinic room to get his hand properly examined. He regaled him with the story but stripped it to the bones; it felt like his hand had been crushed when something reached out to grab him when he was out... yesterday.

'Look Tom, this is the strangest thing, I can feel bony thickening around both distal radius and ulna – it's like callus, and a lot of it, it's like you've got a well-healed fracture. Is that sore?' He palpated along the lower part of the long bones and Tom did feel some pain, but nothing excruciating. His wrist was worse, with marked tenderness of the individual bones and when compressing the arch, Tom winced and pulled away. 'Tom, you've broken your wrist and badly, but not yesterday – this was weeks ago. What really happened?' Mike was full of concern, his big dinner plate hands, equally at home holding a scalpel, a rugby ball, or whatever part of the female anatomy he could get hold of, gently supporting his friend's wrist. Tom stared back at him in silence.

'There's definite trauma here. Go over to the Abbey later on this afternoon, I'll get you booked in for an x-ray and MRI – they'll fit you in as an urgent even if it's out of hours. I'll give Andy Bullman a ring too, I'd like him to come over to meet you.'

'Who?'

'New guy, really good hand and wrist surgeon – did some pioneering work on scaphoid repair, which got him the job last year. Gives a better hand-job than anyone I've ever known, and I've known a few...'

Tom left the consult with Mike feeling like he'd made a positive step forward. He walked down the line of clinic rooms, when suddenly a figure emerged from a room on the far left. A figure wearing a faded brown hoody and navy blue jogging bottoms. It reached the middle of the corridor and turned to face Tom. He absently scratched at his arm as he did so, finding himself staring at this figure that seemed to stare right into him, eyes boring into his soul. Quickly, the figure turned and disappeared off to the right, in the direction Tom had been walking when it appeared. He ran the few steps to the corridor and turned right to look along the ward, but the figure had gone.

***

Tom made his way back to the Research Unit, once again moving unnoticed up through the fire escape, hoping that Mags hadn't shut the fire door tight behind him after he'd left. Finding it cracked open still, he slipped through into the busy scene of the hub, people talking loudly and helping themselves to coffee. Like a stranger arriving through the swing doors of the saloon bar in an old Western, the room fell silent as he moved through to the central desks. Tom smiled and nodded at his colleagues as they muttered awkward greetings. He quickly spoke to Scott, and they brought the meeting to order before everyone could take their seats.

'Thanks for coming today guys,' Tom didn't really know how to start. The meeting was being recorded and, unbeknown to him, a direct web-cam feed being again sent to Henry's office. Despite all his experience of presenting at conferences, and the knowledge that he was speaking to his team, Tom was quite nervous about standing in front of them –because of what he would be saying. 'I must apologise in advance but I'm a little tired today – I guess being dead didn't agree with me.' There were some slightly nervous smiles around the room. 'I don't, however, really know where to start.'

'Okay, well, I drifted with the sedative,' he had his laptop in front of him with his notes written up in bullet form for him to refer to. 'I certainly remember, I guess a typical sensation of falling backwards, the room kind of 'hazed' away, faded away from me as I fell, head over heels. And, at that point, I was really quite scared; I guess it's why it sits fairly vividly with me even though a lot of things happened afterwards. But I was scared because for the first time, I didn't have the option to say no, not to go through with it. We'd been planning this for so long and up until the point where I had the sedative I could still have stopped it. And I guess the voices of a lot of people over the past few weeks were hanging over me, all those people who'd been trying to persuade me not to go through with it, all saying I told you so. A lot of people pedalled a lot of rhetoric to me for a lot of reasons, all with a background of fear, so I was genuinely frightened. I was spinning as I fell, faster and faster, and I got the feeling of being increasingly enclosed – almost like falling down a plughole in a way – where the water would close in on you and spin you faster as it did. The surrounding pressure became so tight it was like I was being crushed and I couldn't breathe. I guess that was the time you guys were zapping me.' People nodded at the logic of that. 'And then I was spat out the other side and I flew up and out of my body. I was up on the ceiling and I saw you guys packing ice around me, and Chloe dropping an ice pack onto the floor as she was stacking it against my chest. I wanted to stay and watch but I was pulled away, up and out of the room, through the walls and roof and out of the hospital, into the sky.' He paused and looked up at the friends and colleagues in the room who were hanging on his every word.

Tom continued to regale them with the story; of leaving the Earth's atmosphere, entering deep space, some of the things he had seen throughout the cosmos, some of which had great clarity, some of which had less. He emphasised to them that he had been gone a long time, that his memory had faded, and he could barely remember any of them as he flew. He described it to them as he had to Sarah earlier that morning. He told them about his view of the Milky Way, and its converging spiral arms, his approach to the centre of the galaxy, and the black hole at the core with the strange star somehow in orbit around it. And then Tom explained how, after being chilled to the bone by deep space, he started to feel warmth for the first time. He described the arm reaching out to him, taking hold of his in its grip and how it crushed his wrist as space and time folded in on itself, presumably when the defibrillator was used on him. Finally, he described the void, the black lake, the sensory deprivation as he seemed to drift almost forever, warm and supported and serenely comfortable after the carnage that had come before. That was the final part of his description before coming around on the bed.

There was complete silence as he finished – nobody could respond. He had spent the best part of two hours telling them about space and time and of all he had seen, and the irony was that he had lost all track of time when he was reliving his experience. Now he had finished, nobody else had any response. Finally, Scott stirred and said. 'Wow. Er, thank you Tom – an incredible account. I'm not sure how I can digest that – how any of us can digest that right now. That's amazing – how vivid. I guess that justifies the experiment in the first place, sending somebody healthy and well into that situation has given us a lot greater clarity than before. We've at least got a good picture of what you experienced, anyway.' There was nodding around the room. 'We need to think carefully about how we write this up, what we write up and when we do it, so it's perhaps not quite so emotive.'

'Yes but surely we write it up ASAP and get it published in a psychology journal, this is groundbreaking, this is what happens when we die.'

'Well, it's certainly your experience of being at the edge of death, yes of course, but you know, one person's experience doesn't make a consensus or mean that this would be the same for everyone, so I'm saying let's be a little careful.' Scott looked at him with a serious expression, Tom turned away, exasperated.

'Okay, why don't we go back through the CCTV footage of what happened? Perhaps,' he said turning to Hatim, 'at double speed, so we aren't here all day.' This was received with a nod and almost immediately the computer monitor to Tom's right sprang to life, the screen split into four quarters with a different CCTV picture on each. The change-over met with a flurry of activity of people disappearing off to the bathroom and to get coffee or water, the desperate need for comfort breaks being overshadowed by Tom's extraordinary testimony.

'Are you sure you want to, Tom?' Chloe asked, still seated and not yet afflicted by an older person's bladder.

'Want to what, Chlo?'

'Want to see what happened to you on those images.'

'Well, spoiler alert, but I reckon I die early on before rising again in a manner that might get the good reverend all excited,' Tom smiled down at her.

'There's no need for the sarcasm, just trying to look out for you.' Chloe pulled a face as Tom turned away.

When everyone had returned, Hatim started the CCTV feed, synchronised so all the pictures played together, but at twice real time. Tom encouraged everyone to narrate what they saw, from the initial sedative, to counting backwards, to him closing his eyes – where he interjected that that was the point where he started to fall and spiral backwards. Aliens took over and described how Charlie had started the cooling pumps and they had shocked him as per the protocol. The ECG on the screen showed that his heart had been shocked out of its normal rhythm. A flatline, like those seen on TV programmes and in films, simply indicates that the machine isn't working properly, since electrical activity remains travelling through the heart for some time after death, and the irregular up and down trace they could see on the recording was testament to that. Without an organised heart rhythm, without synchronised electrical activity to trigger the heart muscle to contract as one and pump blood, Tom was now effectively dead.

'And now we start the timer,' Sigurd continued.

'Yes and you, you fucker, changed the protocol at the last minute.' It hadn't really come up since Tom had been resuscitated, when the immediate concern was his health and well-being, but now Scott wanted an answer.

Tom winked infuriatingly at him.

'Well how fucking unprofessional and reckless was that? We'd based everything on twenty minutes under as a reasonable time to get you back, given the data we had. We had nothing for cases lasting twice as long.'

'We had one.' Tom looked at Scott, almost looking through him, his eyes piercing.

'You're talking about Solomon aren't you?' Scott accused him.

'Yes. No point in doing these things if we aren't trying to push the boundaries is there? Solomon was brought back after about forty minutes.'

'Yes but he was immersed in ice-cold river water, and we could only approximate those conditions. What you did was reckless and put all of us in an extremely difficult position. Andrea was all for sticking to the old protocol.' Andrea nodded over in the corner but said nothing.

'So why didn't you?'

'If it was your protocol for someone else, we would've done,' Chloe said in reply. 'But this was your call, your neck, and your party, so... we went with it.'

The screen showed them packing the bags of ice around Tom's body. They'd emptied one freezer and most of Tom had disappeared under a pile of ice cubes. Chloe returned from the second freezer with four ice packs piled up and tucked them along the side of his chest. In her haste she dropped the third one as she packed it against his ribcage.

'There. Chloe drops the ice pack, just like I saw.' Tom smiled triumphantly. Bob and Chloe exchanged glances.

'Have you seen this footage before, Tom?' Bob asked.

'No, of course not. The only video I looked at yesterday was that clip of the door opening when there was something in the room with me later in the afternoon. I haven't seen anything else,' Tom explained and Chloe nodded her agreement.

'I've only just put this footage together, so it wasn't available for Tom to see until now,' Hatim affirmed.

'It proves that what I'm saying is true,' Tom was beaming as he looked at everyone, inviting dissent.

'It proves something, I suppose,' said Chloe, half smiling back at him.

'It's a start,' analysed Bob. 'But it doesn't prove all the rest.'

Attention returned to the screen, the footage showing the team milling around, nervously watching the clock as time ticked on. Charlie bent over the pumping mechanism between the hot and cold tanks, changing the manifold over, showing it was almost time to re-start Tom's heart. Andrea took up the commentary as all hands quickly started removing ice packs and throwing them into the open freezers. A few missed, exploding on impact, sending ice cubes skidding across the floor.

'This is the reheat process starting and we start the resus protocol.' On the screen, Tom's body was shocked for the first time, his back arching off the bed, arms and legs jerking. 'There was no response from the first shock at one fifty, so we repeated at two hundred joules.' Tom's body jerked off the bed again, back arching further. 'Still no output, so we began the drug protocol with 1 milligram of adrenaline and 300 milligrams of amiodarone, with a re-shock.' Andrea looked at the screen. 'Again, nothing. We re-shocked.' Tom's body arched more tortuously off the bed this time, his back clearing the bed for a split second. Andrea continued. '*Still* no output –'

'So I hit you with a dose of Zol!' Sig smiled quietly.

'Yes, that was another aspect I wasn't happy with, going so far off piste with an unlicensed drug – anything could have happened.' This was Andrea's first real opportunity to admonish Aliens for his actions. One of the reasons Sig hadn't wanted any other medical staff involved was so that he didn't have to justify his use of the Zol. Aliens didn't reply, and the video continued to run.

'I only registered about two or three shocks – they must have been with the Zol – I don't know that I even knew of the ones before,' Tom commented.

'We did a further shock at two hundred joules.' On cue Tom's body jerked once more but just as it did, the top left camera – an overhead view of Tom on the bed – recorded an odd movement. The defibrillator caused his body to jerk violently, but a split second later, almost like a shock wave travelling along his body, his right forearm appeared to bend, to flick around almost at a right angle below the wrist, articulating where there was no joint, being flung out to the side. As soon as the deformity happened, it righted itself, the wrist flicking back like a whip cracking. Tom and Chloe spotted it.

'Hey, did you see that?' he pointed at the screen and got Hatim to pause the footage. 'Can you go to full screen for this camera... thanks... and rewind ten seconds or so... now play again.' Tom used his laser pointer to highlight his wrist as the footage played. The enlargement didn't bring a greater resolution and so the picture suffered from motion blur and large blocky pixels, like sitting too close to an old TV. The replayed footage again seemed to show the wrist flicking out at a right angle to the forearm.

'See.' Tom was excited. 'My forearm gets broken just after I get shocked.' He pointed the laser again.

'I'm not sure you can say that, Tom, it's very blurry,' said Scott, watching alternately with and without glasses to see if there was a difference.

There wasn't.

'There looks like there might be a glitch on the screen, like a digital judder or something,' said Hatim.

'Or my arm bending at a very strange angle for no apparent reason, which would fit exactly with what I told you.' The footage seemed clear to Tom, and he implored them to support him.

'I'm looking at some kind of blurry movement after you've had a jolt from a defib, Tom. I don't know what else to say.'

'Can you clean the images up?' he asked Hatim.

'I can try – I might be able to reduce some of the picture noise. It'll take time.' The screen immediately changed to a Windows desktop, and a cursor moved around. It highlighted and opened several windows and apps as Hatim copied the files across into another format before putting it through a video filter to 'wash' the footage clear of some of the blur seen from the low resolution camera.

'So, moving on, after a further, er, bolus of the drug,' Andrea continued. 'We administered what became the final shock.' Tom's body lifted completely off the bed, his back in a tetanic arch.

'We used one last big dose because you weren't responding – it felt like it was the last chance to get you back – so I hit you with a lot,' Sig smiled at Tom and gave a slight shrug. Andrea frowned.

'Well it certainly worked – the response at my end was huge and it was obviously successful here...' Tom indicated the screen where there was a degree of celebration as they recorded his normal heart rhythms. High fives and handshakes were exchanged around the room along with some silent cheering. Hatim stopped the video feed and the room went quiet as everyone sat around awkwardly.

Tom from the screen to face the group who were all staring at him. 'What did you all want, hmm?' He said, his voice sharp. 'What did you *want* me say; 'do you know what, just a bit of light, tunnel-thing, feeling of well-being, angels singing, job done? Is that it? Would you be happier with that? Well, I did do the whole flying / tunnel / light thing with maybe an angel at the end. I've got more details, that's all. And a snapped forearm. This video feed proves it, with the ice bag falling and my wrist clearly snapping in two.'

Nobody would meet his gaze now, everyone was united in feeling uncomfortable with the morning's events.

'You've seen me laying on a slab for the best part of an hour, but that isn't what happened. I flew, flew up through the sky, into space, across the galaxy, I was flying for... aeons. And as I flew, my memories faded. The things I remembered about my past life – here –' Tom tapped his finger onto the desk in front of him, 'slowly disappeared. Not in the blink of an eye but over days, weeks, months... as time passed.'

'Your brain was dying, Tom,' Bob responded. 'The cells were losing their functionality, links between neurones were collapsing and this would have caused your memory to fade. In the same way that we associate loss of memory with getting older and memories fading with time, so your perception is that you've been away for a long time.' Bob's argument was perfectly and frustratingly reasonable. 'If you'd been gone any longer, you'd have *completely* forgotten everything because you'd have been dead. If you *were* gone for a long time, you'd have had to process so many things to keep your mind active, to stop yourself going mad –'

'I reviewed every single case I've ever had, not just the case, but every time I'd seen the patient, every visit, every conversation, things that had worked, things that hadn't, every surgery I'd been involved with. Everything.'

'Okay, so your life flashed before your eyes, it's one of the most common things –'

'I thought this was all about perception, Bob? Are you telling me I just tick every box, fit into every cliché that you guys use? What chance have I got if you rubbish everything I say?'

'I wasn't rubbishing any –'

'Sounded like it from where I'm standing. I could *reflect* on everything. Nothing 'flashed' if you want to use that term – I could slowly review and digest over time. I thought about all the women I'd slept with, every single pair of tits I'd held in my hands – the weight, the skin, the *taste*, Bob. Not some quick-flash of MTV images of a life in sixty seconds. Sorry ladies,' Tom looked up at Chloe and Andrea apologetically. 'I would see a planet appear in the distance as a tiny speck, and it would get a little closer every day, and then eventually I'd fly past. It would take even longer for stars. And as I waited I could think about these things – imagine having a year to think about what you did last week? And I passed thousands of planets and thousands of stars.'

'Let me play devil's advocate for a second.'

'You usually do,' Tom said with a slightly forced smile.

'Let's say, for a second, that this didn't really happen – I'm not saying it did or it didn't, but let's just speculate that it didn't. Let's say you had a psychotic episode or a dream or something. How do you respond to that?'

'Well, no, it was real, it was so real, only an hour might have passed here, but it was like half a lifetime with me.'

'Dreams themselves do seem very real and vivid, and time can pass in different ways in them.'

'But what could I say that would convince you? I don't think there's anything is there? You have your own view of the world, and the brain, and no other opinions are available.'

'I'm just asking you to consider a for-instance, Tom.'

'And, as usual, of course, it will be a for-instance that will back me into a corner,' Tom was becoming a little heated.

'Tom, please consider this from our point of view, how it sounds, and help us to understand what happened to you.'

'You aren't interested in what happened to me, you just want to tell me it's a dream.' Tom was visibly angry now. 'Well, I don't know about you, but if I'm dead and I'm going to have a last dream before my brain shuts down, I want to have a dream about big tits and sports cars, I don't really want to be having one about being dead.' He looked around the room at the familiar faces of friends and colleagues who seemed strange to him now, people in whose trust he had placed his life and now he wasn't sure if he would trust any of them again. 'Okay. Fine. Go away and think about it, I've got some data to look at.' He turned away from the group, pushed through his office door and slammed it behind him.

***

Tom sat at his desk, the light less harsh in here, and flicked on his desk lamp. He attempted to read the text on his computer screen, but found himself re-reading the same text, noticing out of the corner of his eye people going back and forth outside his window. He got up and closed the blind – something he never did – and sat back down. There was a knock at the door as Tom looked at the data for the dozenth time. He ignored it and carried on.

Fuck 'em. The knock came again, a little louder, one extra rap this time. Tom sighed. 'Come in.' The door opened and Bob Wauberg walked in. Tom looked up, the lamp light framing his face, casting shadows around his features with its yellow-white light. He didn't speak.

'Can I sit?' Bob asked carefully, nodding towards the chair, a mug of steaming hot coffee in each hand, limiting his ability to gesture.

'I don't know, can you?' Tom couldn't stop himself being obtuse. Bob gave a thin smile.

'Okay, you and the grammar police got me.' He set the mugs down on the desk and flopped down into the padded office chair opposite Tom's desk. Tom was looking down at the hugely important pieces of paperwork on his desk – never had pointless HR memos been of more interest. 'I'm sorry if was trying to rationalise things and throw questions back at you – always have I guess. It's what steered me into doing this,' he spread his arms and smiled again.

'Every time someone has an idea or thought process different to your own, it's not compulsory to argue it down with psychology or clever use of words, you know.' Tom looked at his friend. 'Because you *are* a clever bastard.'

They stared at each other in an intellectual Mexican stand-off.

'You could be a little easier on them.'

'They could be a little more supportive of me.' Tom sipped his coffee, which still tasted like shit to him.

'Well, look, they stand in a room for an hour with you going all hypoxic, and then have to listen to you tell a story that sounds just like you've had some kind of brain hypoxia. You can forgive them for putting two and two together.'

'I suppose you're going to tell me again that my experience is just my perception of what happened, aren't you?' Tom's eyes flared again.

'No, I'm just gonna shut up this time.'

'What a refreshing fucking change.'

'We all need a little time to get used to this idea. When the ancient

Greeks were busy not exploring for fear of falling off the edge of the world because they 'knew' it to be flat, it would have taken them a while to get their head around Pythagoras' suggestion that it was round. I don't imagine any of them went sailing that afternoon.'

'Don't patronise me, Bob.'

'I'm not. This is our perception, and our perception is that you can't be right. Einstein says you can't be right, but Quantum theory says you can. If an electron can be anywhere in the universe at any one time, then who the hell knows what a-, a-, a 'spirit' can do?'

They sat facing each other, reflecting on their discussion, their argument. Tom was angry at Bob, having several years' worth of anger to direct at him. It wasn't anything personal, but Bob was one of those frustratingly calm individuals that always came up with a simple explanation for everything, even when you thought it was something far more exotic. Right now there was every need for more exotic.

'I've been experiencing some strange things since coming back, Bob.'

There was a pause now that the argument had settled, a change in Tom's tone. 'I don't think anyone would call that unusual.'

'I keep getting these strong feelings of déjà vu.' He shrugged his shoulders and curled his lip in a resigned way.

'You've been through a hell of a lot.' Bob sat more assuredly opposite him, adopting the more confident upright posture he might take during a consult. He took a sip of his coffee.

'No. I mean I find myself in a situation, perhaps going into a room I've not been into for a while or speaking to someone I've not seen for ages and I know I've just been there, or I *know* the conversation we're about to have.' Tom tried to explain.

'Do you want to listen to yourself?' Bob smiled widely and sympathetically at his friend. 'You know that déjà vu is just a perceptual thing, a feed-forward mechanism. Déjà vu is your sensations – eyes and ears registering something before your brain interprets it – that delay means you have a 'memory' of the experience and so when your brain finally gets round to processing it, you think it's happened before. Everyone gets it in some form from time to time. If I'd been dead for forty-odd minutes and brought back with a whole mess of visions in my head, having a little phasing once in a while would strike me as pretty reasonable. Either that or you've actually gone to a different dimension, travelled through time and are meeting yourself in the same room.'

'From what I've seen, all options are available. And the awareness of someone else in the room?'

'Paranoia, fear perhaps… Or you brought something back.' Bob smiled.

'What?' Bob's last comment startled Tom.

'I am, of course, *kidding*. We Americans do that from time to time, y'know, we call it *humour*.' Bob's American accent pronounced it *yumour*.

***

Hospitals are never empty, even at night, always a porter, cleaner or on-call medic rushing somewhere, but The Abbey was eerily quiet that evening, the day staff and visitors having all departed. It was a small private hospital sitting in a secluded corner of the grounds of the large St Catherine's hospital site. Completely separate, even down to the access road and car parking, so those paying for their care could keep their expensive new cars separate from those of the great unwashed. It wasn't just a clever name, though 'Abbey' was a far grander title for the old chapel that had stood on the same site many years before. Stained-glass windows had been retained and re-used in the main foyer of the private medical centre which also boasted arched, vaulted ceilings of stone and oak, all designed to create the same calmness and serenity as the inside of a church. The polished oak floor echoed with Tom's footsteps, as they bounced around the auditorium and back, making it sound like there was more than one of him walking across the floor. He was naturally drawn to the slightly out of place modern oak reception desk where the evening receptionist pointed him through the main double doors and to turn left for Radiology and the MRI suite.

At 5.30pm, the MRI unit would be quite happily locked up for the night, the scanner having a well-earned rest from its whirling and spinning of the day. Not that the giant superconducting magnet at the heart of the scanner ever got any downtime. The magnetic field was permanently live and strong within the room – shutting it down meant the time-consuming and expensive process of decommissioning and re-charging before it could start again. Tom walked into the deserted waiting area outside the scanning room. He stood for a few minutes, waiting to see if anyone might come for him, pacing up and down, listening for footsteps or voices, but he heard nothing. Finally he walked to the end of the waiting area and knocked on the 'Staff Only' door. He was about to knock again when the door was suddenly opened by a radiographer who had agreed to stay late to scan the hospitals 'poster-boy'. But don't tell Henry.

'Sorry, I didn't know if I should wait...' Tom pointed back over his shoulder to the waiting area, already becoming agitated and annoyed after being kept waiting. He was rewarded by a beaming smile of the most perfect white teeth from the pretty girl whose fiery red curls were piled on top of her head. A week ago he would have been enticed by her, shyly looked at her from the corner of his eye and even tried some gentle flirting, but not anymore. Now he barely recognised she existed.

'Get your shirt off will you Tommy, don't worry, Amy's seen it all before,' leered Mike, who'd been sitting in the control room with the technician. Tom took off his watch and belt and left them next to his phone, coins and wedding ring. He signed the consent form that said he wasn't pregnant or claustrophobic, nor did he have any metal parts or fragments in him that would depart messily through the nearest exit under the pull of the magnetic field. Amy opened the side door into the scanning room and waited for Tom to go through. He approached the movable bed that slid into the large cylindrical magnet, all rounded and cream metal, plastic and vinyl.

'He's right, Mr Boyand, the shirt's got to go, too,' the smile was unwavering as he handed her his shirt and lay down on the bed, adjusting the position of the small pillow as he did so. She bent down and placed a pair of headphones on him. 'I can talk to you through these, but it will be quite noisy during the scan, so I'll put some music on too. Try to keep as still as you can,' she said as she fussed over the exact positioning of his arm by his side, using several small foam wedges to keep it in place. Finally, she was satisfied and handed him a panic button. 'Just in case,' Amy said before retracting the bed, drawing him into the belly of the scanner, his body disappearing inside leaving him alone in the narrow tube of the machine. He tried to relax as he lay there waiting for something to happen, the hard plastic around him cool and impersonal. After what seemed like an age – *but it's all relative I s'pose,* he thought – Amy's voice came through the headphones. 'It'll get a bit noisy now, Tom, as the machine positions itself, please try to stay as still as you can.' Some music faded in – Tom Petty's 'Running Down a Dream', an old favourite of Sarah's, which made him smile.

He heard a whirring sound and a staccato chuga-chugga-chugga sound as the machine kicked into life, drowning out the vocals. The whirring changed and the cylinder around him seemed to clank as if this were an old steam-powered scanner from an alternative Victorian history.

He found himself feeling as good as Tom Petty, humming along to drown out the mechanical sounds around him, but trying not to move – his right foot struggling not to tap along with the Heartbreakers.

'Still as you can please, Tom,' her voice whispered in his ear, fading Tom Petty out and back in again as the clanking of the machine stopped.

Mike stood behind Amy as she sat at the console, engaging the protocol for the scan. The live images of slices through Tom's hand and wrist appeared on the computer screens in front of them. Mike alternated between watching the live pictures, inhaling Amy's scent and staring down her ample cleavage, accentuated by her slim-fitting tunic.

Tom gave himself up to the experience – enjoying eclectic old tunes from The Pointer Sisters, INXS, U2, Mariah Carey and *that* one by Cameo, red codpiece and all. It was like the scanner had been built in the late 80s and the music hadn't changed – maybe Stephen King's Christine had transformed itself into a medical device.

Finally it was over and he was moving, the bed withdrawing from the scanner, revealing Amy-perma-smile standing over him, *and what a sight to wake up to,* Mike would've said.

'All done. Okay? You can get dressed again.' He slipped his shirt around his shoulders and followed her back into the control room where he could see slices of his body on the computer screens in front of him. Andy Bullman had arrived and handshakes were exchanged as Tom finished adjusting his clothing.

'Is there somewhere we can view these with Tom, please?' Mike turned to the radiographer.

'Yes, use the reporting room next door. Have you got a radiology log-in?'

'No.'

'Okay, I'll log you in as me.' She got up from the console having powered down the ancillary systems on the scanner and led the three men into the radiology reporting room. There she logged onto the image-viewing system and located and opened the file containing Tom's images. Amy left them to it and returned to the control room to finish closing things down for the evening.

'Sit down mate,' Mike indicated the chair between him and Bullman, all three crowding around the one computer screen.

'Christ did you see the rack on her? Bloody hell. I'll be down here a lot more from now on.' Mike was like a schoolboy.

'I'm sure Alex would approve,' Tom replied – Mike's previous legendary philandering had supposedly been tamed since his marriage to Alex. Suddenly a familiar female voice came through the speaker on the side of the PC.

'If you press the illuminated red button on the side of the screen, Mike, that will turn off the microphone in the room.'

'Oh shit.' The other two medics laughed at his embarrassment and Mike replied. 'Er, okay – sorry about that.'

'No problem… Shagger.'

***

'Yes, see the oedema in the proximal carpal row, extending distally and into the metacarpals here and here?' Andy Bullman touched the slices of films on the screen. 'There's even some evidence of bony bruising.' He used the mouse to point the arrow cursor on screen. 'I would say there *is* evidence of external trauma, and not from perhaps thrashing your arm around while being shocked and striking a trolley or something. This is a crush injury – not severe – but definitely one from external crushing trauma.'

'But there wasn't any direct trauma – but the CCTV does show the end of my forearm bending at a right angle for a split second.'

'CCTV? While you were out? Jesus,' Mike exclaimed.

'That's as maybe, and perhaps it did look like your arm was bending – maybe at the wrist – because this isn't a fresh fracture. From the look of it, I would say it's about two months old,' said Bullman.

'What? But I only just did it,' Tom was wide-eyed. *But you were on your way back from the other side of the galaxy*, he thought, *and you've been telling everyone you've been gone for a long time.*

'Well it certainly doesn't appear to be a new fracture – there's evidence of healing, and not just soft callus, but it's calcified as well. Look, you can see the bridging happening across the fracture sites – here,' Bullman indicated parts of the screen showing the bony deposition, then seemed to correct himself. 'The callus formation itself is unusual at that end of the forearm. Looking at it again, it's probably more than two months old.'

'Really?'

'And there's something else. The alignment is reasonable – a degree of deformity which is a little disappointing, but it is what it is. There's also deformity within the bony deposition.'

'I'm sorry I don't know what you mean,' admitted Tom, getting lost in the orthopaedics.

'Okay. New bone is laid down in a certain way and is then remodelled to more fit the type of bone and loads it has to withstand,' he explained carefully.

'You're talking about stress-lines – that sort of thing,' Tom replied, as if to say *Hey I'm a doctor too.*

'Yes, exactly that. This isn't like that though, it's... strange.' Bullman shrugged, as if that was all he had.

'I don't understand.'

'Neither do I. It's nothing to worry about *per se* – can't be, there's good healing there and the alignment is okay, it just looks strange. There's been soft tissue trauma as well, some of the tissue, well again, looks a little strange – there's a lot of soft tissue proliferation around the fracture and into the hand as well, so your forearm and hand being bigger, what you're thinking of as swelling, is largely soft tissue deposition.'

'What does that mean, prognosis-wise?'

'I'm not sure, best guess is that you've had a strong healing reaction to your injury and that soft tissue is just a proliferation response to it.'

Best guess? Tom thought.

'Might be worth a CT, to look at the bone a little more closely. Why don't you come and see me in clinic next week. Can I take a copy of the disc from this so I can show a colleague?'

'Of course,' Tom shrugged.

'Look, take it easy with the arm, it's a bad fracture that's healing but you don't want to strain it unduly or put a lot of load through it.'

'Okay, thanks guys, I will,' Tom said with a forced smile, having more questions than answers, but knowing now wasn't the time. He stood and shook hands with both men and left the room. Mike kicked back in the chair.

'So what do you really think, Bull?'

'I don't know. I've never seen anything like that before – no one has. You saw it – he's got greater *muscle* deposition in the arm, and there's more bone formation around the forearm and wrist. And that just can't be.'

12.

Tom sat in his office the next morning, already on his second cup of coffee. It still tasted awful, but it *was* working against the constant tiredness he'd felt since coming round, so needs must. He was still feeling somewhat marginalised after meeting with his team and Bob. Sarah was concerned about him, and had fussed around all the previous evening. It wasn't at all like her, so clearly she thought he was crazy as well. At precisely ten o'clock, as Tom studied some data, he heard Henry breeze, unannounced, into the main office, noisily calling out cheery 'good mornings' to anyone he could see in the department.

Oh great, the day gets better.

The Research Chair for the university burst in through the door without bothering to knock and exclaimed an even louder greeting to Tom. He was already annoyed with Tom for ignoring his calls and emails yesterday, and whilst even Henry recognised that Tom had been busy, he didn't like being given the cold shoulder treatment. Tom, on the other hand, had been so completely drained after all yesterday's meetings, he would rather have done a DIY vasectomy than speak to Henry.

'And a terribly good morning to you too, Mr Boyand,' he said, sitting down uninvited.

Well, it was. Tom looked up from some data printouts he was perusing. 'Hi Henry – good to see you.' *I'm such a lying bastard.*

You're a lying bastard, thought Henry. 'How are you feeling, old chap?

Back to normal yet?' Henry's eyes twinkled with mischief.

'I'm okay thanks – a little tired, but I'm okay,' he smiled a thin-lipped smile to his superior. *Now, just what're you up to?*

'As you know I watched the full CCTV feed of your little show the day before yesterday.' Tom noted the particularly biting tone in Henry's voice as he accentuated *show*.

'Yes,' dismissed Tom. 'All went rather well I thought – just as planned. No need for any of the hysteria.'

'Rather well?' said Henry with raised eyebrows. 'You used staff that shouldn't have been there, you used an unlicensed *drug*, and your findings sound like the ravings of a complete madman. So if that's your idea of experiments going well, I'd hate to be around for those that go badly.'

'If you look at the rosters, Henry, and I'm sure you have, all the staff who helped us on that day weren't due to work, so we didn't take anyone from their front-line posts.'

'And the drug? This... Zol? I think the legal department will be speaking to you about the licensing and future royalties from this, should it get approved. Although given the backhanded way you've gone about trialling it, you might have fucked that up too.' Henry was triumphant, almost spitting the words at Tom.

'Sigurd developed Zol when he was an independent researcher working in Iceland, as an aside to his day job. His university weren't interested when he declared it, so Sig kept the rights and he registered it as his own. The university has no claim to the drug.' Tom explained with a half smile on his face, backing Henry into an administrative corner.

'That's by the by, Tom. This is still an unlicensed drug that you used clinically in this hospital!' Henry's pantomime outrage at this was almost comical.

'It *is* an unlicensed drug, Henry, you are completely correct, but it wasn't used on an external patient, it was used in an internal laboratory study, with the full consent and knowledge of the subject. It was only to be used in this experiment if there was a danger that the standard resus protocols were proving ineffective. I'm not sure how the hospital would have looked if my experiment had resulted in my permanent and lasting death.' Henry was going red in the face, the colour deepening as Tom seemed to have an answer for everything he was throwing at him. 'Interestingly, it was also used with the blessing of the Ethics Committee. The drug is actually listed in the Appendices of our application along with all the other resus drugs we would use. The requirements stated we must disclose all of our methods, and we did. Did your people not spot it, Henry?' Tom looked Henry in the eye, tilting his head slightly, fighting the urge to smile at Henry's discomfort.

'You think you're such a clever bastard don't you, Boyand?' Henry boiled over. 'Well let me tell you this. If you try to publish any of this nonsense, this two-thousand-and-fucking-one fantasy story of yours, not only are you going to sound like you're insane – you'll be a laughing stock. And I'll make sure you never get a research post anywhere ever again!' At that, Henry noisily pushed the chair back and stormed out of the office, not even allowing time for the half-smiling Tom to get to his feet. He paused and turned at the door. 'Your current funding is all very well, but your benefactor's input will soon dry up now that the experiment is done, and your colleagues will be looking for 'proper' jobs in the rest of the university. If you play ball with the press, I'll certainly see what I can do to help them...' Henry left the threat and the offer hanging in the air, before leaving in a cloud of anger.

'Fuck you and all who sail in you!' Tom said angrily after Henry had gone. He would be the last person Henry would ever annoy.

Later that day, everyone was sat in the hub talking – taking a break together like any group of colleagues would – passing around gossip about who was shagging who and whose wife had found out about it, skirting the obvious elephant in the room. Chloe sat staring ahead, not taking part in the discussion, her lack of participation unnoticed by everyone else. In a lull in the proceedings, a quiet time belonging to everyone's thoughts, Chloe finally broke radio silence.

'He's not himself,' she exclaimed. It wasn't a provocation or an intentional start of a debate, it was just something that needed to be said.

'He's changed,' nodded Scott, picking up on the narrative.

"He's not himself' and 'he's changed' are two very different things,' Bob replied, ' 'Dying' and being brought back to life is, well, pretty life-changing, so should we be surprised if his reaction seems strange or even extreme to us? We haven't 'seen' what he has seen, and we can have no concept of the magnitude of the effect of that on his psyche.' Bob was happy for others to lead on this discussion but it was also clear he needed to keep the debate grounded and not hysterical.

'He's acting like someone who's had a brain injury. His personality's different, he treats people differently, he's a lot more aggressive and seems distant. He's become quite strange,' said Chloe.

'It's more than that,' replied Scott. 'He's obsessed by the work, repeatedly going over the same few seconds of video again and again. Now there's being thorough, there's wanting to find something, and there's that. That does suggest obsessive behaviour.'

'You can see from his point of view why he's obsessed with it – regardless of whether you choose to believe what happened to him – he genuinely believes what he's seen and experienced, and nobody else is willing to give it credibility.' Chloe looked at the faces staring back at her. 'So you can see how he's desperately looking for things, looking for evidence to say, 'hey, look at this, this proves it to you'.'

'He's right to an extent,' Sigurd's soft accent added. 'We can't explain his wrist – no one can. Logic says it has to be a fracture from a few months ago, but Sarah is adamant it isn't, and Shagger says it wasn't a minor fracture, so there is no way he could've ignored it and carried on. There really is no explanation.' He shrugged. 'We've backed him into a corner by basically saying 'we don't believe you', and he has obviously gone on the defensive. He believes what he's seen and what he's saying and he is desperately trying to sell the argument to everyone else. I get that. I'd do the same, and I'd probably be working as hard as that to prove something, looking at video and all of that.'

'So wait, Sig, you believe him?'

'No I don't – how can I? I'm saying I understand why he's doing what he's doing. I can understand the drive to work as hard as he is, and that's perhaps not helping his mental state – he must be desperate and exhausted. We can try to interpret what he's thinking and then telling us, but we haven't had that experience and it would be surprising if that experience wasn't massively powerful, wouldn't it?' Sigurd shrugged as he finished.

'It's still early days and it's likely his reaction will ease and moderate in the days and weeks to come,' said Bob, the voice of reason. 'His personality is different, but he's perhaps reacting at this stage as someone under duress.'

'Or he's gone a bit fucking crazy, had a psychotic episode after being starved of oxygen for so long. You couldn't blame the guy, but what if he's just lost it?' Charlie said, after watching one-too many of Tom's repeat viewings of video feeds.

'Really?' Tom walked into the hub. 'Gone 'fucking crazy' have I? Maybe. Maybe? Maybe! Ha – maybe I have. Maybe my brain got fried and when I died it left me with these images of all this funky shit. And my brain getting fried has made me crazy.' He was wagging his finger at everyone in the room. 'Or maybe, just maybe, all this funky shit happened like I said?' Tom stepped confidently into the middle of the group, his posture semi-aggressive and challenging. 'You might not have the data, but what if I'm right and you're wrong?'

'Tom, where've you been, we were wondering –' Mags was interrupted.

'There seems to be a lot of wondering going on about me,' Tom added.

'Yeah, perhaps. Sorry. Where were you earlier?'

'Down in the porters' lodge in the basement, by the power plant. You know the old research facility was right next door to them, and on late nights those lads were the only company I had. It was nice just to have a chat and get out of here for an hour – and not one of them called me 'fucking crazy'. Any thoughts on that?'

On his return he'd seen through the double doors that the rest of the team were meeting in the hub. Since he hadn't been invited, it must either have been impromptu over something else, or it was about him. He'd turned right and quietly entered the side door into the storeroom, making his way to the far end, to the door which opened into the hub. He'd looked out on them through the small arrow-slit window, listening to their discussion before confronting them.

'Tom. Boss. I hear what you're saying, and calling you crazy is a couple of steps too far – sorry Charlie. But you have been behaving quite differently, a bit strangely maybe, and certainly confrontationally. Look at it from our point of view –'

'Oh I am Scotty, I am. We spend months planning an experiment that *every last one* of you fuckers bought into.' He emphasised each word as he accused them. 'Or at least you said you did, anyway. And perhaps it was just better than working in McDonald's and so you went along with it. But, either way, you all invested your time and energy in the project, to look at what happens beyond death. And guess what?' He spread his arms wide and looked to the ceiling. 'It worked. We did it. The people in this room performed the greatest ever experiment on life and succeeded. All of those God-botherers can do one, because you just flipped the Almighty the finger and here I am! But there are going to be consequences, no? As intelligent people – as you all are – you can't expect me to wake up and say that I had a lovely dream and here I am.' Tom turned to face Scott, leaning toward him as he spoke. 'You have to expect that things happen on the other side. You can't go and fuck about with this and expect there to be nothing on the other end. You've heard my account – you can't make up that kind of stuff in such detail – the brain isn't going to fantasise about being a fucking astronaut in its dying seconds, is it? *Is it?*' His face was just a few inches from Scott's, his head turning one way then the other. 'How do you explain my hand? 'Crush injuries' the scan showed. So did I go home and put my arm in a fucking vice in my psychosis?' He stood upright and looked accusingly at everyone, no one returning his gaze. Suddenly he looked haggard and weary as he flopped down onto the blue vinyl couch at the side of the room, rescued from the coffee room in the old theatre block, foam bursting out of the rip on the front seam with a farting noise as he sat. 'You know, you're probably right. It *is* crazy what I'm saying. But you're the only people who could *possibly* believe me and right now I *need* your support. I need to know the people around me aren't going to phone the guys in white coats. I do feel different. Strange. Fucked-up, even. But I'm not crazy, and I need you to believe me...' He slumped back in the chair, head rolling back to stare at the white strip light on the ceiling, its harsh brightness making him squint. A lump rose in his throat like he was going to cry.

'Okay.' said Chloe. 'It is the most fantastical story. But it's you. You always had faith in me and so I guess this is the time to pay it back. I believe you.' Tom let out a sigh of relief and his shoulders relaxed. Chloe looked across at Scott and raised an eyebrow.

'You took me on as a researcher three years ago when I asked you to have faith in me, so okay, I will have faith in you.' Sig spread his hands earnestly.

'Okay, I'm gonna stop this episode of Jeremy Kyle right now,' said Scott sternly. 'Tom, I'll cut you some slack and I'll try to help – you're my best friend. It's true, us sitting around slagging you off isn't helpful, but right now, it's a step too far for me to believe it. Sorry.' He looked apologetic. Tom nodded and gave a thin-lipped smile to everyone.

'Well, it's a start. Thanks everyone. Thanks for your honesty, Scott.' He nodded a smile at him. 'You awkward bastard – this is the last grant I'm gonna get for you!' There was some muted laughter. 'Although in fairness, it'll be hard to get another grant for anyone ever again...' He stood up to leave, nodding to everyone again. 'This crazy fucker's gotta get home. G'night.' A chorus of farewells followed him out of the room and down the corridor. He ducked into the lab, shoving open the double doors with his hip which resisted for a split second and then released with a whoosh of recycled air. The room was in semi-darkness, illuminated only by back lights and screen-savers on the monitors around the room. He stood there, thinking of all that had happened since he was first strapped into the cold suit a few days ago.

What if he *was* going crazy? What if all of it was a construct? Didn't every crazy person think they were sane? Did anyone actually sit there and think; *Yep, I'm crazier than a shithouse rat?*

His mind churned and his eyes focused on the doors opposite, leading to the main corridor and home. Suddenly out of the corner of his eye, he saw it. A hooded figure, in the shadows off to his right, pale skin with shoulders hunched forward, disguising some of its bulk. He spun around to face it, flicking the switch on the wall to illuminate the room, ready to fight, ready to physically and verbally attack. 'What the fu –'

The harsh overhead lights flickered on and there was no one there.

He walked forwards a couple of steps, head turning quickly one way then the other. Flicking on all the lights, suddenly bathing the lab in a neon glow that hurt his eyes, he searched the place from top to bottom. He ran across the room, looking under desks and in cupboards, behind the defibrillator which he shoved away from the wall and he pulled the plastic privacy curtain aside from the small changing area in the corner that nobody used. Nothing.

Maybe I am crazy? He thought and absently scratched his arm.

He left the way he'd come, switching the lights off as he did so, not seeing Scott peering in through the glass doors where he had been watching him.

***

Hatim texted him as he reached the lifts to the car park:

```
Are you still in the office?
Yes. Why?
I've cleaned up the footage. You have to see
it.
Okay come up, everyone's here.
```

'Okay so I cleaned it up as best I could, filtered out some of the noise from the motion blur, zoomed in to about the level where it's at its clearest and tried to clean the resolution up a little. It isn't perfect because these cameras aren't designed for quick movements when zoomed in, but it is a lot better.' Hatim sat at a desk, clicking the mouse. The computer screen opened a window with several different video manipulating options scattered around the outside. He clicked the triangular green Play button. Suddenly the footage window sprang to life and Tom watched the same scene as yesterday, this time upgraded from noisy standard-def to hi-def. The play screen was split into four views from different cameras around the room, and they watched the action play out at normal speed.

'And here it is...' Hatim said, cueing the moment they'd been waiting for, as if to add to the dramatic reveal. He clicked the mouse, and the image zoomed in to one full screen camera view of the upper half of Tom's body, transporting everyone back to the point of resuscitating him. It was disturbing to watch it all over again, how they'd struggled to bring him back. As his body arched off the bed, jerking almost airborne, there was a brief delay and the lower part of his right forearm suddenly changed. The skin became physically indented, and the wrist was squeezed, like an invisible drawstring had been tightened around the end of the forearm for a split second. Suddenly, with a jerk, Tom's forearm bent at a hideous angle, folding at ninety degrees to itself, bending where no bones should ever bend, whiplashing back and forth once as his arm flailed. All those in the room gasped as they saw the wrist fracture so horribly. Then all was still on the screen. The arm looked a little strange, perhaps the immediate after-effects of trauma, but there was no sign of the deformity they had just witnessed.

'Anyone think it's an old fracture now?' Tom turned and left for the second time that day.

13.

Sarah had spent the day at home. She'd originally planned to spend the time looking after Tom and just being around rather than having her focus elsewhere, and was unimpressed to say the least that he'd gone to work as if nothing had happened. In his absence she'd blitzed the house, using housework as therapy more than anything else. As a nice surprise for the kids, she'd taken them to the park to play after school. She needed to spend time with them, to have some normality and not think about the events of the last couple of days. Reserving all of her concern for Tom getting through resuscitation unscathed, Sarah hadn't given any thought to what it would be like after the experiment – how Tom would be, how she would feel. She hadn't thought about the bloody press either. Now she chided herself for over-analysing Tom in the last two days – he seemed a little distracted, but *of course* he was distracted after all he had been through, both physically and mentally. There was nothing more than that, nothing more concerning, and he was bound to revert to his old self when the dust settled. She wanted to sit down with him that evening and talk about what he'd experienced, not because she was particularly fascinated by what the afterlife might look like, but she felt that she needed to support him and whatever he was going through. Scotty had invited her along to the debrief in the research unit yesterday, but she'd declined, not wishing to relive the details of resuscitating her husband for a second time.

Sarah worried about Tom's mental state, particularly that he'd been unable to remember her or the kids when he first came around, after saying a tender goodbye just an hour before. She feared that this might be a symptom of oxygen deprivation to the brain and might point toward permanent brain damage.

When they got home from the park, to distract herself from further negative thoughts, Sarah turned her attention to the laundry. She was folding towels on the kitchen worktop as Tom walked in.

'Hi,' she said, almost too brightly, and tilted her head towards him for the obligatory kiss on the cheek. Tom completely ignored her, walking passed to dump his laptop bag on the counter, shoving carefully sorted piles of clean laundry to one side. 'Hi,' she said again, louder this time, but with a similar response. Sarah decided to continue her own conversation. 'Well, hi yourself, how are you? How was your day? I'm fine and it was great, I spent the day 'working from home' so I got the washing done, the ironing done, so you don't have to do any of that now you've got in – just in case you were wondering or were about to crack on with it.'

Tom looked up from unpacking his computer with a frown on his face. 'What?'

'Ah, a response, we make progress. I was just saying hi,' Sarah replied, not hiding her exasperation.

'Yeah. Hi. Sorry,' he said, having the decency to look sheepish.

'Course there used to be a time when you'd not only come in and actually say hello, but give me a kiss as well. But I s'pose that's too much to ask?'

'Mmmm?' Tom asked as he opened his laptop and typed in his password. Sarah let out a frustrated sigh. 'Fucking press,' he said.

'Tom,' Sarah snapped at him, nodding her head in the direction of the den. 'Language.' Tom looked across at his children for the first time since arriving home, who were sat together on the sofa like two peas in a pod. 'Reporters still out there are they?'

'Uh-huh.' He was scrolling through emails in Outlook.

'How was your day?' she asked enthusiastically.

'Enlightening.'

'Oh?' An edge of concern appeared in her voice.

'Yep. Turns out that when I was being resus'd my wrist *did* snap like a twig.' He looked up and smiled grimly at her.

'Shhhh,' she hissed , 'not so loud in front of the kids, they can't be hearing that stuff.' She was angry at his thoughtlessness but didn't want to labour the point. 'How on earth can that have happened? And what's the explanation for it?'

'It correlates with what I experienced when I was out.'

'Which you still haven't told me.'

'Okay, let's talk about it later, shall we – I'll tell you everything.'

'Alright. Now can you put some food on for the kids while I put the laundry away and hoover upstairs?'

'Erm, I was going to do some emailing.' Tom once again looked down at his screen.

'Or alternatively, you can do the hoovering and I'll feed the kids, what's it to be?' Sarah gave Tom what was commonly referred to as 'the look'. It said that if you were back to normal enough to be in work all day, the least you can do is help out at home.

'Okay, I'll sort them something,' Tom replied switching the oven on and opening the freezer, looking at his computer screen as he did so. He saw a message from Kate Dennehey he had missed from the day before.

Just seen the press statement that Andrea Dent gave. I thought we had agreed to run everything by my office? Kate

Tom replied: It was the only way to create enough of a diversion to get me out of the hospital, and I knew you wouldn't go for it if you knew in advance.

Kate's response was immediate: The whole point of using my office was to prevent the clusterfuck of my not knowing the press statements that come out of the hospital - it's embarrassing. We need to work together and you need to use my office.

Okay. Agreed. In that case can you release a statement that I'm fine and just need some time to rest while I write up the results and we will publish them in due course?

We've already done that - why repeat ourselves?

To get the fuckers off my driveway.

Sarah rescued the folded laundry before Tom could manage to contaminate it with food and disappeared upstairs to put it away. She busied herself by finishing hoovering upstairs, so at least it was done for the weekend. The hoover died as she switched it off and she could hear some kind of commotion downstairs. She rushed down to the kitchen and saw the kids sat at the table with plates of incinerated chicken nuggets in front of them. The waffles hadn't fared much better.

'Everything okay, boys?' she asked, sensing the tension between Tom and her sons.

'They are just being bloody fussy that's all – the nuggets got a little overdone and now they won't eat them. These kids are bloody ruined. I've told them that they aren't going to waste good food and they'll sit there until they're gone.' Tom was so disproportionately angry he was shaking.

'Baby these are so burned they're unrecognisable – they need to be gone.' Sarah picked up the two plates, watching Liam stifle a sob as tears ran down his cheeks after his dad had shouted at him. She turned and dumped the carcinogenic contents into the food waste bin. Tom grabbed his laptop and strode into the den, muttering to himself. 'It's okay boys, I'll put some pasta on for you now,' she beamed at them and their solemn expressions seemed to lift as she put the kettle on.

***

Cylinders of yellow light grew out from the shades of the lamps in the living room. Just as they had before the experiment, they sat together on the sofa, Sarah with a glass of wine, but Tom only wanted water, wanting his head to be as clear and sharp as it could be.

'So', she said, crossing one leg under the other and sitting on it to half-face him. 'Made any sense of what you saw?'

'It's more like having the time to process it. I saw everything, and now I've got to cram it all into this tiny storage unit.' He knocked on his head as he would a front door.

'What happened?'

'I was thrown out of my body. Yep, out of body experience does really happen. Then I left it behind and flew into space, like I was a bird and then a ship.' Tom tried once again to tell what he'd seen as a story, a narrative that would grasp the attention and become embedded in his wife's cerebrum – something so real and profound that, no matter what your view or belief system, you would simply have to believe and understand that the story was real.

'Is there any explanation for how everything seemed to take such a long time – you said you were gone for *years*, when your body was out for less than an hour?'

'I don't think my mind, or my life force, or my soul if you really must go there were particularly connected to my body. I can't have travelled where I did – you are talking about thousands of light years to the galactic centre, and yet there I was. Bob can say it was some previous experience or inference from things I've seen or believed, but the idea of the entrance to the afterlife being some kind of soul catcher is about as far away from what I thought I might see. I can't really convince anyone what I've seen, until they have.' He shrugged and sagged back onto the sofa, aware of the tension running through his body as he told the story again. His wrist throbbed like a heartbeat.

'And so the defibrillator shocked you back into the real world?'

'Jesus fucking Christ, love, haven't you listened to anything I've been *fucking* saying?'

'Don't raise your voice to me, Tom, or you can carry this on without me. It's quite a tough ask to understand the mechanics of all this, you know. On the one hand you're flying through space at way faster than the speed of light, totally disconnected from your body. And then you're back in your bed in the hospital. The sensible explanation is that the one has been an extension from the other.'

'Are you spending too much time around Bob?'

'Or what else?' It was Sarah's turn to raise her voice. 'That you detached your soul, projected it into a parallel universe to become Han fucking Solo and all home in time for tea?' She scowled at him. 'This is why I'm having a hard time with it.'

'Parallel universe, eh? Y'know that's not a bad shout.'

'Oh bloody hell.' She punched him on the arm, with almost too much force to be playful.

'I wish I was clever enough to distil what I've seen, to dictate and rationalise it so science could benefit from it, but I can't. My head is just so full of the ideas, the answers, the beauty of it all, and they are all getting in the way of each other so it's not coherent.'

'Being dead probably has that effect on people.'

'And then when I'm back here...'

'What?'

'Well, there was whatever I saw in the room straight after.'

'Do you really want to dwell on that? That could've been a dozen things–'

'Including a figure that shouldn't have been there.'

'Well okay, if you insist it could, then let's add that to the list of possibles.'

'I think I've seen it again.'

'Seen what?'

'The figure.'

'When? Where?' Sarah could live with tales of nebulae and black holes, but seeing shadowy figures was more disturbing.

'In the hospital – right smack bang in the middle of the orthopaedic ward.'

'What exactly did you see?'

'It was a hooded figure.'

'What – like Death?'

'No, it was like a person in a hoody.'

'And wasn't it?'

'What?'

'A person in a hoody?'

'No!'

'How do you know? What makes you so sure?'

'Because it appeared right before me. And it stood there, staring me down, and then it was gone. And it seemed like the rest of the ward stopped when it was there, but no one else noticed it, during or afterwards, or saw it leave the ward.'

'Did you see it's face?'

'No it had the hood up, it's face was in shadow.'

'What do you think it was?'

'I think.' He paused, he recognised he'd asked Sarah to take in a lot, but he knew this was going a stage further. 'I don't think I'm supposed to have come back... from being dead,' he added after seeing a frown grow on his wife's face.

'I don't think anyone is.'

'But I think this hooded figure is watching me.'

'To what end – to do what?' This new paranoia was causing her own fear to skyrocket.

'I don't know.'

***

Sarah stirred in bed, moonlight filtering in through the open skylight window on the still, muggy night. The room was bathed in the faintest of blue-grey light, making oversized shadows of the furniture, and the bed floated in a sea of darkness. She woke, sensing something amiss. She reached across to Tom's side of the bed – he wasn't there but the bed was still warm. Propping herself up on her elbows, she saw him tiptoeing out of the bedroom, his long thin Nosferatu shadow creeping along the wall like a giant spider.

'S'everthin' k, babe?' she managed to mumble, still half asleep.

'Stay in bed,' Tom whispered, much more alert than her, 'I heard something, there might be someone in the house.' He continued to the door, which they always left ajar so they could hear the kids if they got up in the night.

'What? It must be just a noise, come back to bed,' she said, thinking he was becoming ever more paranoid. She sighed and dropped back onto the pillows, letting him go and reassure himself that nothing was wrong while she drifted back to sleep. Too late – her bladder was stretched tight as a drum and wasn't going to let her settle down again. She got up and padded naked to their en-suite bathroom, yawning as she did so, listening for creaking floorboards as Tom carefully made his way downstairs. She sat, enjoying the relief in her abdomen, wondering how long Tom would be prowling around the house before satisfying himself that there was no intruder. Back in bed, the long arms of sleep were already reaching out to claim her when a loud banging sound jolted her awake – a crashing thud reverberated through the whole house like someone trying to batter the front door down. Two more thuds followed – Wump! Wump! Alert now, she sprang out of bed, senses turned up to eleven, her heart hammering in her chest. She bent to pick up her long t-shirt, discarded almost as soon as she'd gone to bed and pulled it over her head. She ran through the bedroom door – first checking that the boys' doors remained shut – and headed for the stairs.

Wump! Wump! Wump! The banging noise came again, although muffled this time. She raced downstairs, not caring how much noise she made, heart thumping in her chest, not sure what she would find when she got to the bottom. She ran across the den, and, seeing the patio doors open, headed for the garden.

'Tom.' She hissed in as much of a stage whisper as she could muster. Sarah stopped in her tracks as she crossed the threshold onto the patio. Tom stood off to one side, looking down at something on the floor, breathing heavily and looked as tense as a coiled spring. She took a step closer and out of the shadows the shape on the floor emerged as Tom's old cricket bat, or the remains of it.

'What the fuck is going on? Tom?' She looked from her husband to the bat, which had obviously been used to smash against the patio doors, breaking the handle and heavily damaging the face. It was a wonder that the glass hadn't smashed.

'It was here,' Tom said.

'What was?'

'Hoody.'

Oh not this again, she thought.

'Here in the house – I heard it on the landing and followed it down the stairs but it'd gone. Probably to get this,' he gestured to the bat.

'Why would it break in, then leave, then start to smash on the windows? I don't get it?' Sarah shrugged.

'Neither do I. I think it's trying to get my attention.'

'Did you try and stop it?'

'I didn't see where it was, and was checking it wasn't still inside, when it ran at the patio doors, hit the glass a few times and then ran off.'

'And it was definitely this same figure you've seen before?' she asked, not knowing what to believe.

'Yes.'

'How did it get in?' *If it got here from across the galaxy, it might not bother with arbitrary things like walls.*

'By forcing the bottom lock – we didn't double lock the back door before bed,' he shrugged with only the slightest implication in his comment.

I'll think you'll find I did double lock the door before bed, because I always do, and I checked it tonight, just like I always do, she thought but didn't push the issue. 'We might need to get the locks checked or updated then,' she said. 'What are you going to do about this Hoody?'

'I don't know, babe, I don't know what it wants.' He sighed. 'Come on, let's go back to bed.' Tom came back inside and locked the patio doors before making a big show of locking and checking both locks on the back door – which of course he found to be locked. The house secure, they followed one another up the stairs and to bed, but for both of them, it would be a far from restful night.

***

They awoke to the usual Saturday morning routine; the Hornets had football matches, so they would drop Liam at Sarah's parents so he could spend the morning tormenting Grandpa with incessant dinosaur games, while they headed off to the playing fields. Twenty-four teams were due to play, meaning large crowds of parents and other supporters ringed around small pitches, several deep in places. The crowds were even thicker for matches on adjacent pitches. A keen watcher of Ben's team under normal circumstances, and as vocal a parent as anyone else in his support, today Tom stood uninterested. He stared blankly into the distance, then up at the half moon emerging from behind a cloud in the deep-blue sky, imagining flying up into the heavens, longing for freedom. His gaze drifted through the crowds, finding nothing on the pitches to interest him, when suddenly he saw it. Directly across the pitch, Hoody stood facing him down just like at the hospital, its face in shadow, but Tom was sure he could see a smile. Tom maintained eye contact and started to make his way to the end of the pitch intending to confront him. Sarah was concentrating on Ben's game and oblivious to his leaving as he eased his way between spectators, levering himself through tightly packed groups, pushing past those who wouldn't easily give way. He reached the end of the pitch, where the crowd was thinner, and hurried along to the opposite side, always watching Hoody who was likewise tracking Tom's progress. On the far side, the crowd deepened again and Tom excused his way past throngs of parents until he reached the halfway line, exactly where Hoody had been standing, but it was gone. Tom looked up and down the sideline, and at both ends of the pitch, scanning the people, but could find no evidence of his adversary. He looked back across the pitch to Sarah, still watching the game and unaware of her husband's absence. Hoody was standing immediately behind her, looming over her, the threat very real and evident. Cold, black expressionless eyes met Tom's, and fear gripped him as he somehow knew he was looking at a clinical killer who could end Sarah's life right in front of him. Tom hurried back, barging his way through the crowds this time, not caring about the glares and exclamations he caused, ignoring abuse when it was thrown at him. Reaching the far side of the pitch again, Tom closed in on where he'd left Sarah, but too many people ahead of him blocked his view and he pushed them out of the way, forcing his way through the crowd to get to her. Suddenly the supporter Red Sea parted and Moses saw his wife, standing as she had been all along, on her own, studying the game. The final whistle blew and the children all dutifully shook hands with their opponents and, having played their final match of the day, drifted towards their parents on the touchline. Tom barely noticed Ben as he came off.

'Did you see my second goal, Dad?' he asked, drawing heavy, excited breaths.

'No. No, I must have missed it,' Tom replied, still distracted.

'Oh,' said Ben, disappointed. 'My last one?' His voice full of hope.

'No, I didn't.' Reality crowded in on Tom's thoughts about flying through the clouds and seeing Hoody threatening his wife. He started to feel guilty and dimly recognised that this mattered to Ben. It really *mattered*.

'How did I play, though?' Ben was giving his dad one last chance. And although Tom hadn't taken any notice of his son's games and barely even acknowledged that he was taking part, he hadn't left all his tact and humanity at the other end of the galaxy.

'Yeah, sorry I missed your goals mate, but, for me, you played...' He struggled to remember the nuances of football – not that he'd really forgotten, but more universal issues had commandeered his readily available brain-space. '...sharp. You were really sharp today. Like when you ran past that other kid, the bigger kid?' *He must have done that at some stage, right?*

'When I did my step over?'

'Yes, that's it, that one.'

'Didn't even know you saw that. I couldn't see you on the side where you usually stand.'

'I'd just seen someone from work and I went to, er, find them – I watched from further over. That was top class, mate, it really was,' Tom warmed to his subject, Ben beamed, and Sarah eyed her husband suspiciously.

'First one I've done properly in a game.'

And you deserve for me to have seen it. He was angry with himself, regardless of the enormity of what was happening on their cosmological doorstep – people's lives were still going on right here on planet earth, all around him.

Ben then showed him the red mark on his leg where Alex Tilson had kicked him. 'Alex is always fouling, kicks me every time,' he said in a disgruntled manner.

'He doesn't like it when you beat him, darling,' smiled Sarah, ruffling Ben's hair.

'Elbow him in the face next time,' Tom advised.

'Tom. They are seven!' Sarah admonished.

'He won't do it again will he? Little prick,' Tom countered forcefully.

'What's a prick, Daddy?' Ben looked up, innocently, at his father.

'Happy now?' Sarah was furious with Tom's antics.

'Oh, erm –'

'It's a naughty word, Ben, Daddy was silly for using it weren't you, Daddy?'

'Yes. Mummy's right, mate. Sorry. I just get a bit cross about folks going after my big guy is all,' Tom countered with a conspiratorial wink at his son.

'Thanks Dad,' Ben beamed, 'S'okay, won't tell anyone about the 'prick' word.'

'Thanks mate.' Sarah – fuming – just shook her head.

'You've scratched your arm.' She noticed bright red weals on his forearm, and watched him continue to scratch at the skin.

'Must be where it's healing, itches like a bas –' he looked at Ben who was innocently examining his dad's arm with concern. '– yeah it really itches.'

They picked Liam up from Sarah's parents – he had cornered the market in Gramps' attention all morning and hadn't been stuck watching football, so all was good in his world. Tom was withdrawn during the afternoon and struggled to interact with his family – brooding about seeing Hoody. They'd picked up pizza on the way home, but Tom didn't have any appetite for it.

He sat in his usual position on the sofa in the den as the rest of them ate pizza slices from the box, his laptop on the table in front of him. The kids had finished eating and were playing noisily off to one side, taking it in turns for an army to assault the walls of the Playmobil fort. Sarah took the empty cartons into the kitchen and he saw her smile as she periodically looked up from tidying up. Tom focused on his emails, deleting blocks of messages from media outlets requesting statements and interviews.

Tom was finishing typing a message as it was Liam's turn to attack. He had brought his secret weapon in the form of a dinosaur assault group to take down the fort. Tom shook his head slightly, trying to concentrate, to block out the noise and focus on the words on the screen. He jumped backwards as a Tyrannosaurus Rex flew across between the laptop screen and his face, clattering across the table.

'Jesus Christ will you two just bloody stop it!' Tom raged, anger surging through him. He flung his arm out in a wide backhand toward the toys at the end of the table, one large sweeping stroke sent all the toys, fort and all, sailing through the air, narrowly missing the boys. Soldiers and dinosaurs went skidding and sliding across the oak floor, the fort breaking apart on landing. The boys stared at him as Sarah quickly came through from the kitchen.

'And can you keep the bloody noise down, I can't even hear myself think!' He looked down at his already painful wrist, at the red mark the impact with the fort had made. The skin seemed to ripple as he looked. Surrounded by the debris of their game, Ben stood facing his father, a defiant frown on his face having never heard him shout like that before. A frightened Liam had moved behind his brother, his bottom lip quivering like the night before as he fought the urge to cry.

'Now tidy that lot up and play quietly!'

Sarah glared at him. 'Can I speak to you, please?' She marched back into the kitchen. Tom pushed himself up from the low seat, wincing at the pain from his wrist, and followed.

'What?' he asked.

'What the fuck?' she asked angrily.

'I don't follow,' he said with a shrug and a slight shake of the head.

'You've yelled at the kids, twice in two days, and they're upset. You never yell at them, particularly for no reason. So I'll ask again. What the fuck?'

'The things I've seen. It fucks with your head, sometimes I feel like it's going to explode. I don't think I can cram all of this into my brain. And my arm is painful – I think it's making me short-tempered.'

'I'll say. I don't know what really happened to you out there, but you've been behaving really strangely in the last couple of days – yelling at the kids, barely noticing or talking to me. You're not yourself. But it's got to stop – did you see how scared the kids looked earlier?'

'No. I didn't. Sorry. I do think we spoil them too much though, and the odd row won't do them any harm.'

'Now is almost certainly not the time to be reviewing our parenting style. Another time, another –'

'I saw Hoody again today.'

'What? Where?'

'Down on the Astroturf. I saw it in the crowd across the pitch.'

'So not someone from work?'

'No. I went over there and turned back to where you were stood and it was right behind you. It's like it was threatening you, showing me how easily it could hurt you.'

'Couldn't that have been any big bloke in a Hoody, especially from how far away you were?'

'On a day like today, when everyone else is in short sleeves, a guy has his hood up? I don't think I'd be the only one noticing.'

'Okay, well let's think about that later. But you've got to calm down around these two.' Sarah walked through into the den, gesturing to the boys with a wave of her hand. 'Come on kids, Daddy's still tired from work this week. Want to go to Kidzone?' she asked them as she picked up dinosaurs and fort pieces.

'Yay, can we ask Matty and Carla?' asked Ben, his father's troubles quickly forgotten.

***

They decided to have Chinese takeaway the following evening, a fairly common occurrence in their house and a guilty pleasure for 'chef' Tom. Over the years they'd trawled their side of town looking for a decent Cantonese take away, one whose two major ingredients weren't MSG and food colouring. In the end, the place they found was closer to home than they realised. Wong's was a little back street shop, with a dirty window covered with a grill, and the menus barely readable from outside through the rust and grime. Inside was full of Chinese lanterns and calendars – both traditional and tacky in equal measure.

Tom had barely known Wong, until he saw him in his clinic one day, the victim of a mild heart attack. He operated on him, performing a heart by-pass, and within three months Wong was back at work. When Tom next went to get a take away they recognised one another. From then on Tom had rarely paid full-price for a meal. If he had – on his insistence, uncomfortable with being consistently offered a gratuity for doing his job – he had walked out of the shop with far more food than he had ordered. His principles couldn't have been too compromised, however, because they never did go elsewhere – they really couldn't because the food was *that* good.

To stop their kitchen smelling like Wong's, Tom bagged all the cartons and waste food from the mountains they'd come home with, and took them outside to the wheelie bin at the front of the driveway. He walked carefully down the steps from the kitchen, skirting around the side of the house, poking his head round the corner to see if any reporters remained, but at last they'd all gone, moving on to the next story and fifteen-minute celebrity to harangue. Tom lifted the lid of the bin and raised the black bag to drop it in when something caught his eye along the street. An hour after sunset, the yellow sodium glow of the streetlights created pockets of illumination surrounded by shadows of parked cars, bushes overhanging garden walls and large trees framing the street like an arbour, with the soft light washing out the colours from the scene. In the middle of this quiet suburban nightscape, one he had seen a thousand times before, the Hoody stood in the middle of the road, facing down the street towards him but almost two hundred yards away, hands once again held bent at his sides like a gunslinger, challenging him. Tom looked down to push the black bag into the bin and close the lid, looking up again expecting to see an empty street. But Hoody was still there. Tom contemplated what to do and scratched at his forearm, which was itching like mad now. He thought about turning away, forgetting the obvious challenge and rejoining his family. He looked back to the house for a second but he knew what he needed to do. Making up his mind, he suddenly broke into a run, dashing out of the drive into the street. He looked up but Hoody had gone. *It can't be far, it can't just disappear.* Tom ran down the street to where Hoody had appeared and looked in the gardens left and right. He thought he saw movement in the bushes in the garden on his side of the road, and carried on running straight into the driveway. The house was between streetlights, so even the front yard was dark, and he could barely see anything in the gloom. His eyes were focused on the bushes he had seen move, but in the darkness he failed to see the galvanised green dustbin right in front of him. The bin went flying as he ran into it, the lid clattering across the driveway, sounding impossibly loud in the quiet evening. Tom stopped in his tracks, standing like a statue in a kids game, the lid rolling noisily around him, still searching the undergrowth with his eyes. The front door of the house suddenly opened.

'Oi! What do yer think yer doin'?' The elderly owner of the house, whom Tom didn't know, called out toward the rustling bushes, framed in the door by the light of the hallway behind. Tom took an immediate decision; he couldn't be found, he couldn't be caught here in this situation; it would be extremely difficult – if not impossible – to explain this away without him sounding insane. *More insane.* He looked to the garden wall to his left, and estimated it to be just above waist height. Without waiting for any doubts to creep in he broke into a sprint, quickly closing the few steps to the wall and dived over it. His arm and leg led over the brickwork, flying out of the old man's garden and onto the street beyond, landing heavily on his injured right arm as he hit the pavement, his face stopping just in front of a pile of dog shit left by a careless dog-walker. He stifled a cry and cupped his arm, slowly getting to his feet as he heard the owner shouting –

'I saw yer, I know who you are – I'm gonna phone the police on yer! Bloody vandal.' Tom stayed bent over, shielding himself from the gaze of the old man who was still ranting at him from the safety of his doorway. Fear gripped his chest – *what if he did recognise me, what if he knows who I am?* He started to panic about a visit from Her Majesty's Constabulary, and how that would play out in the press, at work and at home. *Even more insane.* Fear gave way to more rational thinking, however, when he realised that he was totally anonymous. The old guy didn't know him, wouldn't have got a good look at him in the shadows, and wouldn't have recognised him as the hood of his old sweatshirt – that he had slipped on to put the rubbish out – had fallen forwards, covering his face and head from view. Keeping to the shadows of the trees and lampposts, and holding his arm against him, he slunk home, occasionally looking over his shoulder. He half expected the elderly home owner to have turned vigilante and pursued him, ready to launch an attack with a golf club or maybe a garden rake.

' 'Take it easy' they said,' he muttered to himself, seeing some black humour in his fall, ' 'Don't put any load on the arm', they said.' He turned into his driveway, and up the steps into the kitchen. Sarah had just finished tidying away, and gave him a quizzical look – *where the hell have you been?*

Tom's face was like thunder and he angrily peeled off his hoody, wincing in pain as he pulled his damaged arm out of the sleeve.

'Are you okay? What happened?' Sarah asked.

'I slipped when I was putting the bins out, that's all,' Tom snapped. 'Landed on my arm.'

'Here, let me take a look at it,' she replied, reaching out to him.

Tom snatched his hand away. 'And do what? It's fine. I don't need your help.' His anger from the incident with Hoody and the frustration of having a knowledge-base spanning the whole galaxy and no way to process it boiled over in his reaction. Sarah just stared at him as he reached up to a cupboard above the breakfast bar and brought down a bottle of Dalwhinnie. He poured himself half a glass and gulped it down like it was water. Sarah shook her head and walked away into the den.

'I'm going to bed, you do what the fuck you like.' It was her turn to be angry – with the situation and with him for going through with the experiment. He still looked like Tom and sounded like him, but his distance, and these mood swings definitely weren't.

As Sarah cleaned her teeth in the en-suite bathroom, dressed only in her underwear, Tom stormed in and wrapped his arms around her, squeezing her breasts briefly before lifting her clear of the ground.

'C-aarrghhh aa gluuggg... ohhhh fuc-ggghhhh-it,' she bent and spat foamy toothpaste into the basin, and tried again. 'Can't a girl get a little peace just to clean her teeth anymore?' She tried to look annoyed, but was secretly pleased he knew she existed.

He stood behind her and they watched each other in the large mirror as she reached up to touch his face. Tom unsnapped her bra and slid the straps from her shoulders before dropping it on the floor. He spun her round to face him, cupping her breasts in his hands, rolling her nipples between thumb and fingers. Suddenly, dental hygiene was not at the top of the agenda any more. He nuzzled her neck and squeezed a little harder. She kissed him hard, thrusting her tongue into his mouth and wrapped her arms around his neck. He lifted her up to sit on the bathroom worktop. She reached for him, pushing aside his boxer shorts to find his arousal, and she found him more turned-on, harder than she had ever known him. He closed the distance between them, pushing forward into her hand and she pushed her own underwear to one side and guided him toward her, wrapping her legs around his waist. He lifted her, and slid inside, pushing forcefully against her, and she craved it, craved him, forgetting how strange he had been, and perhaps for the first time truly believing he'd returned. All of a sudden, he felt physically real. He grazed her hard nipples with his hands then bore down on them with his mouth, nibbling and biting, and for the first time causing her some pain.

'Ow! Too hard.' She slapped him on the top of the head to emphasise the urgency of the point, giving him a reproving look. He withdrew, moving to her neck, nibbling and tickling. He knew she liked this, and she wrapped herself around him even tighter. They pushed together on the worktop, but both realised they would be more comfortable next door, and Tom lifted her up again, their tongues entwined, and carried her into the bedroom. She liked his strength and to be enfolded within it, *just so long as he kept his fucking teeth to himself, right?*

He carried her into the bedroom, throwing her on the bed, bending down to tear her lace panties off. She reached for him as he climbed onto the bed, her eyes full of lust. He flipped her legs, spinning her over onto her front, standing once more to strip off his shorts, before grabbing her hips to pin her down. He pushed into her roughly from behind, holding her down, his injured hand reaching underneath to pull on her breast. This felt rough, too rough for Sarah, she liked him to be forceful sometimes but as turned-on as she was, it was too much. He had barely acknowledged the existence of her or the kids since the experiment, but boy was he interested now. As pleased as she was in principle with that, this was wrong.

She cried out when his grip was too strong, when she felt so claustrophobic that he might crush her. She squeezed his right arm to stop him – just a bit too much, applying pressure in the region of the fracture. Suddenly his thrusting became less forceful, but quicker and shallower as he neared his climax, the pressure eased and he was no longer causing her pain, but she would be sore for a day or two. She was passed the point where she could enjoy this, and she was confused as to her feelings. He'd pushed things too far, caused her pain, gone to the edge of what was consensual. This wasn't like him, like her Tom who had always celebrated her as a woman and a sexual being, who had always put her needs first. Now she felt he was just using her, like his personal fuck toy.

He eased off as he got to the end – had he realised he had gone too far, or was he preoccupied with the urgency of the moment? He tensed, hands holding her hips, his body froze and he let out a wild and unrestrained cry, an animalistic roar as he reached his orgasm, and he thrust into her one last time. He groaned several more times as the spasms in his body subsided, before collapsing on top of her. He had never climaxed like that before, like the ultimate release of a beast. Sarah was even more confused and she carefully rolled onto her side, dislodging him so he slid into his front, his good arm resting on her hip.

***

Tom had agreed to take time off on Monday to relax – they both had – to spend some time together without the kids. In the morning she left him in bed when she got up with the boys, telling them that Daddy was still tired after his special experiment with work last week, and that was why he wasn't spending much time with them (or talking to them, or even recognising them). He'd slept a lot since he came back from the hospital, but would then be up at odd hours of the night. And there was that strange story about something coming into the house. He was also ravenously hungry. Usually when he came home with a takeaway from Mr Wong's they ended up throwing half of it away, but last night Tom practically ate the lot.

On the school run, Sarah was glad to have time to herself away from her husband – the atmosphere that surrounded him and his mood were sucking the life out of her. She decided they needed to sit down and talk – maybe Tom needed to speak to Bob to offload some of what was filling his brain. On her return to the house, however, Tom was too twitchy and wired to listen to even the suggestion of talking. He became more and more preoccupied throughout the morning, refusing to sit down, insisting on pacing around the house, repeatedly checking each room. Was he still looking for Hoody? Just before she went back to the school to pick up the boys, Tom announced that he needed to go into work and look over things; that he needed to keep digging.

'I thought you were staying off work today – that we were spending some time together?' Sarah fumed.

'We have, haven't we?'

'No, we've both been in the same house – that's not the same thing. You've been walking around all day, checking and re-checking every room – for what?'

'You wouldn't understand.' He waved a dismissive hand at her.

'Oh wouldn't I? Why not fucking try me? I understand a lot about you since the experiment, and being preoccupied with work is one thing, acting like you don't know us or *want* to know is another!' she raged – releasing all the pent-up frustrations she'd had with him over the months preceding the experiment and the days since.

'There are bigger things going on, Sarah –' he tried to reason with her before she cut him off.

'Bigger things than *us*? Like this thing in a hoody that was smashing a cricket bat against our windows the other night? The same cricket bat I came out to find at *your* feet? Like the cosmos and how you've flown across it?' Sarah's eyes blazed. 'Fine. You always used to say that we were the most important thing in the world to you. But I guess not the most important thing in the universe, eh?'

'I've seen things you'll never understand – not until your time comes – and I don't expect you to understand. But this Hoody thing is real and it's a part of it. And I need to find out what it is.' He pushed past her, grabbing his keys, phone and laptop bag, rushing down the steps before Sarah could throw another counter at him. He jumped into the Jeep and drove off – thankful for the absence of the press.

14.

When Tom arrived at the lab the office was populated by everyone in his immediate team – Mags, Chloe, Scott and Sigurd. He spent the next hour or so going between his office and the lab, looking over things, checking and comparing the data they had gathered with the CCTV footage. He became caught up with cataloguing the kit, fascinated by the amount of equipment they'd either made / invented or adapted for this one experiment – marvelling at the amount of time and effort that so many people had put into it. He must have walked past Scott and Chloe's desks twenty times without saying a word to them, ignoring everyone else in the hub. When Tom next went back to his office, Scott jumped up to follow him, catching the door as Tom tried to close it behind him.

'Everything okay, mate?' Scott said, friendly but concerned.

'Yes, why wouldn't it be?' Tom's voice was clipped and business-like – almost robotic.

'Oh, y'know, you've been in for a couple of hours, it's the end of the working day and you haven't spoken to anyone, which is unlike you. Can I get you a coffee or something – you've not had one yet, and that's unheard of.' Scott was trying to be as light as possible and he thought his little joke would strike a chord with his friend.

'The world doesn't revolve around coffee, Scott, and as you can see I'm really busy so...' He raised his hands indicating the piles of data readings, CCTV discs and reports from the various departments on his desk.

'Right,' said Scott, totally lost for words. 'Okay. Later, I guess.'

Backing out of the doorway, he turned to look at Chloe with a shrug. The rest of the team looked at each other then slowly, steadily, started to drift away – turning off computers, grabbing jackets and bags. All wished Tom a cursory goodnight, lost in their own thoughts about how he really wasn't himself.

Tom sat in his office plotting EEG data against time for the experimental period, trying to correlate his memories with when his brain was most active. He wondered if he could extrapolate minutes of real time to the time he felt it had taken to fly across one star system and if, without any hard data collection from his experience, he could reasonably say that certain EEG peaks corresponded to certain parts of it. On the other hand, if he *had* left his body, EEG peaks would amount to nothing more than background brain activity, and be completely independent of his experience.

As he worked, Tom became aware of the sound of scratching in the room, like someone quickly drawing their fingernails along a worktop – not unpleasant like on a blackboard – but almost urgent, animalistic. Like a trapped rodent trying to scratch its way out from behind the walls. The sound must have been increasing imperceptibly for a little while, growing in the background, until loud enough for him to take notice.

Scratching scratching scratching away.

He got up from his desk and listened again, turning his head to try to find the source of the noise.

Scratching away, scratching away.

He moved across the room and listened again.

'Scratching scratching scratching away, scratching away, scratching away,' he sang to himself.

Scratching scratching scratching away, scratching scratching scratching.

The sound was no closer. He moved nearer to the door, and yes, it was coming from outside. He'd taken to closing his office door to hide away from the prying eyes, the whispers and heated moments, now he opened it and moved out into the hub, following the noise. Someone must've turned the main hub lights off on their way home, the only glow coming from illuminated fire exit signs and red lights on the door release switches. Tom walked out into the gloom.

Scratching scratching scratching away. The sound was everywhere but in turning left and right he was none the wiser as to its source. He moved across the hub, listening and turning, pushing through the doors into the observation room and the lab itself—into almost complete darkness. The observation room light was still on and the glow from the window illuminated a rectangle on the floor. Equipment stacked high, awaiting removal, cast eerie shadows into the far reaches of the long room. The hot and cold water tanks were shrink-wrapped neatly together with the pumping system and manifold – Charlie had packaged them up at the end of the previous week – and presumably they were awaiting pickup by Engineering. Presumably? For the first time in his department, he didn't know what was going on, and was completely out of the loop. Ordinarily he wouldn't have liked it, he was a control freak and liked to know everything that was happening down to the finest detail, but not now, it didn't seem to matter in the grand scheme of things, in the scale of the universe.

Scratching scratching scratching. The sound was louder in the lab, and was it coming from over there, from the other side of the bed?

'Scratching scratching scratching away, scratching away, scratching away,' he sang under his breath as he crossed the room, the sound not louder but seeming to come from all directions, as if he were surrounded by mice furiously trying to burrow through the walls. His hand throbbed, itching like a limb in plaster. The skin on his arm was red and swollen where he'd been scratching it, but he continued with some enthusiasm, finding it comforting. He slowly skirted around the tanks, their looming mass filling the centre of the room, creating complete darkness beyond. The bed was a dark shape, with the large storage unit and its stainless steel worktop against the far wall. Suddenly the temperature in the room dropped by at least five degrees. Like opening the door of a refrigerator and standing in the cold air. At that moment, he became aware of another presence in the room. He knew he wasn't alone. He hadn't heard the door open and hadn't seen anyone, but in the gloom at this end of the lab and with the light glowing from the Obs room at the far end, he couldn't make anything out. Something was there though.

'Hello?' he said, far more tentatively than he had meant, his voice catching slightly, and he realised how dry his throat was. And how his hand itched. 'Scratching scratching scratching away.' *Hang on, am I saying this out loud?* He wondered as he scratched his arm again.

'Hello?' he said, more clearly this time, stronger. 'Who's there?' He scanned the room, but there was so little contrast in the shapes in the darkness, it was impossible to decipher anything. Moving along the back wall, getting closer to the Obs room window and the double doors, he spun around to look back over his shoulder, checking where he'd been, searching his field of view. The scratching intensified, it was all around him, almost inside him now. He looked back to where he was going and a figure appeared before him, standing motionless in silhouette from the light from the Obs window. He caught his breath in surprise, staring at it, unable to move. The figure was large, well built, dressed in a hooded top and baggy trousers, like jogging pants.

'What do you want?' Tom shouted, trying to keep his voice even and not sounding afraid. 'What do you *want?*' He repeated. 'Get out! Go on, fuck off!' His restraint evaporating quickly as his anger and fear let fly in equal measure.

Hoody was motionless, making no movement or sound. Tom couldn't even see it breathing. In the silence between the two, he realised that the scratching sound was closing in around him, and the irritation in his wrist was unbearable. For an instant, Tom looked down at his arm as he scratched, before looking up again at the hooded figure. It was gone. In the split second he'd looked away the figure had disappeared – he hadn't sensed movement or the door opening and closing, it had just... gone. Tom realised how tightly he was holding himself, felt the tension he held in his body, his heart pounding in his chest. He exhaled for the first time in what seemed like an eternity and sagged back against the wall, trying to breathe evenly. His left hand stroked down over his mouth as his mind raced.

What the hell was Hoody? How had it got in? And more importantly; *how had it suddenly just gone?*

At least the scratching sound had disappeared. Tom gathered himself and decided against working alone any more tonight. Grabbing his coat and laptop, he hurried down the corridor to the lifts and home.

As Tom left through the double doors, Scott stepped out of the shadows from where he'd been watching since the others had left. He'd seen

Tom furtively searching the department, talking strangely to himself, heard him singing under his breath, obsessively scratching his arm, and witnessed the incident in the lab through the double doors – Tom screaming at something, yelling at it to fuck off. Was he seeing something? Was there something going on his head? Whatever it was, Scott was becoming increasingly worried about Tom's state of mind.

***

With shaking hands, Tom slipped the key into the door lock on the third attempt and let himself into the house. He'd been so distracted on the way home he couldn't remember a thing about the journey. But the important thing was that he was home, and it wouldn't be long now before he would sneak into bed with Sarah without disturbing her, and drift off to sleep. He dropped his laptop case on the worktop, locked the door and removed his coat and shoes. Drained from the evening, he went straight upstairs to get ready for bed. The upstairs hallway light was still on but dimmed, and their bedroom door was ajar. He pushed it open to see Sarah, sat up in bed reading, despite the late hour.

'Hi,' he said matter-of-factly. 'Thought you'd be asleep.'

She lowered the book, her eyes meeting his. 'I didn't want to go to bed on a row.'

He stepped toward the bed. 'Sarah, I'm sorry, I've just got to process so much of –'

'The hell with that Tom, look at your fucking arm!' She pointed at him, the other hand to her mouth. Tom looked down at his hands and immediately realised what'd alarmed his wife. His right forearm, was covered in large ugly scratches and red weals. The skin was shredded in places and was bleeding profusely. 'What the hell happened? My God.'

'It was at the lab...' Tom said simply, not really knowing how else to elaborate.

'Okay, come with me into the bathroom and let me look at those scratches.' She led him by the good hand and he, the eminent Cardiology surgeon, meekly let himself be treated by his non-medical wife.

'I saw something in the lab tonight, Sarah,' he said quietly.

'Mmhmm..?' she said scrutinising the wounds, her glasses perched on her nose – some of this was deep and might even need stitches.

'A figure – a person – it followed me into the main lab I think.'

'You think? Who? The Hoody?' she continued her evaluation.

'Yes. But I saw it for what it was tonight, for the first time; it isn't anybody. Or rather, it isn't supposed to be someone.'

Sarah looked up from his arm. 'What does *that* mean?'

He searched for the right words, those that wouldn't get him instantly committed. 'Remember when I first came round, I knew there was someone in the room, their presence made me get up and then I fell over –'

'You mean when you were feeling strange after you'd just been dead? When you were drugged up to the eyeballs? Then?' Sarah struggled to understand a lot of the things Tom had described recently. Yes, recent events must have had a profound psychological effect, but some of this stuff was too much for her to deal with. She took the first aid kit from the under-sink cupboard and opened a dressing pack.

'There *was* something – the door even moves on the CCTV!' he said earnestly, his eyes pleading with her, his soul-mate, to believe him.

'Okay, we've been through this, and there's no point in going over old ground again or starting another row. So, go on, tell me about tonight.' She rinsed his arm under the cold tap to wash away as much of the blood as she could. The white sink turned crimson, and she looked down at his gouged arm, diluted blood running in rivers into the basin. As the water ran over his skin, a large ripple travelled up his forearm, stretching the flesh, distorting it, like something burrowing underneath the surface. Startled, she let go of his arm, pulling away, looking up into Tom's face.

'You okay?' he asked.

'Er, yeah,' the forearm seemed normal again. Well, as normal as it could be under the circumstances. 'Carry on.'

'I got to the lab and everyone was really odd – behaving unnaturally around me. All I wanted to do was to get on – to start properly looking through the data. They acted like it was me that was being off.'

'Really?' She raised her eyebrows in mock surprise as she pulled on a pair of surgical gloves.

'Sarah – ' he began defensively.

'Okay, I'll stop. But you can see why they might go down the 'Tom's behaving strangely' kind of road, can't you..?' she said with a shrug, holding her gloved hands palms up to emphasise the point.

'I could have been a bit nicer I suppose, and Scott and I had a few words. Then everyone started to leave.'

'You argued with Scott?' she asked gently as she poured a sachet of wound-wash disinfectant over his arm.

'About coffee to start with, and not much else – I know I've been more short-tempered lately, but, well it might have cleared the air..?'

'Okay,' she said doubtfully. 'Then what?' She gently blotted his arm dry with several sterile swabs.

'They all left, and I sat in the office looking over some data for a while. I sat there and noticed a... scratching noise,' he looked up sheepishly.

'Scratching?' Sarah's eyebrows had been in a raised position so much over the last week or so, she thought she might never need a facelift.

'Like a rodent or something – kind of coming out of the hub, then in the corridor, then the main lab, and I just followed the noise. And it got worse, louder, fuller, you know?' Sarah had stopped dressing his arm and was watching him intently. She applied some steristrips to the worst of the wounds.

'This looks like self-harming Tom,' she whispered.

'I didn't even know I was doing it. In the lab the noise was so loud, and my arm was itching like anything. I must have been scratching all the time. Then Hoody appeared...'

'What did it look like?'

'A guy in a hoody and joggers.' he replied simply.

'And you're saying it couldn't have been anybody, nobody playing a prank or messing around? The same Hoody from Friday night?'

'No, it wasn't like a prank. It appeared, right in front of me, like me to you here and then vanished. I looked down for a second and, *pwoof*, gone. The same Hoody as I've been seeing.'

'So it left...'

'No, I only looked down for a split second and if anything moved, I would've noticed it from the corner of my eye. This thing disappeared. Like it hadn't been there.'

'Are you saying you aren't sure if it was there or not?'

'No, I saw it...'

Sarah looked sceptically at him.

'I'm seeing it all the time now, it seems that whenever I turn around it's there,' he mumbled, as if embarrassed to admit the number of encounters.

'What do you mean?'

'Remember when I went to see Mike Hughes, the day after, about my arm. I went to the orthopaedic wards looking for him while he was doing his rounds.'

'Yeah you told me about that – you said it just appeared.'

'That's right - it just walked out from a side room and stopped in the middle of the ward with its back to me. I would've hardly noticed but there was something about how it stood, out of place somehow. Then it turned around to face me, staring at me for a second or two. And my arm itched at the time, I remember now. I thought no more about it, obviously, there was no reason to. But now I remember scratching my arm quite hard. I remember because it just stood there and stared me down.'

'When you first told me about that I thought you'd just seen a guy, like just somebody else on the ward. But could it have been a student or someone, maybe, in a sweatshirt messing around, trying to get a rise out of someone – out of you because of who you are now?'

'No, it wasn't staged like that, it just appeared and turned and faced me and it was definitely Hoody, the same as today. It was weird because I didn't realise what it was at the time, and a figure turning wouldn't cause anyone to pause, but this thing just stood there, arms out to the side like a cowboy about to draw, and... yeah it was sneering at me, challenging me. It was looking down at me, maybe pitying me.'

'Isn't all that a bit of a leap, Tom?' Sarah put in. Surely he was reading too much into things.

Tom ignored her. 'Then it turned and disappeared off to the side. It was maybe ten feet from me, but by the time I got to where it was and looked along the ward, it had gone. There was no way it could've walked or even run to the end and got around the corner into the parallel ward in that time – no way. So I walked down the link corridor, looking in side rooms, the laundry store, the sluice, and there was no sign of it. And it wasn't, you know, something you see out of the corner of your eye that you later think; did I see it or didn't I? It was this guy stood right in front of me not ten feet away. I even asked at the nurses' station if they'd seen a visitor dressed like that, but they said no. Not that they would necessarily, but you get a feel for who's on your ward if they shouldn't be there – visitors, staff in different uniforms, that kind of thing. But no, they said there hadn't been anyone.'

Sarah looked down at Tom's arm as she busied herself with his dressing, unable to say anything. After an uncomfortable silence, he spoke again.

'I can guess what the guys in the lab are saying and what they're thinking. But tissue hypoxia and perfusion are where I work every day, and I'm very aware of what it can do to the body and the personality. Yes, it does sound like I've had a hypoxic brain episode and paranoia and psychosis *can* result from that. Maybe I *have* had a hypoxic episode or a big stroke and I'm being paranoid and need help and treatment. But right now, I don't need you doubting me and looking at me like I'm crazy or feeling sorry for me. I need somebody on my side, babe, on my team, because it's like me against the whole fucking world at the moment.' Sarah tried to catch hold of his arm as he waved it around, gesticulating at her, steristrips half applied and fresh blood appearing in parts of the wounds she'd already dried.

'Will you keep still!' she commanded, putting her hand on his arm. He relaxed a little.

'I want you to believe me, or at least believe that is what *I* think happened. That'll do right now.' He looked deep into her eyes, making her uncomfortable with his intensity. 'I want you to believe me wholeheartedly, but I would imagine you can't do that. Not yet. But I need you to try. I've genuinely seen all this stuff, this thing, it was there, it's haunting the shadows of my vision wherever I am. And whether it's there in my head as a projection or something, it's there, because of what happened during the experiment. It's as if... something came back with me.'

Sarah turned away and exhaled, her mind racing, evaluating everything he said and every aspect of his demeanour. 'You're right – what you're saying sounds crazy... like you've watched too many B-movies late on a Friday night. You really don't wanna search my Google history from the past week because I've looked up more stuff on brain hypoxia and the psychological effects of stroke in the young and a load of other things. But you did this because you wanted to mimic the experiences of other people. The one thing that makes me think you experienced this to some extent, whether it's because of chemical changes in the brain like you said or your own perception, is because the whole thing was your idea. This could even be something like you were trying to show in the first place – that chemical changes in the brain occur and affect your experience. So what if this hooded thing is the manifestation of a chemical change in your brain from the prolonged hypoxia?'

'Bob's got a lot more of a point than I thought he had – this is about how you perceive things. But then again it's not. The whole near-death thing, I'm more and more convinced that... we go somewhere. And I don't care what you call it,' he blew his cheeks out in an explosive sigh. 'As non-religious as we are, I'm not calling it heaven, because it didn't feel like that. It just felt like the end, and the folks at the other end of that one-way ticket aren't going to take too kindly to me saying 'no thanks I'll just go back home now'. And that's what I think has happened – something at the far side has come back. Believe me or not, call it chemical changes, call it perception. Whether it's what I used to believe or what Bob still believes – fine, I don't care, I just need you to believe me and not think I'm going crazy and becoming a raving fucking madman.' He had been rambling as she finished his dressing, watching her hands work on his wounds, and now he looked her in the eyes once again. 'Can you?'

'Yes, yes I can,' she smiled at him, stroking his arm above the bandaging. 'What I know for sure is that you are Tom – the man I married. You're still the same Tom – my husband – from before, but something's changed in you. Whatever happened has changed you. I don't think you're mad because you seem perfectly lucid to me, and surely you would have other symptoms – other physical symptoms – if you'd had a significant brain injury, so no I don't think that's the case either. But I don't know what's going on. So, yes I'll be on your side, but you've not got to shut me out, okay?' Their faces were almost touching, and they kissed gently, Tom nodding by way of reply.

And with little else to say, and exhausted on every level, they went to bed.

15.

There was a knock on Bob Wauberg's office door.

'Come in,' his voice sounded clearly in the minimalist room. Many of the offices in the research facility were wall-to-wall glass, but some staff and research subjects confided in him here, as if in a clinic environment. In order to maintain patient privacy, Bob had specified that he needed a more traditional office room. It had white painted walls, two streamlined leather chairs with smooth metal arms and a small desk in the corner with a floating bookshelf behind. He used a similar clinic room in the main hospital for his regular list of patients.

The door opened and in walked Sarah.

'Sarah! Hi.' Bob beamed, getting up from his desk. 'An unexpected pleasure.' His American drawl always sounding charming.

'I'm sorry to just turn up unannounced, Bob –' She had woken this morning to find Tom gone, with precious little evidence he had been there at all aside from a couple of blood stains on the bed sheets where his dressings had leaked. Sarah had seen from the upstairs landing that the Jeep wasn't there either, so she suspected he had left much earlier – somehow without disturbing her – and he could never normally do that. Downstairs she'd found a scribbled note that read:

```
I love you, all three of you, and I'm sorry
that I ever started this.
I have to sort this out. Either way I'm not
```

```
safe  to  be  around  until  I  can  stop  Hoody,
whoever/whatever it is and however I do it.
Will see you all soon.
T x
```

'Not at all, Sarah, you're welcome here anytime, come in and sit down,' Bob indicated one of the chairs. The tight, shiny white fabric was straight out of the seventies and something that Bob had sourced himself to maintain a lightness in the room that black leather would spoil. The American sat opposite her in the matching chair, crossing his legs. 'What can I do for you?' He smiled, meeting her gaze, probing her with his eyes.

'I need to talk to you about Tom. Have you seen him?' Her large eyes were wide, and she was clearly frightened.

'Yes,' he nodded.

'To speak to?' she sounded a little hurt.

'Yes.' He linked his hands together on his abdomen. 'Not in a specific consultation sense, but we have spoken a couple of times since the events of last week.'

'Well, how does he seem, what's he saying, do you think there's anything wrong or anything I should be worried about?' Her exasperation bubbled to the surface.

'I have to be careful, Sarah, because he has confided in me, and so I can't reveal the details of that, but whilst I can't comprehend what he says he has seen, I'm not concerned about his sanity per se.'

'He says he's flown halfway across the universe, Bob, in such detail. And he believes it so much that he gets incredibly aggressive or hurt if you say otherwise,' Sarah was talking rapidly, clearly agitated.

'He's been through a lot. Physically, his body's been on the brink of death. That was the essence of his experiment. So he must recover from that in whatever ways he needs to. Mentally, he's been to a place only a few have been – he'll definitely have taken his own baggage in there with him.' Bob gestured with his hands, like a conductor, to emphasise the points of his argument. 'And brought some back with him too.'

'What if he dreamed it?'

'Yes. A construct of his mind, yes absolutely, something that the brain uses to ease the enormity and fear of one's passing. His is a much more detailed account than any of the other subjects he's studied, but as Tom has said, he was well, healthy, and atuned to recording his observations. So it's entirely possible that it should be detailed. The very validity of his results is open to question because of his own pre-conceived ideas of what he would see, of course. His experience would always have been biased.'

'What do you mean?' she sat forward in her seat.

'Okay, Tom was preparing for this for a long time. He knew he was going to 'die'.' Bob's hands made the sign for quotation marks. 'This meant his consciousness and sub-conscious could prepare in a way that most people's never have the opportunity to do. He may have had detailed ideas of what he might experience, locked away in his head, and just ticked those boxes while he was 'out'.' More quotations marks. 'What I mean is that if Tom believed he was going to see white light and arms reaching out, if his sub-conscious was looking for imagery to feed him at the brink of death, those images may well have come to the fore rather than anything else.'

'The Marshmallow Man from *Ghostbusters*, you mean?' she asked.

'Remind me.'

'The dweeby guy near the end has to choose the shape that the bad guy takes as he comes to Earth to destroy the place, and everyone's telling him to clear his mind, but he can't quite get rid of the image of the Marshmallow man – and that's what appears to destroy New York,' she shrugged.

'Yes I remember – and whilst *Ghostbusters* wasn't exactly a documentary, it's the same idea. It's been my argument all along – perception versus biochemistry.' He smiled – pleased to have almost proved himself right.

'So you're right and he's wrong?' Sarah was a little incredulous that even in these circumstances, Bob would want to get one over on Tom.

'Not at all, what I'm saying is that the experiment couldn't be unbiased, and so we can never say for definite what he really saw. The only way for us to know for sure is to have actual footage of what he's seen or to see it for ourselves, which is obviously not possible.'

They paused as questions hung in the air, the breeze blew through the open windows of the office, gently flapping the blinds, and bringing with it the faint sounds traffic in the hospital grounds.

'There are other things, too,' she whispered, after a lengthy silence.

'What other things?' he reverted to psychologist mode again. Sarah tried to speak, but her throat closed and strangled the sound. She bit her lip and squeezed her eyes tightly shut, tilting her head to the ceiling, wringing her hands and wrestling with herself. Should she go any further with this or not? Bob got up without speaking, walked over to the water reservoir in the corner and filled a small plastic cup. He set it down next to her on the table. He returned to his seat and leant forward, putting his hand on hers in her lap. 'Whilst you're a friend and not my patient, Sarah, I'll naturally afford you the same levels of confidentiality as if you were. So if you're comfortable talking to me, whatever you say will stay in this room.' He had the reassuring face and manner that made people want to talk to him – one of the reasons for his success – and as she looked into his eyes, she felt herself sag with relief as she decided to unburden herself.

'When we have sex...' she paused again, tears rolling down her cheeks. She shook her head to clear her thoughts, took a sip of water and started again. 'We have a really good sex life. We don't do it all the time and we don't do crazy things, but we do enjoy each other physically.'

'It's simple,' he summarised with a shrug.

'Yes.'

'Vanilla sex.'

'Whatever that means,' she half laughed through her tears.

'Nothing kinky.'

'I don't own a schoolgirl's uniform, no,' she did laugh this time.

He smiled. 'Could it be boring?'

'No. No! Definitely not. We make love, yes we do, but sometimes it can be very full-on, you know, like we really *fuck*!' She looked at him defiantly, blushing but slightly afronted. Their sex life *boring*?

'There was no criticism implied in that, Sarah, I just want to establish the scenario, and perhaps how Tom might see things. Anyway, I made you digress. Please, continue.' He opened his hands out toward her, inviting her to carry on.

'We hadn't slept together since he came back. It'd only been a couple of days, and we don't have a routine anyway, it's just when the mood takes. But he would always, I don't know, give me a kiss when he got in, touch the small of my back or let his hand slide over my shoulder as I walked past, little affectionate things, and he hadn't done any of that. And *before*, he was so tender, and... well, horny I guess.' She smiled fondly.

'Channelling some nervous energy, perhaps?'

'Yeah maybe. Still, him being so attentive one day, and the next being so distant, working all the time or exhausted was very strange. He wasn't taking any notice of me at all – or the boys – like we barely existed. But the night before last, he... forced himself on me. No, well, not like that. I wanted to and it started off like it was before, but he seemed to change and he got so aggressive, so rough, like he's never been before,' her voice grew quiet, sounding embarrassed.

'He couldn't have been experimenting, trying something different – a fantasy?'

'No. No. It was more than that, like he wanted to treat me just how he wanted, to use me and that was it, move on to the next thing – and he's never like that. The night before the experiment, we made love almost like we never had; amazing, tender, passionate and considerate. The next time it was like some kind of rape fantasy.'

'But it wasn't a fantasy?'

'No.'

'What do you think, Sarah?'

'I don't really know what to think. Afterwards I was upset, and since then, when I've thought about it – I don't know. I'm angry with him. It wasn't acceptable behaviour. I don't want to share a house – or a bed – with someone who might think that was okay, you know? But part of me wants to support the husband who's done these amazing things, and, whatever he's experienced – real or not – it's still incredible.' She looked up, both hurt and confused. Bob nodded his agreement. 'He's very different though, now.'

'Different all the time – like a TV show that replaces one actor with another – who says the same things but is different in how he says them? Or different some of the time? Sometimes he's Tom, sometimes he's 'different' Tom?'

'Like he's 'I've had a fucking stroke', Tom. Different all the time, in every way – yes like when you get a new actor. I don't know him since he came back. He can be reasonable and pleasant when we do eventually talk, and he wants my help and support, but he's still not Tom. And there's more...'

'Go on.'

'He's seeing things... like someone else is in the room.' This really did make him sound like a crazy person, she thought.

'At home?'

'Everywhere. He says sometimes, out of the corner of his eye, or in a shadow or something, he sees someone else. Then he goes over there, and there's no one. Well, of course there's no one fucking there. It's happened at work, too. The other night I was woken up by this massive sound of banging on the patio doors. I went downstairs and Tom said someone had been there, that someone else had made the noise – but his old cricket bat was on the floor by his feet all broken up.'

'He told me it felt like déjà vu, but he was looking at things from two different parts of the same room at the same time,' Bob ventured.

'Are you allowed to tell me that?' Sarah showed mock surprise.

'Grey area,' Bob rotated his hands and made a quizzical face to emphasise the unknown quantity of the new brand of ethics he had just made up. 'And you think it's just him, he's making it up in some way?'

'As opposed to the other option..? Is it something to do with this angel?' she asked.

'The what?' Bob raised his eyebrows – something new.

'The angel that grabbed his hand when he was out,' *Where have you been, Bob?*

'Is that what he's called it?' he sat forward, interest piqued.

'Yes, he described it, the whole flying through space thing, to the centre of the Milky Way, into that giant star, and there being millions of hands reaching out to guide him in. He said it was so magical and welcoming that maybe this is what angels were.'

'Wow. He hadn't described it quite like that to me.'

'Did something grab his hand, Bob?' Her fingers absently picked at themselves, and he noticed red sores around the nail beds, looking like she had been doing it for a while.

'He certainly has an injury to his wrist – that's been proven on MRI. How did it happen? Did he fake it by going home and crushing his wrist in a door?' He threw his hands up in the air. 'Who knows, Sarah.'

'But the CCTV..?'

'The strange movement of his wrist when he got shocked?' She nodded. 'It could be something happened then, but I don't think that strange shudder of the film as his body is jerking wildly is a definitive indicator of him breaking his arm.'

'And what about the other footage?'

'What other footage?' Bob wore a puzzled expression – he'd watched it on the feed but not with any great analysis.

'On the CCTV of the theatre room, as soon as Tom first comes round, Shirley the nurse goes up to him. They have a conversation – she's obviously reassuring him and she takes his Obs.'

'Okay...' Bob shrugged slightly, not seeing where this was going.

'She lifts up his hand – his right hand – to take his pulse, and as she applies pressure to his wrist to take the pulse – he cries out in pain.'

'Okay. I hadn't noticed that.' *How hadn't he seen that?*

'And it was an old injury.' She added.

'What do you mean? I thought Tom said it happened when he was out?' Further puzzlement.

'Yes, apparently it did, but Andy Bullman, the hand surgeon, said the bone had started to heal and it looked to him like it might be a month or so old.'

'And it can't be, right? That's what you're telling me?' Bob's whole analysis of Tom's perception was being taken apart.

'His hand was fine. He and Charlie moved the water tanks around the lab the day before and you know how heavy they are.' They looked at each other in silence, the blinds flapping and the traffic noise slowly rising to a roar in their ears.

***

The sticky warmth of the late evening didn't relent when the sun disappeared over the treetops. The weatherman on the radio listed statistics about the 'warmest September since records began'. Henry found it interesting that they never actually bothered to say when the records *had* begun. Surely it would be better to say that it was a record for the last hundred years or whatever – at least it would give you some perspective. What if the records only started two years ago?

Henry and Tilda Dawson had once again barbecued on the rear patio of their house after Henry had meticulously mowed his lawn – something that approached a military operation in terms of precision and orders, but usually involved fewer casualties. The whole cutting in two directions at two different mower settings and strimming the edges took two hours on the nose for their moderately-sized garden – a new build in the first flush of suburban growth some twenty years before. These days, even the so-called 'executive' new houses only had postage stamp gardens and Henry always reckoned they would get two houses on their plot if they wanted. As Henry mowed, so Tilda weeded pots and hanging baskets, arranged trailing petunias to fall to meet climbing late-flowering honeysuckle and fed hungry containers of begonias and French marigolds. With precision timing (as usual) Henry finished Operation Fescue and strolled across to uncover his gas-powered outdoor grill; a significant upgrade on his previous barbecue and one that could cook in more ways than Gordon Ramsay. It was also probably bigger than any cooker the TV chef had ever owned as well. *All of this for the two of us?* Tilda had asked Henry of the gas-guzzling monster last year when he bought it, and had then watched the rain pouring off the plastic cover for what seemed like the whole of the summer. Not so this year. Al fresco cooking had been the norm for weeks now, and Tilda looked ever wider afield for new recipes and marinades to stop Henry's barbecuing fetish from becoming boring.

After another magnificent example of dead animals being incinerated to within a whisker of being carcinogens, Henry had allowed his toy to cool before wrapping it up in its cover, while Tilda loaded the dishwasher. *Far more washing-up when we cook outside, Henry,* she always said. By the time they had cleared away it was fully dark and Henry's thoughts turned to getting the cat in.

The figure watched him from the cover of the bushes. The pungent smells of clematis, choisya, and phlox creating a heady, almost sickly sweet smell in the late evening. It watched as Henry bustled into the study room through the open French doors, switching on lamps to illuminate the whole room. The glow bathed the patio in a soft light until Henry went back outside to finish putting away unused barbecue utensils, when the security light mounted on the wall overhead deluged the whole of the paved area in brilliant white light, as if the mother ship were about to beam him up. The figure bided its time and waited, standing motionless, observing human activity with interest. It became aware of a cat at its feet which hissed and growled as it circled around in the bushes before bolting back toward the house with a screech. Surprised at the crazed animal darting for cover under the grill, Henry looked toward the garden for anything that might have startled it.

'Bloody cat,' he said with some affection and ushered the wild-eyed moggy inside.

These days a couple of weekday glasses of wine were enough to see both of them snoring in their armchairs before the Inspector Morse re-run was even half way through, so they both decided to call it a night. Henry went back outside, leaning chairs against the patio table and lowering the parasol in case the weather turned inclement overnight. He still didn't realise he was being watched while he pottered, the figure growing bolder, moving to the cover of bushes closer to the house.

Tilda cleaned her teeth in their en-suite bathroom, looking at her reflection in their large illuminated mirror. They hardly used their master bathroom any more, now the kids had left home. She finished brushing, spat, rinsed with mouthwash and spat again, returning next door to her bedroom. She walked toward the window to close the blinds, something they always did, although for no real privacy reason, the nearest garden overlooking them was so far away that she could dance topless in front of the window and no one would see. *That would be a shame*, she thought, smiling to herself, as she still considered herself in pretty good shape at sixty-five. She reached for the string on the blinds and her gaze drifted down onto the wide expanse of freshly mown lawn. As she looked she noticed something strange in the silhouettes below her, although she couldn't exactly put her finger on what. Then she noticed a shadow on the lawn toward the patio, a shadow that wasn't usually there when she looked from the bathroom. And then it moved, slowly, from the edge of the lawn, creeping forward. It crouched low, trying to reduce its bulk, but was very obvious from above. The glow from the security light illuminated the top half of the figure – it was a person in a dark hooded sweatshirt. Quickly she left the blinds and ran to the top of the stairs.

'Henry,' she hissed in a stage whisper down to where her husband was making a noise dragging furniture around – he had to have everything just so. 'Henry!' she called, more urgently this time, less concerned about letting the prowler know that his cover was blown.

'Yes?' he called back into the study and up the stairs. Tilda didn't reply, so he came back into the house and saw his wife at the top of the stairs, as white as a sheet. 'Is everything okay, love?' He asked, concerned.

'There's someone in the garden.' She hissed in full stage whisper again. 'I've just seen them on the lawn by the side of the garage.' Henry nodded, and turned immediately to go back outside again, stopping at the sill of the patio doors.

'Hello?' he said, his attempt at a strong commanding voice faltering slightly, the words catching in his throat. 'Hello?' he tried again, more successfully this time. 'I know where you are, and I'm phoning the police, so just leave.' He called over to the shadows where Tilda had seen the interloper, watching for any sign of movement but saw nothing. Henry looked into the house at Tilda, standing motionless on the stairs, staring back at him. He shrugged and stepped onto the patio. Fairly confident now that Tilda's eyesight and the Shiraz had combined to find a fiend, he strode out between planters and the sundial, reaching the edge of the lawn. He glanced up at Tilda, who now looked down from their bedroom window, and raised his thumb. Henry turned away from the house and resumed his 'closing-up' for the day. Satisfied that whoever she had seen had been scared off, Tilda returned to her dressing table where she applied moisturiser and body lotion then brushed her hair. She wondered where Henry had got to. The intruder had clearly been scared off, so why was he taking so long? She suspected that he was clearing up cat shit from the borders. Henry loved that bloody cat, and she tolerated it and its indulgences for his sake. If any other animal defecated on his flower beds, however, he would machine-gun the bastard. She heard a noise coming from the direction of the patio. Startled at first, Tilda couldn't work out what it was or whether it was coming through the open window of their bedroom or from up the stairs through the still open French doors. She heard the noise again, and she knew this time it was the cat, making a wild screeching sound at a high pitch, exactly like he did when the other tom cat from down the road ventured into their garden, spoiling for a fight. These fights were apt to happen at around 3am, so at least she was thankful for small mercies tonight, but why were they doing it with Henry around, and why wasn't he putting a stop to it? Tilda decided to give him a few more minutes to come upstairs before going to see what was going on.

Satisfied that any intruder – probably the aggressive-looking shadow of an azalea or something – was now long gone, Henry got out the little metal shovel he used for filling their coal scuttle. It had to be smokeless fuel though these days, or some fucker from the council would be round to wave regulations at you. In the summer months, with the stove in the lounge out of action, he used the shovel to flick cat droppings into a compost bag. As he moved away from the patio, searching in the beam from the security light above, he heard rustling coming from the bushes at the side of the garage. He looked up and saw movement from within – the damned cat – he turned and looked back to the house to see if there was any sign of him. Suddenly a figure burst out of the bushes and raced across the lawn at incredible speed, leaping over a row of flower pots to land on the patio, narrowly avoiding the cat's tail as it did so, the cat hissing angrily in response. The figure landed right in front of Henry who was rapidly retreating towards the house. Startled, Henry looked up at the person in the hooded jumper, instantly recognising the face.

'Tom? What are you do – urgghh.' The figure grabbed Henry around the throat and started to strangle him, crushing any further sound he might make by pressing hard on his windpipe. Henry grabbed at the vice-like hands, trying to claw them free of his throat as the pressure was already squeezing the life out of him. The hooded figure was strong, overpowering him, and despite his struggles, slowly pushed him toward the ground, Henry's legs buckling as his strength waned. He reached up towards the face of his attacker, trying to push him away, or to scratch it – to cause pain and make him stop. The Hoody squeezed tighter and Henry's struggles were like trying to fight against an iron bar, held as he was in a vice-like grip. He kicked and writhed with his body, desperate to free himself as his consciousness began to fade like lowering a dimmer switch. His hand caught against something, and vaguely, somewhere in his recollection he knew it was Tiger, hissing and spitting at the intruder. The faintest of lights switched on in his head as fog encroached his line of vision, his field of view closing in, and he became more and more detached from reality. He grasped Tiger by the nape of the neck and in a moment of pure self-preservation, with all his remaining strength, threw the cat at his attacker, the startled animal flying through the air even more angry and distressed than before. The hands loosened their grip from around his windpipe, and Henry was relieved, believing it to be over. But then he was jolted from his reverie as he realised something was being pushed into his mouth – forced in under great pressure, his jaw being brutally shoved wide open, breaking teeth and crushing the roof of his mouth as it was rammed in, choking him now not from strangulation but from the obstruction of his airway. His strength was fading, but he still tried to claw at the hooded figure, tried to pull at the obstruction to prevent it being pushed further and further into his throat. He was completely incredulous that this was happening, that it should end this way, at his own house, in his own garden. Then he tasted fur in his mouth. His mind faltered further, starved of oxygen, bizarrely aware that the obstruction, as it was pushed further inside him, was writhing wildly in his mouth and around his face. He felt pain all around there, searing, sharp, stinging pain, and it was the last thing he was aware of before he lost consciousness.

Tilda lay in bed, waiting for Henry to join her, but when he still hadn't come upstairs she got up to chide him for getting sidetracked with either the news on the computer or by an article on his desk. She hoped she wasn't going to catch him on some adult chat room again – as if the get-up and go hadn't got-up and gone already in Henry's case. Or maybe it hadn't, maybe he needed a younger model than her to get him going?

She walked from the stairs into the back of the house – the kitchen in darkness to her left, the illuminated study in front of her leading to the brightly lit patio with the French doors still wide open.

'Henry!' Tilda called, not suppressing the exasperation in her voice to have had to come down to find out what was taking him so long to come to bed – the cat or Sexy Suzie?

The harsh blue-white security light illuminated the patio beyond the open doors. Henry lay on his back, one leg draped over a plant pot, crushing the Japanese maple tree it contained. She screamed at the condition of her husband and that he was very obviously dead. It took a second or two to realise what had happened to his face, but, as the later-printed morning papers would report, it seemed that most of their cat had been shoved down his throat. Tiger, in his dying moments and in a final attempt at self-preservation, had kicked and scrabbled with his back legs to try and extricate himself from Henry's mouth. As he'd struggled to gain purchase for his feet on Henry's skin, he had sloughed off most of his owner's face with his claws, taking with it muscle tissue, cartilage from his nose exposing the bone, and excavating an eyeball. The horrific mess containing the one remaining eyeball stared lifelessly back at his wife. The pathologist later said that the force used to push the cat into Henry's throat had been so great as to not only crush the animal's skull, finally killing it, but had also ripped Henry's windpipe apart.

Tilda stood motionless, staring at her husband's body, unaware of anything other than her heart hammering in her rib-cage, the tightness in her lungs enveloping her, constricting her chest and preventing her from breathing. Finally, she shook off the choking pressure she felt and screamed. She sensed a movement in the garden, looked beyond the security light and suddenly saw a figure, illuminated, if just for a second, a small glimpse of the likely perpetrator of this terrible act. Somebody she instantly recognised.

16.

Sarah woke up after a restless night alone in bed to yet another sunny late summer day. She pulled back the curtains, recoiling from the bright sunlight as if she were one of the undead. The boys were on good form and Nicktoons was soon filling the den with noise as she waited for the kettle to boil. On autopilot, she picked up her phone to check for messages and emails, immediately ignoring three missed calls from an unknown number and the promise of new voicemail when she saw the news feed. She opened the web-page with fear clutching at her heart, the headline – Eminent Doctor Slain at Home – screaming at her. Ordinarily this type of headline wouldn't even cause her to raise a browsing finger, but on this occasion the name on the news feed did – Henry. She scrolled down the page, reading what little had been released to the media.

Professor Henry Dawson was brutally murdered last night at his home. Police and forensic teams are at the scene while his widow, Mrs Tilda Dawson, is being comforted by friends and neighbours.

She immediately thought of Tom. *Henry.* They had never liked each other, and didn't Tom say they'd argued on Friday? Feeling numb she took the boys to school and then phoned in sick to the gallery, scrolling past some more missed calls to do so. The past few weeks having taken their toll and today being the last of many straws. She needed some time to reflect on recent events: the offer to Tom to continue supporting him being in stark contrast to the concerns she had for his state of mind; how he was getting worse, his obsessions with this Hoody, how he was seeing things, perhaps even inventing things that happened when he had done them himself; then disappearing and now Henry was dead. It couldn't be Tom, could it? No matter how much he was obsessed with what had happened to him, he couldn't have gone this crazy. Could he? But what if he had been on the edge, ready to snap, and something had tipped him over? She made herself a cup of green tea and took a long shower. She couldn't face breakfast.

Sarah continued to read news updates, repeatedly hitting refresh on her phone, but it brought nothing new. The day reached late morning and the doorbell rang. Sarah answered after the second ring to reveal two men in suits, standing waving badges to announce themselves as police officers.

'Mrs Boyand?'

'I'm Sarah Boyand.'

'I'm Detective Inspector Morgan Archer, this is Detective Constable Kevin Walker.' Archer was the taller of the two and dressed in a navy suit, the shorter man, the constable, in light grey. 'May we come in for a few minutes, Mrs Boyand –'

'*Dr* Boyand,' Sarah corrected – she rarely used her title, unless she needed to demonstrate some authority. Today she used it because she wondered why two detectives were standing on her doorstep.

'I beg your pardon, *Dr* Boyand, may we come in? I have some questions for you.' The inspector smiled a smile that turned into the condescending grin reserved for the condemned.

'Regarding?'

'Regarding the death of Professor Henry Dawson.' The inspector countered, the smile now faded as he sensed a lack of cooperation.

'Okay, you had better come in.' A pair of regulation brown crew cuts crossed her doorstep and Sarah showed them into the den, offering them coffee which they both declined.

'We wondered if we might take a look around, Dr Boyand?' The constable piped up, jumping in with both feet.

'Why?'

'To get a feel for the place, for your husband, to see if we might find anything that might help us in our enquiries,' smiled Archer in a thin-lipped unfriendly manner. *Slimy bastard.*

'Why might anything about my husband help you with your enquiries, Inspector? Don't you need a warrant for something like that, anyway?' Sarah retorted.

'Are you telling me I need one?' he asked.

'Please forgive my ignorance of these things, but it seems a little unusual that two police officers turn up on my doorstep and immediately want to poke around my house without giving me any justification?' Sarah paused for a second or two, about to relent, then did a mental u-turn – she had said she would support Tom, and she would. 'So, yes, I would say you need a warrant.'

'I can come back straight away with a warrant but that would just waste everyone's time.'

'Don't you need good reason to get a warrant, like hard evidence to present to a judge or something like probable cause as the American TV shows call it – am I wrong?'

'Dr Boyand, we are investigating a particularly horrible crime, and your husband appears to have an issue with the victim, which might be a motive. If you help us, we can eliminate your husband from our enquiries sooner rather than later.' Sarah stared at them both for a few seconds.

'Perhaps you had better enlighten me,' she said, icily.

'Last night, as Mrs Dawson was getting ready for bed, from her upstairs bedroom window she saw a hooded figure sneaking around the garden. She alerted her husband. That hooded figure broadly fitted your husband's description.'

'You said the figure was hooded?' she asked.

'Yes that's right.' He looked down to check on his notepad.

'So that means that the figure had his hood up, covering his head?'

'Yes, Mrs Dawson believes so.'

'So how did they 'broadly fit my husband's description'? Other than he was probably a man with two arms and two legs? Have you asked Mrs Dawson how well she knows Tom? Don't bother, because she doesn't. She's only met him once, and that night he was wearing black tie.' She looked back and forth between the two officers. 'So has she seen a picture of Tom in a hoody outside our house in the press and put two and two together? Or has she heard her husband moaning about Tom not playing ball with the establishment at the university, and him describing Tom wearing a hoody on the day of the experiment, and similarly done the maths? Not exactly evidence is it? And then you come sniffing around here? So what exactly are you accusing him of?'

Archer stared at Sarah. 'Mrs Dawson alerted her husband to the intruder, and he went to investigate. The hooded figure seemed to have disappeared. A short time later, while getting ready for bed, Mrs Dawson heard their cat making a noise, as if distressed and involved in some kind of altercation. She made her way down the stairs, hearing sounds of a scuffle, and found the hooded person bent over her husband, and they were choking him with his own cat.' Archer seemed oblivious to inaccuracies in Mrs Dawson's account, and it was a mark of the man that he had taken rather less than meticulous care with her statement.

'Your husband is of interest, Dr Boyand, because Mrs Dawson positively identified him to us last night. We know that Professor Dawson has made life difficult for Tom in terms of his recent experiment – we've found this out from his colleagues at the university. That in itself would suggest motive.' DC Walker added.

'Hang on a second, you've spoken to them already?' Sarah sounded surprised.

'Yes. We would have preferred to speak to you first, and we tried to reach you both earlier this morning but to no avail.' Sarah looked down at her phone and thought of the missed calls. 'So we visited the lab instead to see if your husband was there, and managed to speak to some of his colleagues.' Archer curled a thin-lipped smile and continued. 'Your husband met with Professor Dawson on Friday, I understand. At that meeting there was an argument and some shouting within the confines of Mr Boyand's office. Do you know anything about that?' Archer met Sarah's gaze.

'No, I don't, sorry.' She shook her head.

'Tom's colleagues heard raised voices and saw Professor Dawson storm out of the office. Nobody knows what that meeting was about, however, and that might be crucial if there is a case against your husband.'

'Henry was extremely antagonistic towards my husband – he disapproved strongly of his work.'

'So motive for murder perhaps?' Archer was like a dog finding a scent.

'Don't let anyone convince you that Henry was a saintly victim in all this. He was a brilliant man and I am sorry that he's dead. But he rubbed plenty of people up the wrong way and trampled over many a career to get where he is today. So if anybody is presenting him to be a well-loved popular guy in his death – that isn't the case. If you wanted to get together all the people Henry has stepped on, or who had an axe to grind, you're going to need a pretty big room.'

'So your husband wasn't angry with Professor Dawson?' Walker interjected.

'Henry was all bluster. He did make Tom angry at times, it would be wrong to say otherwise, but Henry wasn't Tom's superior. Tom is a researcher on his own project, so doesn't really report to anyone.'

'It is our understanding that Professor Dawson approved all the research work in the university hospital, and had the power to cancel any work that was being undertaken?' Archer's eyes bored into hers.

'That's true to an extent, but the hospital wouldn't fund Tom's work, so he brought in his own private funding. Once the research got past the Ethics Committee stage, there was almost nothing that Henry could do to stop it. Effectively, all Tom was doing was hiring the room.'

'So Professor Dawson was powerless?'

'Yes, to a great extent. Henry didn't like that because he liked to exercise power over people, and whilst he tried, it didn't work with Tom.'

'But surely as a senior figure at the university and one with a remit for research, Professor Dawson had the authority to stop the research if he felt it necessary?' Archer raised his eyebrows.

'Yes, ultimately, but Tom would have just taken it elsewhere, and Henry didn't want that. As much as he didn't like the idea of what Tom was doing, he wanted the kudos for any findings that the work produced, so the hospital could claim them as their own.'

'So Professor Dawson was little more than an annoyance to Tom?'

'Pretty much, yes.'

'His widow says that Mr Boyand was angry about how her husband tried to bring him into line, and that it threatened him.'

'Well that's a line that Henry and his ego will have told his wife.

Depends on whose wife you believe, Inspector,' she smiled sweetly at him.

'If I can take you back to the day of the experiment. We know your husband was wearing a brown hooded sweatshirt and blue tracksuit bottoms. Mrs Dawson described the hooded individual as wearing exactly the same clothing at her house last night.' Archer quoted from his pocket book.

'Come on, is that all you've got? You've got Tom being annoyed at Henry and a guy wearing a hoody and tracksuit bottoms, which you'd probably describe as clothing that a lot of guys will tend to wear when they aren't in work. Have you got a hoody and jogging bottoms, Inspector?'

'Look, Mrs Boyand –'

'Dr Boyand.' *Don't mess with my wife, as Tom would always say.*

The police officer nodded, standing corrected. 'Dr Boyand, at this stage in our enquiry, we have some eyewitness accounts which we're trying to corroborate and we've gathered some evidence. In relation to this your husband is a person of interest to us. That is all.'

'At this stage Inspector you've got nothing at all apart from a distressed woman who could've seen anything, and you're trying to put two and two together from watching a press conference. Then, somehow, you think you've got enough hard evidence to get a warrant. That's quite a leap.' She had them on the ropes now.

'Where was your husband on Tuesday evening, Dr Boyand?' he asked.

'As far as I know he was at work,' Sarah replied quietly.

'As far as you know? But you don't know for sure?' Archer was very interested now, like a very interested dog spying a very tasty rabbit.

'Yes, he went into work early and he stayed throughout the night.'

'Okay, like a twenty-four hour shift. Wow. Is that a usual thing for him to do, would he ordinarily do that – go into the office and stay for a day?' Walker looked impressed.

'Yes and no, he was very much a living for the moment type of guy,' he *was*, she suddenly realised his presence had shifted tenses – *when the hell did he die again?* 'He had a massive amount of data to analyse from the study, from cameras, life support, medical notes, drugs analysis, tissue samples, and he was trying to relate this to his own experience. He is very driven because this has been his baby entirely, and he feels a direct responsibility to analyse the data and start making conclusions as soon as possible – particularly with the press interest. With this current study, though, all of the data, all of the information gathered was on the local departmental server – something they had done to make sure results didn't get circulated throughout the hospital. Tom hadn't downloaded it because there was such a lot of data. So in order to work on any of it, he had to go in. I would have preferred if he hadn't, to be honest, he's been a little... distracted since the study.'

'So you can confirm that your husband has just been part of an... unusual experiment, which was all over the news?'

'Yes. You've obviously watched it on TV.' *You obviously are a top-class copper, and an intellectual maggot.*

'And wasn't the idea of the experiment to effectively make him dead for a period of time?'

'The experimental design was such as to stop the heart for a defined period. If you therefore define the stopping of the heart as 'being dead' then you could describe the experiment like that, yes.'

'And it is my understanding that, if he was taken to a certain point where there was no circulation to the brain, where it was starved of oxygen, then that may result in damage to it?' Archer was reading most of this, once again, from the notebook, open on his lap.

'No, not really, they took so many precautions, the design of the experiment, the protocols, the fail-safes, and the levels of equipment were so extensive as to ensure that didn't happen. Tom was cooled to avoid his body systems deteriorating, and then reheated at the appropriate time to facilitate his resuscitation. None of this was randomly undertaken, there were carefully researched and written protocols to ensure the minimum risk.'

'But could it have, hypothetically, caused some brain damage?'

'Hypothetically, the world could end today, although I think it unlikely. So yes, hypothetically, I suppose it could.'

'So could your husband have had some form of brain episode that has changed him, changed his personality? Changed him so he would do something... out of character?'

'No. It's not as simple as that – you're making too many leaps and 'what if's. If he was brain damaged he would have had physical symptoms too, like that of a stroke. And, physically he's fine.'

But is he? Is he really? Does scratching the fuck out of his arm count?

'It is possible though? His colleagues have said he's not himself, he's very different, changed maybe since the experiment.'

'You have to bear in mind that an extraordinary thing had just happened to him, and he was still coming to terms with the effects and the feelings of that, so if he isn't quite himself, I think that's totally reasonable... although I'm not a medical doctor.'

'Yes, what exactly is your field, doctor?'

'Ancient civilisations, art and artefacts. Ancient Greece particularly.'

'Hmmm, okay.' Archer scribbled in his notebook then continued with his line of questioning. 'Is it possible, Dr Boyand, that your husband had some kind of hypoxic brain episode while he was undertaking his experiment? And that this has changed him to have a more psychotic personality?'

'To answer our question, yes, he could have had a personality altering psychotic episode brought on by hypoxia. But, again, I would say he has no other physical symptoms so the chances of that having happened are extremely low. But either someone has been speculating a lot with you, and well beyond any evidence that I'm aware of at the moment,' Sarah paused, staring deep into his eyes. 'Or you've spent all morning on Google.'

'Dr Boyand –'

'Detective Inspector, it seems to me that you're fishing around for some affirmation that Tom *could* have changed in some way and that this will add to the 'evidence' of his guilt. Well, here it is; Tom has been through something that you and I will only ever do once and he now has to live with whatever he's experienced. Do you find the idea of death profound, Inspector? Constable? Of course, it would be unthinkable not to.' Sarah's gaze was ice cold as her eyes moved between the two men, but inside she was shaking like a leaf. 'And yes, he has changed because of it. He is finding daily life difficult at the moment.'

'I'll say,' said Walker. Archer shot him a look then returned an insincere smile to Sarah.

'If you are asking if he could have *killed* someone, even someone he doesn't like?'

Could he?

'The answer is no.'

Could he, though?

'He might be a little different right now but his DNA is exactly the same, and killing someone else would be anathema to him. I imagine some unusual behaviour would be perfectly reasonable following being 'dead' a few days before – one might expect a degree of altering of one's perspectives, no?' She smiled at the two officers.

'Is shoving a cat down your boss's throat a 'reasonable' enough change of perspective, do you think?' The young DC seized on her wording to hammer the accusation home.

'Alright, DC Walker, that's enough questions for one day –' Archer knew this had gone too far.

Sarah exploded. 'You can't even place him there. Mrs Dawson doesn't know what she's seen and your motive is almost non-existent. And now you're haranguing me like he's guilty. Is this the way that 'proper' policing is done these days, Inspector Archer?'

'As I say, Dr Boyand, that'll be all for now.' The inspector stood and straightened his jacket, giving his colleague a withering look. 'Thanks again for your time – we'll be in touch. Our forensics team are at the scene now, and we may be in touch to request a sample of your husband's DNA if we find anything. If you do happen to speak to him, can you please ask him to call me urgently so we can rule him out of our enquiries?' The detective concluded with a thin-lipped smile, leaving his card on the coffee table as he and his colleague left the house.

'I'll be sure to,' came the equally thin-lipped response. 'But don't come back unless you've got some proper fucking evidence!' Sarah slammed the door behind them. Her back against the door, she slowly slid down to the floor, her knees coming up to meet her chest as she slumped, sobbing loudly, burying her face in her skirt.

17.

Sarah walked around the house, wondering about her next step, reflecting on their life. It had been a real fixer-upper when they bought it – not derelict by any means, but very much unloved and uncared for. They'd only just graduated, and with their budget not running to extensive alterations, they'd done most of the work themselves – Tom buying the B&Q 'How to' book and using it as a bible. She looked around the kitchen – down at the stone floor Tom had painstakingly laid and she'd grouted – *I always like seeing you on your hands and knees,* he'd said to her. In the den was the wall of fitted bookcases – the 'world's biggest flat-pack project'. She ran her hands over the cabinet and bookcase he'd made – she'd sourced driftwood from a specialist supplier and he'd designed and built these pieces of furniture that were beautifully made. Even now, when they were comfortably off, they wouldn't ever have decorators in – *why pay someone to do a job we can do better?* She switched off the kitchen lights – Tom had even tried his hand at re-wiring – that was an interesting and expensive mistake they never made again. 'Know your limits' became the mantra for the rest of their renovation. Hers was the design influence in their house – everywhere there were touches of her – the paintings, the cushions, the light fittings. That wasn't Tom; he was the engine room, the builder, the tool-pusher, the craftsman.

Standing in the upstairs hallway, bathed by the sunshine beaming through the giant light tunnel from the roof – she threw her arms wide and wondered what it felt like to be Tom, being drawn into that star. Silly really.

She couldn't even begin to comprehend what he believed, let alone be sure of whether *she* believed him or not.

Sarah tried to remember what the original upstairs looked like before they put the roof window in. On a whim, she decided to go into the attic to look for their 'before and after' picture albums from the renovation. The loft hatch was at the far end of the hallway, outside the boys' bedrooms, she pulled it down, bringing the ladder down with it. She climbed up into the attic space, lit brightly by a Velux window – there had been talk about putting an office room up there at the time but they'd never got round to it. Still, the window was far more effective and pleasant than a bare light bulb hanging down. The loft was floored with planks and Sarah walked across to where she thought the albums were boxed up. In front of her, however, were rows of boxes of raw data from the near-death experience survey. She had gone on to Tom for ages to sort them out when they were stacked in the back of the den. They were cluttering the place up, and Tom had obviously just put them up here, and not done anything with them at all. Wanting to get to the photo albums behind, Sarah lifted the first box out of the way. As she did, the base gave way, scattering questionnaires about her feet. Swearing, she crouched down and started to put them back into the broken box. Lifting piles of actual testimonies from people, she couldn't resist looking through the accounts, fascinated by how so many people could have had such similar experiences to one another, now knowing what Tom had seen. Sarah looked through the first survey, but they hadn't had a 'white light' experience at all.

Trust me to choose the exception.

Next, to the second interviewee; no memory of anything, just falling and then blackness. No white lights. The next had incoherent images of their past life, flashes or glimpses. She must have come across all the negatives. She pulled all of the questionnaires back out of the box and began flicking through them, deciding to make two piles – the 'white light' group – which, let's face it, should be almost everyone, given the data analysis of Tom's research – and the negative group, which should be quite small. Sarah continued to read a pile of scripts. No memory of anything. The next one remembered being in pain, then of relief – perhaps as they neared death? The next had images of her kids flashing before them. And so it went on. Sarah had a large pile of negatives, with only a couple having white light experiences or reaching hands or anything remotely like Tom's – and all of these varied wildly. Sarah moved on from what must have been the 'negatives' box to another that she selected at random. The questionnaires all had similar scattergun results. Sarah read through all of these papers with increasing feelings of both dread and anger – nobody had had the same experience as Tom, let alone the majority of people having the same story. The study was a fake, the justification for this whole charade was a fake – he'd made it up. She looked through almost every script, and only on reaching the last one was there a suggestion of a tunnel of white light, a hand reaching out, peace and joy. Just one interview from over two hundred. She looked down to the name of the subject at the bottom of the page, already guessing what she would see. The subject was Kyle Solomon.

Angry now, she got ready to leave the house whilst exchanging text messages with Scott, being deliberately vague:

Scott are you in the lab today?

Yes, why? Is everything okay? Have you heard from Tom?

No, but I need to talk to you about him. Everything isn't okay. Will be there soon.

Sarah stuffed a large sample of the scripts into an oversize shoulder bag – a lot of negatives, some with something vague, and Solomon's on top. She took this and her handbag, pulled on some wedge sandals and opened the kitchen door. As she did she realised it was raining, so, swearing again, she dumped her belongings back onto the worktop and grabbed a jacket from the coat rack. Once again she slung her bag and the raw data on one shoulder and left the house. Annoyed that time was marching on, she turned to run down the first of the three steps, which Tom still hadn't found time to pressure-wash that year.

Tom. Her husband, the man she thought she knew better than anyone.

The sandal slipped as it landed on the second step, the cork bottom having no purchase on a patch of shiny green algae. Her foot kicked up in front of her, taking her other leg with it in slow motion and a now airborne Sarah flew down the steps. She narrowly avoided smashing her coccyx on the edge of the bottom step, but landed hard on the tarmac, her right foot colliding with the passenger side door of her car and being forcibly bent up underneath her, bags skidding across the wet driveway. The force of her landing threw her body violently backwards, whipping her head back against the edge of the second step. She was aware of a wet thud and a crack, like the sound of a large egg being dropped onto the floor from a height. An explosion of pain spread out from the back of her head as mist rolled in to cloud her vision and the world gradually faded away.

***

As Sarah's head was bouncing off their stone steps, Tom walked into Bob Wauberg's office.

'Thought I'd bring you one of these.' Tom leaned his head round the door waving a plastic coffee cup from the shop in the main hospital foyer.

'You've been out in public? You're on the most-wanted list.' Bob invited him in, indicating the white leather armchair opposite him. Tom took a seat and set the coffees down.

'Porter Mike got them, then I used the service corridors – you can get almost anywhere in this building from behind the walls. Skinny latte..?'

'Thanks. Your health,' Bob raised the cup in salute.

'Mmm, about that...' pondered Tom.

'I'm guessing you've heard about Henry?'

'Yes, I saw it on a news feed earlier. It's terrible – I can't believe it.'

'Have you heard from anyone about it?'

'No – I've been quite off grid the last two days, why?'

'No reason.'

They both sipped their steaming hot drinks and enjoyed the comfortable silence of each other's company.

'So, Tom. To what do I owe the pleasure?'

'I don't want to be fighting and arguing, Bob. It seems it's all we ever do,' he replied.

'No, agreed. We are friends and maybe I do sometimes come across a little superior.'

'A little.' Tom agreed.

Bob smiled. 'A little is as big as this olive branch gets, my friend.'

'Done,' Tom raised his cup. 'And I've been defensive, and I don't want to be bickering. But I do want to talk to you.'

'Okay, shoot.'

'I'm having weird dreams or visions – sometimes I'm not sure if I'm awake or asleep.'

'Dreams seem very real, visceral, as you know, and I'd be surprised that after experiencing something so powerful and... er, profound perhaps, if you *didn't* dream about it. A dream about an event that has just happened could easily be perceived as a vision or a confusion between being awake and asleep.' Bob sat back.

'You asked the other day if it could all have been a dream –'

'I was postulating, pushing your buttons. I'm not suggesting that it was.'

'Yeah, a Bobby Ewing moment. You pushed my buttons alright, but it's not a dream, it's more than that, much more.'

'Go on.' Bob interlaced his fingers as he leant back in the chair.

***

Rain drummed gently on her skin, matting her hair to the sides of her face. Sarah slowly came round, realising that she was half-laying at the bottom of the steps, legs akimbo. She looked down and her skirt looked a darker grey at the front where it was exposed to the rain, but, she considered with her dulled senses, it didn't look too wet, so maybe she hadn't been here for too long? She tried to sit upright but saw stars. The world spun around like she was riding on a Waltzer, the fog closed in, the car in front of her fading from view. Shaking herself, she took a deep breath and she suddenly saw Tom, standing next to the car. The fog cleared and the car came back into focus and she realised she was looking at their smoke bush, which had been a chaotically sprawling thing in the spring until it was severely pruned. Now, as a tall upright beast all clothed in purple leaves it did resemble a figure when out of focus. With a sudden urge, she leant over to her side and vomited into a plant pot, her head hanging down with straggly wet ringlets of hair framing her face as strings of puke and snot hung from her nose and mouth. She put a hand down to steady herself from tipping forward into the pot, staying where she was until she felt a little better, with a clearer head. Looking around for something to wipe her face, Sarah realised her bag had slid out of reach, so, for the first time since she was a little kid leaving a snotty trail on a school jumper, she wiped her sleeve across her mouth and nose.

***

'I also keep seeing something, out of the corner of my eye. It's like there's a figure just out of my line of vision, almost hiding in my blind spot.' Tom was warming to his subject, now that he had broken the seal, he felt like he could let all his thoughts out. 'And there's a presence I can feel when I'm alone. Like there's someone else in the room with me when I know there's not.' He set his empty cup down. 'And sometimes –' He looked up at his friend. 'Sometimes I can see through their eyes, as if they're looking right back at me or something.'

'How so?'

'The other night, I imagined I was in the garden, standing in the bushes, watching Sarah up in the bedroom window, undressing ready for bed. I wasn't even there, but I was watching her from the garden. That's what I first felt as déjà vu, like I told you before.'

'Well I think that's perfectly explainable,' Bob smiled.

'You do?' Tom said with a 'this will be good' type expression.

''Okay, so your hypothesis is that the dying brain releases endorphins and other chemicals to create a more euphoric sensation to ease the body into death – like accounts of when people are freezing to death on mountains they record similar euphoria and even warmth?' Bob finished with a slightly quizzical expression for Tom to confirm with a small nod.

'And that euphoria manifests itself as rising towards a light etc that may be a perception of heaven,' he said, finishing his own theory. 'But all those people who've previously described that experience have been medically compromised. They were almost dead, and were being stuck full of drugs; drugs to counteract their medical status of being dead as well as the drugs being used to bring them back. It's a wonder you've had any accounts at all. You, on the other hand, were medically well before they made you dead, and so they needed fewer drugs to bring you back, hence your memory and perception are clearer, more detailed and involved. And it was such a big deal for you personally, it's bound to bring psychological scars and baggage, it's normal that you're dreaming about it.'

'But it's not a dream. They're visions. And what if it wasn't just a euphoric psychological state created by the dying brain?' Tom sounded a little desperate and almost manic, Bob thought.

'All of these things you're experiencing – paranoia, visions, déjà vu – they're all classic manifestations of brain trauma. Your brain tissue has been hypoxic for just about as long as anyone's has without incurring significant and permanent damage. Your protocol, I might add. And it's possible, even likely, that you've had some cellular damage that's changing you a little, and making you experience this.'

'So you don't believe me?'

'It is a bit of a tough nut that one – conceptually.'

'You're saying you don't believe me?' Tom looked crestfallen, like he expected his friend to have some kind of epiphany as he walked into the room.

'I'm not saying that. Look, when we first met we didn't get off on the right foot – it was two guys in a room both competing to see who had the bigger dick. We were both at fault. And I'm glad to say that since then we've become friends, and I'm very happy about that. I know and trust and respect and care about you as much as anyone not called Sarah. But you're asking me to believe that you left your terrestrial body, flew up and away into space, you yourself saying you must have flown many hundreds of light years, to the centre of our galaxy where no human will probably ever travel, taking an undefined period of years to do so, to then be dragged back very specifically and accurately to your body all the way back on Earth, in real time, just half an hour or so later...' He waved his hands in front of him as if to say, it's gotta be 50:50 at best.

***

Sarah sat up, lightheaded. She reached up to the back of her head, to where it was most painful and felt wetness on her fingers, wetter than the rest of her head. She realised that her hair clip had been smashed in the fall and she could see fragments of brown plastic on the steps. She drew her hand back in front of her face and saw that it was covered in blood. Suddenly Sarah was scared. She was sat here all alone, injured, with Tom missing. She needed to get the kids this afternoon, and she wasn't sure whether she could walk or drive. Her helplessness grew within her and she felt completely lost in what had been happening to her family over the last week. Struggling to muster her thoughts, her emotions threatened to overwhelm her and all she wanted to do was lay down on the steps in the rain and give up. But Sarah had never given up on anything in her life. She had to get herself fixed, had to find Tom and get him back to them, and she had the kids to consider. She shook herself and quickly stood, the garden spinning around her again. Leaning forward on the side of the car to steady herself, she reached down to pick up her bags. She unlocked the car and sat down inside, angling the rear view mirror down so she could assess the damage.

Well kid, she thought, *you look like shit,* as she used a pack of tissues to wipe up the rest of the mess from her face. She used another pack to make a wedge to investigate the back of her head. Sarah winced as she used the wadding to blot the wound, bringing it back in front of her to see that the tissues were soaked in blood, and she knew she had to act and act quickly. She turned her head left and right and was at least somewhat comforted by seeing only a little blood on her collar, and that was starting to dry. Whether she was safe enough to drive was a moot point as she turned the key in the ignition. She picked up her phone and texted Scott again –

On the way in – I need medical attention and a gown

She threw the phone on the passenger seat next to her bag and set off for the hospital as planned. Her head pounded as she drove, the vibration of the car, the bumps on the road surface and the regular turning of her head in traffic all made things worse. At least the pain was keeping her sharp – there was no danger of her drifting off with this level of hammering going on in her skull, but with the fog perpetually encroaching on the periphery of her vision, focusing on the pain at least made sure she got there in one piece. Somehow she reached the hospital, but had no recollection at all of the journey itself or whether there was a trail of destruction in her wake. The thought of this frightened her even more, but she had no time to dwell on such things, she needed to get to the lab. She left her mini-SUV more abandoned than parked in the underground car park and took the lift to the research floor, just about remembering the key code. Her bedraggled appearance generated strange looks and stage whispering from the hens on reception, whom she ignored as she strode as steadily and confidently as she could across the small foyer. She pushed through the heavy double doors leading to the research facility corridor, instantly regretting it as the impact of her hand on the heavy door jarred up her arm and neck to make her head throb even more. She staggered down the slope of fibreboard tiles, bouncing off the walls as she did so, and, learning from her mistake, turned to push the lab doors open with her hips. Chloe and Scott were waiting just on the other side and Sarah just about fell into their waiting arms. They exchanged worried glances as they helped her into the lab, which still contained the bed on which Tom had been treated the week before.

'What happened, Sarah?' asked Chloe. Not really in the mood for small talk, Sarah just looked at her.

'Clumsy,' she said. Chloe immediately thought that she might be a little concussed as she looked at the blood matted on the back of Sarah's head. Aliens found a gown in the storeroom and he and Scott left the room as Chloe helped Sarah change.

When they reconvened, all three looked at Sarah's wound together. Ideally they should refer her for an x-ray to rule out any bony damage but Sarah insisted she didn't need one – she didn't want any other unnecessary delays today, and when she was patched up, they could discuss the real business she had with them. Carefully the matted blood was washed away from her hair, and the size of the wound slowly became apparent. Using a magnifier and tweezers, Chloe removed a couple of small particles of plastic hair clip and stone from the wound as well as several strands of hair stuck in the exposed tissue. From time to time Sarah winced but she said nothing as Chloe continued. After a final wash with some antiseptic, Scott used some histoacryl tissue glue to seal the wound. After they finished, Chloe looked at Sarah and simply said. 'Pain?'

Sarah nodded. Chloe produced two Zapain tablets and some Naproxen, along with a plastic cup of water to wash it all down. 'Thought so,' she smiled.

Sarah's blouse was more or less ruined and whilst the hospital gown wasn't ideal, it would serve a purpose under her jacket to get her home later. They adjourned to Tom's office where Sarah could discuss her findings with them.

'Okay Sarah,' said Scott in a friendly-but-firm voice, 'What the hell is going on?'

***

'But this is all about my perception, Bob, what I perceived it to be, my *reality*. Ironic that you should be talking about biochemistry and cell death and I'm talking about perception.'

'But you have to see it from my point of view, from the point of view of all the people who have listened to what you've said, and how plausible it sounds. Your experience seems incredible, when the simple answer, the more obvious and maybe logical answer, is that you were hypoxic.'

'Have you ever laid on your back on a summer evening in your garden and looked up at the stars?'

'Yes, of course, I guess everybody has.'

'And did that ever give you a feeling of how...' Tom searched for the words.

'How small I am? How insignificant? Yes, that too.'

'Well you have to think, that your view, your impression of the universe in your tiny little backyard on planet earth, is something that lasts for fleeting moments when you've had a beer laying on your lawn once in a blue moon. When you see some of this significance, the size of these stars and this universe up close, then this,' he indicated the desk, the lamp the cup in his hand, 'this matter, this *stuff*, is so unimportant, so inconsequential.'

'But it's our stuff, and inconsequential to the universe or not, it forms our existence on a day to day level, minute by minute.'

'But on a higher level – a universal level..?'

'It's still our day to day mantra – the shit we have to deal with every day. I can't influence those stars you've seen or flown by – it's just the way it is,' he shrugged.

'So are you saying I *may* have seen those things?' Tom asked, interested in how far the discourse had travelled.

'I'm saying that you think so, and I believe that.'

'But not the other thing?'

'Honestly? No. I'm sorry I don't believe it happened, that some aspect of you – call it what you will; your spirit or soul, your life essence, travelled all that distance in such a short time on earth – how?'

'It's like you said before, quantum theory could explain what happened–'

'About which I'm obviously an expert –'

'It can. If an electron could be in two places in the universe at any one time, why couldn't an aspect of me, with no mass, fly all that way at those speeds? Who knows?'

'To go where? Some central processing unit where you return your soul like a car rental after you're done? To what purpose?'

'The chaplain might call it heaven...' There was a pause in the air as both men drew breath, comfortable in the debate, but also sure that the next contentious issue was just around the corner. 'But it was so real, so... *tangible*... and...'

***

'He faked it,' Sarah said without pre-amble, dumping both bags onto the desk in front of the others.

'Sorry, what?' Scott asked, having been expecting an explanation of how she'd split her head open. She certainly had their attention now.

'The first study. The near-death survey. Tom faked the results.' Eyes widened as Sarah watched them and they exchanged confused glances. They didn't know.

'I don't understand, Sarah, the data was so comprehensive and compelling. It fit such a tight data band because of how all the experiences were so similar...' Chloe spread her hands, shrugging her shoulders as if to say that should close the discussion.

'Similar, because Tom made them that way – he made them all up.' Sarah opened the shoulder bag and threw a pile of questionnaires onto the desk which slid across to the others, fanning out as they did, staples scratching the wood veneer. Chloe, Scott and Sig each picked up questionnaires and started flicking through them. Sarah pulled up a chair and sat down. As each subsequent survey was read and discarded, the next was picked up with more and more urgency until they'd been through the whole bundle. 'Have you seen ALL of them?' Scott's eyes were wide.

'Assuming they're all in our attic then yes, most of them. All completely different to each other.'

'So Bob's right, it's down to perception, not chemicals,' said Chloe.

'Maybe, but I don't really care about that right now, what I care about is this one.' Sarah threw one more paper down on the table. They read it, more slowly this time, and returned Sarah's gaze when they finished. 'Kyle Solomon?'

'Don't you think it's a coincidence that one of the few people who had the experience as Tom published it became the benefactor to this study?' Sarah leant forward onto the desk, pressing her point home. Her head still throbbed, but the tablets had at least taken the edge off her pain.

'Why though? Why fake all this?' Chloe was so young that the idea of faking any kind of scientific research was anathema to her.

'Do you have his number? Solomon's?' Sarah knew she had to take charge before the debate drifted. She needed them to focus on Tom, so they could find him before he was completely lost to her, physically and figuratively.

'It'll be on Tom's laptop, but we don't have the password.'

'Yes you do.' Sarah smiled at them and they looked at each other – yes they probably did.

'I'll text Bob – he should be here,' Chloe suggested as she opened the laptop and switched it on, Solomon's name at her fingertips.

***

'What?' Bob frowned. Suddenly, a barrier.

'I just feel that… I dunno,' Tom put his face in his hands, wiping them down over his eyes and cheeks as if washing, then he looked across at his friend, having decided which tack to take. 'I can't get rid of the feeling that I brought something back – like you said the other day.' He sat back and crossed his legs, relieved that he'd finally said what'd been on his mind.

'Brought something back?' *Always repeat what your patient says if you are a really good psychologist*, Bob thought, with nothing else to say.

'Like an energy or a force – a malevolent spirit if you want. Something feels like it's here, and it isn't here to help out.' There was a slight note of fear in that last comment, Bob thought.

'This – Hoody?' Tom hadn't mentioned it to Bob, so he realised that he must have spoken to Sarah. 'It's just projection, Tom. You are projecting your thoughts and your impression of this room, or that place, so that you look at it from a different angle – like changing camera angles at a soccer game.' He refused to call it football. 'You project yourself over there and suddenly you're looking back on yourself as if you are someone else. It's very common.'

'Yes but I've *seen* it, it looks like me, it looks like I did on the experiment day, like it 'sampled' me or something.'

'So you're telling me that this person –'

'Oh it's a creature, Bob – no doubt.'

'Okay, this creature, that you may or may not have brought back from the... void, looks just like you and is wearing your clothes..?' Bob waved toward Tom's clothing.

'Clothes that look exactly like mine, not my clothes per se.'

Bob paused and tented his fingers in front of his face. Up to this point he'd felt he was in control of the discussion, like just another consult. But no consult in history ever ended like this one. He raised his coffee cup, feeling like he needed something a lot stronger, then settled back in his chair to re-focus his thoughts.

'Tom, Henry's wife said she saw the assailant and it was you.' He took a sip after laying that out there.

'I've never been there – I don't even know where he lives,' Tom shrugged. 'What did the forensics say?'

'What?'

'Well, his widow has suggested it might be me, but surely there would be fingerprints, hair, bruising or something that would match my hands?' Tom reasoned.

'I don't know.'

'So a distressed woman saw a man in a hoody and tracksuit bottoms. And who knows how she saw him and how good a look she got, and her husband has gone ranting on about me and the argument we had, and she's seen photos of me in a hoody and all of a sudden that points to me?'

'I didn't say she mentioned a hoody,' Bob said flatly, as if he'd backed Tom into a corner.

'But she did though, right? It's like I've been telling you.'

'From what I can gather yes.'

'Do *you* think it was me – do you think I could kill someone, Bob? Come on, let's put the cards on the table right now!' Anger flared in Tom's eyes.

He's so different now, like he's 'I've had a fucking stroke', Tom.

Bob paused, possibly a little too long. 'I don't believe that my friend Tom could kill anybody, no.'

'Good answer,' Tom smiled, noticing the care with which Bob worded his response.

'Where were you last night?' Bob changed tack.

'Is this an official interview – do I need to 'lawyer-up'?'

'I'm only asking what the police will ask.'

'I was here, in the old research rooms down by the porters' lodge, my old patch. I've been down there a lot these past couple of days.'

'Speak to anyone?'

'No. Not really – I don't think I saw anyone that would recognise or vouch for me – I was back and forth the lab so possibly keypad entries and network access with my account might help – but I bet the clever bastard has found a window where there's nothing.'

'What about CCTV?'

'That's only at entrances, in A&E and on the main thoroughfares. I was trying to be anonymous so I used the fire escape and service corridors to move around.'

'And you argued with Henry a couple of days before?'

'I always fucking argued with him – everyone did. *You* did. He was a pain-in-the-arse meddlesome twat, with a frustrated-clinician-mini-God complex. That doesn't mean I wanted to see him dead, though, Jesus Christ.'

'But you know how this looks, don't you?' Bob was becoming a little frustrated as Tom focused on what he had seen, or believed he had seen, when the reality was that his picture was on the news and the police wanted to talk to him.

'Yes I can see it, I can *hear* it in your voice, Bob.'

'I'm not judging you, Tom.'

'Huh. Sounds a lot like you're on the bus to judgement city though.'

Bob smiled. 'I'm your friend Tom, first and foremost. I'll support you until I don't feel I can any longer. I believe that you've seen these things.' Bob's phone vibrated on the desk as he finished speaking.

***

The ringtone was strange to Sarah – one long drone then a pause. It was answered on the third ring.

'Maloney's Representatives, how can I help?' The smooth purring tones of the secretary at Maloney's asked. Eric Maloney was Kyle Solomon's agent.

'I need to get hold of Kyle Solomon, please.'

'Mr Solomon isn't here right now, can I take a message?' Standard rebuff.

'This is Sarah Boyand, Tom Boyand's wife, and I need to speak to Mr Solomon very urgently – it's about the results of the research study Mr Solomon funded in the UK, and the disappearance of my husband. Tell him... tell him I've found the raw data from the first study, please.'

'I'm sorry, will he know what that means?' The question dented the surety of her voice.

'Oh, he'll know alright. Just get him to call me right away please.' She left the direct line number and hung up.

'So, just to be clear, this is the raw data from the near-death survey three years ago?' Bob summarised out loud, holding up a questionnaire.

'Some of them – the rest are in the loft at home,' Sarah replied.

'You know when I first met Tom, I asked him about the raw data. I was interested in the detail of the testimony, but he told me that it had been lost with moving and renovating the house.' Bob looked at Sarah.

'But we renovated the house about eight years ago. We had to finish it because I was pregnant with Ben. Tom kept all the questionnaires in boxes in his office at home – he was worried about keeping them at work – I guess in case somebody read them who shouldn't have. I finally nagged him enough to get rid of them. I didn't realise he'd just put them in the loft.'

They were all startled when the office phone rang, shrill in the quiet room. Scott pressed the speaker button.

'Is that Sarah?' The soft American drawl asked from across the Pond.

'Yes.'

'It's Kyle Solomon.'

'Hi.' Her clipped tone making him make the first move.

'How can I, er, help you?' Solomon sounded off-guard, nervous. *Good.*

'Why did Tom fake the first survey data?'

'I don't know what you mean,' he said.

'Don't fuck me around Solomon, yours and a couple of others are the only surveys that fit his model, yet his published results say almost everyone had the same experience, statistical analysis and all – as you well know. I know he faked the data, I just need to know why?' There was a pause at the other end.

'Notoriety. Kudos. Justification of the next phase... All of the above.' He slipped into the matter-of-fact tone of the guilty by association.

'*This* experiment was the next phase? He was planning *this* all along?' Sarah was incredulous.

'I don't think he planned it when he first started working on the near-death surveys. It just sorta grew in him over time, I guess.'

'And how did you get involved, exactly?' Chloe asked.

'Tom started collecting data in the UK – had quite a lot of testimonies. Then he heard my story and got in touch. He was fascinated by what I saw – at that point he hadn't had any really clear stories about what happened to people, only fragments.'

'Stories?' Chloe seized on his choice of words.

'Did you make any of this up?' Sarah's anger was rising.

'No. No, it all happened as I told him. I don't know why I remembered things better than others.'

'Mr Solomon, it's Bob Wauberg, I'm a psychologist and a friend of Toms. I'm curious. Do you know what results Tom's co-workers were getting at the time?' Bob hoped his voice was reassuring to his fellow countryman, to strip away any remaining bullshit.

'There were no co-workers. There were two other people listed on the research paper. Mike Chu was the trauma doctor who saved me. As you know, Tom came over from the UK to see me, and Tom wanted to speak to Mike, so I arranged the meeting. He was fascinated by how Mike had saved me, and I think he used a lot from that meeting to make his templates for his experiment.'

'So, are you saying that Mike Chu wasn't involved with the NDE survey?' Bob's normally measured, reserved voice couldn't hide his surprise.

'No. He offered to collaborate and pass any future cases to Tom so he could send out questionnaires, but Tom told me there had only been a few cases in total that Mike sent back.'

'So why the hell was he named on the study?' Sarah exclaimed.

'Again it gave credence to the study – it wasn't just some guy in the UK sounding off.'

'Fuck, he just made everything up and fooled everyone – how can you do that?'

'Because everyone assumes you have integrity and your data is honest,' Scot answered.

'And Magnus Stephens?' Sarah asked.

'He was one of the foremost researchers into resuscitation in the country,' Solomon answered. 'And Tom spoke to him when he was out here.'

'He met him too?' Scott asked.

'No, he called him – the day after meeting Mike Chu. He did some searching for major authorities on resus, and Stephens was always top of the list.'

'And?'

'I got the impression that he thought the whole thing was pointless. I wasn't on a conference call like now or anything, but he didn't see how any two people would have the same experience.'

'Exactly.' Bob exhaled in exasperation.

'So, Stephens was actually against the survey, not just ambivalent?'

Scott asked.

'I don't know – I didn't speak to him. But it seemed like he wasn't interested. I know they did correspond for a while by email, but I don't know –'

'You don't know how he ended up lead author on a study that he thought was pointless?' Sarah interrupted.

'I do, actually.'

'I can see how a co-author might not know they are named on a paper, but the lead author would need to know and correspond,' Bob added.

'Not if they were dead,' said Solomon.

'What?'

'Tom worked on the data and writing the paper all by himself, corresponding with Stephens about things, and I think Stephens was helpful but just not very interested.'

Scrolling through email correspondence on Tom's laptop, Sarah could see that Stephens had indeed been good enough to reply to all of Tom's enquiries and suggestions for co-working, but all with similar replies; *I don't see how I can help.*

'The last email Tom sent was a couple of months before he presented at the meeting in Spain.'

'Where we met,' said Bob.

'Wait. He normally replied within a day or two, but here's a reply from Stephen's account two weeks later. It's written by someone else – another doctor – and it says that Stephen's has passed away.'

'Huge stroke apparently,' Solomon added.

'And in response to a further email, there's an auto-response from Stephen's server saying the address was no longer active.'

'Which gave Tom free-reign to use Stephens name posthumously without raising questions.'

'Jesus,' exclaimed Chloe. 'How cold is that?'

Something else was bothering Sarah. 'When he'd got all his surveys together, he said he was going to put all the data together himself, for the sake of consistency. I didn't want him to – I wanted him to get a research assistant or someone to do it – because it was a large number of subjects, I thought it was too big a job for him on his own. But of course he knew that it wouldn't take a long time, because he was going to make them all up. An afternoon of copying and pasting would do it. So if the numbers didn't add up, why was he still so keen to risk everything when there was no basis for him continuing the research?'

'He talks about death like he's particularly familiar with it – it's like a yin and yang thing for him every day at work. Even without the data he knew that people had seen a window into the other side.'

'You mean like you?'

'Yes. It was very clear when we first met he was fascinated by my experience and kept calling me, asking finer details and wanting me to tell the story again. Eventually he told me he had to experience it for himself. I told him he was crazy but he was serious. He thought that, if the results from the first study were compelling enough, the university might agree to his next idea and he might get funding.'

'But he didn't get the money so you fronted it.' The pieces began to fit.

'He was obsessed with doing it and it wasn't going to cost the earth. He'd got me excited about it too, to show someone what I'd seen, so why not? It was amazing to watch.'

'*You* watched it?' Sarah's eyes widened.

'Yes, of course.'

'How?'

'The CCTV feed – I had it patched across to me – it really isn't hard to do. Watched the whole thing – it was incredible.'

18.

The earlier drizzle that had soaked Sarah on the driveway, had given way to a fine and mild afternoon. Now, deep into the evening, daylight faded, accelerated by growing banks of cloud tumbling in from the west, despite the clear forecast.

Sarah, Chloe and Scott continued to go through the sample questionnaires, Sarah having long before texted her parents to ask them to pick the kids up for a sleepover at their house. Sarah's mother had sounded concerned but she had been reassured by carefully worded texts that said all was well.

Yes, everything was fine. Tom was stuck in a meeting with the Trust Board that might extend into drinks and she had had a silly fall, slipping on a wet floor at home that needed some stitches, so she was in A&E. No she didn't need them to come in, Tom's friends from work were with her and she would be fine to drive later.

Only half a dozen lies in a couple of messages. Simple. Her mother sent a few clucking replies as mums do, but Sarah fielded them easily and finished by saying that she had to go because the doctor was calling her in.

After finding no change to the pattern of fragments of experience, and no other accounts as clear as Solomon's (or Tom's for that matter), the three of them sat back, staring at the pile of documents on the desk.

'What now?' Chloe asked, rubbing her eyes.

'Got to find Tom,' replied Sarah. 'I thought he might have come here after office hours, I think he's been staying here somewhere – it's the only place he'd go. I need to speak to him, and before the police do.'

'Why?'

'I need to know who the hell I'm married to!' Head throbbing even worse now as the Zapain wore off, Sarah picked up her bag, leaving the research data strewn across the desk. She didn't have access to the bowels of the hospital so she went out of the main doors and round to the far side of the building, planning to bang on the door of the porters' lodge. She hoped that someone would remember her. Adjusting the bag on her shoulder and checking for messages from her parents, Sarah diverted through the foyer of the research centre to the main umbilical corridor. She looked out through the glass wall, watching thunderheads rolling and growling as they crashed together, racing each other to reach the city. The wind howled along the sides of the building and it began to rain again. She watched as people scurried for shelter from the car park and drop-off area and she stopped in her tracks. There was Tom, cutting across the main car park of the hospital – like most staff, avoiding the longer curved walkway to get around the hospital and preferring to venture outside to go between buildings, despite the rain. Realising this might be her only chance to find him before he disappeared again, she ran along the umbilicus to the lift, which was waiting on her floor. The graceful gliding motion of the glass elevator smoothly lowered her on a cushion of hydraulics.

'Come on, come on, come on, come on, c'mon,' she shouted, elbowing the doors open as she hit the ground floor and burst through a Fire Exit Only door. The warmth of the evening hit her a split second before a huge gust of wind. It came howling around her like a crazed animal, the storm rolling in, the wind whipping up to gale force, trying to push her over as she ran. She sprinted across the tarmac to intercept her husband as he cut across the circular patch of grass by the large blue sign carrying the hospital's name, where Andrea had given her news conference the previous week.

'Tom!' she shouted, hoping to be heard above the roar of the elements. He carried on walking purposefully away from her, not hearing her, or not wanting to. 'TOM,' she screamed at the top of her voice. He definitely heard her this time because he stopped walking – standing stock still for a second or two before turning slowly around. Sarah had an awful memory of Donald Sutherland doing the same at the end of *Invasion of the Body Snatchers*, revealing he too had been taken over. She prayed that Tom would at least know her from whatever dark place he was in.

'Sarah?' He was puzzled to see his wife standing in front of him, wearing a hospital gown. 'What're you doing here?'

'Looking for you, of course!' she shouted over the maelstrom.

'How are you?' he asked, his voice almost floating, liquid, sounding as if he was pleasantly stoned and passing the time of day with someone.

'Just fucking fine considering my husband hasn't been home, hasn't called, hasn't seen his kids!' Her fists clenched and unclenched, all the raw emotions of the past few days coming out at once.

'I've been... busy, I have to find it...' Tom offered by way of explanation.

'Oh that's alright then, that's fucking cleared everything up just nicely, hasn't it.' She was screaming at him now, and not just to make herself heard over the noise of the storm. Lightning crashed overhead, shortly following the thunder that had rumbled through when their conversation started. She closed the final few paces to him, but still needed to shout to be heard. 'What do you have to find?'

'Hoody.'

'Oh not again. When are you going to realise that Hoody is *you*? Your research was all fake, Tom, I found the raw data. You made it all up! You even made up your co-authors – these people weren't even fucking involved in your study but you used their names so you could get published. We checked. Magnus Stephen's wasn't even interested in your work and you added his name when he was dead. It was all a lie.' Sarah almost spat the words at Tom as she jabbed her finger at his chest.

'Not all of it,' he said, as if that cleared everything up.

'Most of what I found, was. The real results were all over the place.'

'It wasn't all a fake. People were just too sick, too far gone to remember anything properly. You've seen the data – if you look through it carefully there are trends and...' he searched for the right word, '...snippets that said there was something, a bigger picture, like little ghosts or glimpses of what people experienced. Like only seeing flashes of the monster in a horror film until you see it all at the end. I knew they'd seen something. They'd had some form of experience, but all the time it was just out of reach.' He explained with his hands as much as with words, imploring her to understand and to believe what he was telling her. Their heads were almost touching, but still they raised their voices over the storm as gusts of wind swept across the front of the hospital bringing rain with them.

'But you lied, you made the rest up.'

'I needed credibility, I needed the scientific community to approve of what I was going to do.'

'But they never did, and, if you think about it, they were never going to. It was never the scientific community you wanted to fool, was it? It was me. It was *us*! If you could fool me then I'd go along with it and support you. Why Tom? *Why*?'

'From what people saw, the window on death...'

'So you decided you had to go and take a peek through?' She shrugged her shoulders, hands spread questioningly.

'I'm a researcher – a scientist – of course I did. Those people... they were just too ill to remember things clearly.'

'And Kyle Solomon just gave you the money?'

'It didn't work like that – he'd just had a lucid experience.'

'So why him? He's an actor isn't he – he makes stuff up for a living – maybe he was just drawing you in?'

'To what end though? And besides, my experience was like his.'

'Wouldn't Bob just say that his perception affected yours – the power of suggestion and all that?'

'Oh, fuck Bob! He twists everything around to be something other than it is.'

'So why didn't you just publish what you had – the snippets – the 'further work is needed' bit at the end of the paper would have pre-empted this work? You had the money from Solomon...'

'Do you think Henry, or anyone – any university – would let me do this with no harder evidence than snippets or moments? The Ethics Committee would've laughed me out of town. And no one would have ever signed up to work with me on it. The only way was to have a more... persuasive argument.' His face twisted with a sneer as he spoke, and he paused and looked at her. His eyes, always so laughter-filled and warm, now cold and calculating.

'And look where it's got you. Look at all this. Is that what you wanted? Was it worth it, seeing all you've seen –' *or think you've seen,* 'having some – thing– running around in your name, having your kids scared of you. Someone is *dead*, Tom! Was it worth losing everything, worth losing *us* over?'

'You wouldn't understand, you haven't seen it. Sarah, it's amazing – the universe, magnificent, completely impossible to describe.' Sarah realised that until now she hadn't had a conversation with her husband about his experience where she actually believed him. He stared at her, wind swirling around him, blowing his hair up and over his face, his clothes billowing, the gusts almost blowing him off his feet, his arrogant posture and manner answering her question for her. He was lost. Her husband was gone.

They stared at each other, and thunder crashed overhead as a squall rained down on them, the rain almost sweeping sideways. Her thin hospital gown began to stick to her body, and his heavy hoody and jogging pants started to mat to him.

Scratching scratching scratching.

Tom said something that was immediately taken by the howling wind.

'What? ' Sarah shouted, moving towards him again. 'What did you say?'

'It's here,' Tom said matter-of-factly, looking around, searching the hospital grounds. He was scratching his arm without noticing. Ripples seemed to move under the skin of his forearm, beneath the dressing Sarah had applied, like something wriggling inside a sack.

'Hoody?' Sarah said, looking around herself.

'Yes.'

'How do you know?'

'Scratching scratching scratching away,' he sang out loud by way of answer, a wild grin spreading across his face, as if he had just revealed his darkest secret.

Scratching scratching scratching, ha ha ha ha. The voice laughed in Tom's head and the scratching was deafening him now, surrounding him, suffocating him. He was furtively scratching at his arm with the vigour of a fast bowler rubbing a cricket ball on his thigh. The skin was so mobile it looked like a party was going on beneath.

'Stop it!' Sarah screamed at him. He looked down, he'd shredded the grubby bandage on his arm and torn apart the dressing beneath. His forearm and wrist were drenched in blood and his fingers kept working away, scratching beneath the surface. He looked up at Sarah, pleading with her – he couldn't stop himself.

Scratching scratching scratching, ha ha ha ha. The voice wasn't surrounding him now, it came from one direction. He followed the sound, looking up at the roof of the main building. Five storeys above he saw Hoody, stood, legs akimbo, arms stretched out wide, laughing silently to the heavens. Lightning flashed through the sky and exploded a neon aura around the creature and Tom heard laughter in his head again. Hoody looked down at Tom and their eyes met. It reached down to the chest of the sweatshirt it was wearing – an exact copy of Tom's – and ripped it in half, discarding the rags. At last it could unwind into its body and it grew, standing up straight, becoming bigger in all dimensions; muscular and taller, looking huge even from a distance. Hoody's face began to change, the features that so closely resembled Tom's slowly dissolving as the muscles and bone beneath returned to their native arrangement, and Tom looked upon its true face for the first time – the face of a demon. The back of its head lengthened and two pointed objects grew down as far as its waist, like horns or keratinised hair, but moving as the thing moved its head and even blowing slightly in the wind.

Tom stared up at his adversary.

'Jesus fucking Christ!' said Sarah.

'Can you see it? ' Tom asked in hope and surprise, not taking his eyes off the demon.

'Yes, yes! Christ it's massive – what the fuck is it?' She was incredulous. No wonder Tom had been so upset, it had been true all along.

'So I guess that *doesn't* look like a hypoxic episode up there? Or are you as psychotic as me now?' he smiled grimly.

'I *do* have had a head injury,' she said, half-joking. 'Not the time to be all superior, dear.'

Scratching scratching scratching.

'You're still scratching your arm, it's like raw meat.'

'I can't stop myself, it's got too much power over me, it's in my head. But I know something else too.' Realisation was pummelling him like a boxer.

'What?' She looked at him.

'I'm dead. I've always been dead. I'm still dead, since the moment they stopped my heart. Once you get to a certain point it's a one-way trip, and *that's* just here to file the paperwork.'

'Don't be ridiculous. You can't be, you're *here*, flesh and blood. What are you going to do?'

'This.' With that, Tom's fingers dug into his flesh, pressing in, razoring backwards and forwards, using his fingernails to open the wounds in his skin wider, creating a flap, pushing his fingers underneath, starting to peel the skin back. Blood oozed between his fingers as he did so, running in rivulets down his arm and dribbling in long red strings onto the grass.

'God no, stop it, what are you doing? Baby, stop, please!' She wailed at him, trying to reach out to pull his hand away but he turned his body to block her, shrugging her away. He grunted with effort and pain as his fingers hooked under the skin flap he had made, and with one lingering look over his shoulder at Sarah, he ripped the skin off the back of his forearm and hand, screaming as he did so, pulling it away like a glove down to the fingers, tossing the discarded tissue on the floor with a flick of the wrist.

'Oh my God, what are you doing? What are you doing? Run, get away from it. We'll get you some help. We'll go to the police then get your arm fixed up,' Sarah sobbed, not knowing what to do or where to look – at the otherworldly demon on the roof or her husband as he mutilated himself. Tom began to peel away the skin on the front of his arm, now, finding it much easier to lift a flap from the glistening muscle and connective tissue now he'd removed the skin from the back. He quickly degloved the rest of his flesh.

'There! See?' He smiled maniacally and triumphantly at Sarah, holding up his arm to show her, turning it over repeatedly, blood bathing the tissue beneath and splashing on the ground. She was horrified at his actions, gagging at the blood and gore. She felt faint, like she was in a nightmare from which surely – any moment now – she would awaken, with Tom sleeping soundly next to her in their bed and this would all have been an amusing anecdote to tell over morning coffee. But then, gradually, she realised what he had *really* done, what he was showing her. Beneath the blood and flesh his fingers looked strangely different, now free from the confines of the restrictive skin they unfolded as if they themselves had been scratching to get out. She was no anatomist, but the fingers were elongated to almost twice their normal length and were pointed at the end, like nails coming out of the bone. His hand itself was bigger, both in length and breadth, the muscle tissue thicker with more bulk, and this went all up the hand and forearm. This thing looked more powerful – vastly stronger than any human arm. Nobody just tears their own skin off to unfold a bigger appendage. Nobody. Tom's arm wasn't human.

'It must have been changing under your skin.'

'I think when it grabbed me and broke my wrist it... infected me somehow, changing me where it touched.' Tom held his arm out again, fascinated and repulsed by it in equal measure, exalting at the power he felt in the limb as well as being in excruciating pain from the still live nerve-endings he had just ripped apart. 'It was *that*,' he nodded towards the thing on the roof, which let out a reptilian screech when it saw what Tom had done, the first sound it had made.

'What do you mean?'

'It was the one that grabbed me when I was dead, it was the 'angel' pulling me in and it let me go when they shocked me.'

'So the light – this star where this thing grabbed you – isn't heaven?'

'No, I don't think so. It's not hell either – just where you go when you're dead. Like a processing plant.'

'Jesus, and that's it?'

'Seems so, babe.'

'Why did Hoody go after Henry and not me or the kids?'

'I don't know. I've been wondering about it myself. Maybe it didn't want to come straight for me – it was there at the house and at football. Maybe it was testing us out. Maybe it wanted to ruin my life to draw me to it, and it knew that I'd been 'infected' somehow and that I had some power. Or maybe it's just a fucking useless amateur at this sort of thing – just like me. That's why it's here – it's been sent to clean up the mess.'

'You can't know any of that.'

'No, but I don't think I'm far wrong – and that's how I can beat it.'

'How?'

'We're the same. I *am* Hoody and Hoody *is* me. We were joined when it grabbed me to pull me into the star. So I'm much stronger now, like a power-up or something.'

'How do you beat it?'

Tom looked up and saw Hoody running toward the far end of the roof, to the top of the stairway for the fire escape. In response, he made a run for the foot of the stairs to cut off the escape route, carrying his arm slightly away from his body as if he wasn't quite sure how to hold it now it was bigger and heavier. The rain washed away most of the blood and he could look down and see the muscles bulging and tendons flexing as he ran along. The fire escape door was firmly shut, but he smashed the glass with one easy punch of his claw, reached in and pushed the bar down to open the door. He sprinted up the stairs with almost superhuman speed and stamina, terrified and exhilarated at the same time – he felt unstoppable. Hoody was waiting for him at the top, a maniacal grin on its face that almost tore its head in two, like some macabre Halloween pumpkin. Tom raced up the last flight of stairs, breathing hard, running straight at the demon with his head down, striking its abdomen with his shoulder. Hoody reached under Tom's body as his shoulder struck and lifted him up and over the banister, using Tom's own momentum as leverage and dropped him into the gap between the stairs. Surprised, Tom fell, missing the first banister rail, crashing off the concrete side of the stairwell, bouncing down to the next floor. He reached out his arm and grasped the rail, wrapping his new hand around it, immediately stopping his fall but almost wrenching his shoulder out of its socket as he stopped. Searing white-hot pain shot down his arm, but stopped at the claw. He dangled for a second, looking down into the void between the stairs, to the ground floor below. Hoody had disappeared back out onto the roof, so after taking a moment to get his breath, Tom clambered over the rail and climbed the last flight of stairs again. He flexed his arm, gingerly experimenting with moving it, the pain subsiding, and concluded that he hadn't injured himself so badly that he couldn't continue taking the fight to the enemy.

Kicking open the door leading out onto the flat roof that extended over the entire footprint of the hospital's main building, Tom could see Hoody, standing in the centre. It was looking to the heavens as the wind increased, blowing hard across the flat surface, leaves and old plastic bags chasing one another in a race to find shelter. He walked out onto the roof, cradling his painful arm, closing the gap between him and the demon. It was still staring up at the sky making otherworldly grunting and growling sounds as Tom closed to within twenty paces. Hoody was standing on the edge of the glass atrium – the large curving dome that arched over the main foyer of the hospital like a jewel, made up of dozens of huge triangular glass pieces. The atrium was precisely engineered so each piece slotted together to form a strong, frameless structure. The flat roof was criss-crossed by ductwork, pipes of varying sizes clustered in different arrangements going here and there. Some of these pipes culminated in electrical relay stations, some in junction boxes, and yet more attached to the bottom of the tower crane bolted in turn to the front of the roof. The crane had been decommissioned after the last piece of atrium glass had been lifted into place. The recent run of good weather, however, had resulted in all hands being diverted to other jobs before the autumn weather closed in, so the crane had yet to be dismantled.

The wind blew harder, whipping and gusting around the contours of the roof. Suddenly the whole sky crackled with energy – the unforecast heavy storm clouds had converged over the hospital, the humidity of the day had inevitably resulted in this thunderstorm, that seemed to be encircling them. Across the park from the hospital there was a flash as lightning hit a tree in the street beyond. Two seconds later a low rumble of thunder rolled across the rooftops, followed by another flash, closer now, with thunder immediately on its tail. Hoody was screaming upwards, arms wide, claws raking at the sky. Electrical charges danced over metal housings, pipes and walkways across the roof. Tom's hair was standing on end as all the static electricity in the sky around focused on this one rooftop. The smell of ozone was in the air, the atmosphere so thick and heavy as to be almost unbreathable.

Sarah watched from below, looking up to where her husband and Hoody were facing off, framed by the glowing sky. She watched as Tom quickly ran at the demon as hard as he could, striking him in the solar plexus in a rugby tackle using his non-painful shoulder. The tackle propelled them across the glass, both landing heavily in the middle of it. Reacting on impulse, knowing she couldn't leave Tom alone with that thing, whatever it was, Sarah too ran for the fire escape. She bounded up the stairs, taking them two and three at a time, glad of the strength in her legs from all her Stairmaster classes to give her some chance of getting to the top before it might be too late…

…Hoody walked across to Tom, picking him up by the front of his sweatshirt and throwing him back across the flat roof. Tom skidded to a halt, picking up a piece of pipe lying nearby, evidently surplus to requirements during the build. He quickly got to his feet and swung, rotating his whole body like a batsman smashing a six, the pipe connecting with Hoody's lower jaw, tearing away some of the flesh and bone from its face.

Suddenly there was a massive crash overhead and the whole sky around them lit up brilliantly. The lightning burst blasted downwards, attracted to the only tall metal structure on the roof. It struck the pulley-cable at the top of the main tower of the crane, above the operator's cab. Sparks fizzed off girders as electricity raced along the path of least resistance. Purple-white energy flowed along the metal, shooting to the end of the jib arm where it exploded like a firework, raining down on the two protagonists below. It was the signal for the heavens to open and torrential rain to pour down, chasing the rest of the electrical charge down the crane's tower to where it was attached to a metal plate and concrete plinth. The lightning blast exploded as it hit the plate and the insulating concrete, buckling both and shearing all the steel bolts, rendering the crane completely free of its moorings. It rocked gently with the force of the blast. The centre of gravity of the crane was nearer the end of the jib arm, which still hung over the glass roof. Slowly, slowly, the weight of the crane pulled it forward and it began to topple. The hook and pulleys descended and struck the glass dome where Tom and the demon wrestled, marking the point where the jib would impact as the metal chains pooled in a random coil.

'Tom! ' Sarah screamed, racing onto the roof from the fire escape. 'Move!' She waved her hands wildly, trying to direct him to move out of the line of fire. He looked up for a second, noticed Sarah's arm signals and saw the falling crane accelerating down with a creaking groan of twisting, fracturing metal. Both he and Hoody recognised the danger and leapt backwards as the jib struck the atrium glass with a sickening crash, the arm buckling as the large pane it struck warped, bending as if it might just hold under the weight, then shattered, raining razor sharp fragments down onto the foyer below. With a scraping groan, the rest of the jib, sticking almost vertically up out of the roof, started to bend and twist, being pulled down under its own weight, pivoting against the bottom end of the tower resting on the ruined roof plate. The behemoth rotated around the hole in the glass roof, breaking more panes and sending an array of large cracks out across the glass surface, the self-supporting structure bending and twisting under the strain. Accelerating as it fell, the huge girder smashed into the edge of the atrium, further buckling the glass and loosening the metal rim that acted as a huge window frame. The force of the impact sent a shockwave across the glass, throwing Tom and Hoody off their feet, the crane coming to rest as an obstacle between them. Like a spiders web, the cracks in the glass spread out across the entire roof from the original hole. Rain poured down and ran in rivulets across them – the previously beautiful curved glass ceiling was now twisted, unstable and straining, visibly vibrating and creaking under the weight.

The two combatants rose in unison, eyeing one another and the ruined metalwork between them, and the demon threw its head back and shrieked in frustration. Tom watched the creature carefully, squatting in readiness for an attack. He spotted a piece of metal on the glass in front of him, part of the main stanchion of the crane arm, wrenched free during the impact. He bent and picked it up, the weight of it feeling comfortable in his more powerful claw hand. Hoody jumped onto the girder between them and, seeing an opportunity, Tom quickly swung with all he had, the heavy bar hitting hard against the side of the demon's leg, its knee collapsing inwards. Hoody roared and hissed, a reptilian sound, and reached out taloned hands to grab him, but Tom spun away, using the counterweight of the iron bar to turn him back round to face the creature again. It stared at him, opening its mouth, baring teeth and forked tongue. The demon jumped down from the jib, screeching again as it jarred its injured leg on landing. Hoody was very obviously hurt and backed away, never taking its eyes from Tom's. It tested the injured leg by putting more weight through the foot, looking down to see the knee twisted at an unnatural angle, pain rising once again. It hissed at Tom, monitoring his movements, tracking him.

I will take you. The voice was in Tom's head.

'Not today fucker.'

Further cracks appeared in the atrium glass, the whole superstructure groaning under the weight of crane wreckage. Tom had levelled the playing field somewhat but, mangled leg or not, Sarah could see no way that he would beat this thing, whatever it was, this monster from the deep. *But from the deep of where?* Deep in his subconscious made real? Deep space? Deep at the edge of heaven and earth, some guardian of the afterlife maybe? Whatever, it wasn't human. It would almost certainly not be as susceptible to physical injury as Tom would be – it was walking around on a fucked-up knee for God's sake – and far too strong for him to beat. And it would only be a matter of time before he succumbed. She knew she should try and help, to stand by her husband in some way, maybe skew the odds in his favour, but as she was just coming to terms with what this thing might be, she couldn't even begin to think how she might fight it. Sarah watched as the two glowered at each other over the twisted metal, soaked by the rain pouring down.

Sightings of Tom in the hospital grounds had stoked the rumour-mill, people had seen the news today and knew the police wanted to question him about Henry's death. The crane smashing into the glass of the hospital roof and what seemed like an altercation up there had further stoked the stokers, and several had called the police and fire brigade.

The sound of approaching sirens could barely be heard over the storm. Tom closed the distance to Hoody as it focused on its wounded leg, hardly noticing him as it prodded at what might be a knee. He got to within arms' length before it looked up and hissed at him, swinging a wild arm in his direction, which he easily evaded. Tom swung the metal bar as Hoody's arm passed his face, smashing it into the end of its forearm, pulverising flesh and whatever passed for bone in the creature. The impact folded the wrist over at a strange angle and the creature roared in agony.

'I guess we're even,' Tom said, hefting the bar as the demon wheeled away on its damaged leg, putting some space between them.

Sarah heard the sound of sirens and looked up momentarily to see an almost continuous line of blue flashing lights approaching through the park. Taking a step forwards to see the creature more clearly through the rain, Sarah's foot collided with a large metal object which she quickly realised was the crane hook, attached to a heavy pulley system and cables which disappeared under the body of the jib. The main hook had disappeared through the roof of the atrium, so this had to be a secondary one. She looked across at the ruined glass dome in front of her, seeing all the cracks and fissures spreading out like a shattered windscreen. She traced the three widest of these, intersecting to form a 'Y' shape that extended underneath the jib, and it was here that the glass looked most unstable, here that all the creaking and groaning was coming from, like ice moving on a glacier, and here that she could actually see movement between broken sections of glass.

And to physically separate Tom from the demon, to break the bubble of their obsession with each other, to save her husband and her family, she knew what she had to do.

19.

Bending down to the crane hook, Sarah tested its weight, recognising that as heavy as it was, she could just about lift it. She strained, veins bulging in her neck, tensing her arms and shoulders. Slowly she straightened her legs and managed to lift it. Her arms wrapped around the metal, the coldness penetrating through her clothing. She staggered out into the middle of the dome, to the edge of the largest crack, and lifted the steel above her head. Like swinging an axe to split a log, she brought the hook down hard to smash against the ruined glass. A further creaking groan was her reward, but nothing else. She'd have to try again, and bent to lift the hook once more. This time she moved closer to the crane jib, where the cracks intersected, and again she swung the hook. Again it made a loud grating contact with the glass, but once again a groan of the glass was the only outcome. Her strength was almost spent, one more try was about all she had left. She bent her knees for a final time, grasping the hook in a firm grip, the cold metal and lashing rain freezing her fingers. She pushed hard with her thigh muscles, knees straining, legs wobbling, her back bent almost double as her body refused to come upright and her arms were forced straight by her lack of strength and the weight of the hook.

'Come on.' She screamed. 'COME. ON!' She roared her determination for one last effort. Slowly, the hook lifted off the ground, slowly she came upright, slowly she tucked her hips underneath her and brought her hands into her chest, cradling the hook like a baby. She set herself in position, and with a final roar she pushed her arms up into the air, raising the metal block above shoulder level, locking her elbows straight. With one almighty movement, she brought the hook down hard, pulling with her stomach muscles, dropping her legs at the last minute so that she fell to her knees, adding her body weight to the force of the blow. The square angle at the top of the housing impacted directly into the fissure in the glass, immediately widening it and sending half a dozen further cracks weaving out from the epicentre of the blow. The main centre section of the roof buckled. More cracks formed and spread, the integrity of the whole roof started to fail as the jib broke through the glass just in front of her. Two massive, long, thin shards fell from the roof, pivoting and curving in an arc to shatter into a million pieces on the floor below. Sarah scrambled backwards onto a more stable section, but even this was vibrating and starting to break up. The proof that this self-supporting roof relied on every single pane of glass to confer its strength was very evident, as the groaning and creaking of a rumbling chain reaction seemed to drown out even the roar of the wind.

'TOM!' she screamed. 'The roof!'

He didn't hear her – his attention all on Hoody. She screamed again, louder this time, and somehow he heard, looking up at her. Their eyes met, and she wanted to tell him so many things in that moment; to tell him she loved him, that he was her perfect man in every way, that their life together was more than she ever imagined, that he was an amazing dad, to say how much she wished she could spirit the two of them away from here, just to be back at home with the boys once more. Too far away and with no time to say any of these things, she hoped in that split second he knew, hoped he was thinking of her as she was of him.

'THE ROOF! Get BACK!' she yelled, cupping her hands around her mouth. Just as she did so, the demon took two limping steps forwards and flung itself at Tom over the girder between them. There was a simultaneous warping of the glass on either side of the jib in a giant wave of bending silica, like the folding of matter across the universe. And with that the flexibility of the glass reached its peak and, despite valiant resistance under the greatest of duress, it finally succumbed. With a rolling growl the whole roof exploded, shards flying all around them, striking Tom across the hand, thigh and face. Sarah threw herself backwards just as the roof buckled, landing heavily on the gravel hard-standing surrounding the atrium. She rolled over and looked up just in time to see the jib disappear into a hole that used to be a glass roof, desperately hoping that Tom had got clear in time too. Hoody had leaped over the jib, but, only having one strong leg to push from, hadn't been able to generate as much power as it needed, just managing to reach out and grasp hold of Tom's leg, pulling him in. The two locked together, struggling and fighting in mid-air. Tom's subconscious had registered the problems with the roof and had been screaming at him to get out, but Tom was too focused on his nemesis. Now, grappling together, neither of them were able to get away, and Tom wasn't about to let Hoody out of his hands. The jib disappeared beneath them and, slowly, Tom and the beast began to fall.

Like a Road Runner cartoon, they fell in slow motion, with tiny diamond jewels of glass surrounding them as if they were enclosed in a razor-sharp blanket. The demon kicked and fought with Tom in an attempt to distance itself. Tom, in turn, arched his body away from it, stretching and pulling himself clear as if that would give him a better chance of survival, twisting his body like a cat in free-fall. He turned to watch as the ground rushed up to meet him, his body accelerating so the ninety-foot fall happened in an instant and he crashed into the polished tiles, fracturing the floor. The force of the landing crushed his ribs against the tiles, his lungs exploding like a bursting balloon. His face smashed into the marble, pulverising the right side of his skull and his pelvis blew apart as his legs were thrown akimbo by the violence of his sudden stop.

Sarah darted forward as the roof collapsed, watching as the two combatants fell, wrestling each other apart. As she watched, the demon faded from view. Tom was falling alone, having turned his body to meet his fate head on. He smashed into the ground with so much force that she swore she felt the vibration up on the roof, his crumpled body damaged beyond belief – arms and legs twisted and broken at grotesque angles, his head and neck turned almost to look up at her, a sunburst of blood and tissue spattered out in a huge arc from him. This wasn't like in the films or TV, where the body lays in place and a thick dark pool slowly spreads out from it as the camera lingers. Real life was visceral – blood and brain and guts and bone in one homogenised mess. There was no doubt that he was dead – nothing could have survived such a fall. Nothing. And there was already very little left of the man that had once been her husband. Tom was dead. Dead and alone. There was no sign of Hoody, no body, no figure limping away. No evidence that when Tom hit the ground he'd been anything other than a lone figure falling, yet he and Hoody had been locked together when the roof had failed. She stared down at him with utter horror, grief and despair.

And then his right hand moved. The right hand, gripped and crushed at the time of his 'death', the right hand that'd pained him and been examined clinically to show trauma and damage consistent with a crush injury like nobody had ever seen before, the right hand that had transformed itself, somehow, into a claw, twitched and reached forward as if trying to crawl. Sarah raced for the fire escape.

The impact and severe pain lasted for a fleeting moment, before the floor beneath him gave way and he fell through, free-falling down into nothingness, his retinas registering an illuminated grid as an artefact from the bright foyer lights which had been the last things he'd seen. He slowly toppled over backwards, head over heels as the lights closed around him, swirling around like an illuminated mesh blanket, like his cold 'suit' from the experiment. It formed a shimmering, shifting vortex through which he fell, faster and faster, the tightness of the tunnel compressing his chest. It squeezed him tighter and tighter and he could no longer breathe, the pressure so great he thought his chest would pop, crush his ribcage and pulverise his internal organs, becoming unbearable and inescapable until –

***

Sarah sprinted down the fire escape stairs, looking through the windows at the collection of police vehicles scattered around the front car park of the hospital, bathing the night air in a kaleidoscope of red and blue. She threw herself down the last few steps and hit the fire escape door, almost losing her balance as she thrust down the bar of the door release and burst outside all in one motion. She ran across the car park as the most direct route to the front of the curved hospital building, hurdling a row of planters containing small bushes and annual flowers, now looking past their best. The flowers jostled for soil space with large families of cigarette butts from those who didn't want to congregate in cancer alley at the front of the hospital.

There were now so many police vehicles in the car park that nothing else could get in or out. An ambulance pulled up behind the gridlock, blasting its siren repeatedly as Sarah ran flat-out across the tarmac, dodging between police cars and startled officers who tried to speak to her.

The wind gusted even though the rain had eased for a moment, blasting Sarah's face as she skirted the last line of bushes to give her a clear run at the main entrance. A uniformed officer in a hi-vis jacket and peaked cap was finishing cordoning off the entrance with tape and Sarah side-stepped him as he reached across to block her – caught in two minds between releasing the tape and stopping the woman. She hit the automatic revolving doors hard, forgetting they slowed down if you pushed them.

'C'mon, c'mon, c'mon,' she screamed impatiently as they started to revolve again. As soon as a gap appeared she squeezed through and ran into the huge foyer, footsteps echoing on the hard floor. The blue girder of the crane jib hung down through the hole in the roof, reaching almost halfway to the floor, rain pouring down around it. Armed response officers stood in a loose circle in the middle of the foyer, surrounding Tom's body, careful to avoid standing directly under the crane wreckage. Two startled officers closed ranks as they saw Sarah racing towards them.

'I'm sorry, you can't come –' one officer started to say, his hand raised toward her.

'He's my husband!' she screamed at him, ducking under his outstretched arm and hitting his armoured chest with her shoulder to barge him aside. 'Out of my fucking way!'

She broke through the perimeter and slowed her run when she saw Tom up close, the crater of smashed and buckled floor tiles now filled with his blood. His limbs were twisted at horrible angles, and his head was turned right round to face her. His eyes were open but she was sure there was no sight there. She looked up at the shattered roof above, unable to imagine that anyone would survive such a fall.

Then he moved again. His hand, lying on the ground above his head, mangled and bloodied and looking no more like a claw and no more out of place than any other horribly injured part of him, twitched, the fingers curling and opening again. The existence of life? A muscle spasm? Involuntary nerve activity? She didn't care. She dropped to her knees beside him, careful not to touch his broken body, but oh so gently stroked his cheek.

'Tom?' she whispered, as if her voice might hurt him. 'It's okay. I'm here. It's all okay.' She stroked his matted hair, as delicately as possible, not caring what she was running her fingers through. His staring eyes were unresponsive, but she sensed he was still there, sensed he might still be with her, or flying through the galaxy somewhere, still her husband. He wasn't gone, not yet.

An armed officer, the one she'd barged passed, moved to lift her away from the body, but another officer stepped across him, the officer in charge at the scene, a plain clothed inspector with body armour pulled over his shirt and tie. He put his arm across his colleague's chest with an almost imperceptible shake of the head to tell him it was okay, to stand down. Morgan Archer nodded at Sarah as they exchanged glances, the police officers taking a step back.

'Tom? I believe you,' she sobbed. 'I'm sorry, I should have believed you. I shouldn't have pushed you away. Oh God, baby I hope you can hear me. I love you. The boys love you. I hope you know that...' She looked into his eyes once more and they were glazed and sightless, and she knew, or at least, she felt in her heart, that he had gone. Sarah collapsed in on herself, slumping down. She slowly bent forward to plant one last kiss on his cheek. 'Goodbye my darling. Safe trip.'

***

He was flung through the vortex, flying up above his body, looking down one last time at his wife, ignoring the crude matter that had once been his physical self, storing the image of her in his consciousness. He could only pause for a second before turning and flying through the massive jagged hole in the ruined atrium, spinning past crane wreckage and up above St Catherine's as the rain lashed down through the hole. Rising above the height of the building, the city revealed itself in all its illuminated glory. The heart of the city centre shone like a beacon, streetlights illuminated roads as they curved gracefully away, like the spiral arms of a galaxy. Illuminated constellations at intersections and industrial estates formed astrological patterns of brilliant white neon. He saw a petrol station, standing out in its garishness, spoiling the soft glow around it, twinkling red brake lights suddenly bright then immediately vanishing as cars manoeuvred in and out of the forecourt like fireflies engaged in a strange dance. The ever-expanding arc of yellow street lights curving off into the distance, skirting black holes of run-down or deprived areas that had become disused or been demolished whilst awaiting re-development. Dark and soulless, absorbing all energy around them, drawing in hope and light in equal measure. He traced the long straight yellow line of Southern Way as it surged away from the city heading home, noticed the new football pitches at the technical college, the brilliance of the floodlights, white like the petrol station. Southern Way rose and snaked back and forth up the hill before disappearing amongst the woods and the poor visibility from the rain. His eyes tried to reach beyond the top of the hill, towards his home, thinking of the boys, thinking of them getting ready for bed, wishing he'd said goodbye to them properly, wishing he'd spent more time with them and not been so driven, wishing his path hadn't led him to the roof of St Catherine's and a face-off with some... thing. In his mind he pictured their faces – while he still could – before the images became too distant and faded. He heard their voices and their laughter, imagined their little hands in his when they were out together. And as he pictured them so close to him, he said goodbye to them, wishing them a good life, asking them to be good, to be strong for their mother and to grow up and have long, happy and fruitful lives. He was gripped by all-encompassing sadness, a feeling of emptiness as he disappeared into the storm clouds, leaving his home behind forever.

As the visibility faded he could faintly hear a voice behind him, coming from the surface of the Earth that he was leaving behind – a woman's voice – Sarah's maybe? He thought it was Sarah's because it made him happy – he couldn't make out the words but whatever they were, he liked that they were the last things he heard. His pace increased and he flew higher in the atmosphere, following the curve of the earth, marvelling for the last time at the brilliance of the oceans, the jungle green and desert red of Africa, and watched the huge otherworldly storm clouds gathered over the UK. He took one last look at the Earth then buzzed a satellite, daringly flying between one of its solar panels and its main hull, before accelerating away from the gravitational pull. He flew around the moon and headed to Mars, marvelling at the red dust of the planet, and wondered if somewhere on the planet there was fresh water and perhaps life. He passed around the rings of Saturn, becoming sandwiched between the two parallel rings and cutting between them and the gas giant itself. He burst through the rings on the other side and quickly left the solar system, ascending out of the spiral arm of the galaxy and being afforded the best seat in the universe once again. Stars exploded and died, others coalesced and formed, new worlds born in the blink of an eye.

Time fell away and faded like a memory, and this time he could recall little from his previous life as he approached the giant star orbiting the super-massive black hole at the centre of the galaxy.

That's because you're dying this time, he thought. *Properly.*

He pushed toward it but a sudden fear gripped him – the demon had come from here, he'd brought it back with him. But he couldn't believe that. This place welcomed him – that was it – it wanted him to come here, wanted him to feel at home, wanted it to be home for him. It had gripped him the last time as he was shocked clear by the medical team because it had wanted to protect him, to keep him safe in his new home, surely that was the only rational explanation? It was the fault of the experiment – his colleagues pulling him free – that his hand became injured. The demon must have been another being simply caught up in their experiment – an interdimensional anomaly that hitchhiked back to Earth with him.

He looked forward to the stars embrace as he slowly approached, this time noticing hundreds of beings flying toward it like small balls of light leaving vapour trails like jets in a clear blue summer sky. Some were way ahead of him and flew straight into the light, spindly tendrils coming out to meet and guide them in. He wondered if he would meet these beings, whether they were the dead from planet Earth or the whole universe? He tried to fly closer to one nearer to him, but it was too far away and his course wasn't under his own control as the gravity of the giant star in front of him drew him in.

As he was enveloped by the heat of the sun, the white light completely eclipsed his horizon. Below, thousands of tiny arms and hands reached out to him, and he reciprocated by reaching out to them, dozens this time gently clasping his arms and legs, caressing his body, slowly drawing him in and down. He was nearing journey's end, in every sense, almost as if he were about to land on warm white softness, like silk bed sheets, and the feeling was overwhelming. The hands were gradually increasing their grip on him – you couldn't blame them after what happened last time, he smiled to himself. Unparalleled joy filled his heart once again as, apart from some precious moments with... someone – he couldn't remember her name – he wished he hadn't left this place last time. The hands gripped tighter now as they drew him down to his destination, his awareness, his clarity and lucidity, his very identity starting to fade. His consciousness was almost starting to merge with the star. The pressure the hands were exerting on him became intense, pulling at him, no longer as soft and... almost feeling like... he tried to blank it from his mind, tried to think only of joy and of softness and warmth – but the hands felt like...

Tom looked down, and if it hadn't been a dead organ on a marble floor a thousand light years away, his heart would have been beating hard in his throat. His consciousness, his individuality was fading but lasted long enough for him to realise that the hands were in fact claws, with one larger broken one in the middle of the rest, bent at a grotesque angle from where the appendage had snapped, and it was leading the other claws as they started to tear him apart.

The last thing Tom Boyand's soul did was scream.

The End

Acknowledgements

On the surface, you'd think that writing a novel is a fairly solitary activity; sitting down at your computer, wherever you choose to write that day, endeavouring to transfer your ideas from synapse to screen before they disappear off into the cerebral swamp. Not so. The number of people who've been involved in 'Team Angel' has become quite a sizeable round in the pub.

In no particular order, I'd like to thank Mr Owain Ennis and Dr Leigh Keen for their invaluable technical assistance in medical aspects of the story. To Mark Manson and Owen Griffiths for encouraging me early on (it's all your fault), and to Mark for introducing me to my editor, Jackie Bates. Jackie demonstrated endless patience and wisdom in the face of lengthy, question-filled emails, and guided me to take the story to another level – thank you.

I'd like to thank two fine authors; Graeme Shimmin and Andy Weir, for their advice and guidance on suggesting the self-publication route – I can only dream of achieving their success.

To my wife Becky, who, in addition to propping up my chaotic life, was the first person to edit *Angel*. Cue many a tense bedtime as she scribbled and annotated as I scrunched up bed-sheets in exasperation of what she must be writing.

To Sam Missingham, Nick Jones and all the 'Loungers' for collaborating in the cover design – I've never been so glad to be wrong. To the people at LodestarAS, for their enthusiasm and professionalism in producing my video advertising. I must also thank all of my friends and supporters, on both social media and my web-site, for their encouragement and interest.

Finally, to you, dear reader! I hope you enjoyed the journey and I hope that we can be having this conversation at the end of another story.

MB

About the Author

Mark Brownless lives and works in Carmarthen, West Wales, UK. By day he is a Physiotherapist, but by night he is an extreme typist – writing when the rest of his household has gone to sleep. When not exasperating his wife or embarrassing his two children, Mark can be found coaching kids football in the winter and cricket in the summer.

The Hand of an Angel is his first novel.

Contact Mark on social media, at:
www.facebook.com/markbrownlessauthor/
twitter.com/MarkBrownless

SIGN UP TO THE NEWSLETTER AT
www.markbrownless.com
AND GET

MARK'S NEW SERIAL FICTION

FREE!

WHY NOT LEAVE A REVIEW AT AMAZON?

30860867R00155

Printed in Great Britain
by Amazon